THE WOLVES OF TIME

I

Journeys to the Heartland

William Horwood

THE WOLVES OF TIME

I

JOURNEYS
TO THE HEARTLAND

HarperCollinsPublishers

HarperCollins*Publishers*
77–85 Fulham Palace Road,
Hammersmith, London W6 8JB

This paperback edition 1996
3 5 7 9 8 6 4

First published in Great Britain by
HarperCollins*Publishers* 1995

ISBN 0 00 649694 6

Set in Caledonia

Printed and bound in Great Britain by
Caledonian International Book Manufacturing Ltd, Glasgow

Contents

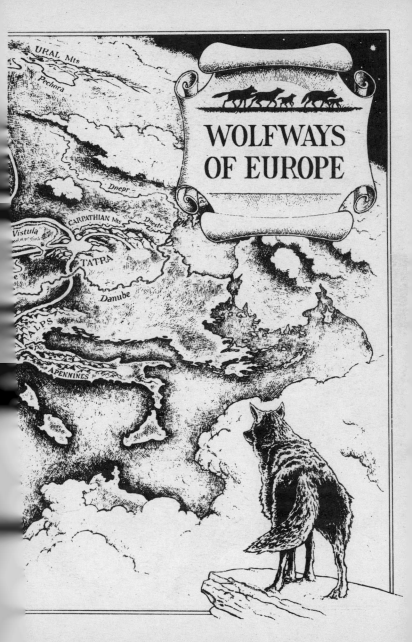

URAL Mts

Pechora

Dnepr

CARPATHIAN Mts

Dnestr

Vistula

TATRA

Danube

ALPS

Po

APENNINES

WOLFWAYS
OF EUROPE

PROLOGUE

AMISTY DAWN BREAKS on this first day of autumn, the traditional day for younger vagrant wolves to leave the pack. Of our small and modest pack, whose name is as obscure as the place about which our lives orbit, a ruined city deserted now by the Mennen, I am the only one who will be leaving. My siblings have found a place within the pack, but I have not. They are content to play their part in what they already know; I have different dreams and wish to journey on wolfways that may take me to the very stars; or to obscurity.

There will be no goodbyes. Vagrants slip away as insubstantial as shadows fading as the sun goes in, for a pack finds them unsettling, and pretends that they have never been. Unless, of course, the vagrant achieves great things, and then they may return to be honoured, to be listened to, to lead the howl.

Until last night I dreaded the coming of this day. My dreams, though different, seemed less inspiring the nearer this day came. My vision, clearer at the beginning of summer, became blurred and confused as time marched on. Yet now, this new dawn, I cannot wait for the morning mists to clear, and for my leader to signal that I may go.

For now, may Wulf be praised, I shall not travel alone.

A week ago, though it seems a lifetime to me, an old wolf drifted in and asked for the protection of our pack. He was the oldest wolf I had ever seen, his fur worn and thin, his teeth all but gone, and his eyes growing white with

1

blindness. Some wanted to refuse him admission to our circle, saying he might have plague, or that he might curse us. My father, our leader, knew his duty and put the wolf under my care, though little credit did I gain for that! Until last night . . .

The last of the summer moons had begun to wane when the old wolf broke his long silence and began to howl, his voice cracked with age, yet, as it seemed to me at least, beautiful in its simplicity and wisdom. The whole pack gathered about him, with me at his right flank, as he howled a story we all knew well, which is the story of the Wolves of Time. The moon arced across the sky with his howling, and the stars turned and shifted in the night. None of us had ever heard the story howled with so much truth. Even my father wept.

When the wolf fell silent, his howling done, my father, much moved, suggested that a pack such as ours would be honoured to care for him as long as he cared to stay; he might, perhaps, find comfort with us in his last days . . .

The old wolf shook his head and reaching out to me, he replied with a question: 'What day is it tomorrow?'

'The first day of autumn,' my father replied.

'The day when vagrants journey forth, and wise wolves do not overstay their welcome. I shall be leaving too. Vagrants must journey and they must wander, and finally they seek. Their seeking is never done.'

The pack drifted away, most to sleep, a few to watch. I led the old wolf to his appointed place and asked him if there was any service I could do for him. He ate little in the day and so sometimes hunger gnawed at him at night and he took food. This time he shook his head.

'Where will you go tomorrow?' I asked. He seemed suddenly so frail.

'There is only one place left for me now,' he replied, his blind eyes searching for the stars they could not see.

I waited for him to continue, and eventually he did.

'Are you fearful of your coming journey?' he asked me.

I said I was and indeed my paws were trembling at the thought of it.

'But you are young, and strong, and you can see.'

'I don't know where to go,' I replied, adding, a little ruefully, 'but you seem to know where you're going!'

I expected to hear his gentle laugh, but I did not.

'Would you,' he asked suddenly, 'care to help me a little along the way?'

'Oh yes!' I said, filled with joy. 'Where shall we be going?'

'Towards a place I left long long ago, and to which I promised I would one day return . . .'

As he said this I heard the wind whisper my name in the grass nearby, and I was suddenly much afraid. I knew then that the wolf who had asked for my help was no ordinary wolf.

'The story you howled for us is more than just a legend, isn't it?' I said, though how I found the courage to suggest such a thing I do not know.

'Yes,' he replied.

'Well then . . .' I began, and I found myself trembling once more. 'And are any of the Wolves of Time still living?'

He stirred and shifted uncomfortably, but finally he sighed.

'One is left alive,' he said.

Then I knew for certain the name of the wolf who had been put into my care.

'What is the name of the place you left so long ago?' I asked.

He turned towards me, the light of stars in his eyes, and the wandering moon in his old fur. I never knew a wolf could look so vulnerable.

'Home,' he replied.

* * *

The mists have cleared and my leader, my father, has stirred. The sun is rising and the pack with it.

The old wolf has stretched and is up. The others avoid us and it is already beginning to feel as if we have never been.

'Come,' he says, 'come . . .'

Was it as simple as this, as the rest of the wolfkind went about its business as if it was just another day, that those great wolves whose names were honoured in our howl last night set forth to join each other and become the Wolves of Time?

'Yes, yes,' he says as we depart, 'it was much like this . . .'

I

SUMMONS

*In which a Bukov wolf dares
to howl down the Wolves of Time*

CHAPTER ONE

The wolf Tervicz, of the Bukov pack,
decides it is he who must try to howl down the Wolves of Time

I T WAS LATE SUMMER, and high in the gorge-country of the Central Carpathian mountains a male wolf stood still at the edge of a rocky bluff, his eyes angry and his head shaking with frustration. He was no longer young, yet his stance was that of one who had not yet been accepted as an adult.

The object of his anger, an old, grey male, had lain down a little way off, two other wolves with him, a female and another male. The ground was rocky and the air was hot and dry, but beginning to cool at the end of a hard day. All around them, near and far, were the rises and jagged cliffs of inhospitable mountains, their profiles softened and turned blue by the hazy atmosphere. Apart from the husks of dried grass and thistles, the only sign of vegetation lay deep in the gorge below where the lone male stood. There a river's torrent roared grey-blue and white, and stunted trees and ferns clung to rocks, wet with spray, dark with lack of direct sun.

None of the wolves looked well or well-fed, none of them looked happy; all seemed stressed, as if they had been under pressure from the combined forces of other packs, of the Mennen, and of a difficult climate and harsh landscape . . . not for days or weeks, not even for months, but for years.

7

For decades, indeed.

These four discontented wolves were the last of the Bukov pack, and their leader was the old wolf, who led them now not by strength of body, but by strength of spirit. His name was Zcale, and he was the redoubtable and ill-tempered father of the other three; the angry male who stood staring now at the harsh landscape as if in hope that he might find comfort there, was Tervicz, a son in whom his father seemed much disappointed.

A dry and bitter wind blew at his paws, spattered rock dust at his face, and whispered at the pale and patchy fur of the other three a little way below him.

'You cannot, wolf, you know that as well as I,' said Zcale, breaking their silence wearily, 'and if you don't you're even more of a fool than you've always been. Howling's not a thing we do any more if we want to survive. Howling gets heard by the Magyar wolves, and by the Mennen. Your fool of a grandfather got killed by the Mennen* after he howled a new moon down. Your mother, Wulfin bless her, died at the jaws of the Magyars after she howled some story or other one night, and that not loudly. Yet still they heard and I . . . I could not save you all and her as well . . .'

Tervicz gave up the argument, shrugged, and climbed away from the little pack to stand proud on a ledge overlooking the gorges where they made their secret home, there to brood in silence, to find space again, to wish he knew how to be angry, how to argue, how to *win*.

Zcale bowed his head. His old eyes showed the pain of that night of terror, when he was forced to choose between herding the three young ones to safety or standing fast and protecting them all, including their mother, against odds

---

* 'Mennen', or, in the dialect of some packs 'Menn', is the word wolves use for men in the plural or Man and humanity in the abstract. The singular form is 'Mann'.

too great for any of them to survive. Perhaps there never had been a choice, and their mother, who fought the Magyars long enough to allow Zcale and the others to get up to safety in the gorges above their territory, had the consolation in death of knowing that her last surviving brood, and the wolf she loved so dearly, had got away, and might still have a chance.

The years had passed and Zcale felt burdened by the loss of his mate. But desolate and punishing though the years had been he had seen through the rearing of their young, and taught them to feel pride in being Bukovian, even if they were the last of their kind. Harsh though he often was, each of them knew in their own way that it was love and fear for them that made him as he was, and that without him none of them would be alive.

But now he was dying, his body growing thinner, his sleeps longer each day, his breathing worse, and all these familiar arguments were final ones with his own young who were – the nearer death approached – plain disappointments to him.

Szaba was well enough, but she was female and there was no Bukovian wolf to mate her but her own brothers and they, well . . . in so small a pack, with such inbreeding in the past, it was not suitable. Nor could she, or would she, take a Magyar to mate – partly because over the generations their tribe had all but killed her own, but also because for her to mate she must first make her way as ledrene of a pack, and what Magyar females would let her rise through their ranks, even had she the ability? Yet for all that, like any female, she harboured hopes of bearing young and seeing them grow strong.

Then there was Tervicz's brother Kubrat, his legs crippled and slow, his body twisted, and only his head whole and good. What a wolf he would have been! For his eyes were clear as spring skies, and his spirit great, and in him the dreams of Bukov might have been fulfilled. But, he was cursed to be weak, and however great a spirit, however bright a mind, with such a body what could he ever be?

Loved, that was all. Loved and watched over, and listened to as well, for his gentle voice could turn dreams to reality for a time, and every ancient tale their mother ever told, he remembered, and could re-tell. In him the spirit of the pack was still alive, and slow though he was, he had in more recent years become their focus. When times were hard it was the need to think of him, to cover his back while he made his slow escapes, that kept them acting as one, as a pack always should.

Which left poor Tervicz as the only whole male, but one who had so far seemed sadly unsuited to the role. He was made well enough, though not as strong as Kubrat would have been . . . He talked and thought well enough, though not as well as Kubrat, nor as imaginatively as his sister Szaba. He knew the territory and its routes well enough as well but . . . not as well as Zcale wished him to. In short, Tervicz was a disappointment, and Zcale let him know it.

There was one other quality Tervicz had, which annoyed his father terribly, but which brought tears to his old eyes as well: for all the criticism he suffered, and the sense that he was not quite good enough, Tervicz was loyal to each of them, he was kind, and if he complained it was at himself and never at them.

'I could wish,' Zcale said that day as Tervicz turned from the old argument about howling to be by himself, 'that he would be angry once in a while, or aggressive, or . . .'

'It's not in his nature, father, and never will be,' explained Szaba for the thousandth time. 'He is a wolf born to care for others, not to lead. He knows it and we know it and all your complaints about him will never change that, nor destroy it.'

'He is a wolf,' continued Kubrat, shifting himself clumsily to get a better view of Tervicz, 'who will always think of his pack before himself.'

Kubrat smiled towards his brother, his eyes pale, his affection warm as a summer evening wind; his love as palpable and unspoken as the approach of night, or day.

'He is a wolf much like your mother,' conceded Zcale, 'and I wish he would be angry with me for I treat him badly. But you Kubrat can never lead us, and he . . . I wish . . . I wanted . . .'

Zcale followed Kubrat's gaze towards Tervicz with something like despair.

'We all understand your suffering,' said Kubrat, his voice a little less gentle, 'especially Tervicz. Why else do you think he puts up with you? Why, if you had treated me as you treat him I would not have let you get away with it . . .'

There was an icy edge to Kubrat's voice before it softened, and a harsh look in his eyes before they grew gentle again.

'Yes, and *you* would have been a worthy leader,' snapped back Zcale, with a miserable nod that took in Kubrat's withered body and his weak and trembling limbs.

'Tervicz is all we have,' responded Szaba, 'but instead of making him more you make him less . . .'

'Well then, who cares for my view now?' rasped Zcale. 'You all know I'm dying and you can fight about such things among yourselves when I'm gone – a female, a cripple and a weakling! Give me a day or two, three days at most, and then shove my useless body over the gorge's edge and let it tumble to the rapids far below. Mind you, I won't have much to say to Wulf when I meet him, for what have I to show for the life I've had, can you tell me that?

'As for Tervicz, all he ever wants to do is howl down the stories of the past, just as his mother did, and look what it

11

did for her! If you didn't tell him those tales, Kubrat, and you did not sympathize Szaba . . .'

'Of course I sympathize,' said Szaba, upset by her father's reference to death and Wulf, and trying to ignore it. 'Kubrat agrees with me, don't you, my dear?'

'He may do,' continued Zcale, 'but then Kubrat has more sense than to howl aloud and bring Magyar and Mennen to us. We can whisper our stories and remember them. We can . . .'

Szaba shook her head.

'Father, we cannot. But of all four of us Tervicz is the only one who honours our history sufficiently to want to risk the present by celebrating the past. Respect him for that at least.'

'Respect him?' cried Zcale hoarsely, staring upslope to where Tervicz still stood alone. 'I do respect him, and I love him, as I love all of you. As your mother did. Nothing in all the world would give me greater pleasure than to hear him proudly howl down the story of the Wolves of Time to us, as it should be howled down: the form of it spreading out into the night sky, its line and shapes of tragedy and hope, of despair and coming triumph, echoing and re-echoing in the gorges hereabout, that I might for a moment forget what I am, which is an ailing, frightened Bukov wolf and imagine what I might be, which is the father of wolves who will fulfil the Bukovian destiny. Ah . . . a destiny that now can never be, never.'

'Then let him howl for you, father. It is the season for the howling down of the Wolves of Time, yet for three seasons now none of us have done it, except mutely into the shadows and the caves where none can hear it, least of all the gods.'

'Your mother died striving to howl down those mythic Wolves. She . . .' He coughed, almost choked, pushed

Szaba away, and then said again, 'She did what I refused to do, and died.'

'Father, she told us that none could make that howl so well as you and she thought that if she started you would be persuaded to continue it as it *should* be done . . .'

'Did she say that?' croaked old Zcale, as if he had not heard it before.

'You know she did,' said Szaba patiently. 'Now Tervicz wants to make the howl, which is his right as the strongest male among us. We are well placed here to escape should he be heard. The winds are petulant and strange and will give no easy clue to any who might be listening as to where we are. Anyway, a bold howling of our most ancient tale will surely serve to remind the Magyars that we still are . . .'

'I said such words to your mother the evening she died, and then refused to do it myself. Such persuasive words they were, and she began to howl, until . . . Anyway, Tervicz does not know all of that great howl. The tradition is already dead.'

'Dying perhaps, father, yet not quite dead,' said Kubrat softly, 'just like you!'

Zcale permitted a brief and bitter smile to cross his face.

'I wanted to see a Bukov wolf set off for the Heartland, just as one was destined to do. One of our kind should have been there when the Wolves of Time came back. But the gods have never called us and now it is too late . . .'

On the slopes above them, with the light of a late afternoon sun on his face, Tervicz moved close to the gorge's edge. Suddenly, light flecked at his head and in his eyes as he turned to look down towards them, a light that sent a shiver down the spines of Szaba and Kubrat, but which their father did not see because he was not looking.

'He's no Bukov wolf,' muttered their father bitterly before wearily turning away from them, lying down and closing his eyes. 'Nothing left now for us,' he mumbled, 'nothing but decline and loss. Nothing but death and the extinction of us all.'

But the others barely heard him. There was something about the way Tervicz stared at them, something neither of them had seen before, and it was more than a trick of light that made him seem to bound in the air as he turned, trotted and leapt down the slope to join them again.

'Feel better?' rasped Zcale who, hearing him, sat up and turned to face him. A leader to the last it seemed, wanting to impose himself. The expression of love for Tervicz he had made but a short time before was now gone from his voice. Even as his son replied, Zcale turned from him, uninterested in anything Tervicz might say.

So he did not hear Tervicz mutter: 'I feel . . . strange, not better.'

Then he went straight to Kubrat and shifted his back-legs around a little in a way so automatic and yet so caring that none who saw it could doubt either that he had done this little service a thousand times before, or that he did it with love.

'The wind seemed to be freshening,' he said turning to his sister. 'And yet it seems uncertain.'

'What was "strange", Tervicz?' she asked in a low voice. 'Was it something you saw?'

Tervicz's gaze was sombre, unusually so, and he looked over at his father and said quietly, 'He looks ill. He looks old. The wind Szaba, it whispered to me.'

'Of what?'

'Of impossibilities.'

'Which are?'

Szaba was less patient than Kubrat with such ambiguities. She was matter-of-fact and preferred straight talk. But then Tervicz said something strange indeed: what he said made her tremble and glance at Kubrat with such concern that he, too, shifted a little nearer. Their father was mumbling to himself, and staring about them as he often did before he slept, with worry and concern, as if he expected Magyars and Mennen to come storming out of the fissures in the rocks nearby.

What Tervicz said was this: 'The impossibilities you ask about are these: first for me to howl down the story of the Wolves of Time and second to journey on alone. That was what the wind whispered that I must do, Szaba.'

'They *are* impossibilities, my dear.'

'They are *not* impossibilities,' he said, 'they are happening already.'

It was said so quietly, so surely, and she had never in all her life heard Tervicz say something with such certainty.

'Are they not?' she asked.

'In ancient times they believed that the wind was Wulf's own voice. I heard more than the wind whispering just now, Szaba: I felt Wulf's gaze upon me in the evening light, and I heard him call my name and command me to howl down the old story, and journey westward . . .'

'To the Heartland . . .' she said faintly.

'I have been thinking,' said Tervicz very quietly, 'that before he dies, and *whatever he may say*, father might like to hear us howl down the old tales as Bukov wolves used to do.'

'Tervicz, you know that is the last thing he wants!' She was shocked, for her brother had never been so outspoken and rebellious as this. Nor so intimidatingly strange.

'It is the last thing he *says* he wants,' said Kubrat. 'If that's what Tervicz means I agree with him.'

'It is exactly what I mean, which is why I am going to howl down the tales, and even the legend of the Wolves of Time, whatever he says. Naturally, I would prefer it if he gave me help, seeing as it's a howling I have never done before. But if he will not, well, I suppose I must try to do it alone.'

15

The wind flurried at their fur, and tore at the heather near the gorge's edge; it carried grit that spattered at the rocks above their heads, and it swirled and turned and dried their mouths.

Tervicz looked at her with something like terror in his eyes – but not the fear of one who is weak any longer, and is unable to do what others can do; this was the fear of a wolf who has dared look into the future and who knows his paws are set upon a way whose routes are uncertain, and whose outcome quite unsure, yet who knows he must go forth.

'My dear, what is it that you saw just now?'

Tervicz looked so strange, and the swirl of the winds was so unsettling that Kubrat hobbled over to them inquiringly.

'Yes, what is it, wolf?' he asked.

But Tervicz barely had need to answer, for the wind whispered about them, and the light was bright and strange, and it was in his fur, and his eyes. He turned from them, looked out across the gorges and said, 'Our time has come, Szaba. The Bukovs' time is now, Kubrat. I . . . I know it, I feel it, it is a river in spate that has caught me and will take me before another day is out.'

'But what . . . ?' began Kubrat.

'The time for talk is over,' said Tervicz in a voice that might have been that of an elder who has heard all the arguments, considered them, and knows the time for action has come. 'Whole centuries of talking have come finally to this, to now.'

He turned away from them and ascended the slope slowly to take up the proud and formidable stance he had before. He climbed into a golden evening sky. He climbed at the bidding of the whispering wind. In him, as he went, was suddenly all the pride and tradition of the Bukov pack.

He stopped at the edge of the gorge and, watching him,

it seemed to his siblings that he was of rock itself, and of the sky, near and far, and of darkness and light.

He raised his head to the sky, he opened his mouth, and he began to howl the first strands and strains of their ancient tale:

'In the distant days when wolves roamed the earth alongside the Mennen, one equal to the other, the wolfways criss-crossed all of Europe. They were the lifelines of the wolves, routes which pack-wolves, secure in their belonging, used to find their way from rendezvous to rendezvous, or to lead them to safety when they were separated from their pack; routes, too, by which the outcasts went, as they drifted from one pack to another; and the routes on which the gods themselves journeyed forth in disguise, to watch over all of us.

'The wolfways were first made by Wulf himself, greatest and most powerful of the Wolf gods, as – from the time of his breaking of the Rock that had entrapped him from the beginning of all time, to the season of his maturing and ascension to the stars – he marked out his earthly territory . . .'

Below him, old Zcale started up out of his slumber, turned, and saw his son, his weak disappointing son, proud above him, howling down the tales of old.

'No! No!' he cried. 'You cannot!'

'Help him, father, show him,' said Kubrat softly. 'Help him as you were surely going to help our mother the day she died . . .'

'I cannot and he must not. The Magyars, the Mennen . . .' rasped Zcale, his eyes wild with all the dangers he had always feared.

'Help him, father,' urged Szaba as Tervicz continued, striving to find the right howlings for the tale he told, 'give him your love now.'

'He does not know . . . what he howls is not right . . .'

17

'It sounds all right to us!' declared Kubrat.

'It could be better, it could sound more . . .'

'Then go and help him,' commanded Kubrat fiercely. 'Do it now! It is all he ever needed.'

Then as Tervicz continued, his voice beginning to weaken for lack of another to accompany him, Zcale climbed up into the light of grace that shone upon his son, muttering, 'No, no, my son, not like that, never like *that!* Here, I'll show you how to do it properly, for Wulf's sake and my own!'

Then Zcale raised his head, opened his mouth, and joined the howl, taking it on and up so powerfully, so truly, that Szaba joined them, and finally, crawling up the slope, up into the light of evening and of Wulf, Kubrat added his voice to theirs, all four, all one, Bukovian, across the gorges of the Carpathians, whose echoes joined them, and brought to that great prophetic howling to the skies the voices of all generations past which had ever howled down the story of the Wolves of Time.

Out over Carpathia, on to the Heartland of the Tatra, and then to north and south, to east and west, the howling would be heard by those who will be the Wolves of Time.

The howling of the Bukov wolves is Wulf's call out to the life he has almost lost.

Their howling, courageously begun by Tervicz, is the beginning of Wulf's last mortal birth.

Listen now . . .

CHAPTER TWO

The Bukov wolves howl down the tale
of Wulf and Wulfin's fall in the world of mortal wolfkind

I N THOSE LONG YEARS when he was finding wisdom
(*the howling of the Bukov wolves began*) Wulf journeyed out from the Heartland wherein he was first
born, to the cold grey Baltic Sea in the north, and thence
to the warmth of the Adriatic in the south. Then from the
dunelands on the Atlantic coast of the Iberian peninsula he
travelled, and right across to the Ural Mountains deep in
the Russian hinterland, which mark the easternmost extent
of his territory. Thus were the wolfways made, and the
places where Wulf rested his weary head were the holy
places, known first by him in their primeval state.

It was then that from rock and tree and secluded lake he
freed the other wolf gods who would form his pack. These
gods wandered in his wake, and helped make the last
wolfways.

As he neared maturity, Wulf felt the yearning for a consort to equal him in strength and wisdom, and help him
lead the pack.

Yet no consort was there for him, and the wolfways all
seemed finished, except the last, which led back to the
place where he began, which was the rock, called the Wulf-
Rock, which rose in the secret centre of the misty heights
of the Heartland.

So it was that, in the hour of his maturing, he came to his

journey's end, back where his earthly journey had begun. There, on the rocks which he had broken out of to be free, the She-wolf Wulfin waited. Whence she had come he knew not, for Wulfin, Mother, the other side of light, the other side of dark, is mystery, as Wulf himself. He knew nothing of her, but he saw her and was accepted, and the pack of the gods was all but complete.

Yet not quite.

For Wulf and Wulfin mated, and decreed that their cubs would form mortal wolfkind and together, all mortal wolves as one, they would be the last-found god – each mortal wolf a part of something greater than themselves whose truth they could only guess at in life, and know fully in death. Singly, by themselves, the earth-bound wolves were but mortal; together, as one, they were another of the gods.

Thus the gods reared the mortal cubs, and each of the gods in their own way imparted their wisdom to them – the lore of rock, of tree, of lake; the lore of life, the lore of death; and the greatest lore of all, which was fearlessness, through which self dies and god-nature is found once more.

The cubs grew, and Wulf and his fellow gods, male and female alike, were excited by what had been made; and some desired them, and others were jealous of them; for gods especially have weaknesses.

So Wulf commanded that no god should consort with mortal wolf, so that mortal wolfkind would forget its origin, and the gods that made and nurtured them would be invisible to mortal wolves, and would watch them unseen. If one of the gods broke this law and sought to consort with mortal wolfkind, their punishment and torment would last as many years as they had spent days with the mortal wolf.

Amidst the ruins of the WulfRock that bore him, Wulf commanded it, saying: 'Let them not know their origins for they will otherwise dream of what they might be and not open their eyes to what they are. Yet they will remind *us* of what *we* are, and teach us by their mortality to honour our state. In return, we shall watch over them, and guide them, as the shadows and light of the forest guided me when I made the wolfways for all to follow.'

'Yet let them have a distant memory of us,' added his mate, Wulfin, wisely. 'Let them see us sometimes in the stars, there to see the patterns of the wolfways you have made, that when they are low and full of fear, and when they dream and seek our courage, something of our grace will come to them.

'Also, let them know in their heart of hearts that together they are a god, equal to us, to be respected by us, to be loved by us. For such faith in themselves will lead them to honour us and all we honour, which is all life, all things as one.'

Great Wulf stared at the cubs he had made, who played among the rocks which was the WulfRock, and said, 'Let it be so.'

Then, one by one, the gods said farewell to the mortal cubs, and watched in sadness as their charges saw them recede before their sight, into the form of rock and tree and lake from which they had once been freed by Wulf, until only the wind remained to whisper of what had been, and the mortal wolves were alone upon the earth not knowing that the gods were so near, in rock, in tree, in lake, and feeling only loss of all that had reared them, and given them love.

Then were the cubs confused, half-remembering what they had lost, half-believing they were more than each other singly was. Then did they try to seek what it was they could not find and from out of the Heartland mortal wolfkind scattered, following the wolfways Wulf himself had trodden, journeying by the holy places where he had rested, forgetting their past and their rearing, finally forgetting that the Heartland had been home, and learning instead to fear it, and never to go near its misty heights where the WulfRock rose.

Yet in each wolf's soul was left a wondrous echo of that fabled place, and in each pack's memory, passed down through the generations, was a part of the truth of what they had been: that wolfkind was itself of the god, and together, somewhere in their past, they had been as one, god-natured, eternal.

For millennia wolves walked unafraid, masters of the territory Wulf had made for them, honouring the rest of life – even the Mennen – as they honoured themselves. Their sworn enemies were the great cats, sabre-toothed and dangerous, led by their war god, Smilodon.

Time passed and shadows lengthened across the earth as the Mennen, carnivores themselves, ceased to hunt and gather and made settlements instead, and so lost touch with the wilderness. It was sometime then that the Mennen became the wolf's curse, the demons, the canker in the wild rose of life. Mennen who had been weak, now became strong.

The Mennen built their stockades and separated themselves from the life beyond, and slept uneasy lest their stockades should fall. They tossed and turned and made nightmares for themselves of what lay beyond, and their fears were embodied in the form of the wolf. Those who had been allies in the natural world, became enemies. The Mennen declared war upon the wolves, and saw in their shining, ferocious eyes, and ravening teeth, a wilderness they now feared.

The Mennen delved and built; they dug and drove; they broke and heaved; they killed the fauna and the flora, and they killed even themselves. But, like the fungi that thrive in fallen forests, they flourished on decay, and grew fat on death.

It was then that the ancient wolfways began to be destroyed, and the holy places as well, where wolves had howled their communion with the gods and wilderness. Even there the desecration of the Mennen penetrated and spread.

The Mennen built their stockades across the wolfways, and where the wolfways had crossed the streams and rivers, where wolves might pause and drink and be cleansed by the clear waters of life, bridges were built which the Mennen made sacrosanct. To those bridges, thinking their ways were still safe, wolves still came in innocence, and the Mennen killed them.

Then did the time of fear and terror truly begin.

Wolves were nailed alive by their paws to the wooden piers of the bridges that others might see and take warning. Some were decapitated, their heads stuck up as marks of the Mennen's strength and resolution.

Wolves were eaten by the superstitious Mennen who felt thereby that they ingested the wilderness itself and so tamed it.

Wolves were blinded and castrated, and the unborn were ripped from their mothers' wombs and burnt alive, in savage defiance of the lupine gods.

Yet few wolves who witnessed such horrors survived. Rather, most lived and died away from the Mennen, never knowing the darkness that was burgeoning in their midst, never seeing or hearing the coming of their enemy until it was too late.

So it was that unsuspecting wolves were taught old lore which was respectful of Mennen, of place and of each other. 'Let your brothers and your sisters have their place as you have yours, and if they take yours from you then remember they leave somewhere that is free.

'To north a wolf may go, my love, and to south; to east, my dear, you may wander, or to west: to all places do the wolfways lead, and a wolf who knows them can always find his destiny.'

Wolves were thus taught that the earth is to be shared, and a wolf who seeks to take too much will not benefit. Nor can a wolf know all the earth, for none but the gods themselves can know all places, or be in all places. A wolf should take comfort from knowing that there is always a place for him.

As cubs learnt these things, they learnt too that, as their mother's belly is a place of safety and comfort and peace, so the Heartland was wolfkind's haven, its beginning and its ending.

A few wolves guessed where this place was, and pilgrims, outcasts or dreamers, sometimes ventured far from their home territory to make their way to the Heartland, to speak out their dream that once they too were of the gods, and desired to be so again. But after the time when wolfways were broken by the Mennen, the way back to the Heartland was lost.

It was said that the last wolf to dare to pray at the Rock itself was of the Hutsul branch of the Bukovian pack of the south-eastern Carpathians whose name was Harbesch. She it was who taught knowledge of the wolfway to the Wulf-Rock to one of her young – though what his name was none ever knew, it being a sibling secret never told. In time he told one of his own young and so the secret knowledge of the way back to the WulfRock was passed down through the generations of the Bukov wolves . . .

'Yes, yes, yes!' cried old Zcale, breaking in the howl. 'You have howled all this well, learning more as you went, listening one to another and to me. But now we come to the fall into mortality of the gods, which is the beginning of the death of wolfkind, a death whose final moments we are witness to, for we are part of it.'

Zcale began to cough once more, but terribly now, for

the howl had been far more than he should have attempted and now he had stopped it was plain that he had exhausted himself.

'No, no . . .' he spluttered, leaning against Szaba, 'I want you to continue. Let me hear my children howl, let me hear, for it is a comfort of a sort, though I wish . . . I wish you . . .'

He wheezed and choked, and tears came from his eyes and for a time he could hardly breathe at all.

'. . . I wish,' he managed to say at last, 'you would get on with it, or else I'll be dead before you ever finish!'

He said this last to Tervicz, and in all their memories it was the first time he ever spoke to him as if he was leader.

'Continue, wolf, for Wulf's sake!'

'Well, then,' began Tervicz, 'it is of Wulf's fall that we must howl, for only after that were the Wolves of Time sent forth from Bukovina . . .'

'From the Heartland, wolf, not from Bukovina . . .' said Zcale most irritably. 'Tell it, tell it, tell it, and before I die I can tell you what you need to add, which I am near doing, and will . . . will do . . . before ever you finish at this rate!'

'But, father, you have told us all you know, or so you told us many times,' said Szaba.

Zcale cast up a look to the darkening evening sky that was almost comic in its weariness, the look of a father who utterly despairs that any of his young will ever display any wolf-sense at all.

'Didn't tell you the secret of the Heartland, did I? Eh?'

'But . . .' began Kubrat, for even he had never guessed that Zcale had not told them all the stories that he knew.

'But buggery,' snapped Zcale wheezily: 'Howl!'

Hastily, Tervicz began and the others followed the lead he gave . . .

*   *   *

Why, then, did the gods not help mortal wolfkind combat the Mennen's rise? Was that not their task? Or was it that they did not see?

The truth is that gods are as fallible and blind as mortal wolfkind can be, and more arrogant. So as the Mennen continued their inexorable destruction of the wolfways, the gods chose not to see that a curse was upon wolfkind.

Yet now the original doom of wolf was near. Amongst the gods the one who should have been wisest, Wulf himself, saw it least. And why? Because he had broken his own law and consorted with a mortal she-wolf . . .

The first time Wulf went with his mortal mate, Wulfin forgave him and Wulf was shamed. The second time, Wulfin forgave him and Wulf was angry. The third time . . . the third time Wulf went with his mortal mate, the sky was filled with shooting stars and the earth shuddered with falling meteorites and the forests were aflame for the whole year of his sin. And his mortal mate conceived a litter. When Wulf's sin was not forgiven by Wulfin he said proudly, 'But I am Wulf and you cannot harm me.'

Nor did she, for she did not need to. The gods' own law had been broken by Wulf himself, and as a rose may be devoured by the worm within, so did Wulf himself begin to die.

As his mortal mate's belly grew, he grew weaker, day after day and month by month, and he lost ascendancy to Wulfin. Gods must live by the law as well – and suffer by it, too, as Wulf himself decreed.

Wulfin had seen the danger of the Mennen's growing strength and the evil nature of their fear, and she was angry beyond measure that her mate had so threatened the pack of the gods itself by relinquishing his own strength in giving it to mortal wolf. She declared what soon would be.

'By the law you yourself made you are judged guilty, and with the punishment you ordained, you shall be punished.

'For a thousand days you went with mortal wolf. For a thousand years, you must run with mortal wolf and know their pain and hardship. You, who should have seen the Mennen's strength grow and corrupt the wilderness, will now suffer its pain for a whole millennium.

'Of the two cubs that shall be born of your mortal mate, you yourself shall be one, and as you made mortal wolfkind not know their origin, so will you forget what you once were. You shall be born of ordinary wolf, to die and be reborn as mortal wolves are, lifetime upon lifetime, not knowing what you were, suffering death after death, re-learning in each life something of what a god should know. Wiser each time you shall be reborn, yet still you will not know what you were. And as your wisdom grows, so shall your suffering.

'Until a lifetime will come to you more than nine hundred and ninety mortal years from now, when you must learn all you have learnt anew in one lifetime, suffer all you have suffered, lose all you have lost; and yet you must still strive to raise your head to the stars and see what once you lost. If then you still have the strength to be the god you were, you will arise as Wulf once more. If not, wolfkind itself shall die.'

The dying Wulf stared at his Wulfin, into her clear eyes, and saw already what he had lost, and that he loved her and, despite all, that she loved him.

'And what of the other cub my mortal mate shall bear?' he whispered.

For a long time Wulfin was silent, unsure that she would say who that cub must be. But then at last she spoke.

'That cub will be myself, that you will not be alone upon the earth, and that through all your suffering one other mortal wolf shall love you true.'

'Will you know who I am?' Wulf asked, as from out of the Heartland of the Wolf, his mortal mate's birthing howls

27

began to call him down to earth, and a dark millennium of mortality.

'I will not forget,' whispered Wulfin, reaching out to him. 'I shall know, but with whom can I share my suffering? Surely I am also to blame for your fall, and my suffering will be to watch the suffering of all your lives and be unable truly to help you until the last of them.'

Wulf saw how deep her love for him ran, and as he died his howl was weak and soft, like the bleat of a blind newborn cub who calls to the she-wolf it cannot see. So did Wulf fall from the gods to the earth, and so did Wulfin follow him, both to be reborn mortal, and live the curse of the dark millennium: one to strive to see as a god again, the other to bring what comfort she might to one she loved who could never know who or what she was.

With the fall of Wulf and Wulfin, and the scattering of the pack of the gods, pack after pack of mortal wolves began to lose their faith. All across Wulf's territory the Mennen found the wolves weak, and more wolfways were cut and the packs divided further. The drive towards extinction had begun with the start of that fated millennium.

Pride and stupidity, faithlessness and a failure of love, these brought the wolves down low and allowed them to be all but destroyed in the time that followed Wulf's punishment. Worse was the forgetting, for when communities break up, when even vagrants cannot travel far without being outcasts of their kind, something of the past slips away with each wolf's death so that each community harbours only fragments of what all once knew and shared.

Even the stories of the gods and the curse on Wulf were almost forgotten, except that somewhere in the past millennium a wolf who is Wulf himself, but knows it not, lives and dies and is born again, each time a little wiser, never knowing what he is, striving to find again the grace he knew, and lost, and will, finally, in his last life, have one more chance to regain for all eternity.

The howl slowed down and finally ceased, until the remnant Bukov pack lay silent, watching night take over the sky, and a slow moon rise. In the gorge far below them the shine of the river's run was the last thing to be lost in the dark, but where it had been its roar stayed on. The air grew cool, and fretted at the meagre grass on the ledges about them.

'Well, then,' sighed Zcale. 'That was good, and it was pleasing. My young can howl after all! And you, Tervicz, pleased me by insisting on it! But I am so tired, so aching, and the night stretches ahead so far. I would have liked to see one more dawn, and feel the rising sun on my face again. That would have . . .'

'Father!' chided Szaba, going nearer to him.

They all moved a little closer, flank to flank, paw touching paw, feeling that with the howling they had become as one, and that they did not want to break apart again. As for Zcale, they could not tell if he was really dying as he seemed to think, or if his strange and restive mood was excitement from the howl they had achieved, and all it promised. But then . . .

'I would like to hear you howl down the Wolves of Time,' he declared suddenly, 'just as it has been done by your ancestors through generations past. The Wolves' time is coming – that I have known for many a year. I have kept you in check, kept you together against this day.

'You know the tale and you will now howl it so that I can die knowing that you know it. When you've finished I'll tell you something about the Magyars, that foul and treacherous tribe that has fed on the Bukovs, just as it has fed on all wolves unfortunate enough to come under its influence. Magyars have been the bane of my life: I wish now to die in the hope that their long and baleful reign is over, which it certainly will be if only the Wolves of Time can return to the Heartland which they left so long ago. But that's for you all to tell me about, isn't it?'

'It is, father,' said Szaba soothingly.

'Then tell Tervicz to get on with it! Centuries can wait, but moments never do!'

'Yes, father,' they said, smiling at one another, feeling closer and more purposeful than they had for many a long year.

'And may Wulfin herself guide our howl,' said Tervicz, raising his head to the stars to begin the howl down whose purpose was as simple as it was awesome: to summon the Wolves of Time back to the Heartland once again.

CHAPTER THREE

*We learn the story of the dark millennium
and witness the howling down of the Wolves of Time*

W ITH THE FALL of Wulf and Wulfin into mortality, the first into the darkness of not knowing what he had been, the second into the suffering of knowing what her beloved had become, wolfkind began its long decline.

Faith was lost. The stories of the gods were lost. The wolfways were lost. Pride was lost. Wolf turned on wolf, pack on pack, and so wolfkind's present confusion and misery was founded, until even the Heartland lost its peacefulness, and was riven by dispute and despoiled with sacrilege. Righteous wars were fought as packs from east and west and north and south claimed that they were the chosen ones to guard the ancient sanctuary.

Of those long wars only one thing need be known and remembered: wolves that kill each other in Wulf's name are always wrong; the only way to counter such wolves and win is with the just assertion of peace. Darkness always spends itself: light always finally returns.

But even when such truths were learned at last by one generation, the next had need to learn them again. In the learning there was much suffering as one tribe advanced upon another; winners in one generation became losers in the next, retreated to regroup and then advanced again.

From all the confusion of the war-torn centuries certain

patterns formed and stayed in place. From the west the Teutons closed upon the Heartland, wolves of strength and purpose, well led, good followers, and ruthless in their fighting.

From the north and east the great Russian wolves advanced, their main group massing in the fabled forests of Bialowieza and crossing the north Polish plain; a second group collecting in the wetlands of the River Dnepr and advancing south and westward towards Tatra and the Heartland over the uplands of Ukraine. Huge were these wolves, and wild, in their way as different from and as dangerous as the Teutons, as rough seas are from the promontories they surge against.

While from the south, out of the scorching vales of the Peloponnese and Phrygia, came the southern wolves, smaller, with fur that glowed red in the evening sun: fractious vicious wolves who remembered the smallest slight down the generations, and who worshipped equally with Wulf and Wulfin, Hrein, god of trickery and mirth, whose laughter could be crueller than it could be kind.

Teutons, Russians and Southerners: these three great tribes of wolves met in the Heartland, bringing chaos and confusion to it for long centuries. Through the passage of that time Wulf was born and born again, killed now as a Teuton, born again to die a Russian, next emerging as wolf of the Peloponnese; each time not knowing what he had been; each time becoming a little wiser; but each time finally flawed and riven by desire and illusion. Learning, learning, and suffering his way into each new death.

While like a shadow, always moving, never in one place for long, went Wulfin, born to suffer Wulf's reincarnations; born to suffer and to love, burdened with the knowledge of what he had been, and to know that he might not have learned enough by the end of the dark millennium to free himself when his last life came.

Many were the names these two assumed, now all forgotten. Yet we know this: sometime in the to and fro, the swing and turn, the fall and rise, of the great Heartland wars, when Teutons, Russians and Southerners all took their turn to dominate, and then decline, Wulf was born into the Magyar tribe.

Unknown and much despised this Wulf that went by a Magyar name – a god who knew not what he was; a flawed god, mortal – saw a truth none other saw: that none of the three great tribes could ever win, for while they fought amongst themselves they failed to notice the continuing rise of the Mennen in the homelands of their tribes.

But this Magyar leader saw it, for the Mennen had already almost driven his tribe to extinction. He simply saw that what had happened to his wolves was now happening to the rest. Then it was that this new leader, the Wulf who knew himself not, led the Magyars out of the valleys and up into the hills of the Ukraine, and thence inspired them to believe that if they took control of the harsher heights of the Carpathians and bided their time, the Heartland itself would eventually be theirs.

'We are the chosen ones,' this false, flawed god-wolf said, and the Magyars believed it, believed it before true faith itself. 'We are chosen to be guardians.' His name was honoured and revered long after he had died. God? Of course he was a god! To the dread Magyars he was good enough that to invoke his name before a fight felt tantamount to victory.

So it was that the centuries of the Magyar rise began, and they went from strength to strength as the other three tribes were each undermined by the Mennen in their original territory. A wolf without a territory is a vagrant wolf; a tribe without a territory wakes up one day and finds it is no tribe at all.

So did the three great tribes discover too late that they

were irrecoverably weakened from behind, and turned their gaze from the Heartland back to their lost territory to regain what they could, only to find that all they had left was the higher heathlands, the sterile places, where the Mennen could not farm, nor even raise much livestock. So the Teutons retreated to the Bavarian heathlands; the Russians to the cold forest lands of the centre and the north; and the Southerners into the dry desert uplands of old Phrygia, and obscurity.

In this way, by biding their time, the Magyars assumed control of the Heartland, and came to call themselves its rightful guardians, believing themselves chosen, and that this gave them the right to destroy any who dared threaten them, whether the threat was real or imaginary.

Meanwhile, unnoticed and almost forgotten, throughout these centuries of strife and self-betrayal one small tribe alone remained true to Wulf and Wulfin, never siding with Teuton, Russian or Southern wolf, and successfully resisting all attempts of the Magyars to invade their territory and subvert their blood.

A gentle tribe of wolves famed for one thing only, and that was not for their strength or cunning, nor their intelligence, nor anything else but this: their howling. Subtle and deft were the Bukov wolves in howling, witty as well, and able to use the rises and heights of the limestone gorges amongst which they lived to swell a howl, to cause it to echo, to make it turn and mock itself if its theme became too serious; or to loom and threaten, rise and warn, to drift and support, if such were what its themes demanded.

Mysterious were the Bukov howls, heard from afar by many different tribes and packs of wolves who, hearing them yet rarely meeting the Bukovians themselves, told others, who told others, so that, through the centuries, that which was best known about these isolated wolves was their howling, and how the most ancient and holy of mortal wolfkind's lore was preserved and re-told by the Bukov wolves better than any other tribe in all wolfdom.

Nor did the Bukov wolves tell only ancient tales. Those who had been privileged to hear them spoke with wonder and not a little awe of the humour and wit of their present howlings, telling as they did of the futile comings and goings of the Teutons, the Russians and the Southerners. Then, when the Magyars began to gain in strength, and claim their rights as 'the chosen ones' and the 'guardians' the Bukov wolves did not spare them their cheerful, distant commentary.

The 'amazing Magyars', the 'Magyar magpies', the 'muddled Magyars chosen by Wulf-knows-who to guard who-knows-what' – such were some of the sarcastic howlings that the Bukovians made, and in consequence such were some of the phrases and tags others took back to their homelands and spread about – none more frequently than the 'magpie Magyars' tag, which is how, by the time the Magyars had taken control of the Heartland, all wolfkind knew them.

Naturally, the Magyars, always a humourless lot, did not take kindly to this mockery, and as their power increased so did their hatred of the Bukov wolves, and their determination to wipe them out. In which campaign, despite the inaccessibility of the Bukov territory, they had steady success.

But still the Bukovians howled, sending forth their tales ancient and modern, and mixing old and reverential stories of the immortal gods with their laughter and mockery of mortal ones. But mockery turned to contempt when the Bukovians heard how the Magyars had commenced a sinister and untoward relationship with the Mennen.

Some said it began when a Mann-cub was lost in the fastness of the Tatra and found by an errant she-wolf who suckled, succoured it, and raised it. Others claimed it was the other way: a wolf-cub was taken by the Mennen, who raised it and taught it to guide them back to wolves.

However, it was in those strange and shadowed vales, in which both Mennen and wolves were cut off from the outside wolves, that a coupling of their divergent spirits occurred and, like inbreeding in a pack that has stopped looking outward for new blood, produced monsters – if not of body then of spirit. Wolves serviced Mennen, and Mennen wolves, and something bestial stalked those covert places for which there is no name but shame. It was sometime then that the Magyars, 'guardians' of the Heartland for so long, themselves became corrupt and in decline, their nature tainted by the plague of compromise to the Mennen; the Mennen plagued by the taint of compromise with wolves. Not all of them, not by any means. One or two perhaps in each generation, which is enough. Let disease break out in one member of a pack and others often follow . . .

It was sometime then that the great Bukov wolf Harbesch was born, perhaps the greatest Bukov ledrene there has been. She it was who foresaw the dangers implicit in the Magyars' fatal alliance with the Mennen – not just for her own kind, but for all wolfkind. Many were the warnings she sent forth in the howlings she led concerning this alliance, through which the Magyars learned eventually to gain favours and food in exchange for leading the Mennen in pursuit of wolves other than the Magyars themselves.

She saw and wept for the way the Teutons in Bavaria were betrayed by Magyar wolves; and, too, how a pack of Magyars ventured south to the Peloponnese and there guided the Mennen to the stronghold of the local wolves, and led to their destruction. Harbesch warned that in the end the Mennen would turn on their Magyar 'mates', and destroy them too.

But always, whatever else she did, Harbesch reminded

her tribe that finally their duty lay in service to Wulf and Wulfin, and to upholding the ancient lore and preserving old faith and loyalties to the gods against the day when Wulf would rise once more out of the mortality to which he had been cursed, and lead a resurrection of wolfkind.

None knew how or quite when Harbesch made the greatest and most courageous decision of her life, which was to venture alone from her own territory to try to find the way through the Heartland to the WulfRock itself. This journey she made, motivated some say by a desire to pray for the life of one of her young, a male, caught for Wulf-knew what foul purpose by Mennen led by Magyars. Here, at last, was the nightmare she foresaw visited upon her own. Others say that it was Wulfin who instructed her to find the Wulf-Rock – and certainly it was Wulfin who guided and protected her there and back through territory watched over by the murderous Magyars.

When Harbesch returned to her rejoicing tribe she was old, and had little time to live. The son lost to the Mennen returned corrupted, foul and strange, but Harbesch, healer now, cured him and proved that the plague of Mennen could be cleansed, the taint removed. To this healed son she imparted the secret of the route to the WulfRock, and he in turn, when his time came to die, imparted the secret to one of his young. In this way the secret of the route to the WulfRock was kept alive in the Bukov pack, against the time when it might be needed once again.

Though centuries had now passed since the coming of the Magyars, still, as defeated tribes will, dreams and resentments remained, futilely resurrected by the young of each generation, the cause of pointless war, and of unnecessary suffering and death. So there came a fateful day when a Teuton leader united the remnants of the three great tribes in one final assault on the Magyars in the Heartland: a campaign which the Magyars won not by confrontation but retreat, leading the united force on too far, straight into the waiting Mennen's guns.

Death and flight followed, and finally disharmony and bloody strife as the last of the ill-fated band met to confer by a certain lake some way south of the Tatra Mountains, which legend dubs Red Lake, or Blood Lake. Here the remnants of the remnant turned on each other as some Magyars, provocative, watched safely from the slopes nearby. Why risk life and limb if the enemy destroys itself? is the kind of code Magyars understand.

One other wolf was there, a male Bukovian, a descendant of Harbesch herself, and himself current holder of the secret. This wolf, on his brave and covert way to the Wulf-Rock, stumbled on this last battle of the great tribes, and watched, and wept. Wolf killed wolf, and where that battle was fought, deep in the Heartland, the rocks are red from the blood of wolves that was shed that day. And the lake turned red with the blood of the slain, and gained its name.

He watched, he saw, and he understood this truth: the Magyars were like vultures, letting others kill themselves that they might feed upon their death: magpies feeding off others' faults and dreams. Magpie Magyars! He saw, too, that Mennen watched, though whether their presence was known to the Magyars or not he did not know.

At last there were only twelve wolves left among those fighting, some from the east, some from the west, some from north and some from south. While up in the shadows the Magyars smiled, knowing that their time had come, but hesitating to descend to where the battle had been fought, for they thrive on others' weakness, not on their own strength.

So it was the Bukov wolf who descended and went among the wounded, tending the twelve still living, honouring the many dead, his paws reddened by the blood that flowed, his eyes weeping tears of pity for wolfkind.

This great Bukov wolf finally stood still, and the fighting stopped about him, and the twelve came to him, a wounded living pack surviving in the midst of death.

'What wolf are you?' one of the Russians asked.

'Of Bukov.'

'Holder of the secret of the WulfRock?' asked a Teuton.

'Yes.'

There was a hush, but for the painful breathing of the wounded, for that one day there would come a Bukov wolf who knew the way back to the WulfRock was a part of wolfkind's lore none had yet forgotten: and here was a Bukov wolf . . .

'Lead us to the WulfRock, that we may find guidance,' said a Southern wolf, speaking for them all, 'for surely we have lost our way.'

'Wulf is not there, nor Wulfin. In losing their way we have lost ours,' said the Bukov wolf.

'Well, we'll *make* you . . .' began one of the others.

'We'll force him to tell *us!*' said two Russian wolves.

'We'll give him no choice but to reveal everything to us alone,' snarled one Teuton to another.

The Bukov wolf listened while they argued amongst themselves all around him, and saw that even the seriously wounded ones argued, that even the ones who needed rest if they were to survive joined in, their greed and lust for power overcoming their desire for life and need for peace.

For a day and a night their argument raged around the silent Bukov wolf, until they grew weary and one of them said, 'And what do you think? After all, it's your life we're arguing about.'

The Bukov wolf shook his head and smiled: 'It's your life, not mine, and mine is worth less to me than yours appears to be to you.'

'So what do you think we should do?' asked another after an uneasy silence, with more courtesy, for they were at last beginning to see that the Bukov wolf was as wise as legends said.

'I will make a suggestion to you all which you may take or leave as you see fit. I am journeying to the WulfRock, just as many generations ago my ancestor Harbesch did, who was the last to visit it for guidance. The secret of the journey there has been passed down the generations until it has come to me, and I see only disarray and uncertainty. Wolves are mortal, including even Wulf himself, I cannot know when I shall die, and nor have I yet got young to whom I should pass my knowledge on. I do not know if I shall reach the WulfRock but I rather think that I shall not.

'Our legends say that Harbesch was the last, until the end of the dark millennium. Well then, that millennium seems still in full flight to me. But it is the journey there, and trying it, that matters. What I shall learn I do not know, but what you have said to each other I shall think about. I can do no worse than you!'

They stared at him, some dissatisfied, some pleading, some aggressive, and a few malevolent.

'Some of you may try to follow me but, well, for one thing I am not sure where I am going and for another I am the only one who is not wounded or injured and you may find it hard to stay with me. Those who are still here when I return I shall tell what I have learned. Meanwhile, help each other heal and be warned of this: up here in the heights around us Magyar wolves lurk, awaiting your demise or flight, or a chance to take you one by one. Healing, unity and patience is now your only way.'

With that the Bukov wolf was gone.

Eight days and nights he was gone from them. Of the twelve he left alive, three had already left to go their own way, having no faith that he would come back, and a fourth had died, leaving only eight.

But the Bukov wolf had also changed, though quite how

was hard to say. He seemed less assured, yet stronger, less certain yet more content; less inclined to smile, yet more filled with joy. He bore himself with more power than any wolf they had ever known and when he came down among them to the lake where they had formed their pack, his paws were sore from the screes he had crossed and his shoulders were torn by the jagged rocks of the place where he had been. None dared ask if he had seen the WulfRock, and nor did he ever say.

He came among them and waited for them to speak, as a great leader waits for his pack to *be*, not needing to chide one or threaten another before all are silent and obedient to command.

'Wolf of Bukov, we will do as you suggest,' they said. 'Speak of what you have learned.'

'Then listen,' he began, 'and may something of Wulf's lost wisdom be with us today, and something, too, of Wulfin's love.'

He paused and lowered his head to think, and they saw that his brow was furrowed with such deeps and shadows as are cast across a formidable cliff by a dying evening sun; and that his eyes seemed to search for a way through the cliffs above, but that the way had already been too long and hard for him to think that he would ever quite complete the climb. They saw in his face that he had not quite reached the WulfRock, but had learnt much on the way.

'The dark millennium will grow darker yet. The Mennen will drive us nearly to extinction. The tales we tell, the legends we have learnt, almost all our lore, will finally be lost. No tribe, no pack, no single wolf can ever remember down the terrible centuries yet to come what wolfkind will need to know if it is to recover its gods, and honour Wulf once more.

'Nor shall a Bukov wolf be able to remember even half of what I know, for the attrition of the centuries will take it away and leave hardly anything behind. Just a myth without substance, a legend without meaning; a tale whose beginning and end is all forgotten.

'It is already happening. I, who have been told the secret of the route to the WulfRock could not find it, but wandered vaguely, like a wolf who is ill and cannot see the way. It was there, but I knew not where.

'I thought of all I had been told, and I came to understand that I was not meant to find the WulfRock – not I, nor my son, nor his son after that: not any of us, for many generations to come. To find the WulfRock is too great a thing for mortal wolf to do, even more so when Wulf himself is in the stars no more.

'But *together*, well, perhaps we might – or our ancestors might when the time is right; when the dark millennium is almost over, and Wulf has journeyed through his lives to wisdom once again. Then, then shall he need help to find again a way back home which he forgot when he fell into mortality. And who shall help him?'

The Bukov wolf looked around at the eight wolves listening to him and asked again, 'Which wolves will help him home?'

The light was grey, the lake ruffled with cool wind, and the heights above were still dark from rain that had fallen the day before. Above them, not far off, in a place they all knew, three Magyars watched, wondering, uncertain, bored.

Higher still, off to the north, unseen by any wolf at all, another stood and stared. Where she was, light gathered and was soft; where she waited, the wind was still; where she who was Wulfin watched, was suffering mixed with hope.

Her mouth moved with the words the Bukov wolf spoke far below: 'Which of you will help?'

'I.'

'I too . . .'

'And I as well . . .'

So, one by one, friend and enemy, hurt and healing, Teuton, Russian and Southern wolves came forward and vowed their help to him who would one day need them all and who, receiving it, would save them all.

'And I . . .' said the Bukov wolf at last, 'I shall be the ninth and last amongst our membership. For we, who fought each other too long, and may have seen the way to wisdom far too late, will journey forth from the Heartland now and take the secret that we share, that none can find the WulfRock by himself, excepting Wulf himself and even he cannot do it without our help.

'Therefore, to save ourselves for this future time at the end of the dark millennium, when we shall be needed once again, we shall journey to the safe places at wolfdom's peripheries, where the Mennen will hunt us last of all. There we shall pass down that part of the lore we know so that in the future, when the time is right, our ancestors can return and bring back to each other what we individually have forgotten.'

'Where shall we go?' asked one of their number.

'To far-off Iberia I shall journey,' began one.

'To the Nordic wastes,' continued another.

'To the distant Apennines,' whispered a third, who had always dreamed of going that way.

'Follow your dreams then,' said the Bukov wolf, 'to northern Russia and to Phrygia, to the Peloponnese and the High Auvergne, to all the places the Mennen will find hardest to abide: there shall we make our homes, there survive, and there await the call of Wulf.'

'And what shall we be, we who leave the Heartlands to the Magyars and the centuries yet to come?' asked another.

'Our pack's name shall be the Wolves of Time, for we start a journey whose ways and distance we cannot guess, and whose ending will be in a time we shall never know, completed by wolves who are our descendants, born of a choice and destiny we made this day.'

Then the Wolves of Time began a howling such as wolfdom had never heard before, which gyred up into the winds, which echoed out among the rocks, which put fear forever in the Magyar hearts: a howling that said: *out of the past we come, in the present we strive to live as best we can, and in the future we of this pack shall return, for we are the Wolves of Time*.

Even before the howling was complete, one by one the wolves dispersed, beginning their long journeys to wolfdom's furthest parts. Until only the Bukov wolf was left, his howl the last, his journey the least far, for one of their number must stay nearby and help, in time, in far-off time, to summon them home to the Heartland once again.

For all would be needed to help the One who must find again the way back to the WulfRock where wolfkind was born, and to where, if wolfkind was to survive, Wulf himself must journey out of his suffering through the dark millennium and journey back on the wolfway to the stars.

CHAPTER FOUR

*Tervicz receives his father's blessing
for the journey, and the trials to come*

A S THE HOWL DOWN reached its ending, they saw
that the stars had begun to fade and that the long
night was over. Below them in the gorges, and
beyond over the Carpathian Mountains, the echoes of the
howling died away. Off into distance and time they went,
borne on the whispering wind, seeking out those mortal
wolves who would make up the pack of the Wolves of Time
once more, to summon them back to the Heartland of the
Wolf, to the aid of Wulf himself.

'Good, very good,' muttered Zcale with uncharac-
teristic satisfaction, his eyes glinting with dawning light.
'Now then all of you, and especially you Tervicz, I have
something to say and I have little time in which to say it.
I linger on, but not for long. I have made it to another
dawn – just! Wulf help me, I shall be glad to see the
rising sun, but after that I trust it will be the wolfway
to the stars for me. And none of your nonsense, Szaba,
about me being well (really!) and recovering! I do not
wish to be well, *really*; and as for recovery, I gave up
hope of it sometime in the night, and very glad I am
too!'

'Father!' said Szaba disapprovingly.

'Daughter!' responded Zcale, with rather more vigour
than he should have done for one who was dying: then he

coughed a good bit, and wheezed even more, swearing and cursing at them all, at himself, and at Wulf.

'Listen then, for I've things to say . . .'

'So you said before!' said Kubrat, winking at his siblings over their father's head. It sounded to them as if his death was not now quite as imminent as it had been the previous evening. There was life in the old wolf yet.

'No respect, no understanding!' muttered Zcale, scratching his flank in something like his old way, except that there was a general benevolence and good humour about him, as if he was letting go of something he had carried for a long time, and was glad to do so.

'Tervicz, you have proved yourself worthy in these past hours, and I shall not fail to give you my blessing when you leave . . .'

'Leave?' said Szaba, though Tervicz himself nodded at his father's words.

'I said leave and I meant it,' said Zcale irritably. 'No reason why he shouldn't. There's usually a Bukov wolf in every generation who does and, well, he'll need to be the one. There's a lot to do out there beyond our territory, a lot of places to see, a lot of wolves to track down and get to know the ways of . . .'

His words were interrupted by a distant howl from the east.

'Bloody Magyars!' said Zcale with contempt. 'But that's what I want to talk about. About time. You've asked me often enough, but until now I didn't see the point in telling what I knew. But now Tervicz is leaving us, there are things you all should know. No need to make a meal of it . . .

'I'm going to tell you what happened when you were born, and why it happened, and then you can come to your own conclusions. Maybe the time will come when this pack has young of its own again, though Wulf knows how. Not in my time now, more's the pity! But who knows what

Tervicz will get up to, and what wolves he'll bring back with him? Because I'll tell you this: he is coming back. Eh, Tervicz?'

Tervicz grinned, a little nervously. The distant howling rose up again, harsh compared to the Bukov sound, and aggressive.

'Well then, let me tell you how it was those years ago . . .' Their father began in a low voice, his brow furrowed, his eyes in pain, his voice often breaking with the tears he had held back through the years: for to show weakness was not what a leader should ever do; nor would it help the three youngsters it was his task to protect and raise to maturity.

Now he did begin to weep, and Szaba wept with him, while Kubrat stared wide-eyed and troubled; while Tervicz, so long the butt of his father's fears and grief, began to see that it had been so because he was not the weakest at all, but the strongest, the one who could take it and survive, and the one who must one day lead.

Then Zcale began to howl his tale, and the three with him began to join in openly as well, adding their voices as codas to his howl, their own tales and memories to their father's grief and fears.

This was no long howling of wolves through the night, no ancient tale of gods and wolves. This was a pack's brief and intense howl of the trials of a recent past, and of the hopes of a future that were coming upon them now with the swiftness of the rising sun above the mountains to the east, into whose western heights and dangerous vales Tervicz must soon begin to journey and find his destiny, and the pack's as well.

Here's how it was, the terrible thing that happened to our pack, (*began Zcale*) and it gives me no pleasure to tell it, none at all. All you wolves have ever known is me, which isn't much to show for the great heritage and tradition of which you're part. So, what went wrong?

Before you were born there were two parts to the Bukov pack: the main part was led by my cousin Goran – you've heard me speak of him. He was tough, and he was stronger than me. That part of the pack lived in the gorges below, where the hunting was better. The smaller part of the pack, who lived in this territory where we are now, was led by me.

As leaders go, Goran wasn't so bad, but he was a jealous type. He didn't want me having my own mate, let alone starting a pack here, and I can't say I blamed him. I got what I could when I could. But it wasn't made any easier by his ledrene, who was one of two sisters. Her name was Dendrine. She was a sadistic bitch and there's no other word for it. She didn't just defeat other females, she maimed or killed them if she could and young males too. Driving them over the gorge's edge was her favourite trick. Bitch.

The funny thing was, if that's the right word, she wasn't all that strong. But she was as clever as buggery and males and females looked into her eyes and felt fear. Of course Goran couldn't do anything about it since she was legitimate ledrene.

I mentioned her sister and that was Amish, and she was the one I loved. And she loved me. From cubs we loved each other. Now, sisters are meant to hate each other but those two were loyal to one another, though Wulf knows they were different. The one was evil and wicked, and the other was true as fresh rain. Dendrine was strongest, but then Amish never confronted her. Nor did Dendrine threaten me, because she knew I loved her sister. I should have . . . I should have told her to her face.

Anyway that was how it was for years and so long as

Amish didn't get with young, which she didn't, and we all let Dendrine have her way, which we did, all was well and no one minded my dalliance with Amish. The only threat was the Magyars, but in those days, though they still felt their traditional hostility to the Bukovians, they had troubles of their own. There are four packs in the Magyar tribe, or used to be. The Tatra pack is biggest and they are the guardians of the Heartland, which is somewhere in the high places of the Tatra. South of the Tatra were the Slovakians, but they had fallen on hard times because they were nearest Mennen places. Proud they were, and hated the Magyars, but had been subdued by them. Magyars liked Slovakian females, good in the rump.

North and east of the high Carpathians was the Ukrainian branch, from whose lands the true Magyars first came. They were loyal to the Magyars and held them in high esteem, thinking them holy and mysterious, bloody fools. Lastly, there were the Maramurians who, as you know, had – and still have – territory to our west and south-west, or, put another way, on the Magyars' east and south-eastern front. Maramurians are cruel, and hate Bukovians, and it has been their wolves through the years who have persecuted us most.

That was the situation when I was growing up, though we never saw much of these other wolves because of the internal troubles I mentioned. What we learned was from vagrants on either side – who could travel pretty freely in those days, and only occasionally got taken or killed. But then, just as often they were absorbed by the other side, maybe because they won favour by warning of Mennen dangers, which vagrants are often good at doing, or because of their own strength. I'll tell you this: no tribe is as pure as it pretends to be, not even Bukovians, and least of all Magyars.

I mentioned troubles. Troubles usually come down to

power struggles. I won't go into the details because I don't know them, and they all passed anyway. All I do know is that a year or two before you were born, a wolf from the Ukrainian side took some supporters into the Tatra, ousted the overall leader, and took power for himself. I don't know what his Ukrainian name was but I do know what name he became known by: Hassler. He was clever, a good leader, and ruthless, and that was all I knew until he came visiting our way.

He sent emissaries to the Bukov claiming that he wanted the years of warring to stop. We're all wolves, that's what he said. From that moment on Bukovians were in trouble. Dendrine had got bored with Goran and volunteered to go and talk to this wolf Hassler. I remember her setting off as if it was yesterday and despite everything I admired her. Needed courage what she did – but then maybe she knew more than I did. Maybe she saw her chance had come and took it when it came.

She was a forceful sort of female, not good-looking but impressive. Her eyes were hard most of the time, but when they softened they softened you. Mostly they frightened you. So off Dendrine goes, and that was the beginning of the end of the Bukovs.

When she came back she was changed; she was more confident, more smug, and she was fattening with young. Needless to say in her absence some female or other – not Amish, she kept out of it – had tried to take her place. Dendrine killed her. Ripped her throat out.

The blood was hardly dried on her mouth before Magyars appeared by routes only Dendrine could have told them. A lot of Magyars, led by Hassler. He was, in his way, likeable. A better leader than Goran, that's for sure.

Well, then, I'll tell you what happened. They said they came in peace but within hours most of the Bukovians were dead. It was Amish saved me – she knew Dendrine better than any other wolf and for the first time in my hearing she said, 'I don't trust her, Zcale, not this time. There's blood on her mouth, and blood in her heart. We get out now. There's murder in her eyes.'

I said that we could not leave. Our duty was to the pack.

She said, 'Zcale, your duty is to your young.'

'What young?' I said.

'The ones you've got me with.'

Well then, that was the first I knew of it. I got her away up into the high places I knew best of all, by routes the Magyars could not follow. The killing must have started soon after we left. To this day you can see the red stain of blood down the gorge-face where the Bukov pack were slain and thrown. Of them all only Dendrine was left, betrayer of the Bukov, consort of Hassler, a murderer for a murderer; leader and ledrene. Oh yes, that's what your aunt became, ledrene to the Magyar, Hassler's mate.

As for Amish, she had lied to me to get me out. Otherwise she knew I would have stayed to help the others. She was not with young, and she didn't get with young for another year, by which time we were the last Bukov pair. That year was good, the best of my life. Up in the high gorges we learned to love, and as Amish said, we loved to learn.

Then you three came – each one loved by us. You, Szaba, because you were always gentle. You, Kubrat, because you were always curious about things despite your difficulties; and you, Tervicz, because you were always as kind as a wolf should be – to all of us. We never howled because we did not want to draw attention to ourselves. We stayed silent and secret.

But then, a few months after you were born, your mother, Wulf bless her, took it into her head to howl down the Wolves of Time. She said someone had to do it. She said there was no sign of Magyar wolves and by the time they tried to catch up with us we could be gone.

'Can't be mute forever,' Amish said, 'otherwise we're not Bukov wolves. We're famous for our howling, so let's howl.'

First time she did it, it was good.

Second time she did it, none came after us.

Third time she did it, Magyars came.

I shouldn't have let her howl at all, but I did. I failed her as a leader. It was my fault alone.

She howled, I stayed aside with you three, and the Magyars must have been lying in wait. Don't ask me how or why, but come they did, unknown to us.

I saw them attack her.

I saw Dendrine among them.

I saw sister rip the throat out of sister. I saw my love killed. I saw the eyes of evil.

I could not go to help her because I had to save you three. I saved you and lost her. It was what she would have wanted. But . . . that night I lost my life. My heart was broken and Dendrine broke it.

That's the truth of what happened, and how Dendrine your aunt became a Magyar. She is a cursed wolf and Amish never did her harm, nor said a bad word about her, though Wulf knows she had reason to. Your aunt killed your mother and I have been silent since, my heart like stone.

But last night we howled again, as a pack, as proud as we *should* be and just as your mother would have wanted. We howled down the Wolves of Time.

Now Tervicz will set off to find the Heartland, and find help for the Bukov. While you Szaba and you Kubrat will move on . . .

'And you father . . . you too.'

'Me? I'm more dead than alive . . .'

Suddenly Tervicz lunged at him and nipped him.

'You'll go with them, father. I order it.'

Zcale stared at Tervicz, wolf stared at wolf, and then all laughed, all rolled, all played as a pack should play.

'I'll do my best,' said Zcale. 'I'll see them safe.'

'So . . .' said Tervicz, and as they said their farewells, and promised to come together again one day, if Wulf willed it, the sun rose on them and warmed the rocks.

'We'll be here, waiting for your return,' said Szaba.

Tervicz nodded and said, 'Yes, yes, you will.'

They all tried to believe it.

'You're our future now, Tervicz, so go carefully as all great wolves should. Remember all that I . . .'

'I shall never forget,' said Tervicz, 'not ever. And one day I'll come back and find you all.'

He could not bring himself to say 'some of you', though in truth he doubted he would see any of them alive again. The others . . . death was in their eyes. But Szaba, to whom life had given so very little, must she die before it gave her something at last? Was hope in him all she might have in return for her suffering?

'I know you will, Tervicz, and you'll have a mate at your flank, and a whole pack of younger wolves following you and we'll know . . . we'll know, my dear . . . we'll . . .' but her voice had begun to break at the mention of 'younger wolves', and the thought of cubs she might have mothered, youngsters she might have reared.

Her eyes filled with tears, and her patchy head, prematurely old, dropped low against his flank.

'Szaba, leave him be with your talk and moods!' cried her father. 'It's time he left, unless he's as weak and feckless as I've always said. Go on Tervicz, Wulf help you, that's enough of goodbyes. Go and show the world what a Bukov wolf can do and don't come back until you've been to the Heartland and found the Wolves of Time. Go on, wolf . . .'

Tervicz turned towards his father, angry at him for having broken into Szaba's tears, still angry at the lifetime of harrying he had imposed upon them all; angry.

Panting, heaving, mouths agape and teeth aglint, they struggled, and Tervicz knew suddenly that he had the strength to win.

'Yes,' rasped his father into his ear so that only he could hear, 'yes, you could . . .' There was terrible tiredness in Zcale's voice, but relief as well.

'But I want more than this for you, Tervicz. I want you away from here before responsibility ties you to this Wulf-forsaken place,' he said suddenly.

The September wind whispered in the rocks and grass nearby, a wind that called his name and said, 'Come now, Tervicz, for we need your help.' He heard it, and his father heard it, and their struggling grip turned from dislike to affection, uncertainty to a moment of mutual affection. And Tervicz knew then what his father was, and always had been: how strong he had needed to be these long years past, strong enough to lead the pack until another grew strong in his place.

'Father!' he whispered in return.

'Go now!' said his father, turning on him with paws and teeth, and driving him back. 'Go and find your destiny and ours! Go, wolf!'

Tervicz rolled away into submission and obedience for the last time, a token gesture. He rose up and stared as an equal at his father.

'I *will* come back and find you,' he said. He stared up the slope he must climb, breathed deeply, glanced a final time at Szaba and half-smiled. The wind flurried at them all, speaking of autumn and of change, and then he was gone, to find the Heartland, and new companions.

'Yes . . . go now, wolf,' whispered Zcale, 'and know that I am proud of you, as of you all.'

Then Tervicz was gone, gone eastward, gone towards the Magyar dangers, gone to the Heartland; to journey towards the same destiny as all the Wolves of Time.

II

LEADER AND LEDRENE

*In which the Nordic wolf, Klimt of Tornesdal,
and Elhana, ousted ledrene of southern Italy's
Benevento pack, hear the summons
and begin their journeys to the Heartland*

CHAPTER FIVE

*We meet Klimt of Tornesdal as he learns
how he must answer Wulf's call*

DEATH CAME HUNTING one windy September
evening among the creaking cranes and corru-
gated iron buildings of the port of Helsingborg, at
the southernmost tip of Sweden. It was seven years before
what some have called the Coming of the Wolf, and the
quarry the Mennen sought that evening was a lone male
wolf, the last of his kind in Scandinavia.

Death comes in many forms to wolves, but this was the
death only the Mennen know how to inflict, which is of
dogs that chase, of bright searching lights and shouts that
confuse, and the sudden roar and spark of the glinting gun
that often maims before it kills.

In Helsingborg that chill evening the wolf had reached
the very end of a flight from the Mennen that had taken
six weeks, and forced him to run and slink and hide and
tremble, and finally to drag his wasted, wounded body,
four hundred terrible miles.

Now he was left with nowhere else to go, and turned to
face the Mennen one final time. To his left was the waste
of stony ground he had just crossed, at whose far edge two
Mennen came now with their growling dogs. To his right
were the harsh rectangles of metal containers at whose
corners more Mennen gathered, shining their lights into
his amber eyes.

Behind, twice his height, was the concrete wall beyond which he could hear the surge and crash of the sea. When he had first reached it he had just had strength enough to leap and scrabble on top of it to see if he could escape that way. But all he had been able to see in the darkness below was the white spray of waves hitting the sea wall, and the turbulent foam as waves fell back on themselves.

Now, back in the shadow of the wall, he watched the Mennen's cautious approach, conscious of the mixed scents of aggression and a lust to kill, the rank odour of their sweat, and the confusing smell of their fear.

Despite his present weakness he was a fine wolf. His fur was dark, his body well-made, and there was about his face and eyes a powerful quick intelligence that no creature, whether Mann, or dog, or anything else, would not feel fearful of. Beyond that there was the shadow of great suffering and loss, and the courage to have survived it. This was no ordinary wolf.

His name was Klimt of Tornesdal.

Klimt drew himself up defiantly, tail out, hackles raised, eyes alert within the snarl and furrows of his face. His natural fear was overwhelmed by sadness that his journey, and the great dream that inspired it, seemed only to have led him to an end in this vile place.

He raised his head to stare briefly at the stars that shone through a parting in the clouds, and whisper the ancient prayer all wolves repeat when they fear that their lives are in peril: 'Great Wulf, as I have come to the very void of death and gaze into its darkness, I give up my will to you. If you show me a wolfway to safety from the danger I am in, I will dedicate the rest of my life to the service of your name, but if it is on the wolfway to the stars that you will have me go, grant that I can do so with courage and with grace.'

As he turned to face the Mennen to his left and they

began to unleash their barking dogs, he took a step forward to be better balanced to respond to their attack, and spoke the final part of his prayer.

'Great Wulf, it is your follower Klimt, born of Tornesdal, in the north, who invokes your name: hear him!'

He looked proud and formidable as he stilled for the start of his last fight, and yet it was not the lights of the Mennen he saw, nor the bloodlust of their hunting dogs he scented, nor even the sound of the pounding sea behind which he heard . . .

At his speaking of the name of his beloved territory of Tornesdal, he saw once more the white of the snow across the fjells, and scented the forest pines, and he heard the summer rushing of the streams; and he recalled the strange impulse, and tragic destiny, that had made him turn from all he knew and travel south to where the Mennen lived.

For a long moment Klimt lingered at this tempting threshold into the sweet memory of a time before all troubles had begun, and he felt a wave of tiredness. He wanted so much to sleep and finally forget, and to have to fight no more.

But he shook himself back into reality, for there is a sleeping from which there is no return and he was not ready for it yet.

'So I still want to live,' he said to himself in wonder. 'Even now!'

The wind fretted at his fur, as if to mock so bold an ambition as to live. It fretted and whispered and rose past him over the wall and then rushed down to the black sea at his back.

'No!' he heard a wolf growl. '*No!*'

It was his own voice, and his own last strength that had him moving forward for a moment to mislead the dog.

As the first dog paused in its flight, and the second began its run, Klimt turned and leapt onto the wall behind him.

The dogs reared up to his left and then, sensing his moment's advantage, Klimt paused delicately to stare down into the swilling darkness of the sea, not frightened any more, nor in any pain, but only relieved at the knowledge that it was all at an end for him. Wulf commanded him to go this way rather than to die in the mouths of dogs, at the feet of Mennen.

Klimt scented and snouted at the surging dark sea below for a moment more, as the dogs leapt up and the Mennen's guns were raised. He glanced at them one final time before he turned and leapt away from the lights, out from the wall to plunge down into the sea's uninviting void; and the world went black.

It was not the cold of the water that surprised him but the power of the current, as strong as a glacial stream in spring. Even as he sank down into its shocking darkness, he felt it suck at him and take him, and he was content to yield to it, content to be overtaken by its power; content to die this way and be released from a struggle for life that was no longer worth living.

Until, thump! And thump again! Then the sharp jab of something in the water, metal, a Mennen structure jabbing him, catching him, fighting him, holding him down.

It was then that Klimt's head cleared to the fact that he was truly near death. His lungs were close to bursting as he discovered that even now, at the very end, his anger was not dead and he had the will to live.

'No! I will not die!'

So he struggled up towards a shimmering light, up, up with a rush of breath out through the surface of the sea into night and a starry sky, and a light that searched the sea behind him, as the current – so hard and swift it was like a cold creature that had him in its jaws – dragged him away.

Klimt struggled to swim, struggled to move, as the cold now began to take its toll and sap out his life. His desperate paws and haunches stiffened and began to fail him, and he knew that even as he had once again found the will to live, now he was dying.

The Mennen were far behind him: ahead was dark sea, and to his left were rocks lit up by lights from somewhere above, lights that moved in pairs. Vehicles. Desperate, he turned towards them. Desperate, he swam.

Desperate, he knew that life was almost gone from him, not drowsily as before, but clearly, here, now, in the icy, numbing grip of cold.

'Wulf, help me,' he gasped, repeating the simplest prayer. 'Oh my god, help me.'

The current eased and a surge of water lifted his body as a wave carried him towards the rocks nearby. The jetty that was now ahead dropped below him and then seemed to power confusedly towards him as, in a mêlée of scrabbling paws and foam he was hurtled into the land again, and he grasped it. The Mennen-made land. His only life.

He pulled himself weakly above the water-line as another wave drove up behind him, turned him, and thumped his left flank onto more rocks. For a moment its falling, foaming withdrawal sought to drag him back into the sea again, but he hung onto the land he had found, and when the water was gone, and before another wave could come, he wildly pulled himself higher up the slippery seaweed covered rocks.

A wave came in, spent itself below him and he knew he was safe. He shook himself and the spray shot up and caught the lights that moved in pairs on the ground above.

He stared at the stars, and they were as they always had been, their meaning beyond him, but yet *there*. Something, it seemed, was permanent, and Wulf had heard him. Wulf was *there*!

Then, whispering, the wind came among the rocks; whispering right into his soul . . .

'Klimt. Wolf. Come now to the Heartland . . .'

And he heard the whisper of the god's call on the wind and knew that he must try to live.

'What can I do for thee?' he whispered in return, for he had promised if he lived he would dedicate his life to Wulf.

The wind whispered again, calling his name then, as if from the stars themselves, and it seemed to say, 'Help us! Help all of us!'

The last wolf in Scandinavia pulled his battered body over the edge of the jetty and found himself in a stopping place of rumbling, roaring trucks. He was cold, and could hear the dogs and the Mennen still. He was cold but he was full of faith. Wulf had called to him to help and there would be a wolfway to the Heartland and when he got there – 'and I will, I will,' he whispered passionately – he would serve Wulf to the end.

But then, a final shock. The tall shadows moved and out of them there came a Mann, who stood suddenly before Klimt, staring at him from eyes that were darker than the darkest shadow thereabout.

Klimt stared, shivering and nearly broken by fatigue and cold, and he knew he could not run.

But the Mann only stared and in a flush of wonder and relief, Klimt knew his scent to be benign. The Mann scented as weak and tired as he himself, and quite as lost. Klimt dared to move nearer and stared up at the Mann, whose eyes seemed then to take light from the stars, and be a part of the night sky.

A roar came from nearby as one of the great trucks lit up and moved out of its line, turning in a slow arc towards the shadows where he lay.

Then, a miracle upon the wind: a sweet scent like the forests of his youth. The wind had whispered and Wulf was showing him what he must do. Klimt rose and ran beside the truck, scenting the great split logs of pine it carried, trying to scrabble up onto them. He fell back, ran forward faster and with one great leap flew through the air and took possession of a territory of crashing, heaving timber. Beneath the tarpaulin, he found somewhere warm, which scented like Tornesdal where he was born, and he knew the gods desired that he begin his life anew.

Klimt raised his head in the jolting darkness, saw a slit of sky and stars, and offered a mute howl to both Wulf and Wulfin, who had found him a way – a wolfway he supposed – which would take him out of hell. The truck turned and turned again and moved south onto a noisy ramp, a boat, and on across the sea.

It was then that Klimt let himself succumb at last to the darkness that had beckoned him so long, and trusted the forgiving gods to watch over him and lead him on.

While behind him, beneath the creaking chains of the cranes and derricks of Helsingborg the men came back to their vehicles with dogs and guns.

'We lost the bugger in the sea,' said one to another who stood there, still.

'The wolf drowned,' said another, angry, disappointed.

The Mann stared at them and knew then that he stared not into the eyes of men, but of Mennen, the scourge of wolves. And seeing them as wolves did, and smelling their scent of sweat, fear and blind arrogance, he turned to stare over the water across which the ferry and the wolf had gone. He knew then that if he was to escape the curse of men and find another way out of human darkness, it was a wolfway he must seek now, and learn to follow.

CHAPTER SIX

*Elhana of the Benevento pack of Southern Italy
finds courage to answer the summons of the gods*

T HAT SAME SEPTEMBER, for days after her defeat
as ledrene of the Benevento pack of the Matese
Mountains in the south, the last viable pack left in
all of Italy, Elhana hurt in body and mind.

Elhana was an elegant fair-furred wolf and despite her
present humiliation and low spirits she was a female to
whom eyes turned. Her own eyes were large, and clear,
and though they carried a natural ledrene's confidence and
power, they were kind and compassionate. Her paws were
perhaps a little large, her legs a little long, so that there
was a curious awkward youthfulness about her movements;
but one made up for by her strength and speed. But for
now she simply hurt . . .

First was the humiliation of defeat at the paws of her
daughter Pescara, whose eyes, from the moment they
opened after Elhana bore her, held a cold and naked hunger
to gain power and displace any female that got in her way.
Elhana had never loved her daughter, feeling that the mis-
chievous wolf-god Hrein had stolen into her womb and
placed the demon cub there.

Second was the anger that she, Elhana, ledrene of a pack
she loved and whose tradition she felt she honoured, should
have been defeated by deceit and not by strength. For she
believed that without the love and help of the pack's leader

66

Abruzzo, Pescara could not have played such a trick on her. Abruzzo had done a terrible wrong: for the leader should never interfere with the ledrene and her challengers. Yet he had pleasured his daughter Pescara, and when Elhana had gone to remonstrate, he had moved in such a way that his body was shield to Pescara's vile attack. So swift, so sudden, so lacking in the etiquette of pre-ritual and challenge, that even Elhana, trained so well in all the ledrene's arts – excepting a daughter's deceit, it seemed – had been taken by surprise.

'Yet it must be said, my dear, that she pressed home her advantage as if god-inspired,' said old Lauria, Elhana's beloved mother, Pescara's grandmother.

'Hrein-inspired,' said Elhana, glancing across the settling ground to see if Pescara saw them, licking her festering wounds to neck and right front leg.

'Well . . .' said Lauria, a former ledrene herself, now a struggling follower with but another summer's strength left in her aged body, 'you have to admit that she has taken on the light of grace.'

Elhana nodded and settled down and remembered when she herself had taken on the 'light' with which most leaders and ledrenes are imbued for a time when they win the fight to lead. In this way wolves who were formerly but equal adversaries become unassailable for a time, and return the pack to its equilibrium. She had come to know that the light is no more than an inner confidence born of success and power and that it can depart from a wolf as swiftly as it comes.

From the rocks beyond which mother and daughter lay, there was a sudden rush as Pescara came to lunge spitefully at Elhana and nipped her haunch before turning, pausing as dust rose about her, staring with wicked, triumphant eyes before slow-stepping away, tail high. All to remind the pack of who she now was; just for show.

But Elhana noted that Pescara did no more than that; a nip was enough to show her dominance; outright confrontation with Elhana now would not be wise, for hurt pride and righteous anger give a wolf much strength, and Pescara was not yet ready to risk losing what she had so recently gained, and so young. Nor was Elhana yet ready to risk a second fight and another defeat, and so lose all chance of ever regaining what she had lost.

Or was it just that? She stared into her mother's warm eyes and knew, as so often in the past, that she was not going to speak what was on her mind. And what was that? Elhana knew, just as she knew Lauria liked wolves to work things out for themselves. Mixed in with the hurt pride and anger, there was relief that now she was not ledrene she need never again yield herself up to Abruzzo's rough and repugnant embrace.

She sighed, and shifted her paw to ease the aching throb, half-closing her eyes as her mother groomed her wounded neck, warm and moist and as loving as when she was a pup. There were benefits in not being ledrene, and this was one of them.

She sighed again, more ruefully, as she admitted to herself that when she had become ledrene she had taken the gamble that Abruzzo would not last long, that her own true love, Umbrio, would defeat him before the season's end, and together they could make the pack great once more. Together . . .

It was not to be, for the gods did not favour Umbrio. Something had died in Elhana's heart that night when Umbrio had died so terribly, weakened by the septic wounds that followed wounding by the Mennen's guns, then finished off by Abruzzo, savage and pitiless. And afterwards, heaving and sweating with the grotesque triumph of defeating his rival, Abruzzo had ravaged her, the blood of the wolf she loved stiff in his face fur.

So romantic innocence died in Elhana's heart, along with much of the hope and faith that her mother had instilled in her through her stories and teachings, that up there in the sky the stars told a story, and it was Elhana's own, that she was mother of a pack, and at her flank, strong, purposeful, just, magnificent, was a wolf who would be great and who loved her, as she loved him. All such hope had almost gone.

The years of duty had passed so slowly, but now that she no longer had to maintain the ledrene's role, she realized she could at least begin to dream again.

'You're looking better my dear,' whispered Lauria a little later.

'I've been dreaming of what might be, just as you taught me when I was young.'

Lauria's eyes smiled and she nodded towards the northern sky where the first star was shining bright, though the sun had not yet died across the range behind them.

'I saw you in the stars the night I bore you, right across the sky, running with the gods themselves and helping to lead them towards a destiny that will save them from the fate that has cursed the wolfways for many a century past,' said Lauria, as she often had before. 'All my life I had been seeing that great vision, but until the night of your birth I thought it was myself I saw. But it is *you* my dear, you who must dare to run with the gods. Your time as ledrene here has been but preparation . . . Did I not tell you that it was your father who . . . ?'

Elhana put out a paw to stop her mother's old wanderings, for other wolves were becoming restless and uneasy with this talk. 'It is too late for him to help me, mother. My father Ambato is long, long gone. I am but a follower now and if I am to be ledrene again –'

Lauria shook her head, and her wise eyes grew serious

in the evening gloom. 'You do not want to be ledrene again, not here, therefore you never will be. Not *here*.'

'But somewhere else?' whispered Elhana, who deep in her heart, beyond where even her mother was admitted, held a smouldering faith that the gods were somehow with her, and would honour her, if only she could find the right way to go forward.

'Somewhere!' said Lauria fiercely. 'Look at the stars, see how they rise and run, and find for yourself which way they tell you to go. I cannot do it for you. No wolf can. It must come from within. But it is known that the gods summon certain wolves. Why, your father . . .'

She journeyed into a tale Elhana knew well, of how her father was not who he *should* have been, nor even he whom Lauria had loved with all the passion and helplessness of youth, but another altogether. It seemed that Lauria's leader had gone hunting and she, grieving with the disappointments of youthful love and hating the sensual brutality of the leader who as ledrene she must mate, found comfort with Ambato, a male of lower rank. He was on the pack's periphery, a wolf of dreams, one who, having no hope of gaining power in the pack, had recourse to wandering, and dreaming of far-off places where he might (in the safety of imagination, as it seemed to Lauria) do great things.

Ambato lacked the courage to leave the pack, but he did not lack the passion to begin to make Lauria believe there was something great beyond them all which, for a wolf who could find it, would make the pack's concerns seem inconsequential indeed. Such dreams and passions easily turn to love and Lauria and Ambato found a love all the sweeter for being forbidden, a thing of moments and of secret, sunny glades. Despite her leader's brutal attentions she had never until then got with young; but in those snatched moments with Ambato, Lauria became pregnant and the litter she bore included Elhana.

Ambato stayed long enough to see his young born, and to assure Lauria that she was right to think Elhana blessed; but not long enough that afterwards Elhana could quite remember him, unless it was memory that put a vision of dark and serious eyes before her, staring from the stars, always reminding her that there was something greater than the Benevento pack, and one day, one distant day, she must seek it.

Lauria told Elhana about the Heartland, and repeated many times those fragments of a greater story which was all Ambato knew of the epic tale of the Wolves of Time, who lived in ancient ages past, before wolves declined and the gods began to fade.

'Who were they?' asked Elhana, just as Lauria had asked Ambato. 'Tell me about them.'

But who or what they were Lauria did not know, just as Ambato had not known, except that long, long ago, before the coming of the dark millennium, a wise Hutsul wolf, of Bukovina in the Carpathian Mountains, sent forth some wolves from the Heartland, out into the peripheral places far away. He sent them at a time when the packs of the Heartland were destroying one another, that they might preserve the truth of Wulf himself, and loyalty to him. One day, that wise wolf said, the Wolves of Time would be able to return, bringing with them ancient lore. Thus would wolfkind be saved.

Upon this tragic, noble theme Ambato, dreamer, had constructed many a tale for Lauria, and she in her own turn recounted these to Elhana, and others of the pack. Whilst Ambato, sensible to the danger that the leader might one day learn whose 'his' cubs really were, found courage finally to leave, and trek northwards, towards where he believed the Heartland lay. If he ever got there, he told Lauria, he would offer his services to the gods themselves and ask them to intercede for Elhana, special product of their love.

'But what can an ordinary wolf give to the gods that they have not already got?' asked Elhana dubiously, rubbing her sore limbs.

'Your life, my dear; your mortality,' replied Lauria. 'Now rest and sleep easy, for you are ledrene no more and do not have to worry about the things a ledrene frets over, not here at any rate.'

The evening advanced, and bit by bit the northern sky lit up with the stars whose patterns held all the secrets of the wolfways, and all of what was, what is, and what will be.

'Tell me of the wolfways as you used to do,' said Elhana, but she had no need to ask, for her mother was already arching her head towards the sky, and growling the ways: Ariano, Vulture, Rionera, Gravinadi and so the way to the holy place of Acri in the south; then due north to Gargano, where the fabled last howls of the Severo pack had been heard, and given strength to the wolf Peschici to venture inland and fight for his right to lead the Benevento pack, and so begin the fortunes of this greatest of the packs of the legendary Italian wolf.

The night sky darkened, the stars grew more bright and the moon began to rise above the mountains and across the eastern sky.

Impulsively, Lauria rose up and padded off into the night, and Elhana, pausing for no more than a moment, followed her. A few of the pack stared after them, several looked Pescara's way; the new ledrene did not deign to acknowledge that she had even seen the departure.

Silence fell about the pack, ears pricked at occasional sounds, and some wolf said, 'I scented Mennen that way yesterday,' and another growled agreement. Lauria, old follower, would no doubt howl, as all wolves in this pack had a right to do when they wished and perhaps others might trot off and join her, standing nearby to enter her dreams and join her prayers. Perhaps.

Pescara flicked her tail warningly. An individual might howl if they wished, and another with them too – like Lauria and Elhana, the one too full of old lore and dreams, the other too low in defeat to take seriously for now. But others . . . Pescara rose suddenly, trotted about the pack nipping at the females and some of the subordinate males, just as she pleased, and then settled down again. This night the others must stay where they were.

The males lazed, and those whose rank was subordinate to hers lay watchfully. The few stronger males chose sleep, as their leader Abruzzo did. Or they tried to sleep. There was a wakefulness in the waiting for a howl. Let Lauria begin and they, who knew and respected her, could stare at the stars and try to imagine the wolfways which they had long forgotten and only she now knew. Once upon a time, long, long ago, their ancestors had known how to see all the ways in the stars, *all* the ways. But now much of the lore was lost.

It was a long time before Lauria's howl came, and it was distant, for she had chosen to take her stand somewhere higher up in the mountains. So when it came it was soft and muted, a lament rather than a call. Yet several of the pack stood up, their ears upright, their snouts turning the way she had gone as their eyes half-closed and they felt the urging of the howl, and the yearning it made in them.

'No!' growled Pescara, 'Nnnnooo!'

Not one wolf moved, not even when they heard Elhana's howl join her mother's, the two gyring up together, first one and then the other taking the lead, first one and then the other falling away.

Then old Lauria began to trace the pattern of the wolfways and Elhana followed her. Up, up among the stars went their sinewy howls, first following the whole patterns the one had taught the other, and then, later, seeking out in fits and starts those fragments that Lauria had tried to learn when young.

'I wish I had listened better, my dear, for some of those wolves knew so much and could tell you all the wolfways towards the north . . . Falmari, Calamani, San . . . Sang . . . Sanguida! But there are so many more.'

'Falmari, Calamani, Sanguida,' howled Elhana gently up into the sky. 'Those places must still be,' she whispered dreamily.

'Still are, and so many more we've forgotten. But they still *are*.'

'Do you think there are still wolves north of here?'

'In the northern parts of these mountains? Perhaps. Why your father travelled north . . .'

'Ambato . . .' whispered Elhana.

Lauria's eyes wrinkled in the starlight as she remembered the far-off time when she was young enough to have been loved, to have made dalliance in the dappled sunlight of the olive groves.

'I can remember his face, his hunted eyes,' she said, 'I can remember so much of Ambato. But one thing has gone from my memory now: I can't remember the sound of his voice when he told me that he loved me . . .'

'Why did he really leave?'

'He said the Great Wulf himself had summoned him to help and he must go.'

Their howling ceased, and they lay on the rock where they had stood, extended their heads along their paws and watched the stars. Lauria's eyes closed towards sleep, but Elhana stayed awake as the lore demanded: one must keep the watch. So she stared at the northern sky and followed the fragments of patterns there, trying to decide which way the wolfways would have gone, and how their patterns might be echoed in the trees and rocks and lakes that lay below, all dark and silent now.

'Can the lands of wolfkind really have been so wide as the skies themselves?' she asked. 'And are there wolves that look tonight at this same sky, and see these same stars, and do not know the pattern of the stars beneath which *I* have learnt to run? I could tell them what I know, and they could tell me, and together . . .'

For a long time that night Elhana dared to dream the outsider's dream, which is the dream of roaming to somewhere new and better to find a new purpose in life and make a new community.

She sighed, and half-dozed, and perhaps even briefly slept, though others would not have known, for as ledrene she had developed the knack of keeping her ears cocked for sound, and her eyes part-open to the world about – or, as tonight, part-closed, and unseeing of what began to spread across the northern sky.

Sometime in the deepest part of the night the sky began to cloud, and the stars were lost in blackness. The wolfways that had been lost to memory now became obscured to sight. Dark clouds crossed the moon. A wind stirred the dry, benighted grass. Elhana did not hear it.

The sky darkened more, and the wind's whisper came more clearly calling, whispering, pleading. Yet still Elhana did not hear.

Dense became the cloud, the stars all gone now, and the air deathly still again. Forgetfulness and sleep stalked across the lands of the Italian wolf, as there came one last stirring of the wind, spiralling up into the night, invisible, and whispering down to where it touched the dark earth, travelling and searching, calling one last time. 'Help usss, now,' it called in the dead grass and deserted clefts of the mountains.

'*Help us!*' it called one last time, and lifted dust and the detritus of the abnormally dry summer and hurled it into the wounded face of Elhana of the Benevento.

She came out of her sleep as swiftly as a river in spate forced between rocks, up and alert. Her back fur ruffled and her jaws opened into a warning snarl. She rose to hear the cry of the wind as it faded away to north again, 'Help ussss!'

'What is it?' whispered Lauria urgently waking also. 'What is it?'

She scented Elhana's alarm and fear, head straight and low. Her daughter was barely visible in the dark.

'Out of my dream I heard the gods call to me . . .' whispered Elhana, mouth flared, eyes staring. 'I thought I heard the voice of Wulfin herself.'

Her eyes were filled with sadness. But as her mother stared back she saw in wonder how the light of the stars began to shine upon her daughter's face.

Barely daring to move, barely able to breathe, Lauria turned her head slowly to the north and stared at the sky and saw a slow revelation of a great pattern of stars.

'Look! Look, my dear!'

Shivering, frightened, overawed, her paws utterly still upon the ground, Elhana looked and saw the great dark clouds had split mightily from a spot directly above their heads to the far and distant north, and at the clouds' riven edges the moon's light smouldered and shimmered, while in the black space beyond, stretching as far as the eye could see, was a pattern of stars that zig-zagged northward.

'Look and remember,' whispered Lauria, 'for the gods are showing you the wolfway that has been lost and forgotten to us so long, the way beyond our great territory. Look and remember!'

Elhana saw the pattern clearly, and pulling back her head, she began to howl its line from where it started directly above them, and slowly, star by star, group by group, to the north she howled. And as she howled the wolfway the clouds closed in, following her, until one last star remained, which was where the wolfway ended. It shone brighter than all the rest, and the clouds did not cover it.

'Where is that star?' asked Elhana.

'I know not,' whispered Lauria, 'unless it is . . . unless that star marks the far, forgotten Heartland. Seek it my dear, follow it, follow for all of us . . .'

Elhana was still as rock. 'The gods have summoned me,' she whispered, 'and they have shown me the way north. I know it.'

'They have. Then go, my daughter, follow it and find what place the last star you can see shines upon . . . find out if it hangs above the Heartland of wolfkind: *that* is your destiny. There you will find a new pack and a new mate. *There* . . .'

Elhana turned back to her mother and made her obeisance to left and right, shoulder to shoulder.

'Go, my dear, go *now*,' said Lauria urgently. 'Follow the dream that was born the night I bore you, and has revealed itself again tonight.'

It was a command that held the inevitability of lore, yet still Elhana hesitated, feeling her mother's body against hers, smelling her sweet scent, hearing her gentle voice.

'I remember,' whispered Lauria in wonder that she should remember so trivial a thing now, 'your father's voice . . .'

'When he told you that he loved you?'

Old Lauria shook her head.

'No, not that, not then. I remember what he told me the night he left; "Tell her I have gone ahead, tell her I shall wait for her . . . tell her that".'

'Who?' Elhana whispered, her eyes upon the fateful star.

'You, my love, you . . . He went on ahead that you might one day find courage to follow. That day is come this night.'

'Yes . . .' whispered Elhana.

She pulled away, looked at her mother one last time, turned and ran into the night as confident as if it were nothing at all she did, and she was gone.

Lauria rose up proud, and howled into the clouded sky. A howl of triumph and of destiny, a howl so compelling that far below, the pack stirred at its first sound, and, much as Pescara sought to keep them where they were, one by one they turned, the strong followed by the weak, for they felt the yearning of that howl, and they raced through the night, wolf after wolf to stand around old Lauria as she bade Elhana farewell.

They howled to tell the gods who dwelt in the northern sky that from their number they were sending a great she-wolf and she was journeying north to seek the Heartland and, as ancient prophecy decreed, to help the gods towards the star they all could see that night when Wulfin called.

CHAPTER SEVEN

Klimt recalls his youth and the loss of all his
family, and is resolved to continue his journey

K LIMT LEAPT OFF the lumber truck which had
carried him out of hell with the same instinct for
survival which had first made him leap on to it.
Nearly a day had passed and dusk had come once more,
and now he scented fresh air.

Wherever the truck had first taken him had been dark
and still, but for a gentle rocking from one side to another,
and the smell of oil and salt sea. Then lights, Mennen
voices, and roarings, before silence once again. Watchful
rest after the earlier sleep, and a time to examine his body
and find he had suffered no more than bruises from the
rocks and protrusions in the sea, with two old wounds on
his flanks, and one on his left paw, seeping and sore again.

He needed to find a safe place to rest and heal and consider how best to travel on.

'Wulf will only help me if I help myself,' he told himself,
nudging the covering which hid him to one side and peering
out. Nothing but a creaking darkness. Best to lie low and
still.

So the time had passed until he heard the Mennen voices
again, and one, no two, came past where he lay, a simple
lunge away. Scratchings, creakings, knockings and finally a
bang and roaring, and the truck shook beneath him and
moved off.

He listened much, but scented more, whiffling at the passing air and wondering that there could be so many scents he did not know.

'At least some of them are food!' he muttered ruefully to himself. 'So perhaps I will not starve!'

The truck's sound suddenly increased and settled to a steady whining roar. When he peered out he saw a grey, dead landscape rushing by, and straight trunks of what seemed to be trees flash against the sky, except that they had amber lights on top. The road he peered down upon went by too fast, so he knew he could not escape without injury, and for a time panic came to him. But then he remembered that this Mennen-thing that carried him had gone slow and stopped before, and surely would do so again. No creature goes on travelling forever.

'But the first chance I have, I escape!' he decided.

So it was that dusk fell and the truck slowed and stopped and Klimt had readied himself to leap; but there were lights and Mennen near, and other vehicles roaring round about. Instinct told him to stay where he was. The truck moved off once more, and gathered speed before settling to its former pace. Klimt had repositioned himself near its edge, muzzle to the air, waiting for the right moment.

It came only as night fell beyond the strange, bright Mennen lights along the way they travelled. The truck slowed, Klimt stared out and saw an edge of dirty grass but a single leap away. He flexed his body, readied himself and then . . . once more the truck gathered speed.

Four times this happened before the time was right, and, what was more, the air scented fresher than before.

Klimt nudged the covering aside, turned a little to face the direction in which they were travelling, readied his paws again, and as the truck slowed he leapt to new life, and new territory. He hit the grassy ground, rolled in a welter of paws and scratchy vegetation, and was suddenly up and still, four paws on the ground, safely in shadow, the truck roaring off into the distance, with other vehicles racing past on the road above him, their approaching lights shaped like moons but bright as suns, their rear lights red as blood.

Lights and more lights, Klimt had never seen anything like it. He scented quickly all about and found nothing much that caused him concern, though some things were curious, not the least of which was the scent of carrion.

It could wait. He crept lower down the slope and stared out across a view like nothing he had seen before. Lights everywhere, almost as many as stars, but not *live* stars. Most were amber or yellow, and they ran in lines, with each point of light diminishing in size to create gentle curves that cut across each other. The lights seemed to roar, and past them, moving steadily, went other lights. The red ones slowly disappeared, the white-yellow ones grew bigger as they roared until they too disappeared somewhere below him to his right.

All Mennen-made, all strange, and not a Mann or scent of one at all. No, no, what he scented was the sea, its robust smell carried on a light wind from the north, and oil. He peered through the haze the near lights made and saw, distantly, the dappling of water above which faint lights bobbed up and down.

He stared upwards at the sky and saw there great clouds of light, soft, drifting, changing except for one place only: straight above his head.

'Real stars,' Klimt whispered, 'not Mennen-made.'

He got up and turned upslope to find the carrion. Rook, fresh-dead. And then another . . . very strange. He scented hard at them for poison, but there was none. He pushed at their squashed bodies with a paw, check-tasted them before consuming them thankfully, but with care. Birds would do for now. He spat out feathers and bones, licked his mouth, and contemplated the unfamiliar fact that he felt good.

'The Mennen are not chasing me!' he thought. 'The Mennen do not know I'm here.'

He stretched his front paws forward and his rear paws behind, and arched his back down. His haunches shivered and his head rose, jaws open, teeth catching the distant lights. The tip of his nose broke the cover of shadow into light and he righted himself and trotted further down the bank to begin exploring.

As the evening wore on the roar of cars and trucks never ceased, though beneath the bridges, or in the concrete channels for water that he found and drank from, the sound eased, or echoed, or whispered.

There was life in the dark. Like the bats he found which lived in the dark recesses beneath a fly-over, and which he watched for a long time as they fluttered in and out of the light beyond their home. He had never seen pale, translucent bats before, only the black silhouettes that darted out of dusk, and crossed the moon.

There were voles, three of which he caught. There was a toad, large and fat and foul to touch and scent, let alone to taste. No dogs though, but for one heard barking in the distance. Instead he scented fox, the only substantial creature he detected, though its trail was old.

He found a duck, rotting, and far from water. Indeed he found many dead things along the verges by the roads the trucks used. And he understood why as he watched the rush of the Mennen-trucks: they came so fast, with such an ear-splitting roar, and the fumes along the way all conspired to dull a creature of his senses. Getting killed would be so easy here.

'Yet I feel safer in the middle of this unnatural place than ever I did when near the Mennen before. Maybe . . .' he thought, '*because* there are no Mennen, only their rushing things, and their innumerable roads, and the lights which seem more striking than the stars.'

He turned finally north, forced to cross one of the roads since there was no other choice, and after much searching back and forth, found a way beyond the flat grey structure onto grass, and from there to rolling dunes, with the smell of sea beyond.

Deep among the dunes there were no lights and he could see the stars above. But on the edges of the sky, and around, he could see the glow of the Mennen lights, and he marvelled at how they dominated the normal sky.

Movement. Scurrying. Rabbits! He had scented their spoor a little way back, and now he heard them near. He let them be, partly satisfied by what he had already found, but mainly because he was too excited by all he saw and felt.

He did not know why he felt so safe, so masterful, lord of the Mennen night. He came onto a rough track and scented a Mennen-thing ahead. Smaller than a truck. Reaching it, he felt its warmth, though its moons had set. He peered from shadows up its flank and saw, dimly, the strangest thing: a Mennen head within the Mennen-thing, still and staring. He circled the thing cautiously and found he could see another head in the other side, this one moving. Sounds briefly of a low voice. He went off into the night and, where waves lapped along a shore he found a safe place to sit and stare across the sea, and think:

'What are the Mennen?'

He had asked this of his father more than once and had discovered that there was more than one answer. Finally, it came down to this: the Mennen *were*, as blizzards were. They came and they went; they killed wolves or they did not; there was no answering what they were, only the fact of it, and a wolf must only accept all it meant.

Then . . .

'When did the Mennen come, before or after wolves?' he had asked his father, as young wolves will, thinking about the answers to one question and then finding another to ask, and another after that . . .

'They came after.'

His mother had said it in that quiet and measured voice she used when there was a tale to tell behind what she had begun to say.

'How long before?'

His mother had smiled and Klimt had relaxed, for he liked her stories of the early time of wolves, when Wulf himself roamed the earth and led his pack of gods from the misty heights of the inner Heartland where, too dangerous for mortal wolf to venture near, the WulfRock rose, out of which he had first come. The WulfRock, which was the portal of gods into mortality, and the threshold a mortal wolf must cross if he was to set his paw upon a wolfway to the stars.

'No wolf knows when mortal wolf first came to earth,' she had begun, 'but we know this: in the beginning there were three kinds of earthbound creature – the great cats, the great wolves, and the Mennen. The cats came first, the wolves came second, and the Mennen came last. The cats began to decline first, the wolves second, and the Mennen are declining last. No creature has ascendancy for ever, unless his gods stay sure across the sky. Eventually all creatures, all tribes, all beings die, to be replaced by others . . .'

How bleak his mother's eyes had been when she had said this, and though he did not know it, how like his own. Bleakness might have been the dust of snow across Klimt's heart in need of the warmth of sun and a love that was passionate.

'I know when the cat gods began to die across the lands we know,' his mother had continued, 'leaving their mortal kin to cast but trivial shadows among the forest trees, and hide from wolves, and you know it, Klimt, for I have told you.'

'It was when mortal wolves defeated their war god, the sabre-toothed Smilodon, in the shadow of the WulfRock,' Klimt had intoned, knowing that his mother liked to precede a new tale with reference to an old one, just to see that he was attentive and had remembered what had gone before.

'It was, my dear, it was so. Smilodon died, and wolves were finally ascendant over cats, whilst the Mennen had not yet found their strength and begun to understand that only by the destruction of the sacred wolfways might they be ascendant over us. But . . . it was long ago, and though we have never descended to the humiliations the cats have suffered – playthings of the Mennen – yet we have been defeated, and our decline has been the more painful that it is within the memory of our tales. But there was a wolf of Bukovina knew it . . . have I told you of that?'

'Bukovina is east of the Heartland, you told me that much, anyway.'

'Ah . . .' and his mother had smiled that slight smile again and told him what little she knew of how the Wolves of Time, inspired by a Bukov wolf, were sent forth from the Heartland that they might hide in far-off places, where the Mennen did not roam, and await the Mennen's decline so that there would be wolves ready to return to the Heartland when the time was right, and Wulf summoned them.

'When will that be?' Klimt had asked, indefatigable; not satisfied with one great story, but always wanting more. 'Did a wolf from the pack of the ancient Wolves of Time come here?'

'It is a dream, my dear, only a dream, for only mortal wolves are left now, and the Wolves of Time, wherever it

85

is they went, cannot now find their way to the present from the distant centuries in which they hid: our decline has been too great.'

'Hmmph!' Klimt's father had said, 'There's always room for dreams my dear, and what wolf can tell they will never come true? Certainly one wolf can never tell another, or none of us would ever journey anywhere, in body or in mind. So don't tell Klimt that the Wolves of Time are dead – tell him they live in sleeping shadows, waiting for the day of their recall. Tell him that!'

'You've told him yourself!' she had replied, for she saw the gleam of hope in Klimt's young eyes . . .

It seemed so long ago, the time when he had been so young, and now there was another lore to think about, more important and more terrible than dreams and prophecies: for all wolves knew that the Mennen must never be killed, *never*. But he, Klimt, had killed a Mann and he felt something he knew his father had never felt, nor his mother, and nor for all he knew, *any* wolf: *he felt no fear of Mennen*. In the act of killing one, his fear had gone.

He mused in wonder now, wondering if it was in losing that fear he had lost another, which was the fear of death itself. Were they the same, perhaps? He had not been afraid to die when he had faced them for the last time before turning to dive into the sea.

'I did that not because I was afraid – no, it wasn't that – it was because I did not want them to have me. Let the sea see me die not the Mennen . . .'

He got up restlessly, raised his head to scent the air, and made his way slowly through the dunes that edged the sea. He turned back towards its sound and found it lapping softly over mud, which sucked at his paws when he went out onto it. He backed off to drier land and wandered the deserted shore, listening to the night clucking of the waterfowl, and somewhere a sharp fluting of an oyster catcher.

Why was it that here, in darkness bounded in all directions by Mennen lights and structures, and the hum of the endlessly moving Mennen-things, such sounds seemed more beautiful to him than ever before?

He stared across the darkness of the sea to the shadow of land beyond and realized he was looking at the territory from which he had escaped. He knew, too, that he could not turn his back on it forever and journey on to seek the Heartland until he faced again all he had lost, and found a place for it in his heart.

He backed to the sheltering haven of a dune, settled into deepest shadow, and lived one last time the memories from which he had fled, and remembered again the prophecy of Heartland and service to all wolves his father had made for him, which had given him the strength and courage to survive.

The river Torne rises in the mountains of Scandinavia's far north and Tornesdal, its valley, runs south-east into the Gulf of Bothnia. Klimt's mother was a Lappish wolf who had wandered down from the fjells of the north-east, and his father was of Norwegian stock with the scent of pine forests in his blood. Both vagrants, they met and mated, and chose the forested lower part of Tornesdal for their territory, a compromise. They had two litters, the first becoming the males and females who helped to raise the second litter of three cubs, of which Klimt was one of two males.

In their different ways Klimt's parents taught him all they knew of lupine lore, and whispered of the Lappish mysteries of leading and wandering, and of the vengeful ancient gods out of whose downfall the gods Wulf and Wulfin came.

'Gods *do* fall,' his father was inclined to say, though with an self-irony Klimt was then too young to understand. Instead, he had stared at the night sky and imagined gods, each made of a million stars, plummeting down to earth.

'Pride, usually,' explained his father, 'which breeds indifference to those for whom a god should care, as a father should care for his young and a leader for his pack. A leader is *never* more important than his pack, never!'

'But aren't they the same thing?' said Klimt, who was inclined to enjoy an argument. 'Didn't you say that once?'

'He may have done – he says a lot of things,' his mother had replied. 'You'll find that truth accumulates, my dear. But . . . a leader and a pack are not always the same thing. There are different packs than this, and different ways of leading them. We have shown you but one way, and that not necessarily the best. Now *my* father, when he was leader, would never have talked as *your* father does. He was too stuck in his ways, too inclined to think he was always right, too.'

'Proud?' wondered Klimt, 'like gods?'

'Just so,' continued his father. 'The ancient gods fell, and Wulf and Wulfin took their place. This was at the time when the world as we know it was made. But in time Wulf himself fell and left Wulfin to wander the wolfways of the stars alone, searching for him . . .'

'You told me *that* story long ago!' said Klimt dismissively.

'Hmmph!' exclaimed his father grumpily. 'Then you understand why mortal wolfkind is in decline. Wulf did wrong by his ledrene Wulfin and mated with a mortal wolf, and in doing that he died as a god and was born as a mortal wolf, born to die and die again in the never-ending cycle of life and death from which there is no escape for any of our kind unless they can ascend the wolfway to the stars and themselves be gods as Wulf once was.'

'How could a wolf do that?' wondered Klimt, staring at the stars. 'Was Wulf really reborn a mortal wolf?'

'If he was not, then what hope can be left for any of us, or for wolfkind?'

'But you said wolfkind is dying,' said Klimt flippantly, too young yet to believe in his own mortality, let alone that of his whole race.

'One day, my son, you will see that we are, we are . . .' said his father, glancing sadly at his mother, who nodded bleakly. 'Your mother left her own pack because she believed that by doing so she might in some small way help all wolves.'

'I thought one or other of the remaining gods, Wulfin herself perhaps, might show me a way. But . . . well . . .'

'She showed you the way to *me*,' said Klimt's father gently, and with great love.

Klimt remembered staring at them then and seeing for the first time that they were the whole world to him, and that one day they would be no more. They were mortal . . . and in seeing that he saw for the first time too that he was mortal as well and that if there were things to be done with his life, they had best be done sooner than later. Such things as this, and many other things as well, Klimt learnt in the peace that was Tornesdal then.

He learnt too of the wolfways, marked out by Wulf himself during his earthly wandering when he was in the ascendant, before he became a god, which were the ancient routes of wolf through forest and mountain, by lake and river to the sea, in all the places of the earth.

'And why do they exist, my son?' asked Klimt's father rhetorically. 'So that wolves may wander safely from one place to another, as vagrants or as lones, or in breakaway packs seeking new territory. And how do we remember them? By the patterns of the stars, which you too must learn so that when you are adult, and if you lead a pack, you will know which way to go.'

That was the hope, but in time Klimt found a different reality: his parents did not know all the wolfways of the stars, only fragments of them covering their own territory, and the places where they were born. He was shown how the stars and the lines and angles between them led a wolf from mountain top to lake, from lake to fjell, from fjell to valley, from the meeting of two rivers up to a mountain pass, and he marvelled that there in the stars, lost now to wolf's memory, was a guide to all the earth.

'No wolf knows all the ways, or can interpret all the stars except for Wulf himself,' his father told him. 'That is why he *is* a god – or was!'

'Not even Wulfin his mate?' asked Klimt. 'Does she not know them?'

'Yes, yes, perhaps she knew them too, perhaps. But amongst mortal wolves, in olden times, each pack knew its wolfways and how they connected to the adjacent territories and vagrants could follow the ways from pack to pack.'

'But packs don't like vagrants,' said Klimt.

'Hmmph!' said his father, 'It all depends. Vagrants are tolerated if they pass on the tales and secrets that they learn, howling out their tales at dawn and dusk, and keeping their proper place. They live on the scraps a pack leaves behind, as they travel in the space between territories.'

'Where do the wolfways begin, and where do they end?' asked Klimt.

'At the place where Wulf began his mortal journey, which is also where he returned at the end, which is called the Heartland of the Wolf. To there do all wolfways lead, and the beginning and ending of all things is at the centre of the Heartland, which is where the WulfRock is. But where *that* is, we Nordic wolves know not. Westward, across the Baltic Sea, probably. Beyond our reach, certainly!'

From the moment the young wolf heard of the Heartland, and the sacred place called the WulfRock, he felt a surge of excitement and awesome mystery. He would stare at the stars and muse that lost and forgotten among their myriad of points was the special wolfway that might lead him to the holy place. For special it must surely be.

Klimt had been born in late spring, as sturdy a cub as it was possible to be. Of the two males in his litter he was dominant from the first weeks of mock-fighting, his clear eyes and solid stance forcing his siblings to be subordinate. Yet let another wolf threaten them, if only in play and, however powerful the wolf might be, Klimt went for them. So from the first he had his little pack.

Until the autumn of his birth year he was happy enough; his rilling with his siblings, his nascent howls, his exploration of the territory, pleasures for all to share. But that October the Mennen came and his sister was shot dead, and one of the adult siblings so badly maimed that he died.

A shadow came to Klimt's strong face then and a loss of innocence. It was then that he turned from play with his father to talk with his Lappish mother, who began to tell him things of which she had never spoken before. She spoke of the gods, and how a thousand years before Wulf had sinned . . .

'What did he do?'

'He broke his own law,' said Klimt's mother shortly, 'and wolfkind's present misery is the result. We are cursed to decline before the Mennen's wrath, driven from our homelands, cursed to wander the forgotten wolfways until there is no place left to go.'

In her mysterious, dark way she told of dooms and

91

curses, gave him warnings, and whispered how the gods were in decline. Again and again she told the stories, each time a little differently, each time helping him to accumulate a little more truth.

'For a thousand years our kind will die, that's what I was told, and then we'll have a chance to redeem ourselves, but don't ask me how or why. The sleeping gods will wake as mortal wolves, whatever that may mean, and they'll have one lifetime to put all right again, and one alone – just time enough to teach the Mennen that they're mortal too.'

'Don't listen to her,' his father would say. 'She's getting old and past her time. She says she was told all these stories, but if you ask me, she made them up!' His parents would laugh then, with each other, full of fondness and of love.

Klimt's first winter was a time of new exploration, which he undertook most often in the company of his brother. Up to the frozen lakes they went, or onto the tundra fjells, to watch out for reindeer that had got separated from the herds on the lower ground. They would harry them if they could, but in no great hope yet of killing one by themselves, as the pack did under the leadership of their father. Sometimes he went off on his own, and it was during such an expedition that he first felt the call from a power beyond himself, which his mother had once described as a 'summoning to the work of the gods'.

'You'll know it when you feel it, and you're the one who *will*, alone of all my offspring. When it comes, obey it as you would a call to save your own life . . .'

There came a day when up by the lakes he felt it, and nothing had ever felt so urgent. One moment he was drinking the chill water of a stream and staring at the pebbles over which the water rippled, and the next the harsh thrill of alarm went through his body and he turned up and around, and poised dead-still, water dripping from his muzzle as he tried to hear, tried to scent, tried to see what caused him such concern.

Then there came what felt like a distant howling to his ears, deeper by far than any mortal howling he had heard, beyond time it seemed, certain as rocks or water or sun; and he felt not fear but power. It was the call of gods, and there was no doubt what he must do. Without thought he let his paws take him up the little bank, back the way he had come, down, down towards the lower ground where the pack must be; where he was needed *now*.

He did not even need to quarter the ground to pick up the pack's scent before he found them tussling about a reindeer carcass they had come across, almost all of them more senior than him, which meant he would have had to wait. One of the adult siblings had found the carcass and, having fully exercised his right to gorge himself first, their father was now leading the others to feed when Klimt arrived.

Despite his father's threats he scented at the reindeer and did not like it. But what wolf would listen to him? He did his best to warn them off but with only two did he succeed. One was his subordinate brother, who had remained outside the feeding circle and the other was his mother, who after a few bites at the meat, yielded to Klimt's snarls and nips and pleas, and regurgitated what she had eaten, before retreating from the feed.

No need now to recall the horror of the howls that followed, when one by one the wolves that had fed died in agony of the poison the Mennen had laid upon the reindeer. Worse was the death of their father, who vomited up his own stomach.

By dawn next day all but one had died, though he, too, was near the end. Klimt's mother was sick and very weak, while only he and his brother, who had not touched the meat, were well. At the end of another day, Klimt found himself leader of the pack – if pack it could be called – of only three wolves. The poison was a powerful one and Klimt's mother did not recover full use of her limbs. It was a hard struggle through the winter darkness waiting for the spring sun to bring her health.

Yet it had one compensation: the way Klimt had sensed something was wrong and come running to help the pack, even if he had been unable to persuade them to help themselves, convinced his mother he was a special wolf.

'The gods favour you Klimt, they are watching you . . . Now, you must prepare to journey north. My father's father was a Russian wolf, and *his* father was born of the famous Mezen pack. I must have told you . . .'

She had of course, but that did not stop her from describing again the great dark Russian wolves of the steppes who are bigger than Lappish wolves. Telling the story made her forget her pain.

'You've got their blood in your veins. Now you promise me that when I'm gone you'll turn north and find them. That's the safe way, as far from the Mennen as you can get. Take your brother . . .'

'But we don't know the wolfways over those cold lands.'

'Great Wulf will guide you . . .'

'I thought he had fallen . . .' said Klimt mischievously.

'He has, he has, but what's a god if not an example, and *that* can still inspire you!'

'Yes,' they said dutifully.

But their mother's sickness never left her even when the spring sunshine grew warm at last. They led her a little way northward, and she lived to see the first flowering of the fjells across which she had wandered when she was young and found their father. She scented at the bilberry shoots once more, and nodded in her last moments to where, as summer came, cotton-grass would blow.

'Promise me you'll go north and find your Russian kin, Klimt, promise it, in Wulf's name!'

What harm could there be in making promises to a dying wolf if it would ease her passage to the wolfway to the stars? Klimt promised it, and even thought they might travel on to Russia to find the Mezen pack itself.

But it was not to be.

The Mennen came and three days later Klimt's brother died, entangled in a simple snare of wire from which he could not be released. Poison, wire, gunshots . . . the Mennen meted out their death in many ways, all of them hard for a wolf to fight. As for counter-attacking the Mennen, he knew the lore well enough: wolves do not kill Mennen.

It was some nights after the last of his kin had died, when Klimt had wandered disconsolately off the fjell and back to the forest in the Tornesdal, that he had a dream of destiny that left the sense of being called far more powerful than the one he had had before.

He dreamt that the stars shone bright above his head, and in them a pattern seemed to form, stretching south over the firmament, and then on into the distance before turning east. At its end was a bright solitary star, and Klimt heard his name called and he knew he must follow the wolfway and find the star, which surely marked the Heartland and, perhaps, the WulfRock itself.

It seemed a dream, but when he woke he believed it was his certain destiny, and so he turned his back on Tornesdal, and on the Lappish lands, to head southwards where the Mennen lived. He believed Wulf had shown him the way, and he would follow it. His promise to his mother he put aside, though uneasily, for she had made him invoke Wulf's name when he promised to go north . . .

*   *   *

'I promised her,' Klimt whispered now, the sea lapping up the shore below him, 'and one day I shall fulfil that promise . . .

  A curlew called; nearby voles scurried; the stars grew dim beneath fresh cloud. Klimt settled down to try to sleep, but could not: the past bore down upon him, and took him in its grasp and all that night would not let him go.

CHAPTER EIGHT

*Klimt confronts his grim past and journeys on
in the hope of finding a better future*

K LIMT HAD TRAVELLED cautiously southward
after his brother's death, following Scandinavia's
central spine of mountains on its eastern side, staying as near to the tree line as he could unless weather and
terrain drove him to lower ground. He was a vagrant wolf,
establishing no territory. He preyed on what mammals he
could find, but never Mennen stock unless it was ailing or
dead. The Mennen he avoided absolutely, their lights, their
scents, their tracks, their homes.

He travelled slowly and overwintered high in the lake-
lands of Hanaven, nearly starving in the final weeks before
life and prey returned to the snowbound landscape. That
new spring, when life abounded and the forests scented of
life and began to shine with light, loneliness began to come
to him, like a thorn that had worked its way into his paw
and would not come out.

He travelled on, sometimes rushing and panicked, frightened of his own shadow; at others not travelling at all, but
slumped and listless, feeling there was no point in journeying on. He had dismissed long since his dream of destiny,
and when it came sometimes to trouble him he shook his
head and whispered, 'No!'

The autumn and winter that followed was a time of darkness for Klimt, when his fur was bedraggled, and his eyes

staring and half-dead. He felt that not only had he lost all his kin and been left forever alone, but that Wulf and Wulfin had deserted him too. He knew despair and felt at last the need to pray.

'Great Wulf, my name is Klimt of Tornesdal and I journey in your name . . . Now I see nothing but darkness before me and darkness behind. Guide me!'

A wolf's prayers to the gods are rarely answered directly and never as a wolf expects, and yet if they are made with faith and an open heart they are always answered in the end . . .

Klimt decided to turn back from his journey south in early February and dropped down to lower ground to make his passage north more easy. His mother had been right, but in truth his despair was such that he no longer cared if the Mennen found him. Death might be release.

It was then in his hour of greatest darkness that his prayer seemed to be answered. For out of the late afternoon of the third day of his returning northward journey he heard the howling of a wolf somewhere in the mountains above him, distant but distinct. He got up and stood quite still, his head cocked on one side, his ears erect, and his tail twitching from side to side. Then he extended his head, half-opened his mouth and, raising his head slowly, howled out a lorn reply, stopped, and listened. He had almost never howled since the last of his pack died lest the Mennen heard, but the excitement of hearing his own kind and the compulsion to make contact now over-rode all caution and fear.

After a wait that seemed an age, he heard the distant howl again. Excited, he ran a little way towards it and howled once more, more powerfully this time. He did not wait for the response but trotted up through the trees and pasture fields, faster and faster until dusk came, his heart filled with longing.

He stopped and waited as darkness fell, listening in hope to hear the howl again. Night came; such moon as there was hid behind the clouds, the stars were occasional and dim. Still he waited. Then suddenly he heard the howl again, much louder and nearer, and just a shade downslope. He answered and ran towards it through the shadows of the night, being careful since in addition to the trees there were rocks, and the gullies made by thaw-water in the spring. As he ran, he scented air and ground to seek to identify the other wolf.

There was another brief howl, now very close, and he had the scent, clear and sweet as hay, and even as she came out from among the trees and he saw her shadowy form, Klimt knew that this was female. For a troubling moment he felt a pang of terrible foreboding which demanded that he turned tail and ran, not for his own good but hers. But her scent was good, and the yearning he felt was more powerful than shadows in his mind.

So he went straight to her, nose to nose, flank to flank, scenting the whole of her. A quick turn and push, and then a growl, and he established dominance. She gave the softest rill and he rilled in response. Again and again they nosed and scented in the night, circled and rilled until the snow where they met was flattened among the trees.

He turned proudly from her and settled down, head along his paws. She ran off, scent-marked a tree, whimpered, and then settled down herself within scent and sound but out of sight. Night deepened and Klimt slept as he had not for months past, excited and content. When morning came, they began to talk.

Her name was Elsinor and she had travelled south as he had, but from a territory south of Tornesdal, along the Bothnian coast. The Mennen had harassed her pack and she had lost touch, or rather, chosen to do so. She was young, had never mated, and her fur was paler and more

russet than his own. Within days of their meeting he felt
the change in his life was absolute and forgot all of his
concerns. There was life in his step, and a shine in his eyes
and in hers as well. Each felt the other to be the most
beautiful creature they had ever seen.

Winter lost its darkness and the coming spring gained
its allure, and Klimt, finding his prayer answered, began
believing in Wulf again. This new spring he was not lonely.

For those first days they stayed in the area where they
had found each other, but soon a new need had come – for
a territory of their own that could support a pack.

'Why were you going south, Elsinor?' he asked one
dawn.

'It felt right,' she answered softly, 'and I felt drawn that
way.'

'Yes . . .' he said, remembering his dream. Was this
Wulf's way of getting him to go south?

'Shall we go that way now?' she asked diffidently, and
that was the moment he understood that he, Klimt of
Tornesdal, was leader of a pack, however small it might
be now, and it would abide by his decisions. Leader! He
felt a pride he had never known before, and a sense of purpose.

'Yes,' he answered. 'We shall follow the wolfways south.'

'Wherefore?' she asked.

Then he told her of his dream of destiny when he heard
Wulf's voice summoning him.

'We shall travel south and later in the spring we shall find
a territory for our young. When they are mature enough we
shall lead them further south to try to find a way to the
Heartland of the Wolf. That is our destiny.' He spoke firmly
and stood proud. She stood up, and waited for him to lead
her out into the morning light.

They mated at the end of February, while they were still
journeying, and by the beginning of April she knew that

she was with cub and they must find a territory. The trouble was that the further south they went the more Mennen there were, and higher up the valleys too.

The first possible area they found did not feel right to Elsinor. The second, five days on and when she was beginning to grow heavy with her young and wanting only to stop and make a den for the birthing, seemed fine. But after only two days there they were sighted and followed by a Mann.

They plodded on, Elsinor growing more tired each day, until at last they found a lakeland place that was sheltered, deserted of Mennen, and offered the chance of prey, small and large.

'It will do,' said Klimt guardedly.

'It will have to do,' said Elsinor as she began to make a den near a stream that ran down to a lake.

Ten days later their cubs were born and named: Avendal and Sturma, the two females; and Torne the male, named after his father's home territory. The days that followed, of feeding and nurturing, of little discoveries, of snatched and blissful sleep, and hours of watching as the cubs began to venture out and play in the April sun, was a time of maturing for them all.

Klimt seemed to grow bigger and more grave, and his eyes were ever watchful. His coat had thickened over winter and now as spring advanced and his family – his first pack – grew, his fur turned darker once again. Sometimes Elsinor would watch him from the den when he allowed his young to mock-fight him, as they tumbled squealing all about, and she felt him to be more than ordinary wolf, for there was the light of destiny on him, bright as summer sun. And yet there were shadows too, though whence they came she could not tell.

Sometimes they heard distant shots.

'It's the Mennen,' she whispered so that the cubs did

not hear. 'I fear them, Klimt, that they will find us, and we will be unable to protect our cubs.'

He nodded, eyes darkening.

'I fear the same. The moment our young are old enough we'll move on to deeper forest lands where if they find us they cannot chase us.'

The shadows they had feared rose up, darkened and took solid form sooner and in a way far more terrible even than in a wolf's worst nightmare. Great Wulf had smiled on Klimt, but now he frowned and turned his back.

It was a day at the end of June when the cubs were well grown that Elsinor left Klimt in charge and went downslope to the stream to drink.

As the youngsters tussled with their father a black rook rose suddenly above the trees by the lake and Klimt looked up in alarm. At the same moment there was a shot, sharp and loud, and then another. And then a third. Then silence. The three cubs froze in fear, and then ran to Klimt who hurried them into the protection of the den. Ordering them to stay there he turned and ran to where Elsinor had gone. Only when he got near did he see her lying crookedly, half in the stream, half out.

Urgently he nuzzled at her flanks and head, and then with mounting horror discovered there were wounds all over her.

'Elsinor . . .'

But even as he whispered her name he saw the way the cold and rushing water took her blood away and knew that she was dead. A numbness came over him, preventing shock and grief from turning to panic. The cubs! He turned from her, swiftly climbed the stream's bank and was about to run back to the den when he saw a Mann, and the movement of its dogs. Klimt stopped short, eyes narrowing and even as he saw the flash and heard the bang he felt pain searing the length of his left flank.

Even that he might have taken and still gone forward, desperate as he was to get to the den and protect his young, but the Mann had given a curt command and the dogs were up and at him, and he was running, fighting, crashing through trees and undergrowth, into streams and falling into the chaos of attack and swift defence.

Then as suddenly as it all began, it ended. There was a distant whistle and the dogs he had bloodied but not maimed turned and were swiftly gone, and he was left shocked and alone, his body ripped and wounded by their teeth, and battered from the knocks against trees and ground he had sustained.

He scented the air, ran this way and that, orientated himself to ground he knew, and making the best speed he could, he limped back upslope to the den. If the Mann was there he would take his chance again . . .

He saw them before he reached the den: Sturma, stretched out one way, and Torne the other; both dead. Torne's head was . . . and now he *was* bereft, his eyes wild and his whimpers like a pup's. He went into the den to find Avendal but she was not there, only the scents of all his pack, all his stolen life.

Wild now, desperate, he searched the clearing round the den but found no Avendal. He rilled softly as he went, hoping she might be hiding, but no sound answered him, nor any scent but death. He turned from his hopeless search to where Elsinor had died but her body had gone as well. They had taken her away. All that was left was the fading sense of the wolf he had loved and the deadly scent of the Mann.

Klimt did not know what to do. He howled out for little Avendal, he wandered around the clearing, he licked at his two lost young, he stared, and he whimpered with grief so

103

great that he did not notice yet the pain of the wounds he had.

Then dusk came, and with it a sense of utter loss.

It was as the first stars shone that he heard a distant squeal, a harsh banging, and then Avendal's far-off cry, short, sharp, and shrill. He raised himself, turning his head and cocking his ears in its direction. Then he heard her bleat again, like no sound a cub should ever make. As he began to head towards it he knew it was no simple bleat: this was a cry of pain and loss, a sound once heard no wolf could ever forget, nor any father be able to forgive.

Then, as he neared the cries he at last grew cautious. They had tried to kill him once and might try it once again. His senses and instincts, which so far that day seemed to have failed him were now acute, and they were warning him to go slow, however terrible his daughter's call. Suddenly Klimt *knew* the Mann was waiting.

He took a route that brought him downwind of the sound and paused. Avendal's bleats were fainter and less frequent. Slowly, quietly, he crept through the trees, using what cover he could find and scenting out what lay ahead. There was Avendal for sure, the scent of fear and acute despair; the Mann, he knew *that* odorous scent; and dogs, they were there as well. Being downwind they could not yet scent him.

Quiet as a lengthening shadow he crept on until he was near enough to hear the Mann turning, rustling, patting at the dogs. And finally, by the bleak light of the stars, he saw Avendal, and what he saw was past belief. Avendal dangled from a tree by her front paws, the rest of her body hanging free. She was whimpering now and her head had fallen back and sometimes her back paws scrabbled uselessly at the thin air as her mouth opened in a mute scream. He stared at those paws and saw that his daughter Avendal was nailed to that branch.

He understood that his own cub was bait to summon him.

One wolf in a million only would have done what Klimt did then: *nothing at all* except close his ears to Avendal's dying cries which weakened and grew more pitiful as the night advanced.

Nothing, as she cried out her last and stiffened towards one final, eternal cry of abandonment.

Nothing as the Mann cursed and rose up from his place of hiding, and bade the dogs follow after him.

Nothing but to think, to know, to repeat to himself, 'The lore is wrong and now I shall break the lore. I know no fear now. I shall break the lore my mother taught: that wolves must always fear the Mennen; wolves must never kill the Mennen; wolves must be subordinate.'

Klimt waited until the Mann had gone noisily downslope through the forest, before he rose up in the night. He went to where poor Avendal's body hung and made a single gentle leap to touch her one last time as if to send her innocent spirit up on the wolfway to the stars with his caress.

'Accept her, Wulf,' he whispered beneath her swinging form, 'and forgive me for what I must now do.'

Avendal swung above him until finally she was still, and her spirit gone beyond all pain and suffering, on towards the stars whose names she never learned.

Klimt stalked silently through the forest after the Mann and the dogs, and he looked not like the messenger of death, but death itself, his eyes fierce, his fur unkempt, his muzzle set. He caught up with the Mann, careful to stay downwind, but near, and his eyes were points of fatal fire on the Mann's back and flank.

They came to a track and Klimt was pleased, for what he needed was enough space to see the ground ahead. The Mann stopped and slung the gun over his shoulder and then went on. The dogs followed close behind until Klimt growled low, but loud enough for the trailing dog to hear. It turned, paused, stepped back to investigate, and all it ever saw was the flying head of the wolf, agape with teeth, and the snapping rip at its throat which sent it sprawling into the red darkness of death.

As the Mann and his other dog turned, Klimt was hurling off the track, out of sight and way past them both among the trees, then out onto the track ahead of them as they went back to the dying dog. Klimt trotted stiff-legged towards the Mann's turned back and only snarled when he was a single savage leap away. The Mann turned and Klimt was onto him, ripping at his round white face and crunching at flesh and bone. Teeth broke free as Klimt tasted the warm blood of one of the Mennen. The Mann began to fall gurgling, screaming cries welcomed into Klimt's receptive jaws. Klimt's grip loosened as the Mann hit the ground and as his scream broke free, Klimt moved down to rip out his soft white throat. His killing was instinctive, but full of savage hate, and the need for it allowed him to ignore the dog's assault on his flank until he knew it was complete.

The Mann shuddered, and his hands pushed briefly at Klimt's face and then fell weakly back. His legs kicked for a moment and then were still.

Only then did Klimt raise his bloodied maw and turn towards the dog. His lunge into it was so powerful that he carried it off the track and into the undergrowth. The dog tried one countermove, fell back, twisted, and was off and away howling through the trees.

Then all was still, and the only sound when Klimt's violent breathing calmed was the wind in the spruce above his head.

'Great Wulf, forgive me,' he whispered up to the stars; but their light was cold and no answer did he hear.

'Wulf, the Mann killed Elsinor,' he pleaded. 'The Mann

killed all my cubs. Wulf . . .' but there were no words that justified breaking the lore.

He stared into the impenetrable darkness beyond the stars and felt that his punishment had begun. Loneliness had returned a hundredfold.

'I have nothing left but a memory of your voice Great Wulf, summoning me to seek the wolfway to the Heartland whose line in the stars you showed me . . . The hope that this is what you want me to do is all I have now. Pity Klimt of Tornesdal, guide him, for he has lost all he had, all kin, all love, all leadership.'

He looked one last time at the fallen Mann, and the dog he had killed, stared up and down the starlit track and then turned south off it, and disappeared among the trees.

That was the beginning of his nightmare trek to Helsingborg. Within two days the Mennen started hunting him. There were dogs again, and Mennen on the roads; there were the moving, dazzling lights of motors, and roaring lights from out of the sky. There was baited carrion and traps; and one day a great line of the Mennen beating the forest to flush him out.

He was shot at many times, and hit twice; he was poisoned once; he was struck by a truck on a road where, fatigued beyond endurance, he had collapsed. The wounds he initially sustained festered and he suffered poisoned blood. Three times dogs came after him, and three times he fought them off.

If he found a place to lie low to recuperate, they found it too; if he tried to hunt they saw him, if he did not, he starved. So that inexorably as he travelled further south he had weakened and they had closed on him.

Yet not once was he tempted to turn back north, feeling

that the night his family were killed and he killed the Mann, when he prayed to silent Wulf, he had renewed a vow to reach wolfkind's Heartland. Only there, and then, would he find expiation for his sins. If only Wulf would let him get that far . . .

Klimt stared out across the sea and saw the first light of dawn touch the land he had left behind. As he watched a mist drifted from the north and the land of his birth and all his memories seemed as nothing.

But not his anger.

He turned to face the east and saw the Mennen's lights on road and way were fading before the coming sunrise.

'I do not like you, Wulf,' he whispered, surprised at himself, but relieved to admit so blasphemous a thought. 'I do not like you Great Wulf, for you failed me. But . . .'

But he would travel on as he had vowed to do, taking routes such as he had already found, which might be wolf-ways for all he knew.

'I do not like . . .'

But he said no more. The sun was rising and he could see trucks and cars moving along the motorway off which he had come the previous night. Soon the sun's rays would reach ground he must cross if he was to get back to the shadows of the deadland around the motorway.

'Deadland,' he mused, repeating the apt word as he made his careful way among the dunes towards the hum of moving traffic. 'Deadland is the land the Mennen make in which they do not go without their trucks, and the trucks do not see. Deadland is good land for a wolf.'

It was an insight that gave him the knowledge of what kind of route he must seek out. Then, as he trotted through the dawning shadows, and his paws and flank fur grew wet with dew from matt-grass, he had a sudden overwhelming feeling that he was not alone. Behind him it seemed as if there was a whole pack of wolves following his lead.

'If I don't look round,' he thought, 'they *can* be there.' It felt rather more than a game. He went proudly, tail up, head high and eyes alert not only on his own behalf, but that of all the others.

But what others? He paused, puzzled at so powerful a sense that he was not alone. He looked round and saw only grass, and scars of sand in the dunes, and a glint of sea from where he had just come.

'I . . . am . . . not . . . alone . . .' he whispered in wonder at the power of his faith. 'There are other wolves. There *are!*'

The sense of leading a pack of actual wolves he had just briefly felt was . . . '*is*' he told himself, of a time yet to come.

'I am not alone,' he whispered once again, and felt a flood of gratitude to Wulf who, but moments before, he had told he did not like. He had said what he felt and Wulf had answered him. *There are others*.

Klimt's eyes widened in wonder and delight and in two smooth bounds which sent a group of rabbits scurrying for cover, he turned from the shadows and moved to the top of a high dune nearby and into the sun. For a moment he could risk being seen to celebrate the realization that he was not alone. He slowly looked east and west, north and south.

'I am not the only wolf journeying to the Heartland, am I, Wulf? No, I am not. But they will need a leader and it may be I am the one you have chosen. Yet I would surely serve you better if I understood why you allowed the Mennen to destroy my kin . . .'

But even as he considered the question he formed an answer, though it was not one he liked: 'So Klimt can know the feelings of loss and despair his ancestors have felt for a thousand years! So Klimt has learnt his lesson not to feel too much . . . for he must lead others and be above their suffering that wolfkind may be strong again . . .

'Great Wulf,' he growled, 'if *that* is your reasoning it makes me more angry still. The saving of all wolves is not worth such a death as my cub Avendal suffered. Unless . . .' his eyes narrowed and his face and stance were as still and formidable as cold, grey ice. 'Unless it is that you wish me to be angry with the Mennen. Is that why, though I broke the lore, you allowed me to live? Is it for this I am to travel east?

'Well, whatever the truth may be . . . I will travel to the Heartland and serve you; and I will lead others to do the same. And we shall be such wolves as *you* will wonder if you are worthy of *us*!'

Klimt's mind was suddenly settled and clear. Last night he had confronted the past and accepted it. He had survived. Today he faced the future and felt he could survive that too.

'It will be hard, but no harder than all I have already known. The journey will be long, and winter may catch up with me before I reach the Heartland. No matter, I will get there in the end and when I do I shall form such a pack that wolfkind will be renewed, and the Mennen shall tremble!'

There was, perhaps, a certain madness in his eyes, an obsession to succeed, but any who had seen him in the morning sun on top of that dune, with the Baltic Sea behind and a Mennen motorway before, would have been in no doubt that this was a wolf whose time had come.

CHAPTER NINE

*Elhana meets a vagrant wolf, who helps her learn
about herself, and about the pollution Mennen make*

A THOUSAND MILES to the south, Elhana of the
Benevento found herself trekking northward into the
kind of harsh winter she had only heard of in legends
of the north: harsh, cold, unrelenting.

The first part of the journey had gone well, for it had
taken her up into the Abruzzese mountains where wolves
had always lived in safety and seclusion from the Mennen.
Here and there she scented their marks and spoor as she
crossed their territory, and twice she heard their howls,
but she avoided them and eventually turned away from
fresher trails, wishing to journey alone and without interference.

All her life she had been a member of a pack, and she
had faith that in the future she would be again: meanwhile
she was content to lead a vagrant's life, to watch the setting
of the sun alone, and the coming of the stars. She felt herself
to be in preparation for a challenge which would begin
when she reached the end of the wolfway she now followed,
whose pattern, ever since she learned it, she saw quite
plainly on clear nights. Why had she never seen it before?
Was that after all, what *all* wolfways were – patterns that
had always been there waiting through the centuries for
wolves to see them? Was that all *wisdom* was? A patient
waiting of a pattern of truth which wolves were too blind,

too ignorant or too frightened to easily see? Were the gods the beings which made those patterns? Or were they simply wolves who had discovered the patience and the love they needed to wait until others, slower and less courageous than they, saw the patterns too?

Elhana asked such questions, but found no easy answers when she stared up at the stars. But then, as winter progressed, there were fewer nights when the stars showed, and fewer still after November passed into December and the winds grew bitter and sharp. She avoided the higher passes, preferring the lower ground and the cover of sweet chestnut woods, whose scents and sounds she knew from her home territory. Except that with the harsher winds, the leafless hazel looked more wan, and the stalky buckthorn more tangled and untidy than she had ever known. In January she felt tired and cold and moved higher again where she found a safe, deserted territory on high ground, with only a single-track Mennen road to worry about and rocky places in which to hide and watch the valley below. She stopped for a day or two, then for longer, and eventually did not move on at all.

It was only with the first stirring of spring in February, and the coming longer days that she felt a new restlessness, and a kind of loneliness. She missed Lauria. She missed community. Her dreams of the distant Heartland and of finding a new life at the end of a wolfway seemed to have palled. The dream seemed fainter now.

For several more days she hesitated about pressing on, and might have lingered at her safe place longer still had not the weather grown more mild; better still, the sun shone bright in the middle of the day and she felt it warm her back again. She marvelled at how even this glimpse of spring sun woke new life in her, and lifted the wintry gloom that had felt like an affliction.

'I can never live without sun,' she said to herself,

suddenly profoundly apprehensive about the northward journey she was on. She had heard her mother tell the legends of the north, where the sun did not rise for months on end and when it did, its rays were weak, and summers short.

But for now the sun renewed her spirits and after a few more restless days wandering along the northern limits of her self-imposed territory, she ventured on. Her route so far had been northerly, following the spine of Italy, but now the grain of the land veered more north-westerly and from those vantage points that gave her a clear view she saw that a vast, flat plain stretched northwards below her on which, at night, she saw Mennen lights, and the white-and-red lights of vehicles along the roads that ran down there.

She began to feel that soon she must leave the safety of the Mennen-deserted hills and cross the plain, though what lay on the far side she had no idea, except that it must be higher ground. Then one afternoon after heavy storms and rain the sky began to clear, and as dusk fell she saw the lights stretching further across the darkened plain than she ever had before. Clearer and clearer the night became, as the stars thickened over the sky and the moon began to rise.

It was on that evening that Elhana first got a hint of the size of the mountain range that lay beyond the plain that she must cross. By the light of stars and moon it showed only as a single huge, dark form, its distance hard to judge, but its mass and extent more mighty than she could have imagined. True, she had passed through the shadows of some great mountains on the Abruzzese range, but what she now saw looming before her made those seem small.

She felt at once alarmed and excited, and watched on into the dawn of the clearest day she had ever known, and for the first time saw the risen sun shine upon the white snows, and dark rocky heights of the Alps. She knew then that she must find courage to journey to there if she was to ever reach the Heartland.

She had never truly doubted that the gods were with her, and she thanked them now with a glad heart that she had been brought safely through winter to the sunshine of a new spring, and prayed they would guide her onwards. She spoke her prayers gently, eyes excited, her fur aflame with light – the easy prayers of those who see no reason not to trust their gods and believe that they will continue to be protected.

She continued to feel that way the very next day when she scented that a wolf had passed her way. She did not howl out, but followed the scent back to see where it came from and found before it faded that it crossed her earlier path more than once.

'So, I am being followed!'

She felt pleasure rather than concern, for the scent was male, though old male, and spring was in the air. She turned and continued on her way, which had been down-slope into the foothills to find a place from which to trek out across the plain. But she did not hurry, and preferring to linger, she circled, she poked about, to make it easy for the wolf who followed, and before long she crossed his scent again and knew him to be close by.

Among the Benevento pack such circumspection was not unknown, but a following wolf would normally have shown himself soon enough, even if he was subordinate. But this was no doubt a vagrant like her and unlikely to be immediately subordinate, and certainly he did a skilled job of keeping out of sight.

It was only when dawn came that he finally showed himself, coming out to where she was feeding and stopping some distance away. She saw with some disappointment that he was old and thin, and his eyes were wary. He was not large as males go, no larger than herself, but he carried himself venerably.

They examined each other for a little time, and when he came nearer she rose and faced him, and then trotted towards him, and they stood for a moment muzzle to muzzle, scenting each other up and down.

'I am Elhana of the Benevento,' she said finally, 'and I am northward bound.'

He nodded as if it was what he expected her to say, and whispered 'Benevento' dreamily.

'My name,' he began, but she knew it before he spoke it.

Ambato, the wolf her mother had known. The wolf who had gone north so long ago. The wolf who was . . .

'You know who I am?' he said softly.

'Ambato, also of the Benevento.'

He shook his head. 'Of no pack now, but yes, once I was a Benevento wolf, and I *am* Ambato. And you my dear . . . you have been a long time coming.'

The word 'daughter' was in the air but remained un-spoken. In packs such as theirs paternity came through the leader, and his protection of young in the time of their nurturing and rearing, not through a secret and illegitimate act of mating. Yet . . . each knew what the other was, and sensed a sympathy that came from ties of blood.

'What made you think *I* was coming this way?' she asked.

He sighed and turned away and faced across the plain. 'I did not know your name of course, but last September I saw a wolfway marked out in the sky . . .'

'With a northern star to mark its end?'

'Just so. Well now, I looked at that wolfway, and knew that part that runs south-east of here very well, for I trav-elled it myself as you already seem to know.'

'My mother . . .'

'Lauria . . . yes, she was Lauria.'

'*Is* Lauria.'

But he looked at her sadly, and suddenly she knew with terrible, terrible certainty that her mother was no more. She knew it and it was like a pain within her heart as she remembered that darkest time before the spring when all was sad and cold and she felt low. Had her mother taken the wolfway to the stars in those grim weeks? Could so important a part of her life be lost without her knowing at the time?

Ambato seemed to understand her sudden grief and though he said nothing, his presence and sympathy suddenly meant all.

'Why are you here?' she asked him numbly.

He nodded across the northern plain. 'I have been waiting a lifetime to find a strength to venture out across it once again. I am not . . . well, shall we say I am not a wolf of much courage. It took your mother to get me going; perhaps it will take my daughter to help me continue.'

He looked almost meek as he said this, but his eyes smiled in humorous deprecation of himself and Elhana understood how her mother could have come to love him.

'Twice I tried and twice turned back,' he continued, 'for I felt the gods were against it. Finally I decided I needed the support of another wolf and journeyed almost back to Abruzzese to find help, but what wolf wants to run with an old vagrant like me? I turned back before I spoke to any wolf at all! You see how weak I am!'

'I do!' said Elhana impulsively, eyes smiling.

Ambato laughed. 'You know Elhana, when I saw that northern star I felt certain that the time was coming for which wolfkind had waited a thousand years. And that you, or some wolf like you, would come to lead me on . . . why, I told your mother so when you were born.'

'What "time was coming"?'

'The time when Wulf begins the last of his mortal lives, at the end of which either our gods will be reborn, or wolves will be extinct. For the Wolves of Time are on their way back to the Heartland from west and east, from north and . . . south.'

'Who are the Wolves of Time?'

'They are wolves who are already journeying to the Heartland, as we journey now. Not all that have started will get there, and of those that do, not all will be chosen to join the great pack which is being formed to run in the service of the gods and help to raise them to the stars again. But surely you know the legends as well as I?'

'I know only what Lauria told me, and that was what you told *her*. She always said that she forgot much of what you told her, or rather, was not able to tell it half so well.'

'Then I must tell you what I can . . .'

'Ambato, you said just now that you could not find a wolf to travel with an "old vagrant" like you.'

He nodded.

'I will travel with you!' she said impulsively.

'When?' he said, laughing at her impulsiveness.

'Now!'

'*Now?*' he exclaimed, dubiously.

She nodded, 'Right now, and you can tell me about the Wolves of Time as we cross the plain from which you turned back twice.'

'Now . . .' he said dubiously, glancing out across the great plain below.

'Now,' she said firmly, setting off before him, and not looking back once, so that either he followed her or he did not, and if he did not then he might never find companion, or courage, again. Ambato hesitated no more, and followed after her.

* * *

Ambato had been right to be cautious about journeying out onto the north Italian plain. Roads and Mennen were so thick on the ground that it was impossible to find a route that gave them full cover, and though they picked their way carefully they had to take many risks. They were shot at many times by Mennen, on one occasion by Mennen they did not even see or scent. Once Elhana was nearly caught by the run of a vehicle at night as they sought to cross a place of racing roads and fumes and lights, for she became confused and stopped in mid-run, right in the vehicle's path. Ambato saved her, running back to where she had stopped in floods of light and sound, confused, unable to see beyond the glare up to the night sky and get a bearing to lead her on.

He bit her flank, shouted at her, pushed her, and then, suddenly she was there once more and had the sense to cry, 'Lead me out of here, show me the way . . .'

Such moments put into the background any attempt by Ambato to tell old stories of the gods, and, as well, any desire Elhana had to listen to such tales. In the place to which their journey had brought them, survival was all they could think of. The feeling they now continuously had was that they were being chased by something greater still than Mennen, though who or what their enemy was they never knew.

It was a primordial fear they felt and it gave them dark imaginings of great dark presences that loomed along behind, sniffing at their scent, hunting out their trail, clawing at the pathetic little scrapes they made along the desperate way, chewing the picked-over bones of what little carrion they found, and spitting it out in black saliva before rearing demon heads and following even closer behind.

It became ever harder to find open ground, or to see the sky at night and gain guidance from stars and moon, for the sky was heavy with a pall of haze and smoke whose belly filled and glared with the horrid lights the Mennen lit.

Even by day, when they might have used the sun, the sky was poisoned yellow and obscure, the sun often diffused and lost, its heat seeming to settle all about them and make them sweat driblets of the poison that beset the land, so that they felt dirty and polluted.

So, filled with panic and the mounting horror of feeling they might never escape, glad even of the moment's respite provided by some dusty field or dried-up ditch where Mennen pipes spewed sticky orange filth, Ambato and Elhana found themselves driven north into territory that grew ever denser with the Mennen and all their works.

Try as Elhana did to gather her wits and restore herself to the calm she had felt up in the hills, she could not manage it, and it was Ambato who kept her sane.

'I shall tell you a tale of gods,' he would whisper when they rested, or when the sense of the imminence of the dark forms following them grew too much, and she would escape into a fragmented world of myth and lore, in which even the face of Wulf himself seemed stained and blotted, like the landscape they were caught within.

Days passed, and nights, and time lost its reassuring rhythms as it became broken up into gobbets of present and past, of here and now, of being chased and hiding in holes, or beneath ruined Mennen-things; and moments of grabbed carrion, or the stench and cloying taste of food, if food it was, they found in red bags that shone and swelled in the sun, and sometimes burst with the maggots that bred and spewed inside.

Time, for Elhana, might be a whole year of watching the maggot she had spat from out of her mouth crawl from the hairs of her paw to the shadows of the bag in which the dead thing on which it fed had first been found; or time became the brief moment (as it seemed) when a sun rose at dawn and arced across the sky and into night. Time was topsy-turveyed and all lost.

Then, one afternoon, the dark shapes that followed them and never gave them up, took the corporeal form of a pack of dogs racing out of waste ground, baying, bounding, accelerating as they advanced upon them in concerted attack.

Behind was the multi-laned road they had been forced to cross, and back to whose embankments there was no escape, as the pack sent some of its filthy members to cut them off that way. To their left was a high fence in whose wire-mesh plastic bags and litter hung flattened by the wind. Ahead, only the undulations of waste ground which gave no sign of a haven except that on its far side, too far to reach perhaps, was the dark rise of the wooden palisade which they recognized as meaning that a railway line lay beyond.

They began their run that way, the dogs closing in, the ground tearing at their slipping feet, their tongues caked with dust, their chests filled to bursting with the pressure of their heartbeats. A cog caught up in a machine of destruction. Elhana turned, snarled, and attacked, and the dog retreated as the others slowed, keeping their distance, panting, snarling, trying to circle round in front and cut off all escape.

They set off once more, Ambato deciding to turn almost immediately after a few paces to rip at the leading dog's flank and cause the other dogs to slow again. Together the dogs were strong enough to defeat them, but singly they were no match for the wolves whose stop-start tactics and sudden assaults seemed to cause confusion, and disrupt their pattern of attack.

This latest assault on a dog having achieved its objective, Ambato hurried off again, and catching up with Elhana, led her towards the only gap they could see in the high rough fence that edged the railway.

Had the dogs themselves been better led they would have had no trouble cutting the two wolves off. But

Ambato's last attack seemed to have caused the dog he wounded to turn in its pain and irritation on some of its friends and this temporary disarray gave the two wolves the space they needed. Elhana was the first through the gap, beyond which she turned and, as Ambato leapt through past her, she came snarling back and savaged at the first dog to try to get through. It squealed, tried to get away, and fell back against the others and Elhana, taking advantage of their confusion, leapt back through the gap and savaged two more dogs before leaping the gap again and joining Ambato, panting and bloodied.

As the dogs re-grouped, Ambato and Elhana had time to find that they were not at a railway line as they had thought, but at the top of a steep slope along whose upper edge the fence had been built, and which dropped and slid in a collection of rocks, and litter, and finally of mud, to the fierce, ruffled flow of a river, bigger by far than any they had yet seen.

Its colour was milky white-yellow, no doubt from the sediment and filth it carried, and if this was not evidence enough of its pollution, the stench it gave off left them in no doubt: a sharp and rancid throat-catching odour that felt corrosive just to breathe. But where they now stood was a place almost impossible to defend for the slightest step back from the fence would take them down the slipping, dangerous slope itself and then, very rapidly, into the river.

On the river's far side, which was a good way distant across waters which swirled and heaved with filth and dangerous currents, were the walls and chimneys, spewing pipes and rusting cranes of heavy industry, whose uninviting complexities stretched upbank and down, as far as they could see.

Then, suddenly, the first dog was up and snarling, and another at his flank, and they knew they had no choice. To go back was impossible, to flee along the fence both difficult and dangerous. Two of the dogs had found a way through the fence, or under it, and were already charging towards them.

'The river is our only chance, Wulf help us!' cried Ambato, and with Elhana right behind him, he picked his way down the treacherous bank, scented over the vile water, peered at the far bank and the rapid flow, turned and added, pointing to a feature some way downstream, 'make for that chimney when you reach the far side. We'll meet there if we get separated . . .'

Then he slipped into the water, Elhana as close behind him as she could manage, and they were swimming for their lives, their first enemy, the dogs, who now gave up the chase as suddenly as they started it, giving way to the second, which was the river itself.

The current caught at them, the foul water stung at them, its taste fetid and dank. Yet it had one virtue: it was cool after the long, hot chase, and they could see their objective. So on they went, each checking that the other was nearby, Elhana soon proving the stronger swimmer of the two, until, as they neared the far side, she was slowing her pace and encouraging Ambato to keep going. So powerful was the current that they were swept past the chimney he had suggested as their rendezvous and only reached the other side when it had disappeared behind them as they rounded a bend in the river.

Then more chimneys, and hissing steam, and obstructions out in the river which created counter-currents that sucked at them, and a Mennen-made wall instead of a bank up which they could not climb. Until at last they reached the slower waters of a tributary that flowed into the river itself, up which they swam through slimy water before reaching some slippery steps onto which they were able to scramble. Far off they could hear the barking and baying of the dogs; closer were the sounds of machines and Mennen.

Filthy and dripping with mud, their fur shiny with oily slime, they slunk up the steps and hid in the shadows of old machinery.

As they began to try to clean themselves they said nothing, but each thought the same: from this new place they had reached, there would be no going back. The unknown future was all they had.

III

WULF'S FOLLOWERS

In which Aragon of Spain, blessed Lounel
of the Auvergne, and grim Kobrin
of the Russias, respond to the Bukovians' howl down:
one for honour, one for spirit, and the last for war

CHAPTER TEN

*We witness the extraordinary first encounter
between a wolf of spirit, Lounel of the Auvergne,
and one more mysterious still, the Mann*

T HERE HAD FINALLY been three of them, all
males, all with the same pale fur and the same thin
backs, and the same pale colour to the eye. The last
three, and no more could ever be: male cannot make young.
The pack had really died the day, a thousand days before,
when the last female died who had clung on so long.

She slipped away from them, though they surrounded
her whimpering, licking her old fur, willing her to live on.

But that had not been the worst.

The worst was this: they could not howl. They could not
call up to the gods and ask them to receive her spirit, which
they had loved so much. Mother to them all, the two oldest
sons of her first litter; the youngest, only son of her last,
by one of the others. It had been a last hope, hopeless and
made quickly, as if what they did was against the lore.

So they were brothers, and one or other of the older two
was also father to the younger. Pale and weak all of them,
worn with inbreeding, worn with being the last of what
they were. Then, when she had gone, terminally sad.

'We must hide her body as she taught us to,' one of the
older ones said.

So they dragged her by night, down the steep slopes,
snapping at the black corvids that came down the sky

because they smelt the carrion, up and into the dripping caves. There they nudged her into the waters that flowed and rushed away into the dark of a gorge, and they watched her leave them for a better place.

Then they returned the long way up the slopes and steeps, to one or other of the caverns where they made their homes and uttered their low, mournful growls, which was the only farewell the lore allowed. Then they slept, and on each of the younger wolf's flanks an older one stayed, watchful.

'We are the last in the world,' the older ones said when morning came, 'the very last of all. We must carry ourselves with pride, and we must hope, or we will die of sadness and not live like wolves at all.

'We will teach our history to you, our brother who is our son, and pray to Wulf and Wulfin that they will send you comfort when we are gone. Come, Lounel, our last kin, and we will show you the wolfways Wulf made, as our mother taught them. Look at the stars and see how beyond the patterns of the surface-ways are shadows of their patterns, like echoes in the caves. See them!'

Lounel, surely too young for such a burden and such a life, looked, and listened, and his brother and his father began to use the time that remained to tell him all they knew of the history of the Malpertus pack of the ancient High Auvergne of France, which was the dead pack into which he was born.

For the most part it was much as the story any other pack might have told of their final years: a story of a cutting off from other packs, of a dwindling of the wolfways, of the inexplicable and all-too explicable deaths of their kin so that, slowly, implacably, their ancient fear of the Mennen had grown until it was unthinking and absolute.

'Thou shalt not kill the Mennen,' was the lore, and it was to be obeyed.

'They are always to be feared, for they know when we are coming, and they know where we shall go, and they can trap us, and shoot us, and kill us almost at their will. Or did!'

'Or did?' repeated Lounel, looking from one wolf to another and back again.

'They stopped you see; here they stopped. Here we were allowed to live. Here they taught us to survive.'

'How?'

'Here in Malpertus, alone in all of Wulf's eternal territory, they became our friends.'

'When?'

'When?'

The two stared at each other and back at Lounel, and shook their heads.

'We can only tell you what we know. But years ago, generations and generations ago, one of the Mennen found one of our ancestors wounded and near to death. That was in the high, secret valley where the Mennen so rarely go. It is our last place of sanctuary, where all our ancestors have been taken as cubs by their packs, and taught the traditions and Wulf's lore.

'There the Mann found our kin, and tended him, and our ancestor survived. When in the fullness of time he became leader of the pack, he was guided by the stars and by the whispers of the wind to take to that Mann one of his cubs, to show him what beauty the Mann had helped create.

'The Mann was pleased and so began a tradition, as sacred to our pack as life itself, for it has helped to preserve us, that in each generation our pack's leader takes his first male cub that the Mann may see it.'

'Are the Mennen immortal?'

'They are always there.'

'Was one of *you* taken to the Mann, to be shown?'

One of the old wolves nodded his head.

'One day soon we shall take you, Lounel, for you are our cub, our future and our life and if we show you to the Mann he will watch over you and help you survive.'

'Why do we whisper? Why may we never howl? Why do we lie low when the moon is high? Why do we scurry and sneak and use the caves above the dry valleys?'

'The Mann taught that to our ancestors, and he has taught it to us. It is for our good and our survival.'

'Why has not the Mann died? If he first came so long ago, why is he still alive? Other Mennen die.'

'This Mann does not die, as the trees do not die, or the sun, or the eternal stars. This Mann *is*.'

'But *we* are going to die. There can be no more of us.'

'Yes, we are the last. But there is always hope.'

'When will you take me to the Mann?'

'When our route takes us back to the high valley where the Malpertus pack was saved by that first meeting with the Mann. By the moon we go, when the time is right, soon, soon . . .'

Soon enough they went, teaching Lounel the ways to cross that wild, desolate country unseen; teaching him what carrion he could eat, such that the Mennen would not know that it was wolf that had eaten. They spoke one after another, endlessly repeating the lore . . .

'Take only what the corvids have eaten first, of sheep, of fox, of any dead thing.'

'Attack nothing living, for it will lead you to places where our presence will be known.'

'Eat nothing that is whole, for others will know a wolf has been.'

'Go not near where the Mennen live, for they will scent and see and know.'

'Travel by night.'

'Lurk by day.'

'Light is your enemy, darkness your friend.'

'Sneak.'

'Until when?'

'Until the Mennen are gone and only the Mann remains.'

So Lounel was raised by two old males, and wandered as they did through the nights of the months of the first year and half the second until his two guardians began to die.

Slowly they went, fading a little each day, recovering, then fading more. One helping the other, the second helping the first, until Lounel had to help them both.

'You never took me to the Mann,' he said scolding them, for if they had, it would have meant he was of age to carry the tradition on.

'No, no, the moons were not right, and the winds did not whisper that we should. Lounel, help us now.'

Until there came a day when the winds did whisper, and one of them, leaning on the other, both so old, said, 'We shall take you to the high and secret valley where the Mann will come, now.'

'Is it far?'

'It is at the end of the last wolfway that we shall trek.'

'I shall help you reach that place, and the Mann will be pleased with me.'

They looked at his gaunt face and his lonely eyes. They looked at his shrunken flanks and his thin legs. They looked at his dried and patchy fur, all pale.

They looked at him and said, 'The Mann will see a wolf, a great wolf. He will be pleased.'

How slow that last trek was, across the high hills of the upper Tarn, down among the steep, deep gorges by wolf-

ways they themselves had learnt as cubs, and taught him
now, their eyes growing dim, ways they could no longer
see within the stars.

Yet he guided them by dusk and by dawn, and by dawn
he found for them a place to shelter where they would not
be found, in scrapes and hollows, and fissures of the rocks,
whose shadows in that bleak, dry, sun-bright landscape
were as pale as their old fur.

In this way Lounel helped his last and dying kin back to
the secret valley of the Malpertus pack, finding what scraps
of food he could, resisting choicer things as he had been
taught, lest he break the lore and be found out.

'Where will you go when you leave me?'

'We shall be with Wulf among the stars.'

'And I?'

'You shall wait for the time when the Mennen shall go,
and then you can be wolf and howl aloud to the moon, and
hunt the living things by day and with the Mann you shall
be equal.'

'Alone?'

'Wulf shall send his fellow gods to hunt with you and
their coming will be in the stars. As long as you believe in
them you shall not be alone.'

Coming from the east across the high Causses as they
did, the final stages of the journey were up through the
wild gorges, or across the arid rocky ground between them,
which made old paws sore and mouths dry as dead skin.
Though they travelled at night the ground was warm to
their paws, but the winds were merciless.

On they went in single file until at last they found they
had climbed back into the very heartland of the ancient
pack, back to the secret valley where Malpertus, founding
father of all French wolves was born, to which, in times of
need, of decision and of triumph its members had always
returned.

With slow and weary steps Lounel was led finally to the valley, there to await the coming of the Mann, fearing that when he came his kin's days would be done, for this was their last task.

It had been summer when they had set off on this fateful trek, and it was the beginning of autumn when they arrived. The birds were already deserting south, and the grasses, already sun-dried and yellow, were beginning to break and die. The sunsets were more red, and when Lounel crept out of the claustrophobic valley up to the cols above, he saw, as dawn approached, white skeins of mist in the greater valleys far below.

'When you see the Mann come,' they said, 'you will tell us, and we will lead you out to him. Be not afraid.'

But Lounel was afraid, mortally afraid, not of the Mann but of death, which he saw was coming like a shadow across the only kin he had.

'I shall be the last wolf in the world . . .' he whispered to himself, and all the lore and prophecies, all the urging to have faith and believe that Wulf would send him god-companions, brought no comfort to his heart.

'Lounel . . .'

'Yes,' he said patiently, as he had been taught, 'yes, I shall chew your food for you.'

'Lounel . . .'

'Yes, I shall help you to the caves above.'

'Lounel . . .'

'Yes, I shall clean you of the mess you've made . . .'

'Lounel . . .'

But against death itself I cannot fight.

'Is the Mann here yet, for we . . .'

. . . are dying.

A night, a day, another night and they were near the end, each clinging on to life only for the other, each reluctant to desert the pack first.

133

A dawn of red skies broke.

'Lounel, listen to us. Today the Mann must come. We cannot present you to him as we should. Go down to the secret valley's end and wait for him. Offer yourself to him. Be not afraid. Surely Wulf will see that he comes. Go now . . .'

So Lounel went, down the dry slopes to the lowest part of the valley where its river, long gone, had dropped over the lip of detritus it had formed and flowed down to the Tarn below.

There he waited all day through and then he returned to where they lay, deep in the narrow caves where water dripped and ran. 'Did the Mann come?' Hope was in their eyes.

'He did not come.'

'Tomorrow then.'

Tomorrow came, and with it their further decline, as their breathing became rasping and hopeless, and their desire for food withered, like their bodies, almost to nothing. As Lounel went down the valley once again at dawn, his hope that the Mann might come and acknowledge him was less for himself than for his dying kin, that they might have their own hopes satisfied before Wulf took them to the stars.

But the Mann did not come, and Lounel's day passed with a sinking heart as he knew he must return up-valley, to find them passed beyond all care and him alone, or to face the disappointment in their eyes.

'Did the Mann come, Lounel? Eh? Did he? Speak up for we can't hear you any more, you're whispering. Come close because we can't see you any more, you're fading.'

He came closer, and shook his head and they, striving to find something good to say said, 'Well wolf, there's excitement in the waiting! There is!'

'Yes,' said Lounel. He looked at them and saw how they leaned now into each other, and how the eye of one was half-closed, and the leg of the second splayed out as if it had become so brittle that it had broken.

'Does it hurt?' he asked, nuzzling it.

'Can't feel it at all, so it must be all right!'

They laughed, and wheezed, and peered up at the stars through narrow eyes when night came, pretending they could make sense of the narrow strip of night sky which was their only view. One of them muttered, 'Wolfways, almost . . .' and both slipped to restless sleep.

The night was slow and black, and all Lounel heard was the squeak of hunting bats, one of which persistently flew back and forth past the cave they sheltered in. Dawn brought dull, grey light, and a small herd of deer grazing their way down the valley bottom below the cave. They did not scent the wolves at all, for the wind, though slight, drifted upslope. Lounel listened to the soft pull of grass and vegetation as the deer fed, and the occasional scut of hoof on rock or soil.

He envied them their numbers, and their freedom. He knew the Mennen hunted them, and had indeed eaten deer when once they found one dead and got at by the birds. It had tasted sweet and good and he remembered it as the highlight of the summer. Now he watched light catch their white rumps, and the russet of their coats as dawn advanced. Then they were gone and his brothers stirred.

'Get down that slope! Today's the day! Yes!' they said, snuffling at each other, grinning, almost foolish in their age. Then serious.

'Today! Lounel! You shall become a wolf! The Mann will come today and the mystery will be solved.'

'What mystery?'

'Who is he!' They laughed and thought it funny and he left, disconsolate.

135

At noon the Mann had not come: he was never going to come, the place had not the slightest scent of Mennen. The place was wilderness. And it had grown hot, and Lounel restless, uneasy, felt utterly alone.

Alone. With sudden terror he pricked his ears and looked about and knew without question he must go back. He knew their hour had come, their moment of death, the time he would be forever alone.

He trotted up the slope, hot and full of dread for what he would find, or what they would ask. They would want to know, they would always want to know. He stopped, turned, and looked down the valley.

'Here was where all began,' he said to himself, 'and here we are all ending. Wulf, tell me what to do.' He raised his head towards the blue sky and opened his mouth as if to howl. Just once, he would have liked to do it, just one time.

'Wulf, guide me!'

He went down on his haunches and stared at the grass, all intricate and dry, the insects less than they were, the autumn coming. Autumn, when he would be alone. Winter, when he would be alone. Spring, when wolves in the old days had a mate.

'No mate for me in all of Wulf's territory. I am the last.'

He remembered what he must do when he was the last for he had been told: go as a wolf goes, proudly!

'Yesss . . .' he whispered, glancing towards the sky as if to thank Wulf for telling him what to do.

He rose high, rose proud, and turned and went on slowly up the slope with the measured gravitas of the kind he imagined a great wolf would have.

The cave loomed and he went slowly up to it.

'You're back,' one of them whispered. The other barely opened his eyes.

136

'You're back early . . . why, what is it Lounel?'

He stared at them proudly, came close and growled in a way he never had before. It was a leader's growl.

'Yesss . . .' one whispered, bowing his head in obeisance to the wolf.

'Yesss . . .' said the other, acknowledging Lounel's strength.

'Did he come?' they asked.

'The Mann came and saw me and touched my head,' said Lounel.

Pleasure and hope was in their eyes.

'Was he pleased?' they said.

'The Mann was pleased with me,' he replied.

They stared at him, their eyes proud and full of relief.

'We have done what we were meant to do,' they said. 'We have fulfilled our lore, you are . . .'

You are . . .

'I am . . . ?' he whispered, staring at them, suddenly as still as death. Their breathing had slowed; their breathing had stopped, and the last look in their eyes was pride in what he was. Then they were gone together, gone forever, gone from him, all gone . . .

He stared, too shocked to move.

'I am the last wolf in the world. I am the last. None shall ever know me. None ever speak to me. None other ever howl . . . ever howl.'

Madness came to him, terror, horror and he turned wildly, without a thought of being seen, turned and fled and came back and fled again.

'Wulf!' he cried, and he heard his own voice echo from one side of the valley to the other.

He stared at the wolves who were his only world, now last of his own kind.

Then unable to stop himself, not even thinking what he did or that it broke the lore he had been taught from the moment of his birth, he raised his head and did what he had never done before: he howled, fierce and passionate and filled with grief.

He stopped, turned, trotted down the valley and took his stance where he had waited in vain for three days past. He looked up the valley, down across the distant vales, and once more the yearning overtook him, and the grief, and he raised his head and howled to the daytime sky, up and up and up, on and on. He was alone: none other could know him or hear him, none but Wulf. But here, here in the world, he, Lounel, was the lore, and leader of all.

If he wished to howl, and he did, he would howl; and he did . . .

He came slowly, and he scented him long before he saw him, a solitary Mann.

How white his hands, how big his eyes, and he scented of things Lounel had never scented before.

He stared, and shivered, and understood the mystery of what they were.

He scented of his kin, whom he had seen die. Both had come back to him in the form of the Mann.

He went forward towards him, head low, and then slowly looked up at him, his brother or his father, one. Lounel knew not which reached out a white hand and touched him as he had always been told he would be touched.

He was wolf and he was the Mann, and he was not alone.

Lounel turned from him and for a moment thought he would go back into the valley which was his pack's own. But no. He was the last wolf in the world, and the world was his.

*   *   *

The Mann watched the wolf finally retreat. The experience in Helsingborg had been one thing, one event, and there had (or so he felt) been observation but no contact. Here, with this wolf, as yet unnamed, the contacts had been more than physical – more than the touch of a man's hand to a wolf's muzzle and tongue.

The Mann had looked at the worn wolf's body, its starved haunches and its wasted legs, and he had looked into its eyes.

He felt that in some strange way, quite inexplicable and unprovable, he saw a part of himself that had once been. The wolf had let him glimpse past time and know for a moment that he himself had lived in some moment a millennium before when this same exchange had taken place.

That Mann then had dared reach out to wolves, and that Mann, too, dared do what others had not dared.

The wolf he had met and which had now left had kin, but they were dead, the Mann knew that, and recently so. He, the Mann who had travelled down there through the centuries of time, had kin as well. Brothers.

The Mann wept at what he had just been party to. He knew then that in the struggle ahead he would have to learn to run with wolves, and few would understand. He would follow the Mann's ancient lead, the led, the leader and the pack.

And the Mann knew that for him, and therefore for the wolves, this Mann would die, just as the wolf's kin had died. Last and first, beginning and end, the long wolfways of time that led out from a place and back to it.

Where?

'Heartland,' said the Mann in a whisper that echoed the wind.

'Mmm?' he said, querying his own word. Heartland? And what was that?

'I must find it,' said the Mann, and he raised his head

and, since he was alone and there was none to see, he howled that he had heard a whispered summons from a god to journey to the Heartland; and he howled that he would obey that summons to the day of its completion, or until he died.

CHAPTER ELEVEN

*The fair Jimena proudly watches as her son, the fated
Aragon of Spain, sets forth to find the Heartland*

I T WAS UNSEASONABLY hot and dry that summer,
up in the high Cabrera of north-western Spain, where
the last pack of the Iberian wolves eked out its life. So
hot that the streams had dried too soon, and the rats along
their banks began to die, leaving the great red kites to
circle the stronghold for days, uneasy in the sky they used
to own, before they flew off north.

South of El Teleno, the mountain that marks the centre
of the Cabrera wolf pack's territory, the pack's ledrene, the
she-wolf Ameria, said again, 'The kites have never shifted
territory so soon before. We should be warned by them
and prepare to move as well.'

She wrinkled her eyes, furrowed her muzzle and stared
down over the distant, dry valley of the Eria, into which
the waterless course of the streams ran.

Baillo, her mate and leader, father of two-thirds of the
pack, growled his protest and lunged at her, his scarred
jaws wide. Ameria easily slipped out of the way and his
teeth only made a furrow in the fur of her neck, which she
shook away. Dust rose off her dry fur, and she seemed to
grin, and none knew whether he would have bitten if she
had not moved.

Only in their ecstasies of mating did she ever let him
bite her and then her howls were loudest when the blood

ran free. The pack said she bore a scar across her neck for
every pup she had borne. Indeed, her whole back was
scarred, and the fur there rough and patchy, to mark
how Baillo had had his way. But no mating now, in this
deadening heat, or with that strange whispered pleading in the wind to trouble a wolf: only the need to move
on, to escape – or the idea of it tossed up like a piece
of carrion by cunning Ameria when she saw the kites
desert.

Now the pack waited for Baillo to catch this morsel of
thought, consume it in his ponderous mind, strain at the
effort of thinking for himself, and then regurgitate it as if
it were his own, so that the pack might know what to do.
As the strongest of them all, Baillo led them, but he seemed
to do it well only because he had Ameria at his flank. Yet
she loved him: for his slow thought gave her as much power
as a she-wolf ever has, unless she is a god.

Together, Baillo and Ameria had kept their pack alive all
these long, dry years past, and in doing that had fulfilled
their vows.

So now the pack stared among the pale yellow rocks,
mostly still, awaiting their leaders' decision. Leader and
ledrene, like gods to all of them, except for the outcast of
the pack. *His* flanks shivered with a restlessness that travelled on the wind, and his head was pushed forward and
cocked to one side as he watched them from the safety of
a thicket, and listened to something that none of them
seemed to hear. A far distant howl . . . the wind, or more
than wind?

He shook his head, forgot the howl, and stared at his
elders and betters – youngers and betters too for that matter. He was the fool, the outcast, the unwanted one whom
all packs need.

'Because I choose to be,' he would say sometimes, as
they snapped at his retreating form, 'because I *let* you.'

Which proved, they said, he was a fool, for if he only 'let them' do what they did to him, why did he do it?

A wise wolf might have known the answer, understanding that some wolves are afraid of their own destiny and, frightened to turn towards it, hide behind the game of a fool. But now this wolf *was* frightened. Because the howl he heard upon the wind was indeed the destiny he feared.

His name was . . . the Cabrera pack gave him many names: Fool. Idiot. Turd-face. Limper.

Yes, Limper was what most called him since he limped. Not that he needed to limp, for the bite which began that habit when he was a cub had long since healed. Once, when the only wolf he loved and trusted had needed help, and he had to leap to save her from the Mennen, the pack had seen that his limp was gone and that he was as fine a wolf as any of them; finer than all of them perhaps.

But the fiction of the limp was needed by all of them to maintain him in his necessary role, and so he had continued to limp. And, anyway, he himself believed in the limp. He had long since forgotten the pretence that had started it. Limping about the place confirmed him in the weak position he chose to hide within.

The wolf he had saved was his mother, Jimena, and she did not call him Limper, but by his proper name, which was Aragon. She had named him so for love of the stories of Aragon, whose pack had once been great, perhaps the greatest in all of Iberia. How she had whispered that name to her only-born, the whispers of a soft spring wind . . . Aragon, oh Aragon!

But in naming him thus she unwittingly condemned him to outcasting and herself to retribution. It was bad enough that he was the product of her moment's snatched pleasure with Baillo – but Ameria would have forgiven that if Jimena had not chosen a name she herself had wished to use on her own next-born son.

'Call him anything but that and I'll not harm you much,' Ameria had said. Cunning Ameria, who knew that such a concession would put Jimena properly in her place; a wolf like her, intelligent and graceful, was beaten only if she was mentally as well as physically defeated.

But no . . .

'His name shall be Aragon,' said fair Jimena who had the right to choose, 'and he is my own and if you harm him while he is a cub I will call on the strength of the gods to harm you.'

'Oh, I'll not harm *him*,' said Ameria, who knew the lore demanded protection of the young by all the pack and felt no hatred towards an innocent pup, even one named, as she felt, to injure her. 'But you . . .'

She was not ledrene for nothing, and Ameria attacked Jimena savagely and terribly, causing her the wounds to neck, face and haunch from which even three years later Jimena had not recovered. Her fur was fair still, but her face, her body, were made ugly. No male wolf would have her now, not if all the other females died or smelt of plague. From that day only one wolf saw the beauty that had been, and that was her growing cub, Aragon, outcast and fool.

For how can a cub see ugliness in its mother when she has been all the world to him, and as he grows she encompasses him, as Jimena did, in the one thing no stronger rival could ever have touched, which was the landscape of beauty that was Jimena's mind and imagination?

'Listen now, my dear . . . listen . . .' and she who had been made ugly, whose scars were like dark fissures and furrows down her fair face, took him when the other cubs, sensing weakness, had hurt and harried him too much to those rich places of tale and legend where a wolf may be as strong, great and content as his imagination allows.

So had Jimena fed her weakest cub the milk of lore and legend, story and dream, and gave him what she herself had, something others could not touch, however strong their jaws, however absolute their victory seemed.

Jimena had learnt these things herself at the teats of her own mother, who was Sainfoin, last ledrene of the most ancient Iberian pack, the pack of Segundera, which ended dreadfully at the hands of the Mennen – poisoned and shot and some torn to death by dogs – Jimena's solitary escape and period of outcasting and her adoption by the Cabrera pack was a story as fine as any of those she had learnt from Sainfoin, and as powerful as any in the canon of the great and ancient tradition that survived with her as it had survived with her pack alone: the lore of the epic age after Wulf ascended to the stars, which ended with the passage that Jimena would sometimes share with all of those that declared that from out of Iberia a great wolf would come to help save all wolfkind:

> Out of this dry land
> This wolf will be great,
> A leader of leaders,
> A maker of gods
> And those of Segundera
> And of Aragon
> And of the high Cabrera
> Will look to him,
> And weep at news of his passing,
> For he was of them
> And their own.

Such old legends and prophecies Jimena had taught her adoptive pack and, valuing them, they in turn valued her even after her maiming and disgrace. She taught such things to Aragon, and taught him more, things the others never knew, nor could have dreamed could live in the night-time whispers of a mother to her weak cub.

Of the stars she taught him, and direction. Of the plants she taught him, and of healing. Of the lore she taught him, and of duty. Of the past times she taught him, and of the future. Of the fall of the gods and wolves' suffering she taught him, and the present.

> For we of the Segundera
> Shall give of our own to the Wolves of Time
> That one of ours shall go forth
> To lead
> Teach
> Multiply
> And help lead all others
> Back to the wolfway of the gods.

Of the wolfways, almost lost now, almost forgotten – what she knew she taught him; and of the wind, and how a wolf must listen to its sound. For it was a fact that three times in a wolf's life do the gods speak to him through the wind, whose whispers, if heard and understood, are the gods' directions through life for him and him alone. If a wolf hears them not – and few do, for most are ill-prepared and only half-believe – then the wolf will have no other easy chance.

Jimena knew only one thing – she dared not yet tell her son that she had heard the whisper of the wind come in the hour of his birth. It had come with the scent of herbs much sweeter than she had ever scented in her life, and she had known that in him she was much blessed. That was the third time that she had heard the wind call – the first had been when her mother was near death, that she might be at her flank when she died, a worthy thing. The second was when the Mennen came, that she might know, alone of all the Segundera pack, which was the right way to flee to find the bleak sanctuary of the Cabrera pack and be safe

146

from the Mennen's harm. Then the third and last time was when Aragon was born. She had never dared speak aloud of what it meant, but in her heart she knew: he was the last male of the Segundera and it was his destiny to help lead wolves back to the wolfways of the gods.

She had whispered to her still-blind cub, 'But in knowing you are blessed, I am satisfied. Three times have the gods whispered to me. Only the lost gods hear the whisper of the wind a fourth time, the gods who travel in their loneliness from east to west, from north to south, seeking a way back to what they once had.'

That had been three springs ago. How swiftly the time had gone since then, and how tired she had begun to feel with these dry and punishing summers they had suffered. Now the wind fretted in the grass and the pack waited for its leaders to decide when and where to move.

'We'll move!' said Aragon the Limper suddenly, growling, mocking, ducking out of the way of one of the stronger wolves who lurched suddenly towards him for his impudence.

'We'll be gone! We're harried by the sun from here and we'll be harried by the Mennen where we go! We will!'

Another wolf lunged at him to shut him up and he limped out of sight into the thickets, crouched down and stared at his paws, cocking his head once more to that strange calling in the wind. He heard it but he did not like it, for it made him see he could no longer play the fool.

Frightened by what he heard, he returned to the thicket's edge once more to watch the pack through the heat, glancing for just one single moment at his mother, risking no more than that lest they see him do it. For, since his outcasting, Jimena had abided by the lore and not spoken to or acknowledged him. If she had, they would attack her; that *was* the lore. She had taught it to him herself.

'North,' said Baillo, breaking into all their thoughts with his decision. 'We'll go north tonight.'

'Better do it sooner than tonight, Baillo!' called out Aragon from his safe place, in his old familiar way. 'Get it over sooner than later lest you leave too late.'

'Shut up,' said one, sweat trickling down his brow and in among the wrinkles of his eyes.

Aragon shrugged and grinned, and stretched, one eye half-open in case he needed to escape.

'Tonight then,' said Ameria, 'and north.'

The pack relaxed, the decision made, and went to sleep. All but Jimena, and off to her left flank, Aragon, so intent on not looking at each other. Hot and lazy hours those, as the relentless sun moved slowly over the sky and the wolves waited for the evening cool.

It came like a clap of thunder at his head, that last soft whisper of wind. It came to him, *'Aragon!'*

It sent a shooting pain inside his heart. His mother said it would be like that: the whispered call of the gods on the wind. Or like rocks breaking in his mind.

'Help . . .' whispered the wind. 'Help us now.'

Then Aragon stood up, his four paws on the dusty ground, his back pushing away the thicket above him as if he had forgotten that it was there. And then, as loud as he could make it, for the wind's call came from a most distant place, he howled. A great howl, a howl to wake ten packs of wolves, and not just the one that lay sleeping all about him.

They awoke all right. Awoke to the realization that the outcast had dared to break the lore of howling. Several went for him at once but this time, and for the first time ever, they stopped, confused. Aragon stood his ground, fierce, his mouth and snout curling into the furrows of an angry snarl. Then he lunged forward and bit and ripped, and the blood of another was on his jaws.

His mother, shocked into forgetfulness, broke the lore and looked at him.

He broke the lore again in looking straight back at her, but in their gaze there was a greater thing than lore, clear and true, and the pack knew no word for it but 'destiny'.

'I heard the wind's whisper,' he said, the new power and danger in his posture keeping those who had attacked him at bay, 'and it was to *me* it came. I am to go east, to follow the wolfways to their very origin. I am . . .'

'He's mad!' roared Baillo. 'Mad and wrong as his mother. We're going north and he's coming with us.'

Aragon stared at his leader and for a moment the pack was aghast, for there was about him the confidence of an emerging leader, and with it an implicit challenge. Not that Aragon would have stood a chance against Baillo yet but, once such a challenge is made, everything changes; the pack shifts and turns and wonders, and a leader may be made weak and vulnerable to other attacks by other males. So all watched, all waited for Aragon's move.

He confounded them again as, for the last time, he chose to look foolish and laughed. He looked at Jimena, and his laugh turned to the smile of farewell, the smile a son makes when he says goodbye to the one to whom he owes the most.

'I am Aragon,' he said, 'I am. Remember me!' And that was all he said. But in saying it he was 'Limper' no more, but a young, strong wolf with a future in his eyes. Then he turned and was gone, and when they searched they could not find him – only the blood of the wolf Aragon had savaged, where it had dripped from his jaw.

'I am,' he had said, and in doing so Aragon would be remembered among them forever. An outcast had chosen to challenge the leader and, not waiting for the challenge to be met, had simply turned his back and gone. This was an outcast no more.

'Kill her: she broke the lore,' said Baillo, turning in his anger and frustration on Jimena.

'No,' whispered Ameria, taking a stance in front of Jimena and staring boldly at her mate. 'No my dear, it is better that you decide we must shed no more blood before we leave this evening. It would not be right. You will decide that.'

'Will I?' he growled. 'First I shall decide that the wolf whom the Limper bit shall be himself outcast.'

'That is wise,' said Ameria, and turned to stare coldly at the wolf who was now more stricken than if he had been bitten a thousand times. All lunged at him. All bit him.

'Enough then,' said Baillo. 'We move now.'

'And tonight, Jimena will tell us the meaning of Aragon's howl,' said Ameria. Her voice was almost friendly and it was the first time she had called the Limper by his birth-name, and the Limper was outcast in their memory no more.

'He'll be back,' howled the wolves, 'back out of the heat of the dried waterways. Won't he?'

It was the dry wind that answered, and it said, 'Not yet, not yet.'

So, led by Baillo and Ameria, the Cabrera pack turned to the north, while off to their left flank, to the west, the hot sun died down and the sky was bloodied by its death.

But it was eastward Jimena looked from time to time, eastward where her son had gone, and though her eyes were filled with tears of loss, her slow, maimed gait was full of pride. She knew the meaning of Aragon's howl and she would tell it to them. The gods had blessed her and told her that Segundera was blessed – for the son she had born, and taught, would be one of the Wolves of Time.

She would howl for them tonight, and the ancient songs would be melded with a new song, telling that there had been among them for a short time a young wolf who would be great, whose name was Aragon. And she would reveal to them a legend that even Aragon had not heard, which spoke of the coming of the Wolves of Time and of how the inexorable tide of destiny may sometimes sweep aside the old, and bring in the new.

CHAPTER TWELVE

*Kobrin, former leader of all the Russias returns to
his birth-territory and he begins to understand
the true nature of Mennen, of war, and of Wulf's call*

I N LATE SEPTEMBER of the year in which Tervicz
and the other Bukov wolves howled down the Wolves
of Time, a vagrant male, bulky, worn and scarred,
crested the northern end of the Ural Mountains from the
east, and stared balefully down across the grim Pechora
Valley.

Where he stood and stared was two thousand miles from
the Heartland, as ravens fly. But as wolves must run, such
a journey would be further still, further even than the epic
voyage Aragon must make from distant Iberia to the west.

Overland he would need to go, right across the north
Russian plain to fabled Bialowieza. From there across the
arable lands of Poland, and southward finally to crest the
Tatra Mountains. A route out of northern winter darkness
longer and more rigorous than any the other Wolves of
Time must take.

Yet this was a wolf who though tired from a hard life was
not tired of living; indeed, from the light in his eyes and
the vigour in his step he seemed one who was glad to have
found a new task, a purpose greater than any he had had
before. Age had marked him, but wisdom, resolution and
purpose had marked him still more, and would take him
on to the very stars themselves.

He moved down the slopes of the Urals slowly and deliberately, and began the tiring journey through the headlands of the Pechora, a route he clearly knew towards an objective he had often thought of returning to: the prehistoric denning ground of the ancient Pechora pack. As he approached, a watching wolf (and there was one) would have seen that his bulk was deceptive: he was more than bulky, he was huge. His fur was dark and shaggy, in places patchy from fights long since forgotten; his face was so scarred and torn about the eyes that one of them seemed a shade higher and wider than the other which, with the permanent frown he had, made it seem that not only was he thinking about attack, he had just decided to launch one.

This was Kobrin – or rather, more accurately, his title *had been* Kobrin. But what does an old wolf do who has been leader of all and has lost his position? He retreats and in the wastes he dies. That had always been the way until *this* Kobrin was defeated. Death was not his destiny, though Wulf knows he tried to find it. Across the icy wastes east of the Urals he had sought it, but wherever he looked he could not find it.

Then came a whispering wind, that called him on and told him that before death he had a task to fulfil, one greater than any he had undertaken in all his life.

'The Mennen are here, I might have known,' he whispered to himself, staring downslope to the thin, grey line of road that threaded its way northward with the river. And a railway line, black against the frost, and pylons, ugly, high, their wires whining in the bitter wind.

'Mennen!' he spat, pondering his best strategy. War, and thoughts of war, had been his close companions, whilst its stratagems and tactics had been his dearest friends. Its principles had been his pleasure, and its central paradox – that a leader and his pack waged war to create peace – was something to which he had never found a satisfactory resolution throughout his long, stubborn, hard-won life. But being Kobrin, the greatest of his kind, he believed that he still could.

'We make war to create peace, make war for peace, war . . . peace . . .' he muttered to himself, the old rumination to which there was an answer he was sure, if only he could see it. In truth, if war and strategy and tactics had been his friends and companions, then that final paradox of his occupation had been his lover, his all.

'War and peace, peace and war . . .' Such were the mantras that Kobrin spoke, and they soothed him, and finally led him on a different path, away from leadership to vagrancy, to loneliness and aloneness, to a life the end of which he would have welcomed if he could find it, but it eluded him. So then, the paradox as unresolved as ever, Kobrin took a wolfway over the North Urals to ancient Pechora, where he was born. Pechora, land of raging, icy rivers, of harsh winters, of endless, thin forests, broken rock and sterile soils. And Mennen, Mennen, and their despoliation of a land already ruined when he was born.

As he stared across his birth-territory again and saw its dark undulations and the roads, and the pylons, and the unnatural scars which a million years would not heal, he knew why he had spent all his adult life avoiding this return, and he knew why he had been wrong.

'I should have come back sooner, but I always put it off. Thought I had so much to do,' he muttered aloud.

He became aware that another wolf was nearby, and then two more. He ignored them utterly.

'I should have come because then I would have found the courage to return to what I most fear,' he told himself miserably. For he saw now what he had known in his heart for so many years: Pechora was just a place, another Mennen-ruined place, and the fears it put into him were but those ghosts left over from a troubled cub-hood, when the Mennen came and broke up the Pechora pack, and destroyed his family. Bloody scenes he would never, could never, forget. His parents killed; his uncles; his aunt crawling to protect him and his sister with her leg all shot away and her ribs showing, sheeny pink and blue the shattered bone, weak and so courageous the last words he remembered her speaking: 'Run, run my dears, run . . .'

Now, years later, the watching wolf howled his summons to others, and they were coming, pattering up from the ruined places below, more and more, to form a timid circle at the edge of the place where Kobrin now stood, staring, thinking, muttering. Oh yes, they knew who he was, they knew their Kobrin. Greatest Pechoran ever born . . .

He felt no fear at all, nor much curiosity. It was his curse that others feared him, revered him, treated him as anything but equal, and since he had turned his back on power all he wished for was to be treated ordinarily.

'Some hope,' he grumbled now, as so often before.

'Lord . . . Master . . . Kobrin . . . ?' began an unctuous-looking wolf, pushed into approaching him by the others. 'I mean . . . we mean . . . you are the Kobrin, are you not? One here, you may remember him, remembers you when you . . .'

Kobrin sighed wearily and tried to focus on the servile wolf with its weak, broken voice.

But he could not and he growled, 'Leave me be a little more, wolf, leave me be.'

'Of course, I didn't mean, I mean to say, yes . . . or rather, no . . .' the wolf stuttered, stumbling over a succession of apologies.

'I won't be long,' said Kobrin more gently. 'No need to move away wolf: be still, that is all you ever need to be.'

'Yes, Kobrin,' said the wolf.

Kobrin returned to the memory that coming back

evoked; trying to run away, his sister at his flank, the shots and Mennen shouts, and the confusion. And being caught, and taken then to a place whose name he only later learnt: Collage.

Here in Pechora, the hell of Collage began for Kobrin, the hell to which he had no wish ever to return.

Here in Pechora, the wolves who had awaited his return so long, waiting on him still in a circle of silent awe and respect, *here* he dared to say again the name he had not spoken since the day he fled when he was still young enough to run that fast: Tula.

Here, now, Kobrin faced again all that he had fled from, all that he had left behind, all the dark, rising horror of Tula that had driven him so far, so high, to be Kobrin of all the Russias.

'Tula,' he whispered, his voice trembling, and knowing even as he spoke it there was more.

One more word.

One more fear.

Which was finally all he remembered having, and truly, *was* all he had left behind in Collage.

His fear was a name he dared not speak. To speak it was to open once more a wound made of shame and grief at what he left behind.

One more name.

One last fear.

'Wolf!'

The waiting, servile wolf came to him, and the others who stood watching stirred, fretting restlessly, all uneasy. The Kobrin had come back to the pack that gave him birth. What would he ask of them?

'Kobrin?'

'What wolf am I?'

'The Kobrin!' said the Pechoran wolf with pride.

'What was I?'

'You were . . . you were a Pechoran wolf,' said the wolf
with still more pride.

'And my parents?'

The wolf named them.

'My uncles?'

The wolf named them.

'My aunt?'

She too was named.

'Wolf, come nearer still.'

Nervously the Pechoran wolf did so.

'Kobrin?' said the wolf, almost in a whisper.

'My sister, speak her name.'

'Your *sister* . . . ?' stumbled the hapless wolf. 'I am not
sure . . . I did not know . . . I cannot remem . . . I was
never told of a *sister*.'

'Her name is Yashka,' said Kobrin, speaking the name at
last.

'Yashka,' murmured the wolf. 'She lives still then?'

'In Tula.'

Now Kobrin dared to speak the name with the full mixture of savage loathing and despair he felt.

'I know it not!'

'I know it well,' said Kobrin heavily, the lines of his face
more shadowed, the tone of his muscles more set. 'Mennen
made it. Mennen live there. Creatures die there.'

'Creatures . . . ?' stumbled the wolf, not understanding
anything at all but that Kobrin's eyes were dark as acrid
smoke, and the lines of his worn face like the shadows of
chimneys, of factories, of dead and poisoned trees, of a
place so lost to nature that nature knew it not.

'And creatures live there. They can be called no more
than that.'

'Live . . . ?'

'Incarcerated, entombed, their eyes as dead as the stagnant, poisoned pools about them.'

157

'I do not know this place, or creatures such as these.'

'They are wolves like you or I,' said Kobrin.

'And your sister . . .'

'Yashka is still there, where I left her,' said Kobrin blankly. It had taken nearly a whole lifetime to say as much.

The two wolves eyed each other.

'So, you are leader,' said Kobrin. 'Changing the subject.'

'They have said so for today. I am the wolf who speaks for them. I was the one who said we should meet and welcome you.'

'Your name?'

The wolf shrugged self-deprecatingly as if his name was of no consequence. 'Semenov of Pechora.'

'Wolf, tell me about Pechora and what has happened here. What the Mennen have done. Tell me of the wolves who live here still, and how the pack made a life for itself after most of us were killed or stolen.'

'We shall do it better together than if I try to tell it all myself,' said their appointed leader.

Kobrin nodded. 'Let them howl it then. And when you have finished I shall tell you what you should do, and what I must do.'

That night they howled, and each had a tale of loss to tell, a tale of how their kin survived that they themselves could be born. All were younger than Kobrin by far, but all had tales to tell.

When dawn came, Kobrin commanded them to show him the Mennen places they had told of: the lost forests, the valleys that were no more, the flooded places, and the places made foul with chemicals, and inaccessible with wires.

Of the minefields, where Mennen sometimes ran and crawled and died.

He listened, he saw, and he thought.

158

'Is not the Pechoran pack a chosen one?'

'For suffering,' said one. 'Not for the triumph the lore predicted.'

'For sadness,' said another. 'Not for the glory old tales tell.'

'For sickness,' said a crippled one simply. 'Not for health . . .'

'For triumph and for glory and for health,' said the one they appointed as their leader: Semenov. 'One day, one day . . .'

Kobrin smiled and said, 'Truly, your pack chose you well and I shall serve you, Semenov . . .'

There was a whisper of astonishment at this.

'Oh yes. I was born a Pechoran and I shall die one, however far away I may be. The Kobrin may be leader of all the Russias, but he remains always a servant of his home pack, for better or for worse.

'Now then, I shall teach you the arts of peace, which are no different from the arts of war, except that those who talk of suffering and sadness and of sickness incline to war; those who speak of triumph and glory and health are inclined to peace.

'For myself, I am something in between and know something of both. I cannot stay long, for my journey must turn southwards now, to Tula where my sister awaits my return, as she has waited many years. Then I shall complete what I left unfinished. Before I go I shall teach you what you need to know to begin to prepare yourselves to wage peace through war in the difficult times that are coming.

'I shall serve your leader, but I shall remain your Kobrin, and yours alone: a paradox like peace and war themselves!

'I ask for loyalty and obedience, for the time is coming when wolfkind shall need the Pechoran pack once more. Out of the unknown, icy wastes you shall come, hardened through the dark millennium and having suffered the Mennen's curse, but still a pack, still together. Still with the wisdom to appoint a leader worthy of the name, for Semenov is such, of that I am sure.'

Kobrin noted the wolves' dismay.

'He's leader only in name!' declared a large bully of a wolf. 'We just told the bugger to go and greet you. He's never defeated another male in his life!'

'Your name?' said Kobrin coldly.

'Me . . . ? Why I'm not challenging you or anything I mean . . .'

'Your name?' repeated Kobrin.

'Gorodok, I . . .'

'It takes as much courage and wisdom to speak as leader and control with words, as it does to fight all comers and win,' said Kobrin. 'So far, what I have seen of Semenov, suggests he speaks well, and with courage. Eh, Gorodok?'

'If you say so,' said the wolf.

Kobrin smiled, pleased to see some spirit in the pack.

'I have a feeling this wolf likes you not,' he said quietly to Semenov.

Semenov shrugged and said, 'He's all bluster, but none care to stand up to him but me. So far I've avoided fighting him because he'd win, and he's avoided fighting me because if he does he'll have to lead . . .'

Kobrin laughed. 'Very North Russian that! Now, back to what we were talking about. Where was I?'

'You said the time was coming when the Pechoran pack might be needed,' said Semenov. 'So tell us when, and where and by whom . . .'

Suddenly they all had questions and Kobrin had to silence them to be heard.

'I'm not sure when you'll be needed. In a year or two, or even more perhaps. Which gives you time enough to teach each other what you need to know. When the strongest of you falters, the weakest must have the will to carry on. When the most experienced of you is bereft of new ideas, the most humble must be allowed to speak. When your leader is unsure, allow the outcast to find confidence. I shall teach you how to learn these things and then I shall journey on, leaving you to learn and train; to seek faith, maintain purpose, and never doubt that I shall send a summons to you when the time is right.'

'And how,' said their appointed leader, 'shall we know when we are needed?'

'I shall send word to you, or come myself.'

'How shall we know your messenger can be trusted?' said Gorodok dubiously.

'Come here, wolf!' commanded Kobrin.

A little nervously, Gorodok did.

'Look me in the eyes.'

For a few moments Gorodok did so before his gaze faltered.

'Do you trust me?'

'Yes,' said Gorodok.

'If a wolf comes who claims to be an ally, look into his eyes and you will know if he speaks truth. It is the only way. This you must learn. Sometimes enemies are more trustworthy than friends and will serve you better. This you must learn.'

'This place you are going to,' said Semenov, 'sounds dangerous.'

'It is a journey into death.'

'Is it safe to go alone?'

'No.'

There was a longer silence and finally Semenov turned to the pack and said, 'Perhaps there is one here who will go with Kobrin?'

The pack was suddenly very silent indeed, and looked

everywhere but at Semenov and Kobrin. Gorodok slid into the shadows, eyes averted.

'Then I shall go, for how can a pack ask another to serve it which does not give its members, however weak, however strong, support when it is needed?'

Kobrin looked at Semenov, thin and weak as he was, his flanks shaking with nervousness at what he proposed for himself, and he looked at the others, most of the males being larger and stronger than the one they had appointed leader, now all with heads down, looking away.

'Truly,' he said, 'the one who leads you is the most worthy here. He shall come with me and I shall teach him to teach you on his return. And you shall obey him.'

Three days later, as the two wolves said their farewells, Gorodok found the courage to speak.

'Lord Kobrin, we have been shamed by Semenov, a wolf we despised and who in our cowardice we appointed our leader. We have talked and we have decided you cannot go without support. Ask all or any of us and we shall come . . .'

Kobrin stared around at them, seeing that their eyes were no longer averted, but were open and on him, nervous for sure, but filled now with purpose and coming courage, and was content. He had not learned the arts of leadership for nothing.

'Listen, wolves, and listen well; and Semenov, most courageous of wolves, listen especially. You are right; I shall need more wolves than Semenov alone. Six to eight is the best number. I shall need three fighters, the best you have. I shall need three foragers, the best you know. I shall need two route-finders, cool and trustworthy.'

The wolves clamoured forward to volunteer, each claiming to be best at everything.

'No, I shall not choose the eight. *You* shall. Gorodok has spoken for you, Semenov has already shown his worth. These two know the pack better than I. Let them choose without fear or favour. Do so before light fades.'

Never had the Pechoran pack known such a thing and it brought them excitement, and argument, despair and hope. Throughout which Kobrin sat and rested, eyes half-asleep but observing all the time. The final choice was made only as light faded, and it was Semenov and Gorodok who made it, and a united pack who supported it.

Eight were chosen as Kobrin had advised and their names were recited by Semenov and they came forward, Gorodok among them.

'They are our best,' said the pack. 'Lord Kobrin, these are the ones we trust to help you most.'

Kobrin looked at each of them in turn and finally said, 'And yet is there not one more who is more worthy than all these?'

'Which one is he? Name him!' they cried.

'No, *you* name him.'

It was the great Gorodok who came forward, and stood by Semenov. 'This wolf, our appointed leader, is the worthiest amongst us.'

'Yet you did not choose him among the eight.'

'We wanted to but . . .'

'. . . there are better fighters, Kobrin, than I can ever be. Better foragers than I. Better route-finders as well . . . there is no place for me among the eight.'

'There is no better leader,' said Gorodok quietly, and he made obeisance to the puny Semenov, and all others did the same.

'Wise indeed,' said Kobrin. 'It is best your leader stays behind, for he has much work to do before the eight get back. Teaching others to learn and prepare for coming days of destiny.'

So it was that the Pechorans found a worthy leader, and the eight, led by Gorodok, followed Kobrin to help him with a task too terrible to think of.

'Come back my dear, come back in safety to us . . .'

So those Pechorans left behind called out into the fading light, tears for the loss of friend and kin mixed with tears of pride. And then . . .

'Come back Kobrin,' they said.

The last farewell was silent: the embrace of Gorodok and Semenov, warm now, and with respect.

'Come back,' said Semenov.

'To serve *you* wolf, I shall.'

So Kobrin and the Pechoran Eight (as they became known) began their epic journey, and eventually arrived by night at that noisome park in Tula, and there beheld the creatures of the zoo.

They saw and were appalled.

Rotten fences, a city in decay, keepers drunk, a place from which all nature fled but city birds, the mite-laden pigeons, the broken-toed thrushes, the black corvids, their feathers brittle, their eyes diseased.

Mennen died beneath the teeth and claws of the Pechoran Eight, died that creatures might be freed.

Kobrin led them, his first war against the Mennen, terrible, lore-breaking, bloody.

For, in the cages where long-lost creatures were kept, was a remnant pack of wolves. Thin and haggard, the dull light of hopelessness in their lost eyes, the grim traces of a poisoned industrial atmosphere in their fur.

Old wolves, beyond hope and among them one, as old as any of them, lame, her fur almost gone, her ears and flanks flea-ridden, and only one thing proud: her stance.

Despite all the years of suffering, all the years of pain inflicted by the Mennen, she stood as proud as that day long ago when she cried, 'Kobrin, run! Run my dear! Run as once our aunt told us to! Run . . .'

And so he had, but before he had left her sight, he had turned and said, 'For you I'll run, but one day I shall come back for you, one day . . .'

'I know,' she had whispered as the Mennen came where she lay, lamed by their shots. 'I shall wait for you.'

'Yashka, sister, I have come.'

'I said you would, my dear,' she whispered then.

He looked into her eyes and saw they had not changed, not deeply where the love and faith in him were held, not there.

Then she embraced him, and he her, and no memory was sweeter in all his life.

'Come and bring those who can travel, for we must leave.'

'What wolves are these you lead?' she asked.

'Pechorans, and I serve them. Gorodok is leader of this group.'

'Pechorans,' she whispered. 'Take me back to where my brother and I were once born, take me back to where I still belong.'

Such was the saving of Yashka of Pechora, Kobrin's sister. And such the memory he took on for inspiration as, clear of the cities, some way on the route back north-east, knowing she was with good wolves, he turned at last from them to Wulf's call out of the Heartland.

'What is he, your brother?' asked Gorodok, as Kobrin set off towards Bialowieza, and that onward journey to Carpathia. 'For surely he is more than the Kobrin, far far more.'

'My brother,' said wise Yashka, 'is one of the Wolves of Time.'

'Will he come back to us as he said, to lead us in the coming time?'

'He will, as he came back for me,' she said.

CHAPTER THIRTEEN

Aragon, on his journey to find the Heartland,
meets another of the Wolves of Time

ARAGON OF THE CABRERA PACK, son of the fair Jimena, had begun his heroic journey across Spain to the Heartland with the nicknames of Turd-face and Fool, Idiot and Limper ringing in his ears. Nine months later they no longer applied.

Somewhere across Spain he shed those former selves to become the resourceful and sometimes overly-proud Aragon.

He had been on the periphery of his pack for so long before he left that the high, dry plains of Castile across which he had to find his way alone seemed no special hardship. When times got hard, and food was scarce, and safe drinking sites away from the Mennen harder still to find, Aragon had no difficulty retreating into the dreams and memories Jimena had so long fed him.

> Out of this dry land
> This wolf will be great
> A leader of leaders . . .

Not that Aragon believed that these ancient lines referred to him; rather that they were about a wolf whom one day he would serve and who, though surely he came from some-

167

where across his own Spanish homeland, he would not find until he had journeyed to the Heartland.

Many were the trials of Aragon's journey through Castile and thence into the territory after which his mother had named him, wherein there were no wolves now, nor ever likely to be again. Here he was shot at by a Mann for the first time, and harried by dogs, and lay ill in a makeshift den among rocks above one of the gorges of the River Gallego, poisoned by bait left out for rats.

His strength and courage were born of the years of subjugation to others stronger than himself. Instead of fellow-wolves his enemies now were heat and thirst, the sharp-beaked ravens that scented his distress, the Mennen who sometimes came dangerously near; and finally, as winter set in, the bitter cold.

'Mother, pray for me now in this time of need, let me not forget my destiny . . .'

So prayed a son through a time of suffering; and thus a mother answered him:

> 'For his name is Aragon
> He is my only son
> His is the task of a whole millennium
> To be our strength and voice
> At the very Heartland of the wolf.
> Wulf summoned him
> I heard him myself
> And Wulf will not suffer him to fail.
> Such is my son Aragon
> Son of us all
> Who will be our glory and our light . . .'

So cried Jimena, sensing her distant son's need for her, and leading the others of the Cabrera pack in a howling across the plains.

Aragon survived that winter, his eyes clearer for the confusion he had seen, and his body stronger for the weakness it had known, and he left the place that had been his haven, turned upland from the gorges of the Gallego and ventured at last into the Pyrénées, last barrier to France.

There, one clear, cold day in spring, Aragon stared for the first time across the alien territory of Gascony and thence, though he knew it not then, to the far distant heights of the Massif Central and the Auvergne. There on the Pyrénéan heights he howled at last, for the fear he felt at having soon to leave the hot, dry homeland that was all he knew for the vast and alien lands that lay northward, and through which he must travel if he was ever to make his way to the Heartland. He howled and hoped another might howl in reply, for isolation is a dreadful thing and loneliness a blizzard in a wolf's heart, that robs his mind of strength, his body of purpose, and his eyes of hope.

'Wulf!' he howled.

But to such despair Wulf often does not reply.

'Wulf . . .' he may have whispered. 'Give me courage now to continue with the journey.'

For weeks Aragon hesitated, travelling eastward amidst the Pyrénéan peaks, casting fearful glances northwards down to the plains where he knew he would be alone, and so in danger. Up here, where the air was clear, eagles soared and were worthy company.

'Wulf guide me . . .' and though perhaps Aragon did not then realize it, Wulf did. For in those weeks of dallying, of fearful procrastination, as winter gave way to spring and the snows about him melted to reveal plants of such bright delicacy that he could almost lose himself in their dew-dropped light, his fur thickened and grew more light, and his body stronger. In those weeks the last traces of the wolf that had been Limper left him, and if a weary sorrow for what he was leaving behind sometimes came to his eyes, so did a look of strength and – and for this wolf the word is right – beauty.

So it was that when one dawn Aragon nodded his head in recognition of what he must finally do, and dropped downslope to the north away from the mountains that had been his last haven for the past, and his protection from the future, there was surely no wolf in Iberia's long history who better represented all that was finest and most courageous, and worthy to take that great spirit to the very Heartland itself.

'To *there!*' he told himself, taking one last look towards the distant rise of the Auvergne. 'To there I'll go. Take it in stages. Bit by bit. Real glory, triumph, fulfilment . . . all are found in a succession of single steps, never in one great bound. So to there I'll go!'

With this only half-remembered quotation from one of his mother's epic poems from the Great Age of Wolves, he lowered his head and set off downslope, his next destination ever in his mind as he began the hard work of finding a route that would take him there.

Meanwhile, all that same summer that Aragon had journeyed, and that winter through which he struggled to survive, Lounel of the Auvergne, last wolf in France, and in the world too, so far as he was concerned, had circumnavigated the only territory he and his lost pack had known, and listened for the wind to send him a call from the gods.

Up to the time of the final loss of his pack, Lounel's life had been one of suffering and shadows. For a short time thereafter, until he had stood proud before the Mann who had come and felt his touch and known his scent, Lounel had known real and crushing grief.

But since then, after the Mann had left him and he had

begun his wandering time through summer and winter, and back now into spring, Lounel had known strange liberty. Believing as he did that he was the last, the last ever, he had felt lift from himself the burden of historic responsibility. He was, as he often thought, like something that floated in the air, here and there on a wind none could see which blew from place to place in a way none could know or pre-ordain.

A dry leaf, perhaps, or the seeds of willowherb; the feather from a young dove's belly, a snowflake that drifts against the run of all its mates; or the shine of a piece of dust, caught drifting for a time across the shaft of sun through an olive glade, or between a fall of rocks amongst which a wolf might muse for a day or two, or three or four . . . These things and many more Lounel found himself to be.

Lounel had lost his sense of time, of rooted place, of purpose, of fear. But most of all, lacking company or any faith that he would ever know any again, he lost his sense of self. If he stared at the stars, he was there among them, far, far from the earth upon which he lay; if he felt the earth, his body was its mountain ranges, and his limbs and claws and all his extremities were its river valleys, and they stretched away for ever. If he drank the cold waters of a mountain stream, he was the water that flowed within himself; if he was hungry, his hunger was all life's; if content, his contentment was (so long as it lasted) eternal.

But Lounel had something beyond these vast things: he had a mind that thought and began to understand obscurities, which ran through the words of the ancient lore that was his heritage, as a line of stars defines a wolfway through a myriad of stars on a cold, clear night.

Yet though it was mind and intelligence that saw these things so clearly that sometimes he wept before them, the words he whispered to himself about them were . . .

obscure. Not words so much as sounds of wonder and delight, astonishment and awe, fear and disbelief.

One night he came upon a Mann, no more than a leap away, and the Mann did not know he was there. Lounel stared at him and wanted to laugh, to say words to him, to tell him that he and Lounel, living and breathing and on the way to death as they were, as all things were, were one.

What words could express so strange a thing?

One day Lounel watched two ravens blind a lamb and pick at its struggling head, and tear at its genitals. He felt a pity he had never felt for himself, on a scale as great as winter skies; but for the ravens he felt no shame, no anger, nothing but . . .

What words are there to express such troubling thoughts?

One dawn Lounel knew a rabbit would round a rock, and that it would be white on its left flank and that when it startled at his attack it would veer right, then right again, then stop, then start and chase off to the left before doubling back. All these things Lounel knew before the creature first appeared at the spot where Lounel, who had hardly moved at all, had been waiting to take it: waiting, as he felt, in that spot for that rabbit from the very start of time.

That was the first occasion when Lounel knew with certainty what would be.

What words need a wolf use to describe such certainty?

So by the time a new spring had come, Lounel had journeyed far beyond the confines of his own self to places and landscapes few wolves ever reach. While in the real world of the high Causses of the Auvergne he seemed hardly more than a shadow of a wolf, barely seen by the ravens, and never by the Mennen amongst whose fields and ditches he sometimes roamed at night.

But when the new spring came the wrench of loneliness beset his heart once more and he knew he needed company. The time of reaching out with body and mind to the very stars was over, for now; *he needed company*.

Despite his powerful conviction that he was the last – he was the *last* – he also, conversely, felt that he must seek to evoke the company he lacked and sorely needed. Some might call so strange an impulse to will another wolf to come, when he believed that none existed, an act of faith, or madness, or delusion. But to Lounel it was no different, except in degree, to that same growth of conviction before he could have known that, say, a rabbit would come round some rocks.

Unsure of quite how to make a wolf come to him, Lounel began to tour his lonely territory once again, but differently. He had no strategy, no journey plan, no general intention at all. Rather, he drifted from place to place, scenting at the ground, softly howling and barking out the echoes of the valleys and gorges that so deeply dissect those parts. He did not pray to Wulf for help or guidance but searched from secret place to place for something he could not name. He knew that here and there, but daily more and more, he was rediscovering the lost wolfways of the Massif Central. Once or twice he felt sure he was in a place where Wulf himself had been when he first came to earth and made the world that one day mortal wolves might walk it.

April came and the streams and rivers roared with the last melting of the snow, with April rains, and the air began to warm with sun and new life . . .

There is a river which flows out of the High Auvergne whose name is Allier and whose gorges through the limestone in its higher parts are so ruggedly deep that a wolf, peering down them, sees only shadows and the swirling mists of river-races in places quite unvisited, even by the Mennen.

'Yet not unvisited by Wulf,' whispered Lounel with that strange certainty with which he now sometimes felt such things.

The journey down into that gorge is one no mortal creature should ever make, least of all a gangly, unkempt, clumsy kind of wolf like Lounel. Yet down he started, peering out a way ahead, tumbling down the screes and falls of rock, clinging as best his torn paws could above the voids and precipices to whose edges that route took him. Down and down so deep that at last there was no sun, and still the river raged and roared far below.

'Down that I may see, that I may find . . .' he whispered to himself as his paws slipped on the cold, wet rocks untouched by living paws, depository only of the dead and desiccated claws and bones of birds from the cliffs high above, whose last flights had been downward to irrecoverable death.

'That I may see and find . . .' But *that* he could not name.

His whispered musing echoed away above his head, carried upward with the River Allier's raging roar as he sought to see no thing or place, but something of the Wolves of Time.

Each stumbling, slipping step he took brinked on a fall out into the chill winds that blew up from the waters whose white-grey racings he could now more clearly see far below. Each step from the sun above was a year back into the decline all wolves had lived; each glance above to where he had been safe was a lost hope for a place which he, or any wolf, might never find again; each breath one less towards the certain knowledge that it was not he who was the last wolf at all, but all of them that lived now, all were the last to have a chance, all who would be called the Wolves of . . .

'Time! Give us time, great Wulf!' he cried, his forepaws slipping further down, and chill spray from the river now carried up upon the winds.

Once only did he try to turn back then, reaching up a paw precariously to try to gain a hold on the crumbling, slimy, rotten rocks above and heave himself away from the driven destiny below. Once was enough to know he never could go back.

Then Lounel turned, and almost fell the last part of that drear and dread descent, with its torrential noise, icy cold darkness where light had fled to somewhere far above, a cleft between rugged black cliffs of rock that showed only sky so bright it was a blinding merciless light from a place where gods might once have lived, and mad wolves roamed within their lost poor minds.

There, lost at the very foot of that inaccessible gorge, Lounel's eyes sought out shapes and sights of fallen rocks, and racing hidden pools, all comfortless, all meaningless, and he knew, he *knew* that here too, once upon a time, before mortal wolves were made, before the wolfways were complete, Wulf himself had been.

'*Here!*' cried Lounel. 'Here am I. Guide me now.'

He wandered for a while among the huge, fallen rocks and found himself in a place where by some configuration of the flow of water, the rise of cliff, and the shelter of great rock, there was no sound at all; except for himself and his own movement.

He found a pool. Stared down into it. Saw a wolf all huge and staring, and beyond him the sky, muted and made dark by the deep, dark mirror that water had become.

'I,' whispered Lounel, and a drop of water fell from his fur and the image of himself was gone into a thousand rings

175

of light, which flowed off, caught in currents quite unseen, and were gone.

'You,' whispered Lounel in awe and love, for there, when the ripples of light were gone, he saw in the water that was now his only sight of the line of the cliffs above, where they nearly met and were divided only by the sky itself, the image of Wulf on one side, and of Wulfin his beloved mate upon the other.

'*Us*,' Lounel whispered.

He moved, he stared above, he tried to see what he could only see if he stared away from it into the pool beneath; and even then it fled away, shimmering into different shapes formed where the cliffs edged into the sky; shapes of mortal wolves, shapes of the wolves that Lounel dared to call 'us'.

Then Lounel felt a pity for the gods who now needed the pack of which he was a part, for it was not he who had been alone but they, Wulf and Wulfin, separated this past millennium by a gorge that reached down to mortality, seeking a way to reach out across the void to touch again, and make all things whole.

Lounel poised himself above the pool and stared a last time at that cleft of light he had climbed down so many lives to see. He stared and howled a howl up to the gods, of pity perhaps, of prayer, of shame for all wolves had not done, and of hope of all that might yet be.

His front paws fretted at the cold, wet rock, he leaned forward into the drop below, and dived down, down into the great cleft of light above, that he might try to find a wolfway there.

Dived as once Wulf himself had dived from this same spot.

Dived from all the illusions and protections of all past life, as wolves must dive if they are to ascend up to be gods.

While below him, before him, beyond him, above him, that last howl he made gyred and drove up among the rising cliffs, echoed and re-echoed on itself, and was the raging, roaring sound he heard as the chill race of current and river, water and suffocating depth, took him, dragged him down, carried him from where he was, and away from all he had ever been.

Aragon of Spain, poised in the late spring sun by a river whose name he could not know, nor knowing why he had been impelled for long days past since leaving the Pyrénées and venturing into France, to trek up into the high Auvergne, driven by an urgent need more powerful even than the burgeoning of spring all about, startled at a sound, and stared up towards the impassable cleft of rock which marked the gorge from out of which the dark, deep mountain river flowed.

Startled, and was mortally afraid.

For the sound he heard was the howling of a pack of wolves, a howling down through time. A howl of wolves not threatening, but lost and uncertain where to go; yet knowing that if they did not find the right wolfway, and if they failed to find the courage to make the journey they must make, and if they failed to watch over one another as a great pack must, then all would be lost, *all*. It was that sense of 'all' that put such fear into Aragon's heart and, too, the sense that he was of that pack himself.

So he stood and faced the distant cleft and with beating heart heard the howling die away. He ran upslope along the river's edge, now on sharp boulders, now on crumbling bank, up and up to be nearer where he might be needed, staring ahead at the cleft, and then at the white water that raged out of it, down the length of the stream-bed towards him, and then right past, its sprays and spatters on the sudden turn of breeze and wind that lashed at him, and was painful at his face and eyes.

There was panic in him but not the kind that made him want to flee and hide. No, no, this was the panic of a wolf who knows he has a task he must fulfil, a task that is imminent, but one the gods have failed to warn him of.

The surging waters turned again and spurted out of the great, soaring cleft at whose highest point the cliffs leaned dark and sheer and almost touched each other's brow. Aragon's gaze dropped back to the spume of water that had shot up above the common run, he stared, and then he knew what he must do.

A shame no other wolf was there to see.

Limper, Turd-face, Runt, was certainly not that wolf he had once been. His fur was longer now after the over-wintering, and his power plain, his gaze sharp. He knew now what he must do and the panic was gone. He stared along the river above him and below, searched out a shallower part where he could see rocks which might give him support and a way back to dry land. He found a site, appraised the treacherous fall of white water immediately downstream of it and knew that if he slipped, if he faltered for a brief moment, he would be lost, and *all* might be lost as well.

Aragon breasted the rush of icy water, and its chill force almost took his legs away from him in the first moment; but then, facing upstream, he gained some semblance of balance and, moving sideways across the river, searching out paw-holds, reached the place where they might have the best chance. *They* . . .

Like mist clearing off a Castilian plain, the knowledge of what had so long impelled him to come to these parts, and now to risk his life in the middle of a dangerous mountain river, came to him. A wolf had summoned him, a wolf who needed him as much as the pack . . .

Then the waters upstream rose and surged towards him, their dark bulk bearing down in confusion and water and spray the lost, flopping, clinging body of another, and a head, its mouth open and loose to the water, its eyes half-open, weeping with the mountain stream, its sodden fur dark with the reflection of the cleft out of which it had come.

Aragon saw it, felt it borne heavily into him, got his teeth to its neck, was turned and torn off his feet, struggled to pull it, was taken under, twisted and pulled, the only certainty being that his teeth held on, and the rocks he had thought might help him were there pushing, buffeting, battering at him, as the water tried to drag him over them and past their help.

Aragon pulled his head and the load he carried clear of the water, sucking in air through the clench of his teeth. He glimpsed about until he saw the bank and then, more under the water than across it, he used his last strength and breath to drag clear the wolf whose call he had answered.

The river bottom shallowed, rocks pierced and tore at his struggling paws and he heaved the sodden body out of the river's grasp, then with one final push of legs and pull of shoulder he got himself and the wolf almost to dry land, and fell. He felt himself slipping back, and rose once more, his grip never loosening, and then finding some strength he never knew he had, he dragged the wolf up the bank, over the screes, and into the sun.

It was a male, long-limbed, cut, bruised and battered wherever Aragon looked. No life, though, in the eyes; no breathing in the chest; no movement in the limbs. But in one flank a tremble of life, and in the way water flowed out of his mouth, and his head turned on the slope, and the sun shone upon his fur, there was not yet death.

Aragon licked the wolf's face, he nudged him more into sun. He breathed on him, he put his flank against him, he urged and willed him to survive. And the wolf responded with a groan, a sigh, a gulping, choking gasp for breath, and a sudden vomiting of water that left him struggling for breath.

'Live!' commanded Aragon, and the wolf obeyed.

'Open your eyes, stay awake!' urged Aragon, and the wolf opened his eyes weakly, stared at the broken soil on which he lay, stared down at the river's flow and struggled for a moment to rise.

'Yes,' rasped Aragon, 'that's right . . .'

Lounel turned his aching, battered head to the voice's sound, and stared into the eyes of the wolf that had risen out of the river and he knew that it was into the amber eyes of Wulf himself he gazed.

'Wulf,' he said.

The great head's eyes stared down at him, his paw touched his face, his breath was the breath of life and his voice as gentle and as strong as a distant roar of the wind across a sheer cliff-face. The light from his amber eyes seemed as bright and blinding to Lounel then as the light he had seen between the risen cliffs above the gorge.

'Great Wulf,' he whispered.

The wolf shook his head and smiled, and Lounel knew what he saw, knew what wolf it was, not Wulf, but part of him, part of them all. Lounel sighed and said, 'You heard my call.'

'Yes,' said Aragon, 'I think I must have done . . . Now, wolf, get up and move, crawl if you have to but move, away from the river and up into a warmer place, *move* . . .'

Stumbling, shivering, weak, hurting, Lounel obeyed, and rejoiced; his time alone was over and he knew now what they must do, once he had rested for a very long time.

'We shall travel . . . to the Heartland . . .' he whispered at last, seeking to settle himself into the warm protection of a south-facing overhang above the river bank. 'Yes, yes, we shall . . .' Finally, clumsy with fatigue, he fell. He banged his head. He shivered into pain, and then far beyond it, knowing he was safe and would be warm and was with the wolf he had summoned to his side and who for a moment he had been sure was Wulf himself. Then, for the first time since death had taken all the wolves he had ever known, which was the best part of a year, Lounel slept with the deep, abandoned carelessness of a wolf who knows he is not alone.

It was several days before Aragon decided Lounel was fit enough to travel, days in which each learned to respect the other. Aragon assumed the role of leader without difficulty. He was physically stronger and swifter than the awkward, long-legged Lounel, and, as soon became apparent, his hunting skills were far more developed.

Yet from the first, though it was Aragon who appeared to make such decisions as when to move, their relationship was that of equals, never of superior to subordinate. Aragon's assumption of day-by-day leadership, and Lounel's acceptance of it, was more to do with a natural deployment of their combined strengths than of the power of one over the other. Aragon sensed from the start that Lounel was no ordinary wolf, that he had strengths and insights which made him less a wolf to lead than to protect. To protect, indeed, to the very death, for in Lounel, Aragon recognized a power of spirit that might lead others to the very stars.

Lounel's strength recovered each day, and every day each got to know and like the other more and more, with the time to journey on upon them.

'You shall take us to the western edge of the territory you know,' said Aragon, 'and then we shall find a way on towards the Heartland that has called each of us in so many ways for so long.'

'We shall,' said Lounel, his head jerking a little to one side as it often did when some decision had just been made and there was the prospect of carrying it through.

'It won't be too hard, once we get started,' said Aragon sympathetically, for Lounel had long since confided how nervous he felt about finally going beyond the ancient territory he knew. 'I dallied a long time before I left the Pyrénées behind, but once I got going . . .'

'Want to show you somewhere before we go,' said Lounel. 'Won't take long.'

'Well . . .' began Aragon reluctantly for he wanted to get started now.

'Important that I do,' said Lounel. 'It's where I lost the last of my kin, it is the Heartland of *our* pack. Where the Mann came that I told you about. We shall have to learn about the Mennen and their ways: all of us will have to learn. Must show you. Must say goodbye. Must know where we may one day come again. Wolves must know where they start from if they are truly to leave; must know their first place to appreciate their last. So . . .'

So, talking to himself more than to Aragon, Lounel set off across the plateau above the Allier and took his new friend to the upland valley where his family had died. He avoided entering the place itself, though Aragon went in and stared sombrely at the intertwined skeletons, the rags and tatters of skin and dried fur.

'Taught me all the lore I know and more,' said Lounel, 'and now I am their heritage. I have seen the light of the sky that separates Wulf from Wulfin, and I have felt the coming of the Wolves of Time. We shall complete that pack, Aragon of Spain, and your name will one day be cast across the skies.'

'And yours,' said Aragon, only half-believing.

But Lounel was not listening, or rather listening to the wind.

'Well then. I have shown you that you may remember. Remember this place Aragon, remember the wolfway that brought you to it, and that along which I shall lead you out of it. One day you may have need of it. Remember . . .'

It was a hot, late spring afternoon, yet Aragon shivered at Lounel's words, spoken with strange compulsion and urgency as if he saw what others could not see and knew what others could not know.

'I shall remember,' said Aragon. 'Now, wolf, lead me away from here.'

'I'm ready now,' said Lounel. 'Ready to say farewell.'

Then, softly, he howled, and tears trickled down the fur of his face for all his kin were gone, and though he was no longer the last wolf in the world yet he wished to weep for the voices and love and companionship that he could never know again.

'Come,' said Aragon gently, and Lounel nodded and stared at the ground, and led the way forth.

CHAPTER FOURTEEN

*Elhana and Ambato rediscover the natural world
and share pleasures of the past, and dreams of the future*

I N THE LIFE OF EVERY wolf who sets out to reach
the Heartland, there comes a moment when they must
give up hope of ever returning to their home territory
if they are successfully to complete their journey. It is with
the giving up that the journey truly begins.

For Ambato and Elhana, wolves of Italy, that moment
came with their crossing of the River Po. Though it be true
that in reaching its banks at all, they had had to journey
halfway across one of the plains in Europe with the greatest
concentration of the Mennen and its industries, yet until
they reached the northern bank of the Po neither quite felt
they had cast off their ties to the home territory in the
south.

Not that, as they left the baying of the pack of dogs that
had chased them to the river bank itself, they had time for
such reflections. For one thing, as they clambered out of
the mud and filth on the far side of the river, there was no
mistaking the alien nature of the environment into which
they had been forced to flee. The very water of the river,
and of the tributary up whose bank they finally climbed,
was acrid with pollution, stinging like an infection at their
eyes and mouths and all their tender parts.

Then, too, there were the hissing, steaming buildings
into which their escape had brought them, prefaced by

slimy stone steps up towards levels of concrete and metal structures which they could not see and assess until they reached them, and whose full extent they could not judge even then.

There was the immediate, frightening sense, as they lost sight of sun and touch of normal wind within the cavernous Mennen maze in which they found themselves, that there was no escape route such as wolves always ensure they have in a natural environment. They had come, indeed, to the kind of place Ambato had feared during his years of procrastination up in the hill-lands above the plain.

Here, where there were no trees, no soil, no natural things at all – except the tattered husks of dead plants and the twists of strange, foul-smelling weeds amongst the fissures of the Mennen-made walls – they felt utterly vulnerable, quite unable to make sense of what they saw and smelt, or know which way to turn if danger came.

So they hid in the shadows of the rusting hulk of an old crane, and from its vantage point studied what they saw.

'Are you all right, Ambato?' Elhana asked when she had caught her breath.

He nodded wearily.

It was only at such moments that she realized that he was old and tired, for when he spoke the ancient legends, his spirit was not old, and when he gazed northwards towards where they both hoped the Heartland lay, his eyes were those of youth and invincibility.

'We'll linger a while and see what turns up,' he said firmly.

She was happy to obey. So often it was her impulsive energy that had kept them on their way, and his prudence and common-sense that kept them alive.

Night came, an extraordinary, frightening but finally exhilarating night of roars and scrapes and nearby thundering, and the flares of flames from chimneys, with the scent of the fire not of natural things dying, but of dead things dying right down into sterility. Flames that carried fumes, and fumes that carried flecks of dust and still-burning ash like fireflies into the cavernous corridors of concrete and industrial detritus in which they lay.

The sky was no sky they had ever seen before. Billowings of purple-ruddied smoke, no moon, no stars, except far to their left – whether north or south they could not then tell – where regularly through the smoke they saw the gathering glare of the white eyes of a Mennen bird, like one of the road vehicles dropping at an angle from the unseen stars. These things were always lost behind the rising wall of a tower that rose before them, usually after a roaring sound that died, though by the strange acoustics of the place it seemed to be behind them by that time.

Another dawn came, and slowly, hour by hour, the two wolves began to realize that they were not being chased, nor harried at all. No creature, not even the Mennen, showed any sign that they even knew that they were there. In the place of poison and decay into which they had come there was the safety of indifference and anonymity.

'And in that, my dear, we may find a freedom we have not found since we left the hills south of the great plain we are trying to cross – a freedom even greater than that we found amongst the hills where always Mennen roamed, and we could be seen, or hunting dogs could find our scent,' said Ambato some days later, after they had ventured out of hiding and begun to pick their path away from the industrial riverside and learn to utilize sewer and dyke, channel and pipe, huge, clattering, empty buildings whose doors hung loose, and underground ways which seemed to serve no other purpose but that their walls supported structures above which throbbed with machines, or whispered with the silence of dereliction.

'And yet,' said Elhana some days later still, 'I can't

believe that such routes as these might not have dangers which we have not yet met, or we cannot suspect because we do not recognize them.'

'Then we must watch for them. These Mennen places cannot go on forever. When they stop we shall be back in natural surroundings once again and then . . .'

'. . . then I shall be glad of some fresh air, and to be able to see the stars clearly, and not through the obscurity of Mennen lights and fumes . . .'

'Hmmph!' said Ambato, who had lived long and hard enough to know how to enjoy respite on a journey when Wulf gave it.

They watched and learnt much from other animals. From the foxes that inhabited these deadlands and even raised their young there, seemingly oblivious to the apparent dangers all about, they learnt the art of crossing roads. Watch, wait, watch; feel the ground for vibration, watch for the sudden arc of light at night that heralds the approach of vehicles, choose a starting point not by its ease of access to the road but by its proximity to a safe place on the far side. Then, cross quickly and smoothly, in a straight line, not looking at lights and always with a place behind or under which to hide, *however* short that route might be. The Mennen were unpredictable and bolt-holes always needed. The trick the foxes taught was not to be seen, and if seen, not to be found in the same place for long. Plainly, foxes knew their travelcraft and the two wolves learnt much from them.

They learnt much, too, from the calm indifference to the Mennen and their vehicles of the carrion-feeding rooks – who moved away at the last minute to let them pass before resuming their feeding, with such indifference. Plainly, here along the Mennen ways and in the shadows of their buildings the Mennen did not seem to see, or behave as they did out in the open, natural world. Here wolves could survive if they stayed invisible, for there was carrion about, and rubbish tips where food might be found.

Which was where, finally, along with a motley of seagulls, rats, stoats, wild dogs and many other urban-living creatures, the two wolves found some respite from the oppression of concrete structures and dank tunnels: a rubbish tip over which they scavenged for several days, whose edges were defined by a railway track and road, and a stream flowing in a conduit, whose water, at its upper end at least, before pipes fed foul water into it and the rubbish bags spewed their contents into its course, was almost clean.

They learnt the skills of scavenging in tips, shaking bags loose of their debris, sniffing among the filth they found in the hope of finding something they could eat, their faces and paws festering from the cuts they received from broken china, opened tins, rusting nails in shattered wood, the points of needles, and shards of broken glass.

Ambato became ill and surly for a time, fighting with Elhana over the carcasses of rotten chicken and putrid offal in swelling white bags. Then, when he recovered, Elhana began to vomit, and for a time he had to tend to her, chewing her food, flicking away the flies that infested her face and eyes, watching night and day from the flea-ridden scrape in which they lived, lest dogs and other animals took advantage of Elhana's weakness and attacked her.

It was days more before she began to recover her strength and after that she was silent for long periods, as if mourning something she had lost but could not name.

When she was better Ambato took to exploring by himself, and was sometimes gone for hours at a time, until he came back covered in vile-smelling muck and rubbish, or stained with oil, his shoulder torn, his paws cut, his face scratched from fights with Wulf knows what. Ambato said it was a dark demon of the night that attacked him, one which had been chasing wolves so long, too huge for wolf to make out its form, though its teeth and claws, metallic in their harsh precision, were stark enough.

Elhana saw a gleam in Ambato's eye as he told her this, and the glimmer of a smile, and she touched his wounds, and cleaned them with her tongue and said, 'You've been seeking a way out of here, haven't you, my dear?'

'Maybe,' grunted Ambato, dead-tired.

'Well, and have you found one?'

'I have not forgotten that it is to the Heartland we are journeying. I have never forgotten that,' he mumbled as he fell asleep.

She looked at his lined, lean face, his greying fur, his half-open mouth and she understood that in some things he was stronger than her, far stronger, and that in leading her to him, Wulf had made it possible for both of them to have a chance, however slight, of one day reaching the Heartland.

So time passed by, in which they learnt of demons and of how to keep hope alive, and each other.

Then suddenly one morning Ambato woke to the scream of circling gulls against a rising sun, as another load of rubbish was delivered, and he sighed.

He looked at Elhana, and she at him, and he said simply, 'Let's get out of here: time to journey on. I have no wish to scavenge in this rat-infested place any more. A wolf should die with the bright stars above his head and the sound of wind in trees.'

She nodded, wordlessly, and got up to follow his lead knowing he must have found a way beyond.

Their crossing of the great river into an urban and industrial hell had brought great change to both of them but now, like a snake that sheds its skin, they were ready to move on: tougher, wiser, more knowledgeable about Mennen places, more knowledgeable about themselves.

'Remember the route we take as best you can,' was all

he said as they left. 'Or if not the route then the nature of the route, which is better still, for it will be more lasting. Remember, my dear, for if you ever return this way you may need to know.'

By tunnel they went, underneath roads, across a gravelly waste where Mennen sat by trees at night, singing; then into a canal and down its length for a time, swimming with the hiss of pipes above their heads, and the sudden clatter of a fiery place whose chimney belched out sparks.

They travelled fast because, whispered Ambato in one of the few halts for rest he allowed, 'I want to get out of the city before dawn, out and away . . . before its places and machines wake up.'

It was dawn, and the sky was beginning to grow pale, before, quite suddenly, Elhana knew they would be free. From the north towards which they were travelling, she felt the fresh breeze of cooler, purer air upon her face and she gulped at it, remembering all she had begun to forget.

'Not far now and then we can rest, not too far,' said Ambato, and he loped along, under a road, leapt a wall, and their paws were on wet grass and though the sky was clear and there were few clouds, there was the sound of sprinkling rain.

'Mennen rain,' explained Ambato nodding towards a sprinkler in the ground that sent a huge spray of droplets in the air, swaying first one way and then another: 'Mennen grass.'

They settled into a trot through shrubs and lawns, past cream walls and windows whose glass caught the rising sun and a fleeting image of themselves, and then, finally, out past the barking of a dog and into a rise of woodland.

'We'll stop here for the day.' Ambato led her to a wooden building beneath whose floor they crept, the damp earth cool on their tired paws, and their view unrestricted from under the building in most directions.

'Bliss,' said Elhana, too excited to sleep or even rest.

'You've not seen the best yet,' replied Ambato with a smile. 'Rest now and I'll tell you when they come.'

'What come?' she asked.

'Rest, wolf . . . rest . . .'

She did, waking only when he nudged her and whispered, 'There! Look!'

What she saw, caught and dappled in the sun, seemed to her then more beautiful than anything she had ever seen. It was a herd of deer coming through the trees, slowly, without concern, foraging as they went, listening to some distant sound, staring suddenly over at where the wolves lay unseen, catching their scent perhaps . . . or perhaps not, for the deer settled again, foraged some more, and drifted on.

'What are they?' said Elhana in wonder: she had almost lost faith that such richness could exist.

'They are . . .' began Ambato, and he whispered slowly of what the deer were to wolves, which is most ancient lore, for what were the gods of the world in distant days without the immortal deer they chased and fed upon? Strength and cunning feeding upon beauty. Never before had Elhana understood so well that prey were not separate from wolves but part of what she was part of too, and in that, and in the world whose Heartland they now sought, everything was one. In the Mennen world they were leaving that truth was all destroyed and what was left was hunting with no honour, destruction with no sense, death with no return.

So began the second part of the journey of Ambato and Elhana through northern Italy. The day after, they set off beyond the parkland that had briefly given them sanctuary, always avoiding the Mennen and their towns as far as they were able. They felt no need to hurry, letting caution be their guide, yet it was not many more days before the air felt fresher still, the night sky became clearer and they knew they were climbing up at last out of the great and dreadful plain they had been forced to cross.

The land was undulating, though with little natural cover and a lack of easy prey, so that when they finally reached the foothills of the Alps both were relieved. Elhana left the route-finding to Ambato, whose knowledge of tales and legend included fragmentary pack-memories of journeys north by wolves in times gone by, which he used in conjunction with the stars above, and their combined knowledge of the wolfway north.

One thing was certain – the lines and small constellations of stars in the wolfway they sought to follow reached a climax somewhere amidst the Alpine peaks ahead whose mass they had seen from across the plain, and whose details of peaks and valleys, now they were starting among them, only slowly revealed themselves. It was to this wilder and more dramatic part of their route that Ambato was now leading them.

'I never heard a name for it among the Benevento wolves,' he said, 'but the Abruzzese vagrants had memories of such a place, which they called the Dolomites. It is up there somewhere that when Wulf first walked on the earth he punished three of his followers by turning them into solid rock.'

'Do you believe such legends?' Elhana asked.

Ambato nodded and said, 'They are our only link with our ancestors. After all, it may be that in the tales of future generations, what we do may play a part even if the names of Ambato and Elhana have been lost along the way. It is in tales that something of our spirit may live on.'

'How far do you think we must travel before we reach the place called the Dolomites?'

'Days or weeks, what does it matter? We are not travelling fast. I have taken much of my lifetime to get this far, and *you*, all the time since late summer.'

'I don't think the call to the Heartland demanded that we got there fast,' said Elhana, 'but rather that we bring with us as much as we can learn on the way. If there are others as you say . . .'

She was beginning to talk and think as he did.

'Oh there *are* others, Elhana, a good few others.'

'Well then, the others will each bring knowledge of their own to contribute to the new pack's lore. The knowledge you have of Wulf may be what you give.'

'And you my dear?'

'Me? I want more young. I want to mate with a great wolf, a vigorous wolf . . .'

Ambato laughed.

'Not an old wolf like me then?'

'No,' said Elhana matter-of-factly, 'but you can help me choose.'

'I think *that* will be a matter for your mate who will, I trust, be leader of the pack to you as ledrene. We want no furtive liaisons in the pack we form.'

'Hmm,' mused Elhana, thinking that she was the product of just such a liaison, and he its progenitor.

'Quite so, "hmm". I think we had better get there first!'

'I hope the one I find is young, and passionate and likes the sun!' said Elhana impulsively. 'I hope he's everything. Come *on* Ambato! Father!'

Ambato laughed again and watched her bound on ahead of him, as beautiful a female as he had ever seen, and in her prime. It was a journey of wild faith and dreams that they were on and perhaps it needed mad wolves to dare to undertake it. He himself was of course sane, and ordinary . . . he shook his head ruefully and went upslope after her.

Elhana paused and looked back. She felt excited, and

confident, and the lust of spring was in her blood. But not for an old wolf like Ambato, whom she now watched with affection as he climbed up towards her, the light bright in his grey, grizzled fur, and across the lines of his wise face.

She scented at the air and remembered wistfully the young loves she had known. All too few. She wanted a strong young wolf again. 'And yet he must not be too inexperienced or he will not be a worthy leader, and I do want a wolf who can be leader, which means I suppose he'll be older, and scarred from fighting and, oh! I don't know what I want!'

Ambato caught up with her.

'Still dreaming, wolf? Dreaming that you can have everything?'

She grinned and rubbed her head affectionately against his.

'You can't have everything, Elhana, no wolf ever could. The ledrene of the pack must have the leader, and he must have her. That is the lore, and must always be so. Without that a pack has no integrity and its leaders lead it badly.'

'But Abruzzo of the Benevento had other females than me! And sometimes I had other males when he could not see.'

'Well, yes, of course, especially if a pack is large. Instincts are instincts and being out of sight *is* out of mind, and a wolf may forget himself or herself for a time. But the wistful shine in your eyes was not for mating but for love, and *that*, if it exists at all, is a most disturbing and unpredictable thing. I know it to my cost.'

'I was ledrene to a wolf I did not like, nor much respect. I was only . . . hoping, that the gods might be good enough, if it happens again that I am ledrene, to find me a leader I can love as well as respect.'

'And if they don't?' asked Ambato quietly.

'Then I must do my duty by the pack,' said Elhana without enthusiasm.

'You can *learn* to love,' said Ambato. 'Some wolves hide the truth of themselves very deep.'

'Well, all I can say,' said Elhana lightly as they set off into the Alpine hills, 'is that I hope he's all he should be *and* young *and* strong.'

'So do I,' muttered Ambato following behind her. 'For if he's not, you'll find a wolf to love who is and then we'll have trouble no pack needs.'

They went on in silence, with hope in the eyes of one, but shadows of concern over the face of the other.

Such imaginings were soon forgotten in the excitement of the journey, which carried now the ever-present expectation that something new was just around the corner, or over the rise beyond.

It was certainly true that there was exhilaration in the rediscovery of natural things – the freshness of a breeze, winds that came in due order across the fields and amongst the trees, rather than sharp and whistling around concrete corners and bitterly down the gorges between towering buildings; the larks that sang high in a bright sky, and the rippling water of the streams, fresh and cleaner now.

Yet for all this they felt a greater sense of danger than they had felt within the Mennen city at the end of their sojourn there. Dogs scented them, here, and Mennen had better sight than in the city, where they had seemed to have no sight at all. Several times dogs gave chase, their barking once seeming to attract a Mann who shouted after them. Three times they were shot at, the pellets rattling over the cover they had taken and into the trees behind.

'The worrying thing about *that* one,' observed Ambato, 'is that I did not even know the Mennen were there. It happened to us once before, before we crossed the river.'

'It came from above our heads, not from somewhere across the fields,' said Elhana, puzzled.

'Then why don't we stay just where we are, and observe, until we know what it is we *should* have known to avoid . . . Such knowledge may save our lives and others' in the future.'

They stayed quite still through the afternoon and into dusk. Then they heard sounds somewhere in the trees above, and the voice and cough of a Mann. It was too dark to see what part of the tree he came out of but they crept close and watched him descend to the ground only a short step from where Ambato lay, with Elhana some way beyond. The Mann trekked off and at Ambato's signal the two silently tracked him until, after a drop from the scrubland beyond the trees, he came to a vehicle hidden off a nearby road which they had passed earlier and sniffed about at. He climbed in, its roaring started, and he was off.

Ambato insisted on waiting back at the tree until dawn came and they could see properly once again. Then, peering up, they could make out a structure of wood and green material which would have been invisible among the leaves had they not been looking for some sign that the Mann had been there.

'Well, now we know,' said Ambato. 'He was waiting for us to come.'

'For *us*? How could he have known?'

'If not for us, then for some other creature.'

'I never thought to search trees for Mennen before,' said Elhana wryly.

'Nor have *I* thought to ponder what a vehicle off a road might mean. But now I know: it means that Mennen are about. Come, let us go: we have learnt all we can here and others might come back to such a place as this.'

Here and there along the route they took, when prey

was scarce and they came near a town, they would scent out a rubbish tip such as the one they had lived by for so long, and scavenge over it. The towns themselves held little fear for them now, and their dark underground ways, or the courses of the rivers and streams that ran through them, polluted though they often were, offered safe routes. Indeed, Ambato, who had the greater curiosity about learning where the Mennen might and might not be, observed that the more polluted and stinking a place, the less likely it was that the Mennen would be there.

'They make these places but don't live in them, or go to them,' he would say with wonder. Even at the dumps Mennen were rarely seen, only their great machines which roared back and forth, interminable by day, dead and still at night.

'Such places are havens for us if we need them, and do not let them poison us. We must remember that.'

Suddenly, one morning, as they climbed up more rugged ground they knew the bigger towns were behind them now. They travelled on among foothills clothed with trees, between whose valleys roads snaked along upslope and out of sight. There was, especially at night, the sense that not far ahead now real mountains rose. Their scent seemed to be on the cold winds that drove down the valleys towards them: the scent of height, of snow, of rock, that rose above the final trees, and the earthy smell of scree.

They travelled on above the roads, hidden among the trees, both now fit and well, though Ambato, even on his best days, moved more stiffly than when Elhana had first met him, and breathed more heavily after the longer climbs.

Then, too, it seemed to her that his fur was paler and thinner than when they began their sojourn in the city places, so that the form of his body was more angular, more spare, like a tree that has half-shed its leaves in autumn while the rest had begun to wither, revealing not just the passage of time, but the inner form and strength, as well. Elhana guessed that more often now Ambato felt the aches and pains of age and noticed how he would settle out of chill dusk and dawn wind's way, and how, after a rest, he would rise stiffly and wince.

But the moment the sun shone bright and warm he perked up and moved more easily, and if they could find a warm place to rest for a while then Ambato, basking in the sun, was at his very best, and would talk of his distant youth among the Benevento, and a wolf he had once loved but whose name he never spoke. It was only now, after all this time, that he brought himself to approach a truth they had not spoken of seriously since they first met: the fact that he was her father and, to Elhana something as important, that he had loved her mother Lauria.

'For you did love her, didn't you?' asked Elhana.

'Well,' Ambato replied after a brief pause, 'it's time we were moving on my dear . . . I really think it is.'

He did not want to speak so openly of Lauria, nor of love, though Elhana yearned that he would do so. Among the males, she knew such love was a concept rarely talked about, and a word rarely spoken. She had been ledrene all those years but never once had her leader spoken of love to her. That she had been born of a loving union meant much more to her than Ambato knew.

'Ambato! Ambato!' she called out one day then, when, upslope ahead of him she saw through the trees a view that took her breath away. 'Oh, father, look!'

He had come faster up the slope at her call, alarmed for a moment but then intrigued and curious, for it was not fear that raised her voice, but wonder.

Ambato came to her flank and stared as she did, through

the trees and then on across the river vale to where the landscape opened over verdant, soft pastures beyond which, stark, rising massively, enough to strike two wolves quite dumb, rose formidable white towers of rock. Limestone, rugged, pinnacled and blunt, gateways that once seen, a wolf must hurry to reach and pass in among.

'The Dolomites,' whispered Ambato, certain of what he saw. 'We have reached them at last. These mark the end of the wolfways from the south, and are the portals to the north that all wolves of Italy must take if they are to reach the distant Heartland of the Wolf itself. I never thought that I . . . I never thought . . .'

Ambato was so moved by what they saw, so thankful that Wulf had guided them in safety so far, so awed by the journey yet to come, that he bowed his head and wept.

'Father!' cried out Elhana, unsure whether to laugh or cry until, quite overcome herself, she did both at once.

'Just as your mother would have done,' he said later, when they had found a place to rest and wonder at the journey they had made, and the place to which they had come. If this was but a stage upon the way, what wonders yet awaited them in the Heartland itself . . .

CHAPTER FIFTEEN

*Klimt journeys on towards the Heartland
and comes to the aid of another wolf*

KLIMT'S JOURNEY from the Baltic Coast eastward across the north European plain to the first inland mountains could have been much swifter than he made it, but once he had established that the Mennen deadlands were safe places for wolves he saw no reason to hurry.

For one thing he found them endlessly interesting, especially at night when the lights went on, and for another they were a good safe source of prey and carrion. He quickly discovered that he was not the only carnivore to use the deadlands – fox, mink, polecat, badger had all preceded him and had well-established territories.

Sometimes there were areas where the Mennen had huge structures in which there was noise, and fumes and more Mennen; sometimes there were places where no light shone nor Mennen went; and sometimes he peered through impenetrable fences at distant lights or stretching darkness.

There was plenty of water in streams and Mennen-made canals, though he was cautious and always tested it before slaking his thirst. Often its odour and colour were doubtful, and where he could he drank from rain-pools, or water in natural places, though sometimes this turned out worse and left him ill for days. But as the journey continued these episodes got fewer and he guessed he was getting used to Mennen pollution.

He was never aware of Mennen seeing him, and though once or twice he heard shots they were far from him. Sometimes, and always at night, if he heard Mennen nearby, he ventured towards them to observe what he could.

He learned that their voices could be hard or soft, that they rarely journeyed away from their vehicles, and that their dogs were usually weak. He watched and mused and wondered why Wulf had put them on the earth. They were stranger to him than other elements like wind, or fire, or rain. They shaped the earth and then did not live in the places they made.

So it was that travelling slowly and with curiosity Klimt learnt more about the Mennen, though it meant that he did not reach higher ground until December. When he did, it was the upland mass of the Harz Mountains he entered, whose nature and extent were shown well enough in the wolfways of the stars. He had seen the mountains coming for weeks past, but finally only went among them in pursuit of a herd of deer which he found feeding in the deadlands and which fled when they scented him.

The Harz Mountains were unimpressive compared with his homeland ranges, except for one great round peak of harder rock at the north-east end of the east-west crescent they formed. But the range was at least well-forested, with deciduous trees in quantities he had not often seen before. Leafless as these now were they provided less cover from the weather and the Mennen than he would have liked, and he was glad to find sanctuary in plantations of coniferous trees when he could. But their straight lines made him uneasy, and he was disturbed that Mennen seemed to order trees with the same dead precision that ordered their routeways. Why?

He lingered only a few days before he felt a hunger

for more natural upland country, and, with some regret at leaving the deadlands of the northern plain far behind, he journeyed on. His sense now was that he need not go to lower ground again, for the grain of the land was high and easterly, and he believed that the Heartland lay that way.

Cautious as ever, Klimt continued slowly and steadily, risking full daylight only on ground he had already reconnoitred at dusk or dawn. He sensed the journey might be long, so he would pace himself, and he felt now in awe of the place he was trying to find. Down in the deadlands he had been himself alone; up here, where the air was colder, the nights darker, and the snows thick on the peaks to right and left, he felt again that he was part of a great enterprise for wolfkind, and that others were already heading towards where he was going, so that he travelled in the lost shadows of others before him.

It was afterwards to Klimt's regret that he could not remember the precise route he had followed, but it is hard to remember features whose names are unknown, and which lie under a covering of snow. But the real reason was that he found himself now thinking of his parents, and the pack of which he had been a member.

He did so seriously and with intent, for if he was going to lead another pack it was best he thought through how he might do it, and what might be learnt from all that had gone before. In retrospect, his home pack had not been as happy or enjoyable as a pack might surely be, and this he attributed to the differences between his parents, and their lack of union.

'A leader must accept whichever female emerges as dominant,' he mused, 'unless it will be as in my parents' case, and Elsinor and me, where we were each a vagrant pair with no other choice. If we had stayed undisturbed in Tornesdal other leaders and ledrenes would have emerged.'

He remembered his father's growing interest in his older female siblings.

'Perhaps he would have helped them become ledrene . . .' Perhaps, and yet the thought did not feel quite right. 'But then there can be no one right way towards the perfect pack, nor can perfection last, for we wolves are growing and changing all the time. So a leader must see the changes coming, or even make them come . . .'

Such thoughts became almost obsessional for Klimt in those short days and long harsh nights of winter, and it is no wonder that he barely noticed the passing mountains, the dark shadows of the fir trees, or the rushing icy rivers he often had to cross.

He looked back at his own short experience as leader – first after his father and the others died, and then from the time he met Elsinor – and saw how differently he might have done things, and most of all, how much more cautious he would be now.

'If a leader loses his pack he is no leader, so survival is the first thing. But that is the beginning, not the end, and perhaps if wolves see survival as their only purpose then they will not survive.' A paradox, but only the first of many that he was to find.

One morning he found himself drinking from a dark, still pool whose northern edge was ice, and saw his own reflection, and was shocked. How dark and impenetrable his face and eyes, how fierce, how serious; and, too, how scarred he was and old-seeming.

'Is this the face of a wolf others will follow? Wulf guide me! Wulf, teach me, for you have been the leader of us all.'

Sometimes he saw a flight of birds, one in front of all the others as they turned, and he envied it; or a tree taller than the others on a rise, and he thought that that was how a leader should be.

'But why me?' he wondered, for he knew that leadership is no easy or pleasant thing, though he hungered for it. He did not know, but when he posed himself the question it was anger that he felt, and Mennen that he saw ahead, and he, Klimt of Tornesdal leading a pack of dark wolves towards them.

'The Mennen took our trees and land and now we must win them back if wolfkind is to be strong again. Wulf wishes it, for he is coming to this earth and we must be ready for him when he comes!' Such was the burden of Klimt's thoughts through that time of winter journeying.

It was in late February that he came across his first evidence of wolf, and it brought to an end his long period of introspection. After the Harz Mountains he had travelled south-east through the Thüringer Wald until he had reached the Fichtelgebirge, that sterile and desolate conjunction of the two great upland chains of central Europe. South-east of here the Böhmer Wald takes the vagrant wolf down through Bohemia and then into Austria at the western end of the Alps.

But north-east the wolfways lead through the bitter reaches of the Erzgebirge* and then, by increasingly obscure and mysterious mountain heights to the great Carpathian Mountains which lead finally to the unknown south where seas and mountains meet, and rivers run inland, and history is said to be older than time itself.

Of this last Klimt knew nothing, but as he scented towards the deeps and shadows of the Erzgebirge, he sensed dangers for wolves and their past mysteries, tragedies and lost triumphs, and felt that that was the way to

---

* *Wolves use the Teutonic dialects in the names of places west of the Heartland. Erzgebirge means 'Ore mountains'.*

go. What he found was an upland scarred and abandoned by Mennen who, centuries since, had hacked and delved their way into the mountain sides. These old mines and tunnels, and the spoil tips associated with them, were overgrown with roots and vegetation of generations of plants, and many had fallen in and all but disappeared. But as Klimt made his way north-eastward he found deeper tunnels, undisturbed for decades except by the smallest mammals, and these he used for shelter and respite.

One of their attractions was precisely that they had been made by the Mennen and were but an older part of the deadland he had begun to know – but a deadland that was no longer dead. The Mennen had been, had cleared and dug and killed, and yet the decades had passed and natural life had returned. The Mennen were not invincible: time and faith in their destruction were more powerful than they.

So it was that in the Erzgebirge Klimt had the powerful sense that he was in a place where wolfkind had lived before. Here, he felt, were some beginnings; here wolves had lived *before* the Mennen came.

As Klimt travelled, he felt the sadness, anger and respect any creature feels when he goes where his ancestors were destroyed. Sometimes at night he could imagine the mountains and valleys running with wolves, and their howling gyring up like great avenging eagles in the dark. At such moments it was not hard for him to believe – to *know* – that one day wolves would return to this ancient place, and that he was but the forerunner of the packs that would come back.

It was in just such a powerful mood of nostalgia for what was, anger for what might have been, and hope for what was to come, that he first sensed that a wolf or wolves had passed that way recently. The signals were mixed, and depended on nothing more than half-scents and disintegrated spoor in one of the tunnels in which he entered.

Klimt could not tell how old these signals were, or what sex the wolf had been, or really to tell if there had been more than one. The spoor being inside the tunnel might mean that the wolf had been old and dying, or hiding from the Mennen. One thing though: if he came across the wolf he would know him by his scent.

He quartered the ground outside the tunnel, not in any hope of finding signs on the snow-covered ground itself, but to see if there were other tunnels or excavations nearby that might yield more clues. But there were none.

When he returned to the original tunnel, as if to say farewell to the wolf who had been and gone, he felt the shimmer of a breeze upon his face from further down the tunnel, further than he had ventured in. He was careful of these diggings and shafts since a wolf could turn a corner into darkness and find dangerous drops or icy pools of water.

But, curious, he proceeded until the light grew dim and the entrance behind him receded. Vowing at each step to turn back at the next, he had almost gone as far as he wished, though the cold breeze suggested a way out ahead, when the tunnel turned abruptly to the right. There were strange, distant wind sounds, and random rustlings and knockings that might have upset a lesser wolf than Klimt. But he scented no danger, no life at all, and guessed the sounds were something loose caught and shaken by the wind.

He peered round the bend and saw a glimmer of light, heard the drip of water, splashed through a series of chilling pools and turned a second corner to find the source of the light. A shaft went up through the roof and broke the surface above and there, through a tangle of vegetation he could just see the pale sky. Roots and plant-growth hung down the shaft and it was these which rattled and scratched in the wind.

Because of the sudden light the tunnel beyond seemed like a solid wall of darkness, so it was only when Klimt reached it that he saw he had come to the very edge of a short but vertical drop, a pit in the tunnel floor. Klimt suddenly had no wish to go further, and was just turning to go back when a pale glimmer in the pit below caught his eye. He stared until his eyes adjusted fully to the light and only then saw the pale green-white bones – the vertebrae, the ribs, the tangle of femurs and shins, and the staring skull – which lay in the murk below in the ragged semblance of what had once been a wolf.

Klimt felt deep sadness. He had hoped the wolf had been alive and that he might catch up with him . . . but there he lay, dead, gone, unknown. Klimt trembled and then felt even more determined to journey on and find living wolves to . . . to lead. There would be many more to die before his quest was done.

The wind rattled bitterly above him as he stared on, taking in the dried and twisted pelt whose grey fur lacked lustre now, but vibrated minutely in some subterranean draught.

It was not hard to see what had happened: the wolf had fallen into a place from which it could not climb out, and starved to death. Had it been dying of disease, or maimed by Mennen shot, and not known where it was wandering? Had it sought to hide, thinking it could get back out? Or – and here Klimt looked past the pit to the tunnel's continuation – had it hoped to find another way of escape or simply slipped?

Even as he looked down, the moist soil at the pit's edge began to give way around his front paws and for a brief and terrible moment the pit and the wolf's bones seemed to tilt up towards him. Klimt half-turned, arched his back, thrust out his paws over the void and scrabbled round and back to safety. He took a bound back into the light, panting with exertion and shock before he paused and stood absolutely still. He stared back down the tunnel he had come in by, but what he saw was something he had briefly glimpsed in the pit beyond the wolf. A form that shocked him; a shape he knew. He had seen what it was made the wolf first look in the pit, and he had begun to slip, just as the wolf had, but he had been luckier.

Klimt turned back, stole forward with infinite caution, and peered again into the fatal pit, seeing what he *thought* he had so briefly glimpsed. Beneath the wolf, half-buried in the floor but a dull phosphorescent green where it protruded, was the shape of a Mann. Skull, spine, and the long, thin reaching paw bones. Dead Mann, dead wolf, both doomed, both lost and forgotten inside the earth.

'Great Wulf,' whispered Klimt in the echoing tunnel, 'grant that both have known the wolfway to the stars and know the peace only the gods can grant.'

The prayer was quickly and instinctively said and only afterwards, as he turned from the strange, disturbing sight and exited thankfully the tunnel, did Klimt begin to ponder its significance.

'Why should a wolf pray for a Mann? Yet *I* did!' he muttered to himself, unable to rid his mind of the image of creatures which had been apart in life, but in death were together, and in time would surely be as one. 'Wulf, why did you show me this? Why?' He could find no easy answer, and only slowly did the disturbing light and shadow of what he had seen give way once more to the sense of encouragement he took that he had found sign of wolf. Along the way where one had come, more would be found. This thought, and the first stirring of spring in the plants on the lower south-facing slopes, put renewed life into Klimt as he continued his journey.

A few days after this, when he was nearing the northern tip of the Erzgebirge and the hills were falling ominously away to the valley of the River Elbe, Klimt woke from deep sleep one dusk imagining he heard the howl of a wolf.

It was not the first time, and always the dream was the same: Elsinor summoning him to help her as the Mann began to shoot. But this time there was no accompanying dream, only the sense that a howling wolf in the waking world had summoned him from sleep. Then, having woken into a state of alert alarm, Klimt felt that same sense of being called that he had experienced once in Tornesdal. He needed no second prompting to answer it.

The moment he was up, he noticed that the wind had shifted eastward, that the sky was unsettled and the trees shifting and nervous. Since he had been forced to come down to lower ground he had dropped out of the cover of the spruce, down through hornbeam to a wood of mixed oak. Far, far downslope through its leafless trees he could see the lights of a Mennen town, beyond which was the wide sweep of the river itself.

He thought for only a moment before turning eastward, thinking that if there had been a sound it would have carried to him from that direction. As he ran he scented at the ground, which here was less icy than on the upland slopes, though the snow was thick enough, and in places had formed great drifts. He contoured round to cut across any scent track he might find, thinking that if there was one he would have missed it before, or the scent and sound of any creature making it, because when he denned down for the day the wind had been the opposite of what it now was . . .

Almost at once he found the scent of Mennen and dogs, and then their trail. He followed it briefly, seeking out the dogs' scent since that was easier to interpret. Hours old, going upslope, two dogs, two Mennen. Then, but a short way off he found what they were following: wolf. A single-ton. No sign of more. Old or tired wolf – distressed wolf. Hours old as well. Mennen hunting, wolf hunted, the old story, but one that had taken a millennium to find a new ending.

He began to follow the trail and then stopped suddenly, thinking. If he had heard a wolf's howl then it meant that it had been near, probably somewhere not much beyond this earlier trail. He left the direct line of the trail and continued to contour, stopping to listen occasionally but unable to pick up much against the blustery wind as it rushed among the trees. He increased his pace, cutting back on himself occasionally to double-check, though the light was good enough still to see tracks as well as take scent.

Then as suddenly as he had found the first trail, he found a second, and it was fresh, and urgent with fear. It was the same wolf's scent and, after swift confirmation that it was the same Mennen and dogs in pursuit whose tracks had disturbed the snow and fallen leaves, it was the wolf's he followed.

The first sign of blood he got by scent – a smear over a tree root, but a second was more grim. Fresh and red as wild roses, it spattered the snow where the wolf in his haste and growing weakness had run into a sapling's trunk and had been thrown off-balance. The signs were all there to see, and here the odour of fear was strong. But not just fear: anger and dismay as well, and determination, for though the injured wolf had fallen, the tracks showed he had leapt up despite his injuries and bounded on downslope.

But more than all of that: this was the scent of the wolf he had first come across in the caves, the one he had assumed had been the one he saw dead. Hope and purpose leaped in his heart. The wolf had been searching for others as he had been, and now he needed help.

Without a moment's hesitation or doubt Klimt turned downslope after the tracks and as swiftly as if he had the prey in sight he was off after the wolf and his pursuers.

It was not long before the scents gained in freshness and he saw that the wolf was following a deliberately twisting route, using the roots of trees, or fallen trunks to lessen the tracks, whilst in other places he had dared to circle on himself to confuse the dogs still more.

It was only as he found more fresh blood that Klimt finally heard the chase through the trees below, and the dogs barking and baying as if they had found their quarry at last. He abandoned the trail and went by sound alone, leaping downslope in great bounds, twisting and turning past all obstacles in his path. He veered downwind, but only enough to reduce his early detection by scent and sound – there was no time for anything subtler. And then he was onto them, and as the first dog sensed his approach he just had time to take in the scene and decide what to do.

The wolf, a thin youngster less than three years old, had turned finally to face the Mennen and dogs, his back in the angle of a fallen tree and its upraised roots. On one side the wood stretched on, and on the other the ground dropped away to the gully of a little stream which gushed away beneath banks of snow.

As Klimt arrived he saw that one of the Mennen was raising a glinting gun upon the wolf, just as a gun had once been raised to his Elsinor, a gun which shot her dead. It was a final spur to action. With a low and dangerous growl Klimt powered past the dog that had seen him and landed hard on the Mann's shoulders, bringing him crashing to the ground and sending the gun flying. Before the second Mann and dog could take in what had happened he ran back over

the first Mann's head and shoulders and tore at the arm of
the second Mann, pulling him round and off-balance and
hurled him down the bank of the stream into a mess of
snow and running water.

Only one dog had the courage to confront him, and this
he dealt with savagely, feeling his own jaw and teeth strain
and crack as he caught hold of the dog's head and shook
him. The dog collapsed and Klimt needed only to bare his
now bloody teeth for the other to retreat and begin whining
submissively.

Having created this brief moment of opportunity Klimt
turned finally to the wolf whose life he had saved and commanded him, 'Follow the stream down as best you can. Do
not go far from it. Answer my call when you hear it that I
may find you again. Go!' But when the wolf stayed staring
at him in mute astonishment Klimt came near, looked as
fierce as he did with the Mennen and the dogs, and roared,
'Go!'

The wolf needed no third command but staggered to its
feet with new life, turned and ran down into the stream
where the other Mann was already struggling to recover
himself, and was gone, crashing downslope in a welter of
snow and spray.

Nor did Klimt hesitate now. The first Mann was still on
the ground but reaching for the gun and so he went for
him once more, growling and mauling at his clothes. Klimt
did not wish to kill him, and he sensed they were dead
coverings, like old ivy on a tree-trunk, for he tasted no
blood as they tore, though he felt the Mann's body beneath.
The Mann rose lumbering, turned away from Klimt, roaring and screaming, stenching of fear, his gun out of reach.

Klimt continued the assault, wanting them only to flee.
The Mennen he would not harm but the dogs he would
kill if he had to.

The second Mann was up and out of the stream-bed and,

having kept hold of his gun, was seeking to raise it when Klimt went for him again, so powerfully that Mann and wolf flew, threshing, into the stream. The gun splashed into the water, the Mann screamed and scrabbled away and began running and Klimt turned back to the first who, hearing the low growl again, and seeing the bared fangs and furrowed face, turned and fled after the other, blundering down into the stream and crashing away through the trees.

Klimt followed them, one of the dogs at his heels, and snapped and hustled at the two Mennen until the fighting need draining from him, he finally turned and dealt with the dying dog. Two swift bites, a violent savaging, and the dog lay bleeding and shaking in the snow.

It was over, and all that was left was the running of the Mennen out of sight, and the brief death-squeals of the dog; and somewhere, upslope, the abject whinings of the other one.

For a moment Klimt was still, breathing heavily and feeling a soreness around his mouth and the tenderness of two loose teeth. Then he raised his head, gathered himself together once more, and made his way back to where the fight began. He went to the stream, splashed down into its cold, reviving flow and followed the other wolf downslope, staying in the water as much as he could to leave no scent.

The wolf had made good ground and it was only at his third soft howl, made a long way downslope, that Klimt got an answering call. By now the dusk was gathering towards dark. Stars were already showing, and downslope beyond the trees the fixed Mennen lights were shining bright, and the amber and red of cars on a road were visible.

But there was light enough from the snowy ground to see things close to, and wanting to get his breath back, Klimt permitted himself to trot slowly the final distance to where the wolf stood waiting, midstream.

His first act on seeing Klimt emerge out of the gloom was to rill softly; and his second was to lower his head and tail submissively and wait. Klimt came to him, and stood with his flank abutting the wolf's muzzle, but he held the position of dominance only for moments and did not reinforce it with sound, or more aggressive display. It was all quickly and elegantly done and when it was over, and the two looked into each other's eyes, one knew he was dominant, and the other not, but both held themselves with pride.

'That was close,' said the young wolf laconically, with rueful humour and gratitude in his eyes.

Klimt stared at him, uncertain quite what he meant. It was so long since he had talked to another that he had almost forgotten how; and the last thing he was used to was levity.

'What's your name, wolf?'

'I am Tervicz of the Bukov pack,' he said; and though it was said lightly there was a myriad of shadows and dreams behind these seven words, and the story of how so young a wolf came to be here, and alone.

'Bukov,' mused Klimt. He knew the pack name, of course: who did not? The legends were certain enough of one thing: it had been a Bukov wolf who, before the dark millennium began, had been the last to find the route through the Heartland to the WulfRock itself, and then away again. A Bukov wolf, too, who had sent forth the fabled Wolves of Time; and one of that pack as well who, in some future time, would lead wolves back to the WulfRock . . .

All this Klimt knew and thought of as he stared at the strange wolf whose life he had saved – and he felt disappointment. The wolf was unremarkable and bore no resemblance at all to that legendary Bukov wolf who had first stalked across the landscape of his imagination when his parents first howled the old tales to him.

Klimt said, simply, 'Well then, Tervicz of the Bukov, I am Klimt of Tornesdal in the north. Tell me, how did you come to be so separated from your pack?'

'Do you want the long or the short answer?' said Tervicz hiding behind flippancy.

Just as Klimt had felt disappointment, so did Tervicz, for he understood in an instant of Klimt talking to him something he had not even considered in all his long months of searching: the Wolves of Time might not know what they were, otherwise, on hearing he was of Bukov, he would surely have welcomed such a meeting more.

'What are you doing here?' asked Klimt impatiently, for he was unused to banter of any kind, least of all talk of 'long or short' answers. He wanted the truth, and he wanted it quickly, so that he could properly decide if they were going to travel on together. Either way they should leave this dangerous place as soon as possible.

'I was seeking some wolves,' began Tervicz cautiously, feeling as he said it that even that was giving away too much.

'Which wolves?' asked Klimt, stiffening and looking about him suspiciously.

'I think that you may be one of them,' was Tervicz's strange reply.

'Hmmph!' muttered Klimt, relaxing and quite misunderstanding what Tervicz meant. The wolf wanted company, that was all – but why not? He did himself, and this wolf might give him useful information about the way ahead, or whether there were any packs with territories hereabout. Also, it might be safer having companionship.

'Come, wolf, we must get away from here and it may be better if we leave this area together . . .' said Klimt judiciously. 'You can tell me about these wolves you say you are seeking as we go, and why you think I am one of them. After that we shall decide what we should do and whether it shall be together or separately.'

Klimt did not smile, nor did his voice give the other encouragement. Anything more could wait.

Klimt turned and left, Tervicz following in his tracks at a distance, and any one watching them would have been in no doubt about which was the leader, and which the follower.

Where doubt would have lain was in deciding which of the two saw his future clearly and without fear, and which wolf had a long way to go before he understood his destiny. It is not always leaders who are blessed with the clearest vision.

CHAPTER SIXTEEN

*Klimt and Tervicz join forces to continue their journey
together, but are confronted by the Magyar wolves*

I N THE COLD, DARK DAYS that followed, as Klimt
and Tervicz began to trek south-eastward through the
high passes and forests of the Sudety Mountains, it
turned out that there was little time for talk, nor, more to
the point, much inclination either.

Perhaps each felt that real talk could come later, when
trust had been created, and the purpose of their journey
was more clear. The way was hard, and prey scarce, and
to Klimt, used as he was to the pines and lakes of Sweden,
the twisted and rugged terrain into which they now travelled, with older deciduous forests and high Mennen
summer pastures, was strange and disconcerting.

Such wild prey as had been available in the previous
weeks, mainly rabbits and the lesser mammals, was getting
harder and harder to find; while the bigger prey whose
scent they picked up was mainly deer, but its herds and
strays moved higher and higher up the mountain heights
away from them, or, worryingly, downslope towards the
Mennen places where Tervicz warned Klimt against trying
to follow.

'We must not let the Mennen know we are here,' he
said, fearfully, 'or they will come in vehicles, in dozens.'

Klimt nodded his agreement gravely. 'It is certainly too
soon for us to confront the Mennen – for now it is better

217

to stay in silent retreat, as wolves have for so many centuries. But one day, Tervicz, we shall have to make our stand.'

It seemed a strange thing for a wolf to say, and so radically different from anything that Tervicz had ever thought or heard, that he wondered if he had heard aright, and stayed silent. But one thing was plain, and it was shocking and exciting: Klimt was not afraid of the Mennen. He was, like a pretender to a pack's leadership, biding his time concerning *them*. Well then, this was indeed a wolf among wolves.

On such matters Tervicz pondered as they travelled on into an increasingly bitter winter landscape, in which even carrion was harder to find. The chill winds seemed to have driven all ailing creatures from these parts long since, or else they had already died and been taken by fox and wildcat.

Which left the verges of the roads and their victims, and some of the lower fields where, sometimes, they found a newly dead sheep, and once a horse. Tervicz found to his surprise that he was better at finding such food than Klimt, something the Nordic wolf readily admitted.

'Why, wolf,' said Klimt after an enforced fast of three days ended only after Tervicz had insisted on a long diversion because he rightly sensed he might find food, 'you can scent out the broken body of rabbit from nothing, and the scattered black feathers of a shot rook from even less, and it was you who found the body of two of the three fallen sheep. As for this fallen horse . . .'

Klimt pulled another strip of flesh off the animal before yielding his place to Tervicz.

'It was a skill my father taught me,' grunted Tervicz between mouthfuls, 'which kept us all alive a good many times.' He said this modestly, but he was flattered to be so praised. He could not quite understand this Nordic wolf, sometimes so silent and suddenly severe, sometimes generous in his praise, and often willing to listen to what was tentatively offered as comment or advice, where Zcale would have not listened at all.

'Not too much, never eat too much,' said Tervicz interrupting himself and his thoughts, as Klimt went back for more. For another thing that Klimt was not used to was the need to disguise their predations upon such animals that came their way.

'The Mennen will know that we've been if we eat our prey as wolves should do. Rather seem to be a fox, or badger, or wildcat than known to be a wolf, for then it's them they'll seek, not us.'

'And our pawprints? And our spoor?' asked Klimt, unused to such lore and not much liking it. Had he escaped his own land at the bidding of Wulf, and started his trek, only to emulate a . . . a fox!

'Spoor to be buried, or lost in the stream . . .' said Tervicz, intoning the words just as he had been taught them.

'Befouling streams . . .' growled Klimt, disgusted. It seemed to him sometimes that Tervicz was an unclean wolf. 'What wolf taught you such habits, or is it that you've been too long alone . . . ? We should mark out such territory we take, even in passing.'

'"Mark out and die!" *That* was what *my* father taught!' snapped Tervicz, much affronted. He suddenly grew fierce, protecting the memory of his father who, despite all, had done so much to help them live – as Tervicz had begun to realize in the long months past since he had howled down the Wolves of Time and left on his search for other wolves and the Heartland. He snarled towards Klimt despite his more powerful bulk, before Klimt frowned and with a subtle flick of tail caused Tervicz to retreat and look abject.

'My mother and my father taught me what I know. We

survived, didn't we? The Mennen in our home range were amongst the first wolfkillers, and deadly skilled. We had to learn, and we of the Bukov pack learnt best for we alone survived in our chosen area. How many other packs were lost! What wolves now roam your Nordic lands?' He faltered and then added apologetically, 'But you are my leader now and I shall follow your command alone. You are my father and my mother, you . . .'

'All Mennen are wolfkillers,' said Klimt with matter-of-fact gentleness, seeing that he had been insensitive, and pleased rather than annoyed that Tervicz had wished to defend his own kin. It augured well for the future; and anyway, perhaps the wolf was right, after all. He, himself, had much to learn, as leader and as wolf. 'Tervicz, you are right to practise what you have been taught, until another way is proved better. Nor, though I may be your leader, am I your mother and your father. Finally it is Wulf and Wulfin who are those, and they alone . . . I assume the burden of leadership only until another comes who is stronger, but the gods are always there: as it was, as it is, and as it always will be.'

He calmly fell silent, staring at the weaker wolf, and was pleased to see his anger at the accidental belittling of his birth-pack and parents had subsided.

'We will continue the trek through these lower passes by the methods *you* dictate,' he said finally, restoring Tervicz's pride and confidence, 'and for the time being I shall follow you without question. You seem to know this kind of country and its Mennen better than I.

'Thus far we have travelled without talking overmuch except to agree that it is the Heartland that we both seek. This is wise. Wolves need time to create trust and successful packs need trust and loyalty before all else if they are to survive: before strength, before numbers, and certainly . . .' He fell silent for a moment, remembering one other quality he valued, and then reflecting that it had saved neither his birth pack, nor that little pack he had begun to create with his first and only mate, Elsinor. '. . . and certainly before love. Loyalty, duty, trust: these are things I prize before all others. Well, then, perhaps we shall inspire such virtues in each other. Meanwhile, the day is coming when we should talk more about how we came to be journeying as we are: you from Bukov, if that is where you've come from, and I from Tornesdal. For myself, I had a vision I would like to share with you . . .'

'And I!' said Tervicz, forgetting his earlier caution before the strange power and appeal Klimt had as he spoke like this . . .

But Klimt raised a paw and shook his head saying softly, 'Not quite yet, wolf. But I think we can agree that it is for the Heartland we are looking, and within the Heartland for something that may be unobtainable to mortal wolf – the WulfRock itself.

'However, when an evening of long rest comes, and we have time to talk properly, you shall tell me why it is you think that I must eat only a part of the food Wulf offers us, and why I must despoil the running waters of the land. You shall do more than tell me, wolf: you shall convince me. And if you do not then thereafter we shall trek my way: so prepare your arguments!'

'I shall do so and prove you wrong!' said Tervicz, a little too exuberant at his leader's confidence, and certainly unwisely.

Klimt lunged at him, nipped his flank and sent him tumbling amongst the trees before he himself turned and stood proud, staring back across the ground they had travelled, and then forward the way they must yet go. They had both made their point and it was almost time to journey on.

'One day wolves will eat their fill without fear of the Mennen; and they shall leave their spoor to mark out boldly where they have been; and their pawprints will once more reveal the wolfways without fear that the Mennen will follow destructively in their wake. Meanwhile, Tervicz, think hard about the lore you have been taught, for the day will come when you must teach it to others younger than me, some of whom will accept all you say, while others will question every word. Think hard for I am the questioning kind . . .'

Klimt smiled grimly and signalled Tervicz to press on, which he did with a frown, his mind racing as for the first time in his life he asked himself why lore might be lore and found that 'because it is so and has always been' was no answer at all.

So as they travelled they began to question and talk, with the growing sense as they went, that theirs was no ordinary journey, but the first step on the way to the formation of a pack whose coming was in the pattern of the stars. Tervicz knew more about the lore and legend of the Wolves of Time, more perhaps than any wolf alive except his father Zcale; but as leader, Klimt felt the truth of it all in the marrow of his bones, even if he did not yet know what he himself might be. Destiny seemed to shine across the winter night skies before them, and in the sun and with the mists that slanted across the trees and rocks about the ways they went.

Higher they climbed, always steady and careful, ever more glad of the companionship each gave the other: the one as leader and the other as subordinate, each helping the other to see more and more.

At the end of February, when even the brightest days felt dark and malevolent and they were beginning to doubt that winter would ever end, they were forced from higher ground by heavier falls of snow, and vicious blizzards. They came down through the forest trees into lower vales, and from there along routes that crossed Mennen ways and fields.

Klimt was uneasy, for though he no longer feared the Mennen, he liked the high, freer spaces. But Tervicz knew the better feeding opportunities that proximity to Mennen ways and places brought. What was more, he knew that it was easier to make no pawprints on the roads and tracks along which vehicles had passed and whose fumes masked their scent from dogs.

This drop down to lower ground coincided with a general increase in the height of the mountain mass north of their route, so that though they were now more distant from the mountains, yet still they loomed and lowered over them, seeming to grow darker and more awesome with every passing day.

Klimt, used to the plateau fjell-lands of north Scandinavia, found this change disconcerting and became uneasy and withdrawn. By now he had taken over the route finding, as a leader should, and though he kept to the lower ways as Tervicz preferred, his eyes were always looking up to his left, where the mountains now soared, their highest peaks lost in mists and blizzard winds.

'Up there, we should be up there,' he would growl, as he reluctantly followed the lower route. Though he now led he was still content to confer with Tervicz the moment the route forward felt uncertain and far more ready than Tervicz's father had ever been to concede that he might be wrong, and change his mind. This at first confused Tervicz, reared as he was to the tradition that the leader was not only right, but was never wrong, a very different thing. It unsettled him to be consulted, and that the silent and awesome wolf whose command he had so readily accepted could accept that he sometimes needed advice.

Yet since Klimt showed no other weakness, and reinforced his rule without compunction if Tervicz seemed to overstep some boundary not always obvious to him, the weaker wolf began to accept his leader's strangeness. More than that, he began to enjoy the trust the other so unexpectedly placed in him, and so to gain a growing confidence he had never felt before.

In this way, and perhaps not quite understanding what he did, Klimt began to develop his own powers of leadership by building up the confidence and strength of another, and to start the beginnings of a pack that might in time know great self-reliance as a group because its leader showed trust in its individual members, however weak they might seem to be.

As winter grew more harsh, Tervicz was gladder than ever to follow in the protective shadow of Klimt, whose silences grew longer, and pace a little slower. Tervicz now lost interest in the mountain heights to their left, which seemed to him even more remote and dark, even more unattainable. More than that, if the blizzard winds that beset them were anything to go by, the conditions higher up must be quite impossible.

Food grew scarcer still, and often they went for days without anything at all. Tervicz had to use all his scavenging skills to find some paltry carrion along a Mennen road, or root out the carcass of a sheep which other predators had long since found, and abandoned.

Here and there in the lower vales, they scented the sweet smell of bowered livestock, hidden from sight in a Mennen place whose lights shone out yellow at dusk all the way to the ditch where the wolves hid and watched. Tervicz had never in his life taken bigger living prey than rabbits, and even then generally ones that were so ailing that they stank of disease and coming death. Larger living prey, let alone Mennen's beasts, seemed as unattainable to him as the mountain heights he no longer bothered to look at.

But Klimt had taken larger prey and told of the reindeer that lived in the northern parts where he came from, and how, just once, his parents had shown him how to stalk a herd, and spy out its weakest brethren by chasing them all, and how the weak might be taken.

'Blood on the snow,' whispered Klimt, 'and a living-dying scent as pure, as ancient, as thaw-water off the glaciers. But warm, Tervicz, living, potent, and I had to wait until my father said that I could eat, and then to offer up a prayer to Wulf and Wulfin before I could touch a morsel myself . . .'

Tervicz nodded and, eager to please, whispered dreamily a prayer his mother had taught him out of the ancient lore she had spoken to him, and which he doubted he would ever offer up in any proper way to great Wulf and the stars through whose ways he ran:

> 'Deer to scent in the gorge's lee
> · Deer to chase from the gorge's rise
> Deer to kill in Wulf's great name
> Deer to eat in Wulf's honour
> To scent to chase to kill to eat,
> Deer now, wolf tomorrow
> In Wulf and Wulfin's honour always.'

'Just so,' said Klimt appreciatively. 'So for deer, and all its kind, but different for the fox, and the polecat, and the mole . . .' he continued, settling down upon the snow, his snout filled with the scent of prey they could not take. 'The spirit of each is taken with its carcass only when it's fresh-killed.'

'You have hunted and killed openly with your birth-pack?' began Tervicz, enviously. The Bukov wolves had been too hemmed in by the Magyars and the Mennen for anything so bold.

'That one time only,' said Klimt tersely, closing the subject and then rising abruptly to continue on their way. But after a short distance he turned snarling and irritable, for Tervicz had not risen immediately to follow as he normally did. Tervicz had begun to understand that memory sometimes turned Klimt's smiles to snarls.

The snarl died in Klimt's throat for he saw that Tervicz had risen, but had not moved. Instead he stood stock-still, his neck fur a little ruffled as if he sensed some threat, and staring across the vale and up towards the darkened mountains, the last fastnesses of which were fast disappearing into the swirl of night and grey, winter clouds.

'What is it, wolf?' demanded Klimt, closing to his flank and turning to face whatever danger loomed.

Tervicz continued to gaze into the high darkness of the mountains as if to keep sight of whatever it was he had seen; and when he finally spoke it was as a wolf afraid: 'I . . . I saw . . . I thought I heard . . .'

'What?' demanded Klimt. 'Tell me, wolf, for the fear that silences you might kill us all.'

'I thought I heard the wind whispering my name,' said Tervicz, shivering.

'You probably did, wolf, as I have seemed to do these hours past. Is it that the Heartland is near us now?'

The wind flurried and whispered about them again, and they fell silent, each sure that they were near now, very near.

That night they spoke together of their different pasts, voices in a dark night where faces went unseen, and eyes were no more than moments of shining, teeth no more than the glints of stars; behind them the stir of leafless trees and below them the sparkle of Mennen lights.

Of Bukov, Tervicz spoke, and of his family: his father

Zcale, his sister Szaba, and his crippled brother Kubrat. Then he told of the Bukov view of the Wolves of Time, and how he had howled them down, and begun his journey to find them.

Later Klimt spoke, finding it easier in the dark. Of Tornesdal and how he missed it. Of Elsinor and their cubs, and how they died.

Of his killing of the Mann, and the taste of its blood and flesh. Of Helsingborg and how Wulf called his name.

'Or was it you, wolf, was it your howling down I heard?' Tervicz did not know.

Of their meeting they spoke and in that dark and equal night they spoke too of how they had learned to trust each other, slowly.

'So you think I am one of the Wolves of Time?' said Klimt at last.

Tervicz nodded, certain of it.

'And you?' continued Klimt, 'what are you?'

'Me?'

Klimt nodded in the dark.

'If I am then you are too,' he said and Tervicz sighed, hearing affirmed what he had so long feared, and now unsure if it was an honour or a curse, a blessing or a doom. It was one thing to herald the coming of the Wolves of Time, another to be one of them.

'Am I?' whispered Tervicz again.

It was not Klimt who answered but the wind, and the wind sighed, 'Yesssss.'

The following day, which was cold and crystal clear, they turned north, back upslope among the trees, away from the Mennen ways. They went slowly, conscious as they climbed out of Mennen fumes and scents, that the mountains ahead were higher and more formidable than they had thought.

The air was colder, harsher, the valleys they crossed deeper, the distant views slow to come nearer; and the snow and ice had the sheeny, dusty look that said it might not thaw until the spring. They wound in and out of lower hills, they trekked up through Mennen plantations of coniferous trees, they rested and took what food they could.

Then, in early afternoon, both breathing heavily, they climbed a rise, passed some rocks and knew quite suddenly that in the last few steps they had crossed a boundary. Where they had come from was wolfdom, ordinary, stretching away for miles, to plains, to sea, to mountains; ahead, intense and rising, dark and challenging, as unknown to them as adulthood is unknown to a cub, was the Heartland.

'Well, then,' growled Klimt, looking around at Tervicz, 'we are here.'

Tervicz peered up at the trees, round at the rocks, to seek out the view that was not there and replied, 'And where do we begin?' He grinned, shook his head at the enormity of their unnamed, unknowable task, and sat down.

'Reconnaissance,' said Klimt. 'Steady, watchful, learning all the time.'

Tervicz nodded and muttered with wry weariness, 'Reconnaissance!'

Of the long days that followed neither could afterwards remember much, for they were learning ground that in time they would know almost better than themselves. Familiarity breeds forgetting of the time when the bend ahead seemed fearful, and the gorge below filled with mystery, and shadows.

Some way to the west was an undulating fell crossed north and south by a Mennen way, black, icy and busy enough to avoid. Eastward, to their right flank, the ground was broken by winding river valleys which rose the further north they went. Somewhere in these, they learned from the trails they found, and spoor, and howlings in the night, the Magyars had their territories and places of rendezvous. Of *that* Tervicz left Klimt in no doubt at all.

Northward rose the main mountain mass which was the continuation of the Sudety Mountains down from which, far to westward, they had come weeks before. These they guessed were the Tatra Mountains in whose higher, secret regions the holier places of the Heartland must lie, where rose the WulfRock, guarded, hidden, dangerous to reach, mysterious.

These things they established in the next few days, the name and location of the Tatra confirmed for them by three vagrants they met, Polish wolves from over the Tatra whose routes home had been overtaken by the same severe weather that had first driven Klimt and Tervicz to lower ground.

The two groups stood off from each other for a time, each thinking the other to be Magyars, but came together at last, talked, rested, and then drifted apart again. For a time Klimt and Tervicz had dared to think they might be wolves on a quest for the Heartland as they were, but mention of the Heartland stirred nothing in the Polish wolves' eyes, and their conversation held no dreams beyond food, survival, rest and the coming spring. Yet the encounter cheered Klimt and Tervicz, reminding them that there would be other wolves yet to find; and that other wolves believed what they had sometimes begun to think might never be – that the winter would end, and warmer weather return once more.

It was soon after this that they found themselves in rough Mennen-hewn ground, though abandoned now, the Mennen scents all gone. The place had the sense of dereliction which the Mennen alone of all creatures leave behind: old buildings, long overtaken by trees and shrubs; broken machinery whose harsh, unnatural silhouettes broke up the night sky, and whose creaking sounds in the winter wind added a sense of desolation to the place. Past these, the terrain was flat, unnaturally so, and covered with pools of water beyond which rose up the sides of a quarry, its north face the highest.

Klimt had checked that there were ways out, for a wolf, let alone a leader, does himself and others ill if he chooses a stopping place from which there is no escape. To be trapped in such a place was unthinkable, with its dark, rising clefts and rocks whose wet, shadowed faces were broken only by the dank vegetation of old fern and bracken, and ancient yews whose roots had delved into the clefts and disappeared within.

They explored together and separately, satisfying themselves that to right and left of the steep main face of the quarries were turns and clefts that would allow a good defensive retreat, and whose ways beyond would offer escape. While here and there, on the north-eastern section of the quarry the faces were more broken, and if they had ever been worked it was many centuries before.

Here there were no tracks nor any obvious exit and yet Klimt found himself staring up into the overgrown recesses, feeling that here were surely old ways indeed. One or two of them he even began to climb up, scenting at the heavy, woody air, and feeling the slight downdraught of colder air that told him there might be a way through.

'Wolf!' he called, but Tervicz was far across the quarry floor and by the time he turned and came over, Klimt had himself turned back from the spot. Yet still he occasionally looked back over his shoulder, for it reminded him of something or somewhere he could not place.

Night drew in rapidly, cold and clear with little sound but the light breeze playing in birch branches down the slopes from where they lay. Tervicz watched for a while, and then Klimt, until both grew used to the scents and sounds and slumbered together with an ear half-cocked, or an occasional scenting at the air as they shifted and moved in repose.

Both were tired, but though they had found carrion along the way it had not been much, not enough to satisfy their deepest craving, and they were restless with hunger, and dreams of prey. Then peace of a kind took them, and they lay flank to flank to keep warm against the cold, one to east and the other to west, their breathing growing deeper and more regular, their fur fluffed out against the bitter cold.

Then it came, out of the pitch-black silent night, as sudden as the sharp jag of a broken stone into an unwary paw: the howl of wolves. Nor was it distant.

The howl and bark of hunting wolves, the chatter in the night, the creep of paws through clefts in rock.

Klimt was up and at full attention immediately, Tervicz only a moment slower. Still flank to flank but standing now, their haunches slightly ashiver, though more with tension than with cold, they each surveyed the ground about, quarter by quarter.

Then the howls again and somewhere off to the east, on Tervicz's side, the crash and break of vegetation, and a warning bark.

'How many?' whispered Tervicz, whose voice was gratifying calm and whose shivering had stopped. In that moment Klimt knew he had as companion one whose loyalty he could trust.

'Six? Eight? I'm not sure.'

'Four,' whispered Tervicz quietly, more expertly. 'Maybe two wanderers nearby, but only four howled, they . . .'

The howls came again and he stopped to listen once again. Klimt made out more than four voices and said, 'How do you know? It is important . . .'

Tervicz nodded in the dark as Klimt turned slowly alongside him, their snouts almost touching.

'Magyar wolves,' he sighed, with a mixture of respect, dislike and concern. But there was not one trace of fear. 'They mimic other's voices to make their group seem larger. The attack will come from . . .'

Had he had time to finish what he had been saying he would have been proved right: the attack came from the out-runners who after their deliberately noisy running about had moved to a point just outside the quarry near the track up which they themselves had come before night-fall, and where the downdraughts from the rock-faces carried their scent away.

It was a sight Klimt never forgot: two wolves, one follow-ing the other, loping out of the shadows, speeding up and coming straight at them; and it was an attack those two unnamed wolves never forgot either. For Klimt did not hesitate for one moment but, half-pushing Tervicz to one side, he came snarling out of the shadows and lunged hard at the first wolf, catching him between muzzle and throat and rolling him over straight into the path of the other who, forced to swerve and jump was thrown off-balance so that, though he was heavier than Tervicz he too found himself thrown and bitten, this time in the leg. Yet he struggled up and turned with a deep roar onto Klimt who was strug-gling to gain absolute ascendancy over the other.

This was no ritual warning-off fight but, as Tervicz had predicted, a savage and well-planned assault – though one that was very quickly going very wrong for the Magyars. For now Klimt, untrained in group fighting and therefore bound by no rules at all, let go his first opponent and turned on his second with absolute savagery. Heavier, more angry, more focused, his attack needed but moments to take effect, yet even when the other sought to turn and submit Klimt ignored him and bit his leg hard where Tervicz had already caught him, the spurting blood warm and sweet in his mouth.

Then he backed off and snarled, preparatory to lunging forward again, his brow furrowed in the dark, his teeth touched with light.

There was no need for more: the two wolves had had enough. They turned and fled, one limping badly, both frightened, leaving Klimt and Tervicz to stand together, breathing heavily, watching, calculating.

A kind of silence fell, but it was restless and overtaken at last by the chattered barks and runs of pack wolves beyond the quarry's edge, re-grouping, conferring, preparing.

'They do not give up,' said Tervicz, and Klimt did not doubt it. The wolves they had driven off were strong and powerful and held the scent of a pack that was confident and bloodied with the routine killing of prey; there had been confidence in their run, and perhaps the complacency of wolves used to having their own way.

The surprising brutality of his response might have driven those two back, but it was unlikely to do more than win a brief reprieve. There was anger and a killing mood in the dark air beyond the quarry's edge where the broken buildings were, and even as they waited and watched something changed in the sky above, and so across the ground before them which added a curious starkness to the isolation they felt. One by one the clouds had turned and shifted and now the bright light of the moon came out and with it the light of a myriad of stars.

The radiance shone down, bathing the gaps between the trees with light, shining from the patches of snow and ice, glistening in Klimt's fur, glinting in Tervicz's eyes.

'Time to go,' said Klimt calmly and even as he said it (and if either of them had doubted it), confirmation that discretion was now the better part of valour came out into the moonlight and stood staring at them.

A powerful male, leader no doubt, his fur like grey sleet

in the moonlight, his stare cool and formidable. Not young, but with the power of cold experience in his movements and his stare. As they looked at him, caught still by his appearance, faint points of light appeared amongst the rock and vegetation from which he had emerged: the eyes of his pack. Five wolves, including the leader, about what they thought. Too many to take, but few enough to escape from.

'Which way?' muttered Tervicz, afraid now, but in control.

'The track left of the main face,' said Klimt, moving forward into the light so that the other might see him. 'Go now, wolf. Go!'

As Tervicz turned to leave it seemed that the last veil of cloud before the moon drifted away and the light about the quarry grew brighter still, awesomely so. As it did, Klimt took his eyes from the wolf who stared with such confident malevolence across the clearing and glimpsed up at the sky. Then he did more than glimpse, half-turning his body to get a better look.

Right across the north-eastern part it ran, this way and that, certain as a Mennen way through trees: the wolfway they had seen some nights before.

As the leader of the Magyar pack began his charge, his haunches straining as his front paws came suddenly forward, and as his pack surged out into the light and followed his lead, Klimt turned slowly from them, his eyes following the wolfway's line, on and on past what he already knew, on to that deep pattern of complex stars Tervicz had too briefly seen.

The stars seemed to reflect their acknowledgement of his recognition of them and he was astonished at their beauty and their mass. He saw in that moment the line his life must take, and he felt that he had the confidence of the gods.

He wanted to stop still and stare, to howl the line into his memory forever.

'Klimt!' came Tervicz's call, '*Leader!*'

He saw that Tervicz had reached the escape route's entrance, and was waiting for him; and he saw something more. Beyond him, up among the clefts, he saw the shine of far more eyes, and of bigger wolves, and the glint of teeth. Nor were they only there, but at the entrance to the other way of escape as well. It was all a trap, the howling a fooling and a feint.

But right across the sky above the wolfway ran and led him, from his heart and pulse to run, up into the night.

'No, Tervicz!' he roared, for now he saw the way they must go. He turned as swift as light and charged across the quarry and up into that time-worn cleft that had whispered its ancient secrets to him earlier that day.

'But . . .' began Tervicz, for where but to an impasse could so steep and broken a cleft as that lead?

'Follow . . . !' called Klimt softly, and then all the fear Tervicz felt, or fear he had ever known, seemed to leave him, and time became his and theirs; time to glance quickly back and see the confusion of the pack as he and Klimt seemed swallowed up into the rock itself; time to see the wolfway as Klimt had seen it; time to feel the floating strangeness of paws that knew exactly where to run, and a head and shoulders that knew which way to turn and what to avoid though he had never been that way before; time to hear Klimt's triumphant never-forgotten call as he followed after him: 'Come, wolf, for we *shall* be the Wolves of Time: the gods shall favour us!'

Time to pause panting at the far top of the quarry and look down on the moonlit scene below, where a pack of wolves searched for them in confusion, and fought each other as they wondered what pair of wolves it was had so escaped them, and how a rock-face could swallow wolves.

Time, finally, for Klimt to stand and howl their name across the sky, and down below as well, that the Magyar wolves would know that the Wolves of Time were on the move at last, and these newcomers to their territory were but the first of a great pack that was now beginning to form.

'Howl louder!' cried Klimt. 'To east and west and south, that our voices may join the summons already sent out by Wulf himself, and be heard.'

Then it was time to turn away by moonlight onto the rough fell beyond, and escape into the starlit night along a wolfway as ancient as time itself.

CHAPTER SEVENTEEN

*Elhana and Ambato arrive at the Heartland
and know the stench of death*

FOR A TIME that high summer, Ambato and Elhana
had made the soaring Dolomites their own. Feeling no urge to travel on, finding small prey and
larger carrion amidst the limestone peaks and fallen
rocks, they felt themselves to have the freedom of the
world.

Behind them lay their past, long and dark as it sometimes
felt, sweet and lost as well, while before them, uncharted,
barely imaginable, frightening, lay their future. For one
the journey onward would be the beginning of the end,
and he felt no compulsion to begin; for the other it would
be the beginning of new life, and she wanted to rest for a
while, to learn to love the world about, to listen to the wise
and foolish words of an ageing wolf who loved to bask in
glades among the trees, and climb, huffing and puffing, up
through the screes and clefts above, simply for the pleasure
of looking down. But as time went by they became so close
in thought and aspiration, so close in the way they moved
and paused, so close in silent understanding, that often
they seemed as one.

'Ambato,' she sometimes began, for she wanted to speak
of her mother to him, to hear of love; but he was not the
wolf to talk of it. Not today. Not now. Not quite yet . . .
Let it be unspoken between them lest to speak it, spoil it;

to live it through words rather than silence, might lose it. Let it be. Let it be.

They found the Dreischwesters at last, the three, huge risen rocks he had told the legend of and which were something in the shape of wolves, their shadows spread across the valley with the setting of the sun like the advance of a mighty female pack.

'Let it be a warning to you, wolf, not to defy the gods, and always to show respect to your elders and betters!' warned Ambato with a smile, telling the tale again as the stars began to show one early September night, and they murmured their talk of tales and hopes until they slept.

Then they woke at last to a dawn which brought the first dews to the grass, and the hint of autumnal mist in the valley below. There was no need for words for they knew the time had come to travel on.

Now it was Elhana who led the way, and Ambato who was content to follow and dream along behind. By the Dolomites they had come, and now to the west of the Hohe Tauern they went, by the Niedere Tauern and then, downland to the wetlands of the Danube, and the dangers of the Mennen living there, and cities and towns that had seen no wolf in two hundred years.

Without their long experience in the underworld of the cities of Italy's northern plain they would surely not have survived. But as it was, now they had no fears of Mennen cities, and understood the dangers and opportunities they offered, and could make sense of what had seemed so alarming at first, realizing that for prudent wolves such areas offered opportunities that existed in no other place.

'Would it not be possible,' mused Elhana one morning, hidden in the comfort of one of München's northern sewers as the city's Mennen bustled and rushed about overhead, noisier than usual, 'for a wolf to raise young safely in a place like this?'

'Possible, but possibly not wise,' responded Ambato. 'What would such wolves know of the mountain winds, and the lowland trees? What would they know of hunting natural prey? And they might not thrive well in fetid water and the polluted slime that eats at our fur and whose stench takes days to leave us.'

'But they would be safe,' said Elhana. 'Safer than in Mennen-infested country.'

'They might indeed be safer for a time,' conceded Ambato. 'Now, do you think it will be safe tonight to journey on?'

Even as they began to talk about when to move, they heard above them, somewhere across the city's streets, or up among its buildings, the rat-tat thump of guns, the shouts of the Mennen, and their running feet. Roars of machinery, vehicles turning heavily about, and Mennen's screams.

For two days after that Ambato and Elhana did not move, until silence came, strange silence, and the first of the Mennen bodies they ever saw, drifting in a sewer. Then more, bloated and staring. Then, out in the open, along a canal, they scented the stench of more of them, and saw other Mennen, like rooks among carrion, plundering corpses. They watched and scented from the shadows, shuddering at the horror they felt about them.

'And you want to raise young *here*?' said Ambato, not yet knowing that they were silent witnesses to the beginning of the strife that would spread across Europe, a plague of war to end the dominance of Mennen.

Elhana was silent, her normal gentleness overcome by the disgust she felt at the smell of dead Mennen, and then by something else, something far beyond Ambato's aged simplicities and good nature. Elhana's eyes glinted at the thought that here, at least, a mother would have no trouble finding food. Dead Mennen were not so fearsome as living, and dead Mennen might smell, but still a mother needing food for young would not be choosy, nor need to be.

She voiced her thought and Ambato was appalled.

'Not I,' said Elhana, 'but others perhaps. I simply said it would be possible.'

They travelled on out of the violent mysteries of the fighting Mennen in München, heading north-west for a time to over-winter in the safety of the Bavarian forest. Elhana remembered long, cold days there and the first time they, as all wolves began to then, saw Mennen shoot Mennen and so die. The dead they had seen already; now they witnessed death.

A whole pack of Mennen, a hundred or more, smelling of fear, headed by others, trailing into forest land and then that same ra-tat-tat and thump of guns. Sweat and blood upon the frozen snow, and Mennen corpses whose pink-white hands clutched at sky, and whose curled fingers turned grey and then livid black where the winter winds shrilled through them, and into the caverns of their half-open mouths.

They did not think about eating the Mennen until the ravens came and pecked and hacked at the half-frozen rotting meat, and the stench of flesh travelled the wastes and lingered in their muzzles where they lay and watched. Still, they did not eat. Then Ambato shook his head and turned away to ask Elhana to seek out for him a place where such things might be forgotten. They drifted on for days until they found at last an overhang of rock within whose caves they made a wintering place, and slept. Let the ravens eat the Mennen if they must; there was nothing to stop them eating the ravens then. Feather to flesh, flesh to fur, winter only slowly into spring.

No, there was not much to remember of that long winter

beyond those Mennen deaths: surviving, dreaming, waiting to get on.

Then, as sudden as all the previous breaks on their journey, they knew when the time was right to carry on. The days had lengthened, the dark nights of winter begun to recede, and the streams to unfreeze as the last of the blizzards passed the mouth of their cave, and were gone.

On then to the east, on high above the course of the Danube, on to what wolves once called the Tatra where, Ambato hoped, they might find a clue to where the Heartland was.

'We're being followed . . .'

'We're being . . .'

Wolves! Howling in the night, coming near, letting their tracks be seen, and then one day three of them, paused on a rise and looking down at where Elhana and Ambato travelled. Dark, strong of haunch, cold of eye, terrible in their ungiving self-assurance.

They retreated when Elhana and Ambato advanced; they mocked in their howling when the two wolves called; they snarled from out of the shadows of the trees.

And then, one dusk, when Ambato was trailing too far behind, they attacked. Swift, sharp, bold and bitter, and he too stiff and cold to flee or fight effectively. Sweat and blood upon the waking earth: Ambato's.

'They said not a word, Elhana, not a single word.'

'Are they the Magyars of legend who protect the Heartland? Have we arrived and must we now prove ourselves to them? Are they sent by Wulf to test and try us?'

Ambato shook his head. 'Surely they are wolves,' he whispered, 'without the dreams that drive *us* on, otherwise they would welcome us, or talk to us at least. Such silence bespeaks fear. These may well be the Magyar wolves of ancient times who infested the Heartland, took it, and now guard it selfishly. They are wolves who drag the dreamers into death, as they always have. I may not get through now, though we are almost there. But you my dear, you *must* go on. Leave me now, let them take me while you escape . . .'

'No,' she said in a low, warning way that almost made Ambato forget his pain and limp. 'We shall reach the Heartland . . .'

Shadows moved. Dusk shifted. Eyes advanced and then a massive wolf, his face rough and his eyes crooked from fights and leadership.

'What wolf are you . . . ?' growled Ambato.

The wolf did no more than growl in reply, and stare indifferently, assessing them as a pair and then eyeing Elhana's flanks. Everything about him spoke power and confidence, and cruelty as well.

'My name?' he said, seeming more to muse than mock. 'My name is Hassler and I am Magyar.'

He said 'Magyar' with disconcerting ambiguity, as if he might simply mean what tribe he was – and Wulf knows that was bad enough – but also to indicate that in him the tribe was personified. Ignoring Ambato, who indeed was no wolf to him at all, he gazed upon Elhana's flanks once more with open and unfeigned desire. Then, with no pre-liminaries at all, he shoved past Ambato and tried to scent at her hind parts, aggressive and quite indifferent to normal etiquette.

She turned snarling on him, annoyed, confused, embarrassed.

'Hassler generally has his way,' he said, his voice deep and threatening, his voice mocking. Then, suddenly savage, and quite plainly aroused, he charged on her, turned her, and sought to mount her there and then.

Elhana twisted and slid away, snarling again, and snapping at his face and flank.

Suddenly he laughed, mocking and confident.

'You'll join our pack,' he said to her before turning to

Ambato dismissively. 'As for you, old wolf, I'll let another kill you for the practice, and the fun. Run if you will, but my wolves will find you.'

'What wolf are you?' hissed Elhana with contempt.

'Leader,' said Hassler matter-of-factly, 'and guardian. The Heartland's friend and enemy of its enemies. And you, female? What are you, eh? Breeder of cubs or sterile and useless as female vagrants usually are? Be proud that it is Hassler speaks to you and wants you.'

He came nearer once more, muzzle to muzzle, his flecked brown eyes staring calmly down into hers. He scented her again, and she stood stiffly as he did so: turning and twisting away was undignified and ineffectual.

'Mmm. Not as sweet as some, nor as eager and fertile as others. Unpromising, but not a complete waste. And I like the spirit of an older, resisting female better than the young ones. And I like to wait. In time I will have you, wolf; oh I will.'

This last he almost purred, and, despite herself, Elhana felt desire. It was hateful, and vile, she knew, but she felt it.

'And have you no ledrene?' she challenged, knowing that this might test him, and tell her something of the pack he led. Which indeed it did, for an uneasy shadow came over his eyes and a flash of annoyance at her effrontery.

'The ledrene of the Magyars hereabout is Dendrine. You will know her when you meet her. She will not like you, *that* I know.'

He laughed, turned away, and said, 'She will hate *you*, which makes you all the more worth waiting for!'

Then he was gone heavily away, twigs cracking under his weight, vegetation parting at his advance, and then closing back over where he had been.

Elhana watched after him, heart beating, disgusted, intrigued and filled with desire in the night, but restive and ill-tempered by the morning. She and Ambato lay up until nightfall came once more, nervous, and uneasy. No sound or scent of wolf. Hassler and his unseen followers had moved on.

Then, suddenly restless again, Elhana urged poor Ambato onward, for where they were no defence could be made. Up a mucky stream they went, pasture fields beyond the darker line of old forest, but far upslope, and too steep for Ambato to climb easily. They rested until dawn and then, readied for the run, began to climb slowly.

But suddenly they knew it was too late, and Ambato too slow, though Elhana might have made the sanctuary of that old place alone. For it was on this awkward open slope that the Magyars caught them, deliberately no doubt. They emerged from scrubland to right and left, and then upslope of them.

Eight or nine dark, thick-set wolves; Hassler not among them. Others nearly as large. One the leader of this group: brawny, narrow-eyed, sudden in his starts and stops, unnerving in his watching of them, staring, eyes yellow as a hornet's rump.

Elhana and Ambato backed off towards a fence that ran down from the trees to the gully of the stream below. The wolves advanced. Ambato slipped, fell, cried out in pain, and Elhana helped him to the last place he could go, against the fence, too high for him to leap, only a place to die. And that, they suddenly felt, was what one or both was going to do. Ambato certainly; Elhana possibly.

'It's all right Ambato, it's all . . .'

The pack of Magyars began to speed up their killing advance, first one, then another and then a third, eyes narrow, tails flicking, all ready for the kill.

Elhana turned on them and began to try a bluff: 'Hassler, your leader . . .'

'Fuck Hassler,' said the one with yellow eyes, 'Hassler

is not here. He's gone. "Kill the male and take the female", is what *he* said. He can't be everywhere, thank Wulf. Well then, we'll kill the male and we'll take you, but not quite in the way he meant. We'll *have* you, and leave you dead.'

The others laughed and carried on their wary advance as Elhana and Ambato backed against the fence. The air smelt of evil and impending death. Elhana was almost sick with fear; Ambato limp with despair. He could not fight; he could not help. Their long journey to the Heartland was ending here and now, terribly. Seekers of truth and enlightenment, killed by its professed guardians. The dark millennium had caught up with them.

It was then that Ambato turned and howled, a strange primeval howl, up into the sky, a howl that was a prayer to Wulf himself, that howled down the long time of the wolfways they had taken, and asked not for guidance but for help. In a semi-circle all around them the pack of Magyar wolves advanced, dark, silent and malevolent, and the biggest and the fiercest of them, whose black eyes they knew, whose dark form had been in all the shadows they had feared from the beginning of their journey from the south, he was at the head: the first, the last, the embodiment of what a wolf might fear.

Up went Ambato's howling prayer again, up towards the skies . . . but when its echo came back to them, it came not from the grey forbidding sky where gods were said to live, but out of the ancient wood whose sanctuary they had failed to reach. Too distant perhaps to save them, too far for Elhana to do more than glance that way before she narrowed her eyes and hunched low to take the first assault as best she might.

Yet not so hopeless that Ambato, fallen now, weak from loss of blood, too weak to howl again, did not hear the returning echo of his howl, and look upslope across the pastures, for dreams to come true at last, for a wolf who had always had faith to dream them.

But still the Magyar wolves advanced, and on their breath there was the stench of death.

CHAPTER EIGHTEEN

*Klimt discovers both an ancient wolfway and
new-found strength of purpose*

K LIMT WAS QUICK to consolidate his escape from
the Magyar wolves with Tervicz in February, putting as much distance as he could between them
in the following days, and changing direction frequently –
an erratic northward journey which criss-crossed stream
courses and bogs to reduce their scent trail and took them
higher and higher into broken upland country.

This was no simple range of mountains such as they had
imagined it must be when they had first gazed at it with
such trepidation from the Moravian plains. The rocks were
banded in great strata of shales and limestone, and the
vegetation was mixed forest or the rough pastures of summer grazing, largely deserted of active life now, whether
that of other natural creatures, or the Mennen, for even
they had deserted the few stone dwellings in sheltered
nooks across the fells, and gone to safer lower ground.

But on some days and nights, when the wind came from
the west, they could hear the steady roar of Mennen
vehicles and knew there must be a major road running
north, so they stayed well to the east of it. Occasionally
they came across other abandoned Mennen quarries and
mines, a few much bigger than the one they had been so
nearly trapped and ambushed in.

Though Tervicz was now nervous of such places, fearing

another Magyar ambush, Klimt was not. The escape out of the quarry through the deep and ancient cleft, impelled as he felt it had been by some sense of direction from the wolfway in the stars, affected him deeply, making him wish to find other ancient places which held the same resonance of wolves, of Mennen, and the stars.

He had tried several times explaining this to Tervicz, saying, 'Did you not feel at home in that place, at one with yourself and the place?'

'I felt nothing but the desire to get out of there!' Tervicz would reply.

So Klimt could only shake his head and feel the sadness any wolf feels who, having experienced something deep and lasting, yet inexplicable, wishes there was another to share it with but finds only incomprehension. Again and again Klimt sought such a place, or such a route, along the ways they went, and here and there he thought he almost found it, always in places where the Mennen had shaped the landscape by delving or building but had long since moved on.

Eventually, by accident it seemed, though Tervicz was of the view that Klimt had led them deliberately back there, they found themselves above the original quarry once more, at the head of the steep and narrow defile up which they had escaped, and which had occupied so much of Klimt's thinking. Its feel, its scent, its sense of time and place were all he had experienced before, and all he had been searching for in vain.

'You'll not get me going down there!' declared Tervicz, fur ruffling.

'You can keep watch,' ordered Klimt, glad to be able to explore the strange place again, but alone this time, and in daylight.

They had little fear that the Magyars were about, for several days before they had crossed their tracks heading north towards the Tatra and such had been their route that they would have known if they had been following them.

So while Tervicz was content to rest and watch, Klimt slipped between the steep sides of the defile, straight into the strange, musty air, and the undisturbed snow and leaf-litter on the ground. Walls of rock rose on either side, not vertical, nor smooth, but rugged and ingrown with vegetation, the rock-faces themselves luminescent green where the winter light came down from the sky above, much darker, even black, elsewhere.

The place was quiet, almost silent, yet not eerily so, not to Klimt at least. He looked up past the old, gnarled trees and the steep walls to the sky beyond, the movement of whose clouds, drifting overhead, added to the cleft's sense of stillness, and his belonging. Instinct rather than scent told him the place was Mennen-made, or at least Mennen-shaped, but it spoke to him of even more than that.

Belonging, returning, the sense of this being a right place for him to be, or to have gone; a safe place. The sense that this Mennen place, ancient and still, was where wolves had been at home centuries before, a millennium before perhaps: Mennen *and* wolves, wolves and Mennen. With this thought clear at least, and secure in his mind as affirmation of all that he had hungered after in the long weeks since he was first here, Klimt began the winding descent towards the quarry floor and found himself surprised and disappointed when, far sooner than he expected, he emerged out of the past into which he had seemed to slip back into the present, which was the quarry floor where he and Tervicz had first chosen to rest.

He barked a quick signal up the rock-faces to tell Tervicz where he was, and that he was safe and would be a little while yet. He had no wish for his companion to come looking for him while he sniffed about, first to check that there were no wolves present, and then to ascertain that the different scent, of Mennen and a vehicle, was not fresh. No, no, they had come and gone days before, still . . .

Which left the disappointment, and yet Klimt found himself searching on, glancing back frequently at the nondescript dark entrance down which he had come, and then at the quarry wall on either side that scarred the hillside. As so often in the weeks and months past, he searched not knowing what he searched for, and aimlessly now, wandering among the trees and lichen-covered rocks, peering here and there, his attention wandering away ahead of him, or lost in the details along the way.

Time passed and Klimt peered up the quarry face, wondering mildly if Tervicz was getting worried. No doubt he was. Not wanting Tervicz to disturb him yet, inspired by no more than the thought that there might be something here after all, there might . . . sudden energy overtook him and he ran back up the cleft he had descended and called up to Tervicz: 'I'll be a little longer. Stay there! Stay there, wolf.'

Tervicz appeared on the quarry edge high above, stared down, nodded his understanding of Klimt's command, and turned back towards the top once more and disappeared from view.

It was as Klimt turned from this brief and seemingly anonymous moment and trotted back down the cleft's narrow way that the sense of having been *here* and *now* in some far time and life gone by overtook him, sudden and violent as the wind that heralds the coming of a cold front of air. It was more than here and now, it was the sense of having done *this* before . . . for he had involuntarily started forward, faster and more quietly with each step, as if stalking that mysterious thing he had sought and which eluded him, and which might never quite be seen.

Faster and faster across the quarry floor once more, straight towards an ancient tree that was all that remained standing on the far quarry's edge of whatever vegetation had been there before the Mennen came, perhaps centuries before. It stood bent and leaning amidst the ruined buildings they had come among the first time they came to the place. Straight into the tree's shadow he went, and straight back into that musty scent he had thought only the cleft could hold. Then on he went, across a short way of less ancient wood until he saw what that part of him that *had* been there before must have known was there, and waiting.

In the dull light it seemed no more than a dark gap between roots and rocks, less than a wolf's height, unremarkable and so unseen by either Tervicz or himself when they had first come this way, taking the Mennen route.

'But this is a route as well: it is the continuation of what I have just come down, and I know it and that once, a long time ago, I was here, like this, searching, seeking, I was here . . .'

Cold sweat trickled at his neck as he reached the gap and once more peered through it and beyond and saw a way more ancient than any he had ever known, a wolfway of wolves and Mennen, an old way to where he came from, to where he was going.

His heart beat faster for having found the way to which he felt sure Wulf himself had led him, as once before he had led him there and that he must go on down, race on down, for the past and present were calling him, and the future too.

'For we are the Wolves of Time . . .' he whispered in awe at feeling in his deepest being the truth of it, the power of it, and the terrible, frightening knowledge that the challenge to him and those he must seek out was almost too great for wolves to bear. But the summons came from that primeval, original place that lay beyond even the deepest fear: the place where all wolves run free, and the stars themselves, the place where gods themselves may live, and wait.

Aghast at this sense of awesome destiny, and the fateful ways on which he felt sure it must take him, Klimt turned back up towards where Tervicz fearfully waited unseen and roared, 'COME NOW WOLF! COME! WE ARE NEEDED! NOW!'

Then, even as Tervicz heard his desperate call and turned to answer it by running down the fearsome cleft on the upper side of the quarry, Klimt urgently repeated over to himself, 'We are needed now as we were needed before. We are needed now. We are needed . . .' And most terrible of all he knew that before, long before, the same urgent and desperate call for his help that he felt now had come to him, and he, or the wolf he had been then, *had failed it*.

About him the trees seemed to grow bigger and to loom in as barriers upon him, the sky above to darken, and the earth below to weep the blood and pain of his own kind.

'WOLF, WHERE ARE YOU! I CANNOT LEAVE WITHOUT Y . . .'

Tervicz arrived at last, his eyes wide with alarm and uncertainty, his head low in expectation of a fight, his final progress slow and stealthy until he caught sight of Klimt himself, and saw how he stood tall, but not proud, for his fur was streaked with the sweat of fear and stress, and ruffled with apprehension as he strained to see or hear, scent perhaps, something he had not yet placed.

'What . . . ?!'

Klimt's head turned slowly to stare at Tervicz, and his wild, forbidding eyes silenced him.

'Wolf . . .' he began in a trembling voice.

Klimt felt a breathless panic before this sense of driving certainty that seemed to come out of the very rocks and trees, a struggle to keep calm, an urge to turn and follow the impulse to run to where he was needed even before Tervicz had come . . .

'. . . as I did before, as we did before . . .'

Time had passed *here*, time enough for Mennen to come and go, and wolves, and a quarry to be delved and then abandoned leaving only lost scents and shadows of all that had once been, mulching down through time like the leaf-litter on a forest floor, until hardly anything that was identifiable was left, except this feeling now, and then.

'Wolf . . .' whispered Klimt, and Tervicz went to him, touching his flank with his muzzle, scenting his bewilderment and terrible deep concern. 'Speak my name and that of my pack territory!'

The command was almost a plea.

'You . . . are . . . Klimt . . . Klimt of Tornesdal in the north.'

'And you, wolf . . .' and the fur the length of Tervicz's spine seemed to rise in apprehension, for he sensed that if Klimt spoke his name it would be acknowledgement that now he was of that pack of wolves of whom Klimt so strangely talked.

The sky darkened still more, and the trees about them seemed to tremble and shudder in the thick chill air.

'You are Tervicz, Tervicz of the Bukov pack. You are a great one of your kind, and once you were here before.'

'Here . . .' whispered Tervicz, trembling like the trees with the weight of a memory he could not yet quite reach, and looking about with the same slow recognition of identity of place, and self as Klimt had felt. '*Here* . . .' he whispered, stepping forward to peer through the gap between the tree-roots, and beyond down into the cleft from whose depths an ancient, desperate, still call came to them, and lingered all about.

'Our ancestors went to Tornesdal, and to Bukov, and to . . . to . . .'

'To east and west, to north and south, our mothers and our fathers, leaders and subordinates,' continued Tervicz in a low and certain voice, the words coming back to him from the very rocks and tree-roots themselves. 'Now we, who were the Wolves of Time, are returning once again.

'So many things that we did wrong then, that we could not reach out and touch . . .'

'That we did not understand, Tervicz, or for which we had not the courage, or the skill . . .'

The trees trembled more and the darkness of the sky seemed to bear down upon them savagely as they saw far down the cleft below the first stirring of a wind amongst the undergrowth. A frond of snow-broken bracken shivered, a low branch stirred, and then, nearer to them some leaves were picked up, held for a moment against the black, contorted trunk of a long-dead tree, and then, freed by the wind, driven towards them.

'Klimt . . .' began Tervicz in wonder, and speaking as much to the gods as Klimt himself, 'what wolf are you?'

Even as he spoke they heard the first roaring of that coming wind, and it was not just from through the trees below, but above them, and behind them, and right through the world in which now they were beginning to travel.

'Tervicz,' replied Klimt, his eyes gentle, the brief touch of his paw as reassuring as an older brother's when fearful trouble looms, 'what wolves are we that dare reach back to what we were, and dare invoke that past again into our present lives, and more than that . . . more . . .'

Leaves, branches, driven snow roared up the cleft into his face upon a violent threatening wind that sought to drive them back, but he turned into it and advanced a paw beyond the gap into a place from which there would never be a turning back.

'. . . More than that,' he roared defiantly, 'what wolves

are we that dare turn now into the future and make aright what we and our kind did wrong?'

'The Mennen come!' cried out Tervicz, not in fear, but in absolute defiance.

'They always came and we always fled, until now, now Tervicz, we shall run into our own future . . . what wolves are we?'

'I can hear a call,' said Tervicz coming close to Klimt, shoulder to shoulder, his own paws now beyond that barrier of time and place, the cleft that would take them to their future, steep, wild, full of the noise of a destructive wind waiting below. 'I can hear her cries . . . as long ago I heard them and I failed. And you, leader, you failed too . . .'

His dark tears of anger and pity were streaked by the wind across his face as powering forward and down Klimt cried out the furthest wolfway constellations that he knew, as if their very names would give each fearful, driven step he took more power, and more success: 'Pechora! Auvergne! Wolves of the Apennine!'

'Of Carpathia! Of Vardar and of Lapp!'

'Of wild Basque and the holy Dolomites; Abruzzi and far Castile . . .'

They spoke or gasped, panted or cried out the names they knew, each from the lore he had been taught, many times using names of which the other did not know, but each name giving them strength. As if, lost and deserted of wolf though those places might now be, the lupine power they once held could still be invoked by this appeal through time, so that now with each step towards their new destiny they gained strength and purpose from glories past, and slow, suffered tragedies as well.

As they spoke Klimt led Tervicz down the second part of the ancient wolfway they had found, their cries, the shouted names, their tears, the past and the present and

the call to action here and now that the future might be
served, rising from them and about them like the ancient
trees among which they ran.

So it was that Klimt of Tornesdal led Tervicz of Bukovina
crashing down that ancient track, used once alike by wolves
and Mennen in a time before fear and hatred put them
apart.

They crashed down through the rough, dense vegetation
of the cleft into a mixed wood of huge and ancient trees.
The wind began to die as if they had conquered it, and
from somewhere far beyond they heard with their ears what
they had heard before only with their hearts: the cry of a
wolf, the struggle and the fight of the weak against the
strong, the baying triumph of the cruel who know that they
will win, and the beginnings of the bleak despair of those
who fear that soon they will die, and the gods they trusted
all their lives, the dreams they held in darkest times, the
faith that held them from the void, were worth less than
nothing before the last fearful journey into oblivion they
now took.

These were the dread familiar sounds the two wolves
heard from beyond those unfelled, ancient trees through
which they surged, and hearing them, they knew themselves to be the agent of Wulf himself, with Wulfin at his
flank.

How deep and wide the forest seemed, how slippery and
yielding its dark, fungoid floor became the more they
sought to hurry and bring aid. How confusing the route
became as the track they had followed so well began to
change and modulate, overgrown now by the lichen-
covered fronds of light-seeking plants; crossed and made
difficult by the rotting trunks of trees that had fallen
through the decades and the centuries.

Still the cries for help came, and still they ran, but slower now, panting, beginning to believe they might not get where they must be in time; beginning to feel what both had felt in former lives when, running this way as they ran now, they were too late; beginning to think they would see the bloodied, broken bodies of their once-companions, lost in time forever, as through the undergrowth living, darker forms slipped away, their victims' blood upon their fangs, licking wounds that would heal, casting glances back in shame but brief for the wrongs that they had done. And the Mennen, the Mennen . . .

Klimt could smell them still – through centuries of forgetting – he could smell their odours well, their triumph, their ascendancy.

'Tervicz!' he cried to encourage his slower friend. 'We must go on now for there is no more time! Keep up with me!'

Then gritting his teeth against the pain in his chest and his failing, aching limbs, Tervicz found strength to carry on. Ahead the trees thinned at last, the final obstacle was cleared, and the horrid sounds of nearly-beaten wolves came clear.

Klimt stopped for a moment, listened, and signalling to Tervicz to follow him, lowered his head and neck as he began to stalk forward through the undergrowth, ears pricked, haunches powerful. They came out of forest onto rough, undulating grazing land, covered here and there with grey patches of old snow that sloped down from them to a line of scrub that appeared to mark a stream's course, though it was buried too deep in its own gully to be seen; but its roar could be heard plainly enough, and this chill, wintry sound was background to all that followed.

Stopped still once more, low, barely breathing, Klimt and Tervicz surveyed the scene and saw immediately the fierce wolves that conquered, and those they were about to kill. They were off on Klimt's left flank where the ground steepened running to a crude wooden fence.

To a wolf that was fit and healthy the fence would have presented no barrier at all; but to one who was injured or stiff with age, the fence would have been less easy to get by, perhaps impossible. It was against this slight barrier that a female was now ranged against a mixed pack of eight wolves that formed a half-circle about her, with a ninth creeping downslope, along the fence's edge, his ears cocked and eyes alert as if he was bravely stalking a great and fearsome prey, not a female in the last stages of exhaustion and defence.

Klimt command's were frightening in their directness: 'We use speed, surprise, and all our power. I take the biggest. You take another as we reach them. You will not hesitate for one instant, Tervicz. Choose one, and kill. Then another . . .'

Tervicz felt a thrill of fear, and then the chill of knowing there was no alternative, and finally the calm of knowing he would do exactly as he had been told.

They began their advance low across the field, not using cover, for the pack all had their backs to them except for the creeping one. They took in the rest of the grim scene. Here and there the patches of snow were scuffed and scattered, and stained with blood. Amongst the leafless branches of a tree rising from the stream's gully a blackbird hopped, pinked out its worried song, and was gone out of sight to ground again. Somewhere far behind them, across the sky, a Mennen bird was heard momentarily before the stream's winter flow took precedence again.

Then it was, as they increased the speed of their advance, that they saw the female was not alone. For now, as her front paws pushed and stressed against the stones in expectation of the coming final assault that half-seen shape behind the female turned and stood up shakily, his face bloody, one front paw hanging useless beneath him. He was a male, his face-fur grey with age, and it was spotted and clotted with blood.

Now Klimt increased his pace so that he began to bound across the grass, with Tervicz a shoulder behind, like two dark fearful shapes emerging out of a nightmare forest.

It was then that the old male saw them and grunted a strange sound of recognition, as if he knew them, and knew that they would come. Then, in that silent moment before final killing and death, he raised his head and howled, the weak, croaking howl of a wolf who has almost passed his time, but has lived to know at last not despair but that hope may not finally be in vain.

As he did this, and the first of the bigger wolves began his final charge, the female turned towards Klimt and Tervicz and saw them for the first time, her pale, brave eyes locked for a still moment in Klimt's gaze: and as they did, and he powered into a raging leap, his claws readied, his jaws open, his brow furrowed in concentration for what he must do, he knew what wolf she was.

Not by name; not by sight; nor yet by scent, or touch.

Klimt knew her by the inner sense that overtook him that here, now, some essential part of him was coming home, and discovering once more a place within his heart that transcended all the senses, and knew not present time at all, unless it be the past and present and future from which, through which, into which, he had run that day. The wolf whose eyes locked into his was ledrene to his leadership, he knew, he knew, he knew . . .

Klimt's bounding leap began from behind the encircling wolves and was like a blizzard storm over them, which, as he turned from that brief moment of recognition of the wolf he had come to save, and drove down onto the back and neck of the wolf that first sought to kill her, was a blizzard that turned into a rain of blood.

Nothing that any of those wolves had ever seen was like Klimt's attack then. It was so powerful, so sure, so absolute that the wolf he took had his back ripped open, his dying body hurled past them all against the fence, his blood scattered flying in the air. It was so shocking that every other wolf there but Tervicz froze in astonishment and fear. Even the female, who turned to stare bemused at where her attacker gasped and gurgled his last breath against the fence, his blood dark red against the palings and the snow.

Except Tervicz. He had slowed at the last moment, he had chosen, and as the others stilled in shock at what Klimt had done Tervicz locked his jaws on the hindquarter of a lagging male, crunched and ripped as he pulled him over, rolled him squealing, others knocked flying as he rose up and turned to hurl him violently against the fence as well, the sound of breaking bones and sinews, and the screams of pain, all one.

All one, and then continuous with the attack Klimt immediately launched on a younger wolf, shocked and staring still, his right shoulder caught in Klimt's jaws before he could draw breath. His body heaved and lifted, as his own jaws tried to lock on Klimt's leg. He was lifted, shaken, thrown and then attacked about the throat by Tervicz, before Klimt turned, snarling, on another.

The wolves retreated and the female they sought to save came forward, snarling too, so that for a moment she and Klimt stood flank to flank. Then Tervicz joined them now making three to six: then one of the females backed away and the creeping wolf who had been coming along the fence fled; making three to four.

Klimt did not allow hesitation and recovery to take grip but launched forward at the nearest one. For a brief moment this wolf, his fur paler than the others and his face scarred by past fights, stood his ground. But then Klimt went for him and he snapped, turned and slipped away and out of reach, turning back to face Klimt from a safer distance.

It was enough. The others around and behind him fled towards the stream and this old, experienced one, casting only the briefest of glances at the wolf Klimt had killed, and the other who lay dying, shrugged and backed away, beaten, yet not defeated. Indeed, he stood quite boldly staring at them until the advance of Klimt caused him to retreat to the edge of the drop down into the gully formed by the hidden stream.

'What wolf are you?' he demanded of Klimt.

Klimt was silent, frowning.

'What *pack* are you?' he persisted, addressing his question to all of them, assuming that Klimt and Tervicz were with the two so far unnamed wolves they had saved. As he spoke, two or three of his companions came up out of the gully to stand at his flank, though it was plain enough from the way they cast their glances, and watched over their safe retreat, that they had no intention of trying to attack Klimt, to punish him for killing and wounding senior members of their pack.

Klimt's silence deepened, and he came forward a little, forbidding in his staring-down of them, the stillness of his body showing that he felt no fear at all.

'You know what wolf it is you've killed?' said the bold one, his voice gruff and assured. 'You know who'll be after you now?'

Still Klimt was silent.

'That's Hassler's eldest son you've beaten and he'll not let you alone now until you're all taken and killed,' said one of the other, weaker, males with something like pleasure in his voice.

'Hassler!' exclaimed Tervicz.

'Leader of all the Magyar packs,' the other whispered slowly, evidently fearful even to mention that wolf's name.

'Wolves like you might have joined us, but now . . .'

Several of them shook their heads and one even laughed mockingly.

'Shut up!' snarled the older wolf, not sharing in their glee. 'I'll ask again, for it is the custom in these parts to say who you are.'

'Did you ask who *she* is,' growled Tervicz, pointing towards the female and then adding, as he looked at the ageing male, who had now slipped down onto the ground, his mouth open and panting with pain, 'or *him*?'

'They wouldn't tell us,' said the Magyar wolf dismissively, 'and anyway what can such wolves offer us? But you . . . What wolf are you?'

He tried to hold Klimt's gaze but could not and looked away, and then at the others, and there was respect in his face, and perhaps at last a touch of fear and awe.

'Us?' said Klimt at last, looking around at Tervicz, and then the other two as well. 'We are the Wolves of Time.'

It seemed as if the very sky itself spoke, and the ancient trees behind Klimt too.

He lowered his head and stalked forward as if to charge and the Magyar, even the bold one, hesitated but a moment more before they turned, and fled down into the gully behind, and splashed unseen across the stream and were gone.

It was then, and only then, when all surprises and dangers seemed gone, and Klimt felt ready to turn back to Tervicz and the two wolves whose lives they had saved, and talk with them to find out who they were, and where they had come from, that he saw the Mann.

Not standing or lying still and watching, and hoping he might not be seen, as Mennen often did; nor moving about the place quite ignorant of wolves' presence, as was their more normal way. This Mann was emerging from further down the gully, quite openly, moving slowly and deliberately towards them.

Tervicz saw him immediately, and rightly went straight to a point halfway between Klimt and the others, awaiting a command. As for the other two, they simply froze, but for the shivering of the old wolf's flanks.

But Klimt gave no command, or not immediately. He simply stared, and snouted at the air to catch the Mann's scent, to see if he could ascertain what his eyes told him, but which he could not believe: that he had seen this Mann before.

The Mann came on inexorably in a way Mennen never did, or had never done to Klimt's knowledge. Slowly, openly, almost lightly across the grass, in a way that Klimt felt certain posed no threat. Yet, yet . . .

Klimt turned and nodded Tervicz towards the female that he might watch over her while he himself went to the male.

'We're leaving . . .' he said.

'He cannot rise . . .' said the female, the first words she had spoken.

'Go with my friend,' commanded Klimt. 'Go now!' His voice was suddenly harsher. 'Wolf,' he said addressing the stricken male, 'you shall rise and you shall run with us. If you stay here we shall leave you, and it is likely you will die. The Mennen come now . . . But you must not die. We need you. Therefore, take strength from all your faith in Wulf, and feel the love of Wulfin in your old, hurt body. Rise, wolf, and we shall see you to safety, and recovery.'

The wolf struggled to get up and had nearly done so when he began to falter once again, his wounds almost too much for him.

'Wolf,' whispered Klimt, 'what of all things do you seek?'

'I seek . . .' said the male, his eyes moving from Klimt to the female, and then past her towards some place beyond *them all, 'I desire . . . there is a place . . . and we . . .'*

'Come with me now, and you shall find that place,' said Klimt, turning back to stare at where the Mann came on towards them, ever nearer now.

'I am not afraid of him,' Klimt whispered to himself, so lost in the memory of this Mann, and his familiar scent, which was of Helsingborg, which was of that wolfway that started then and they had found again, together, wolf and Mennen . . . no, no, wolf and Mann. So taken up with this sense of union and destiny was Klimt that he barely noticed as the male, inspired by his words, or afraid of the Mann, struggled to rise once more and finally succeeded.

'Yess . . .' whispered Klimt, at the Mann perhaps, or possibly at the old wolf, 'yes . . . we shall go now, we shall go.'

Then he led them upslope along the fence, and into the undergrowth where it abutted the trees, then on along the top of the next field by the forest edge. Once only he stopped, to stare back at the Mann, and he saw far below that the Mann had stopped still as well, and was staring back at him.

Then he watched as the Mann turned from the path they had taken and set off upslope towards the forest trees, towards that very place where he and Tervicz had emerged: the wolfway they had found, the wolfway that had scented of Mennen as well as wolf, a way back to a distant past before disunity which led back further still to the future to which they all were striving to return at last, and must find, and must overtake.

Then Klimt turned from the Mann and that ancient vision, and led his growing pack to safety and to rest.

CHAPTER NINETEEN

*The Mann discovers a new and unfamiliar species:
himself, as human being*

THE MANN WAS.

*His name is lost now, lost within the spirit of the pack that
was the Wolves of Time. Lost, then, in the light and shadow
of Wulf himself. Lost in that one place wherein a Mann's
nature may be found.*

This solitary Mann was a German zoologist, trained in
Freiburg, and what he had just done was even more
remarkable than what he had just seen, or felt he had seen.

He had seen the male wolf who led the others before
in Helsingborg, Sweden, in circumstances he had never
forgotten, but had never thought that he might see him
again.

He had hoped to, perhaps, and dreamed that he might,
certainly . . . And so the Mann, deputy director of the
German Mammal Institute of Freiburg and as experienced
a field worker on the larger carnivores as any in Europe,
had broken all the rules of his training and broken cover,
leaving his equipment where it lay and his binoculars hanging untouched from his neck, he had stopped observing for
the first time in his adult life, and simply walked towards
the wolves, to join them.

To join them . . .

'It's ridiculous,' was what he whispered to himself as he watched the great wolf quickly lead the others up the field, round the fence, and then along the edge of the trees beyond until, having paused briefly to stare back down at him, he had finally disappeared from sight. Then, like shadows when the sun goes in, they were gone.

'Ridiculous,' muttered the Mann again, shaking his head in astonishment at himself.

Yet, his absurd behaviour continued.

He should have gone back to the equipment he had left. But he did not.

He should have gone on to where the wolves had fought, to see what evidence of their presence and the fight they might have left behind, not least the body, still warm no doubt, of the slain wolf. If it was dead.

But even this he did not do.

He should, perhaps, have felt just a shade nervous that there were hurt and wounded wolves about the place, for they might be a threat to him.

But this he did not feel. Fear was very far from the Mann's mind and heart. For he felt more alive than he ever had, more at one with what until now had always been distanced and scientifically objectified by observation. Something so profound had happened to him as he had watched the wolves that afternoon that he felt now in a daze, that same daze that had made him get up and try to . . . well . . . try to run with them. To join them. To be of them, not as the Mann, zoologist, but as the Mann, fellow creature.

'It surely was ridiculous!' he told himself once again, shaking his head as he turned upslope just as the wolves who had won the fight had, though now he was not trying to follow them. Instead he set off for that spot which he had noted much earlier, where the two wolves had first emerged from the forest.

'Yess . . .' he whispered, peering up towards the trees and finding the little holly-bush that marked the place . . . 'Yes!'

He thought ruefully that perhaps, after all, observation had its points, for how else would he have known how to find the place again?

The Mann smiled briefly to himself, his tanned face showing lines both of worry and of laughter, his hair ruffled by wind, his eyes, which were normally restless and searching and reading the vegetation and landscape, seeming a little lost as his smile faded and he pressed on.

He was in his mid-thirties, spare but strong, and he moved with the smooth, steady grace of an experienced hill-walker. He wore boots and breeches of a nondescript green, with a thick, worn, army buff anorak, equally unremarkable. The Mann carried nothing but his binoculars, which were black. All his other gear lay on the ground in the gully below where he had made his temporary hide and watched the wolves.

He had been there since early morning, having tracked the Magyar wolves to an area some way below the gully the day before and then camped out in his van down by the road, which was a kilometre or so away. He had climbed up silently at dawn, the wind in his favour, located the wolves with surprising ease and then taken up a position to observe, using the experience of years of watching and observing such mammals in the field.

His choice had proved good, for the wolves had been in and out of the gully and up into the field all morning, and then they had rested for a while. The Mann had felt a little tired himself, and hungry too, though he avoided eating any of the food he carried lest the scent warn the wolves of his presence, if they did not already know it! A drink of hot water from his flask kept him going.

The day was dull, the light going grey just after midday

*and staying that way. Another cheerful Slovakian day!
Then, suddenly, all changed, and the Mann's years of
observation, many hours and days and months of which
had so often been without significant incident or event paid
off in this most spectacular hour of his wolf work.*

*The pack, or most of it, was visible, and then he saw one
of them rise suddenly up, alert, scenting at the air, listening. Whatever it was the wolf had sensed the Mann could
not yet know, but he turned to look across the pasture the
way the first wolf, and then its companions, looked until
the first went down low, and two more slipped back down
into the gully and out of sight.*

*The Mann knew at least where these would go – directly
towards where he lay hidden. He kept still and they trotted
past, so intent on stalking whatever it was that was coming
that they did not notice him.*

*Whatever it was . . . prey possibly, thought the Mann.
Another wolf perhaps. Or . . .*

*He dared look up again, but very slowly, raising his head
by degrees.*

*He saw her immediately, a vagrant, not a Slavic wolf. A
wolf of southern type, clear against the patches of snow she
passed, travelling slowly and, unusually perhaps, leading a
male who appeared weak from hunger, or injury.*

*The winter wind harried at the grass and branches of
the shrub in which he hid and they cut and wavered across
his view for a moment, the wolves slipped downslope and
into hidden ground. When he saw them again they were
nearer, and alarmed. His scent perhaps, or the other
wolves'.*

*The female paused, the male behind her, both uneasy.
Then they grouped, snouting side to side with the wind,
then forward across it, and seemed to sight a movement
beyond where the Mann lay, barely breathing. So near, so
strange, the female was so strange . . . so beautiful.*

To him all wolves were beautiful, all to be honoured. But this wolf, fair, nervous of her surroundings yet in command of herself: more than beauty went with her . . .

She moved nearer and paused again just upslope of him. Then, slowly, she turned her gaze to where he lay hidden, and she stared, and even from that distance he saw that in her eyes was a constellation of amber stars and it seemed then that it was all wolves that looked at him, through the dreadful centuries past, looking into the eyes of the men who had harried them, hunted them, killed them.

'Observe,' he ordered himself, appalled that his science was under assault from such emotions. She was a wolf, an animal, a pattern of biological responses. She could not look with the eyes of all wolves, any more than he could feel with the heart of all men.

'Obser . . .' he tried to tell himself again, before he was lost into that feeling her stare invoked, and slow tears.

Her neck fur ruffled in the breeze, but her eyes were so still, and her stare took him across a void of feeling he had never dared enter and it rose up above him, cliffs of it, clefts and cliffs with a sky beyond he wanted to reach.

Not for the first time in his adult, scientific, life Jakob the Mann felt tears well up in his eyes, but this time he let them flow. The wolf looked at him from a thousand pairs of eyes, each one a myriad of lives, lost now, gone, residual only in her, and she was more than he could ever be. The Mann looked away, and his tears fell onto his hands, and trickled then into the grass and earth below.

'Only observe!' he told himself again, but he knew then that he would never ever only just do that again.

How long was that moment? Hours? Days? How far back did its beginnings stretch in his life? Three decades or more, to when someone had asked him what he wanted to be when he grew up, and someone else said, 'He wants to work with animals,' and someone else said, 'Really?' without interest, without pleasure; and his father, large, dark, smiling down from his height, said, 'Tell them what you saw today,' and he tried.

But how does a six-year-old describe the glory that he knew through an open bedroom window before anyone else was awake . . .

'I saw . . .'

Saw the sun come up, and the stars die.

'Saw . . .'

Saw a squirrel pause up on a branch, and its tail all light, all . . .

'Saw . . .'

'What did you see, son. Tell them!'

Saw a whole hour of rising light and life in which, from his window, he wandered free; and he saw . . . he saw a wolf come out of the shadows, and its young, and they played across the grass and birds above, black, and . . .

'Saw . . .'

'He saw the fox. There is one round here – it's been seen a lot this year. We're hoping it'll breed. He thought it was a wolf!'

Oh, they laughed, their laughter sleet across the rising dawn he had lived, spoiling it.

'Saw . . .' but he felt it fading now.

'I showed you a picture of a fox. That was what you saw, wasn't it?'

Bleak, the shadow of their sleet in his grey eyes, and the young boy had nodded and whispered, 'Yes . . .'

It was, and it wasn't.

'He can say "biologist". Say it, son.'

He said it and felt he had betrayed all that he had seen and felt.

Later in his room, staring out at the dusk, and a garden that held nothing of what it had he told himself again, 'I did not see a fox, I saw a wolf . . .' For he felt a wolf had come to him, to summon him, with a voice that was the whisper of the wind, for a task that would stretch across the earth and sky, and it was, among the adults, he denied.

Then he cried as he cried now.

Thirty years had passed, and now at last, as sudden and unplanned as happiness, the window had opened once more and a new dawn was upon him, and the fox had become the wolf he once saw.

So now, the Mann observed no more, but watched, and felt, and sensed that what he saw was more by far than what he might ever have observed, however carefully.

The two Magyar wolves who had raced surreptitiously past him emerged, pretend-attacked, and played the game of finding out what wolves these were. The Mann knew their game and understood it, and was bored, as he felt the two arrivals were bored.

And intimidated, as they were. And fearful, for far more was at stake than games.

The female and male retreated from the Magyars up towards the forest edge – the forest at which the Mann had barely looked until now. Older than he might have expected, very old indeed, its edge following the line of a private Slovakian estate whose only enterprise had been, two centuries before, some quarry work. That died, and the forest trees were left to live and die and reach the climax of their growth just as they wished.

The initial phase of growth was so far over that it would have been pointless looking for it, even in the subsoil. It was a millennium since silver birch had grown in that area, shooting up for a century before they fell, and rotted where they fell, and slower-growing trees found their time. Oak, ash, beech here and there, and larch grew and formed the climax vegetation, which the Mann saw and recognized. Except that climax in this context meant ancient and broken, new and old combined, rich and orderly chaos.

271

He had done his research before this trip and knew what patterns of vegetation to expect. The site was not virgin, Man had had his way. But as forests went it was as natural as was reasonable to expect. This was no Bialowieza . . .

The Mann whispered the name of that hallowed, ancient place which chance, and history, had left as the sole intact original forest upon the North European plain. Poland's glory, more glorious than its now doomed fight for democracy in his view, more glorious even than the dappled horses that worked its flat farmlands. Too docile and domesticated, too cruel, when they grew old.

'Bialowieza,' he whispered, and it brought back memories of love and of discovery. Phallus impudicus. Stinkhorn. The first place he had seen it, and smelt it, and it was glistening and erect as he stood hand in hand with the girl he grew to love, and whom he lost. Love like that comes but once, he thought, just once, and when it has gone, snatched away by others cleverer with words and deeds than him, can the sun shafting through the trees, or the sound of horses' hooves, or a hand holding yours, ever feel the same?

Nothing was the same. The fox of his childhood had turned into a wolf in his adulthood. Disease and disharmony had spread across all Europe and beyond; there were eighteen deaths in Freiburg in the week before he left, all violent, none attributed. France was suffering civil war in all but name; Italy was splitting up, and Venice, impossibly, was no more. Denmark, Britain, even Switzerland . . . the countries, the cities, the people themselves, were sick now, and wild in their sickness, and so many were dead.

But in truth, where in Europe was there that was not scarred and desecrated by man, the most predatory and unnatural of creatures? Where was there that nature, a worm turning at last, was not killing man? Disease, pollution, the most virulent cancers science had ever seen, Europeans turned back from airports in Africa and Asia.

Boats sunk for fear the Europeans would bring not a plague but a whole syndrome of disease. Mankind eating its own feet, ripping its own chest, breaking its own bones; mankind blinding itself; mankind acting out the final cut which it made for real long years ago when it turned on the land and began to destroy it, never knowing what it did.

The Mann sighed wearily and turned his attention back to the wolves, whose ritual attacks and retreats to test each other's strengths and weakness to establish a status, he knew well. Just like humans, and like them too, as the afternoon wore, the play began to be nasty, the pack to group, and the pair that had arrived to want to get away.

The Magyar pack's leader had emerged. He was a brute male, not the strongest but the most confident, and unusually for a wolf he was . . . cruel. It was not him who went in for viciousness first, but it seemed encouraged by him. Usually, in such a situation, the leader disciplines the one who has gone too far, and does not encourage him. Usually, too, the vagrants would have made good their escape, but this time they did not. Was it the old one, too tired to run? Was the female staying loyal?

The Mann grew interested and more than that, he felt a mounting horror in his chest. The viciousness drew blood, the female counter-attacked, two went for her; the male tried to intervene, two went for him; and then, suddenly, the visitors were being harried along the contours of the field, towards the fence that lay less than two hundred metres away.

The leader went in hard at the male, he taunted him, and the male sought to turn away but could not. Across the grass the Mann heard the crack of bone, a shin perhaps, and a grunt, and then his horror was real. Ritual play was turning to ritual killing and he knew the pair did not stand a chance.

The Mann felt that temptation which to science is a sin:

*he wanted to intervene. Make a sound, stand up, advance
towards them and they would scatter and be gone. Wolves
do not attack humans, whatever amateurs might think.
Wolves are programmed to fear all men, and all manner
of man.*

*But no, it was not right to interfere with nature. Let
nature take its course. Nature knows best. Nature . . .*

*Then the female howled, a strange, brief howl, as near
to a call for help as the Mann had ever heard a wolf make.
She had backed to a pile of stones just before the fence,
shepherded her companion behind her and turned to face
the sliding, sneaking, darting pack, and its stolid sadist of
a leader.*

*She howled a howl that seemed to turn in the dull air,
and flee upslope among the trees, and echo there, down
arboreal corridors of time. The Mann lay still as death, for
the help she summoned was of a kind far greater than any
he could give.*

*Slowly the pack tightened its semi-circle about them,
while one of the smaller males began to creep towards the
male on their right flank.*

*The Mann watched, numb, witnessing what seemed the
final stages of two brutal deaths among the million million
that had taken place since time and life began. Let nature
take its course and the strongest will survive.* Mein Sohn,
musst du niemals . . . *no no, you must never interfere . . .*

*For a moment his father's cold voice spoke to him again
and he subsided. His father was right. A fox is not a wolf;
two and two make five.*

Saw . . . the sun rise.

Saw . . . the dew like lights in grandma's eyes.

*Saw . . . a mother wolf play with her cubs across the
lawn . . .*

Nein, nein mein Sohn, es war ein Wolf nicht, es war die
Füchsin.

But it had not been a fox to him when he was six, and it was certainly not a fox that was defending an old male as if he were her cub, and who would die before his eyes, for lack of a god who might answer her cry for help from the valley of the shadow of death to which life had brought her.

It was then that the Mann noticed movement at the edge of the trees. It seemed to him then that the ancient forest cleft open, as out of its shadows emerged not one wolf but two, the first large and strong, the other of medium build, but lithe and fit. But it was the leading one that held his attention, and almost caused him to gasp aloud in disbelief.

It was no ordinary wolf he saw, for such light as there was that day, and God knows it was dull and fading that afternoon, seemed to focus upon the wolf's form, and shine from it, so that its fur was luminescent against the rough pasture and the dark trunks of the trees rising behind.

The Mann felt sure he had seen the wolf before and, raising his binoculars once more for a better look, was quite sure he had. It was the Scandinavian wolf, the rogue wolf that all but he had believed was drowned in the Baltic Sea at Helsingborg. That seemed so long ago now, before the world came out, and showed itself to be insane. Before, in Sweden's case, a team of six men and two women shot and incinerated most of its parliament dead.

The Mann's heart hammered in his chest. If his identification was right, there was no doubt that this wolf had killed a man in Norway, and several dogs. Also, though he had kept these suspicions to himself, from the description of two forest workers who claimed they had been attacked by wolves in the western Erzgebirge – a claim dismissed by most wolf experts as a hysterical fabrication by men who were out hunting when they should have been doing harmless maintenance work – this was the same wolf.

Always, always, the descriptions had stressed the

strange, shining paleness of the wolf's fur: luminescent, like this one.

Now the wolf began a charge across the ground, and was more magnificent than any charging predator the Mann had ever seen, and it was all the more transfixing because the animals he was charging, the other wolves, had not yet seen him. He charged straight onto the Magyar leader and in a display of ruthless savagery he killed him. His companion went for another of the pack, and between them, in a matter of bloody seconds, the pack was in retreat, and the female's call for help not just answered, but answered brutally.

It was in those extraordinary moments that the Mann involuntarily stood up, the habit and training of a lifetime thrown aside, and leaving his binoculars to hang by their strap from his neck, he simply stared.

It was astonishing, and the Mann felt a continuing tremor of excitement not so much at what he had seen, as to be here, and now, and witness to it all. He stood, he stared, and some last reservation to be a part of it left him. He was observer no more, he was an animal like them, and he wanted to join with them, to . . . run with them. He wanted that.

Once, in Canada, he had met an old Inuit who, it was said, knew something of wolves. The man, the Mann was told, was an Inuit shaman, or so some said.

'You have a totem animal,' the Inuit had told him, 'and you know what it is?'

The Mann had not been sure what to say. He had been deeply moved by his meeting with the man, and had sat in silence with him, smoking and drinking, and listened to the old man's tales.

Perhaps he had a totem animal, he was not sure. A fox perhaps?

The Mann afterwards swore that he had never spoken that thought, only thought it.

But the shaman interrupted him as if he had spoken and said, 'There are many animals, all different, mostly helpers on the journeys we must make. Some may not seem like helpers. Some may not be helpers!' He had laughed then, rather wheezily, and the Mann had laughed too.

'Have you ever thought that you may run with wolves?' the shaman had said suddenly, laughing still except in his eyes, which were serious and in earnest.

'I . . .' the Mann had said, not knowing what the Inuit meant.

'You will know when you know, and that will be when they offer their help to you. When they do you will be ready for it, and maybe then you'll need it. Then you'll try to run with wolves and many times you'll fall.'

The Inuit had laughed again, infectiously and they had drunk some more of whatever it was he put in the Mann's tin mug. It came from a beer can, and it had been sealed until the Inuit opened it, but the Mann swore that it was rather more than beer.

'Falling down reminds you of the ground where your feet are, and your rear end too, so it's good for you! Getting up reminds you where you're coming from, which is the earth. Falling down and getting up, again and again and again, is good for men.'

'Yes,' the Mann had muttered.

'One day you'll get up and know how to run with wolves!'

'Will I?' wondered the Mann.

'Mmmm,' mumbled the Inuit.

Now, eight years later, the Mann understood for the first time what running with wolves might mean, and he understood it with a shock of relief and an intoxicating sense of liberty.

So then he had started, walking towards the four wolves, at first slowly and steadily, not knowing what they might do but not caring, for his head and heart felt light, and his feet felt that they wanted to begin to run across the grass, to run that he might join them . . .

They turned suddenly and stared, and the front paws of the second wolf began to fret and his tail to frisk preparatory to some kind of charge or feint. The leader moved not at all and staring into his eyes for the first time the Mann felt small, and the world of the pasture about him felt suddenly wide, and getting wider, and without escape or defence.

The wolves broke, turned, and the leader got the old male onto his paws and they were all gone off upslope.

The Mann stared after them, relieved perhaps, disappointed certainly, sweating, fearful, and exhilarated all at once. He watched until they had reached the trees, rounded the fence and had gone along the forest edge on the other side and all were gone but the leader, who turned and stared back down at him.

'So . . .' sighed the Mann, knowing that the incident was over, and that it had transformed his life, or rather, set it off in a direction whose goal he could not know or guess, but that it would take him out of his present life for good and drive him more and more towards where wolves might run, that he might learn one day to join them. Whatever that might mean. Yet what had he to lose? The world was mad and there was no value in declining into insanity doing something normal. Let Europeans fight each other, from now on he would try to run with wolves.

He felt physically and mentally more tired than he ever had, and for a time he stood quite still, tempted to fall back into habitual ways and go and examine the site where the *wolves had fought. There would be something there worth keeping and examining later: fur, blood, spoor . . . something.*

But he was beyond that kind of biology now, far beyond, and looking across the grass towards the place where they had been it seemed to him that he was looking back to a time where Jakob the Mann had only existed, for years, mute in any real sense, without feeling, but with too much thought. But where the wolves had gone, why, there was a future time there, a better time, and he could reach it if he could discard himself.

He shook his head, turned away, and looked up towards the cleft among the trees from where the two males had come, and he saw it with the new eyes which now saw a different world – but which another, looking at the same place, might have seen as no more than a slightly wider gap between trees that formed a shadowed wall beyond which rose a silent forest, now beset by still winter dusk.

The cleft was there, and down it the wolves had come, and the Mann, still quite unconcerned about the equipment he had left at the top of the stream's gully, turned upslope towards it. The climb was a steep one and he took it steadily, that good habit, at least, not abandoned. No running here! The gap between the trees grew nearer, bigger, and it seemed to soar above him into the arches of an unlit cathedral as he entered in, and continued to climb.

It seemed self-evident which way to go, though why he chose to go left of one tree and right of another, or over one fallen trunk and round another, somebody watching him would have been hard put to say. He simply knew the way, as he had known the wolves he had seen today were special to him, and to the world, and he clambered and climbed on upwards, pausing sometimes, turning to look back, his eyes growing accustomed to the forest gloom even as that gloom deepened towards night.

He was astonished at the evident age of the forest cover he was in, and at how it could have been that so unmanaged and ancient a place as this, where trees had fallen untouched over the centuries, and the fungus that grew from them was of a kind and spread that bespoke a place undisturbed for long decades, was not known to him; or mentioned by colleagues who knew of his visit here.

It felt as if the forest was lost and forgotten, unstudied and unexplored; and yet it felt that where he went now was a trail upon which he had been before.

'Ah . . .' he muttered.

A paw-mark in a spot of exposed soil; wolf, left hind leg, the only evidence of their passage he had yet found.

He climbed on up through the trees, pausing only once more, this time because he felt himself watched, a not uncommon thing in forests such as these.

It was twilight when the Mann emerged into the quarry and the small road there, and for the first time he knew where he was. He had read the map during the days before and had planned to venture up here at some time. Quarries have all kinds of interests for those who know what to look for . . .

'But not at twilight, not when the wolves are running free . . .' he told himself ruefully. He was not cold yet, but he knew he soon would be if he did not keep moving. The air had got cooler during the climb, and not just because night was coming, and he was a little higher up. No, the sky had cleared a little, and might yet clear more, and the temperature was dropping faster as a result.

He looked about, advanced into the quarry proper, pondered for the first time seriously about his equipment and his situation which was, well, unprofessional to say the least of it. No hope of rescue services these days, not in Slovakia; these days a man was more likely to be found by death squads, and shot.

'What the hell,' he said aloud and instead of turning back downslope he turned his back yet one more time upon the life he had begun to shed that day and from that same instinct that had led him to the cleft, he turned to the darker broken end of the quarry and saw almost immediately the route's continuation.

The sky between the rocks and trees was now blue-purple, with a drift of slate-grey clouds whose underbellies were lit by the last of the lost sun's light. He stilled, knowing he was being watched, and listened in vain. A flap of wings, but what watched him was still there, and at his level: wolves. He was perhaps afraid, but it was the atavistic fear a social man feels when he is alone, in an alien place, and other creatures may be about who are more in their element than he. He breathed deeply and calmed himself; fear in such a place does not help nearly as much as doubt and caution; fear leads to mistakes, doubt to prudence.

'I'll go on up,' he muttered, for he saw it could not be far and he need only find his way back to the quarry road to know he could find his vehicle again. Keys and equipment . . . The spares were taped underneath the rear, his equipment would have to wait overnight, and suffer perhaps.

The Mann pushed on up through the darkness almost urgently, grasping at roots in the dark, clinging onto slippery, lichen-covered rocks, a kind of panic overtaking him as if to stop meant being overwhelmed . . .

Eyes watched him, amber eyes.

The Mann stopped and felt the ancient past lives of the route he was taking bounding up behind him to the present, and then overtaking, overwhelming him as the present, which was all the past and now, surged upward past him to lead him on.

'Men have walked here, not just wolves,' he thought and he was overwhelmed at last to know that he was watched, and need not feel the fear.

*He breathed slower and deeper, and then climbed more
slowly up the remaining part of the cleft route back into
open air. He was in a high place, and he stopped and
stared. Below and behind, from the quarry face's edge, he
could dimly see the tops of the trees through which he had
come.*

*Before him, pale-dark in the night, stretched a fell of
grass and rocks, in which, perhaps, animals moved, and
watched back and forth, near and far. Beyond, far, far
beyond, he could see the outline of the Tatra range, black
against dark purple sky. Above that, and stretching
towards him was a broken sky whose moon was hidden,
and whose clouds obscured all but a few stars to the
east.*

*Tired now, the Mann sank to his knees and then, growing
wet and uncomfortable, perched on a rock. He sat until he
was shivering with cold. Had the season been a warmer
one he would have sat until dawn.*

*He rose stiffly, pondered which was the best way to go
down to the road, hesitated before the cleft and decided it
was too dangerous. Then, taking advantage of the lighter,
more starry sky, and now occasional glimpses of moon, he
made his way cautiously along the quarry top, found a
track, followed it down, and reached the road he had
crossed over earlier.*

*Then, his steps light and rapid, the Mann set off back to
find the campsite and his vehicle once again, his day's work
as a human being done.*

Above him, where he had been, Klimt watched, and
Tervicz too. The female rested, her body warming the
injured male.

'The Mann's gone,' whispered Tervicz.

'Mmm . . .' growled Klimt, 'but not his scent which is

sweet as bilberry . . . Tervicz, in the morning we talk, and we plan. These wolves . . .'

He nodded towards where the female, and the injured male, kept each other warm.

'He'll not last long,' said Tervicz.

'Wulf has sent them to us, and we shall find the reason why,' replied Klimt tersely. It would not be an auspicious start for his now expanded pack if one died so soon.

Following his lead, they all fell silent, and, slumbering, began the long wait for dawn.

CHAPTER TWENTY

Ambato accepts Klimt as leader
and Elhana finds strange comfort outside the pack

K LIMT WOKE ABRUPTLY the following dawn
with a renewed sense of energy and purpose. This
was surprising, since he had slept but fitfully until
shortly before dawn, worried about what the future might
now hold for him and his new companions. But the long
weeks of travelling with Tervicz, during which he had
begun to learn about some of the burdens of leadership,
had helped to prepare him for the new challenge he now
faced. There was much to do.

He glanced at the others. The injured male had barely
moved and lay under the lee of a bush, with some rocks
rising behind him and dead grass pulled up in front. They
had ascended by a roundabout route to the edge of the fell,
taking up a position adjacent to the highest part of the gully
which Klimt had chosen as his route downslope, and in the
environs of which he felt such comfort and destiny.

The female appeared to have risen moments earlier and
was stretching, first her front legs and then her back,
haunches shivering for a moment. She was well-made,
light-furred, of middle years, and when she turned to gaze
briefly at Klimt in acknowledgement that he was leader,
before looking away without expression, he saw that her
gaze was a confident one, and the concern she held in her
eyes was more for her friend than for herself. Was he more

than a friend? Her mate perhaps? Certainly, he must be in some way more impressive than he looked to have attracted and held a female so much younger than himself. Daughter then? Mmmm.

Klimt looked about for Tervicz and moments before he saw him, heard him trotting up through the undergrowth of the gully from the quarry below with that eager nonchalance which denoted that he had found food. And so he had, for a rabbit, half-eaten already, hung from his mouth. He placed it on the ground near the old male and then looked around at Klimt and came over to him.

'Had your fill first?' said Klimt.

Tervicz shrugged and grinned. In some ways Klimt was easier than his father had been, for *he* would have insisted on taking what he wanted from such prey, whoever found it; but in other ways Klimt was far more complex and difficult for Tervicz to make out, and perhaps he should have presented the food to him first.

'Do you want it?' he began.

But Klimt shook his head distantly, his thoughts elsewhere.

Tervicz, who had been afraid of Klimt's power and strength from their first meeting, had felt a growing awe for him, an awe greatly increased after all that he had done the day before. Now Tervicz waited, only casting a regretful sideways glance at the female, for he knew that such a wolf as she could never be his.

It seemed likely, indeed, that *mating* might never be his if he stayed in the shadow of such a wolf as Klimt but then . . . Tervicz looked out across the fell, and the Tatra beyond, and reflected that the awe he felt for Klimt was mixed with loyalty and growing respect, all the greater now that they had other wolves with them. But mating . . . ah, well, he might surreptitiously take his chances when they came. In some ways he had been surreptitious all his life.

Klimt stretched, went to the quarry edge and stood where he had stood after the rescue and before trying to sleep the night before. He wondered briefly about the Mann whose scent he had recognized. The Mann had been there at the horror of Helsingborg, and yet he smelt benign, and he did not follow them . . . then the scent of bilberry and the briefest moment of nostalgia passed through him: Tornesdal in the spring when he was young; the melting of the snows, the running of the streams, and there on the fjells the bright green of bilberry leaves.

The memory of the Mann nagged back at him. *What was the Mann? What did he represent? Where had he gone after he entered the ancient wood?*

Klimt turned abruptly from memory and questions, went straight up to the female and scented at her, then to the old male who struggled, as previously, to get up.

'No,' growled Klimt. 'We'll talk where you are, wolf.'

'He will get better,' the female said, but it seemed unlikely and Klimt ignored her completely, continuing to look at the male.

'Well, and where are you from?' asked Klimt without ceremony. Had the wolf been mobile they might perhaps have journeyed for a while and kept their distance before interrogation. As it was, the evening before it had been all the wolf could do to travel up above the quarry through the trees with them, and the last part they had taken the Mennen-way, with its easier gradient.

'I am Ambato of the Benevento and she . . .'

'Benevento?' queried Klimt.

'Benevento is far south, down the wolfway of the Apennines.'

'South of the Tuscan stars?' said Tervicz whose great-grandfather had learnt of those constellations from an alpine wolf of the Stab.

'Much further,' said Ambato quietly, his voice troubled

by pain and yet with the authority that age and journeying can bring. He made Tervicz feel young.

'Listen now, and I shall whisper to you the ways to the Benevento . . .' and he did, telling them the ways he had travelled, and how it was that he had been gone so long from the pack. Elhana listened from a distance, always alert, and studying in her own way this great wolf who had saved their lives, and his restless youthful companion.

'. . . beyond the Tuscan stars you must travel, thence to Umbria; linger there, know its mellow mists and gentle vales, and ready yourself for the trek south to the myriad stars of the Abruzzi, dry, shining, pointed and glorious and yet, wolf, you must not stop. Go on, through the dry lands of the south and reach at last the Matese Mountains, marked by a single star; there, if you howl, you shall hear the Benevento pack's answering call. But beware if you are not worthy, beware . . .'

He finished and rose with a struggle, and lay down again wearily as Tervicz nudged the food nearer him. Ambato chewed at it for a while.

'You speak well, Ambato of Benevento,' said Klimt with respect. It was a long journey he had heard described – as far as his own in distance perhaps, and plainly hard. Certainly a brave venture for so old a wolf to make.

'Why did you leave your pack?' he asked at last.

Ambato understood well how important the question was, and, too, that he must phrase his answer right.

He shifted and lay down again, letting out an involuntary gasp of pain, frowning, and muttering to himself. He felt so old now, so very old. But . . .

He brought his mind back to the question the leader had asked him: why had he left the Benevento pack? Why *had* he? Once, when he was young, the question and its answers seemed easier, and of a piece. But now, and since his journey with Elhana, and the way they had been saved from the teeth of the Magyar wolves, no question was easy, no answer obvious.

He had never been much of a pack wolf, not truly. He had been a dreamer, he had striven to worship Wulf, and Wulf had comforted him through the years. But until Elhana, his daughter by Lauria, came to him he had found no way to serve Wulf, not as his heart desired, and he might have wished it. His life had been one of waiting, hoping, dreaming . . . and then she had come and he had known what he must try to help her do.

'By herself Elhana could not have come to you. No, no . . . she couldn't by herself, you see . . .'

Ambato was muttering and talking to himself, his haunches shivering once more, not knowing that he talked aloud, not knowing that he was sharing his thoughts with wolves he hardly knew, not even realizing he had spoken Elhana's name.

'Know them to be good; know these to be the ones I was looking for . . .'

Elhana tried to go to him, but Tervicz stood in her way. By Klimt's stance, and the way he had lowered his head near that of the Benevento wolf, he knew the two must not be disturbed. Surely the old wolf was dying and had things to say; and Klimt was his leader now. Let him say them without fussing then . . . Elhana was still, understanding, but nearer now, near enough to hear Ambato's gentle voice, racked with pain.

'This wolf's asked me why I left the Benevento pack. Why does a wolf up and run with stars? Eh? How do I tell him that, if he doesn't know it already? They don't know I'm dying, but *I* know, I can feel it, the slow draining away of life and interest . . .

'Wulf . . . *Wulf*. . . you put a dream into me, you showed me the wolfway to the stars and then you made me wait all through my life until it was nearly too late, and I too old to get there. Then she came, and I knew you wanted me to help her get to that place, but I have not the strength . . .'

'*What place, Ambato? Tell us of that place . . .*'

Was it Klimt who spoke then? Or was it the wind that came whispering up through the cleft in the rocks of the gully, up from a long time past, and was among them, now here in the old winter grass, now there gentle and insistent about the rock in whose shelter Ambato lay?

'You *know* Wulf, it is where you and Wulfin and the others used to live, and it is vaster than the stars which lead there, though to mortal wolves it seems only a rock. The WulfRock. But you showed me the way and you put its dream into me and when she came . . . I knew that you had shown her something of it too. But not all of it, and so I had to help her, but not tell her . . . not tell her that it was love that led me forward, and led me on again when she came . . . you put the form of her mother Lauria in her gait, and the light of her mother in her eyes as well and I would be in heaven . . . but I have not got there yet and I am dying . . .'

'*What place, Ambato?*' whispered the insistent wind.

'Rocks, rising like no others rise; rocks where Wulf had his beginning, and Wulfin and all the gods. Rocks as bleak as winter ice and confusing as a blizzard to those who know not how to look; rocks which are a womb of life to those whose heart is pure. You showed me that place when I was young, just once you let me glimpse it, and it's near, it's so near . . . but I have forgotten how to find it for it was not in this hard life I knew it; another life, another . . . *Wulf! Why did you take my life from me and make me born again? Why did you make me forget what you showed me, and where it is?*'

This last was a cry of pain and grief and Elhana would

289

have gone to him then if Klimt himself had not stood firmly in her way. There was the voice of Wulf himself in this, and Wulf would guide them all. The old one must speak, he had so much to tell.

'*Near here?*' the wind wondered, playing about them once again, easing Ambato's pain. His breathing grew easier, and he turned to look into Klimt's eyes and said, 'It is near, wolf, but none of us is ready. We are too soon, or too late perhaps . . .'

He smiled wanly, accepting now that death stalked near. The wind that had flurried up the cleft, from the past to the present, had brought for all of them the voice of Wulf, but for Ambato it seemed to have brought as well the shadow that waits in the future for all wolves. It was already upon his face, and was draining the light from his eyes.

'Elhana . . .' he began.

But once more Klimt stood in her way, and when she strove to get by him he turned, snarling, on her. She might have gone for him then but Tervicz hustled her back, nipping at her, his paws tangling with hers, his strength tumbling her.

'Ambato!' she cried desperately. 'Father!'

Ah . . . she is the daughter then.

'He's right!' called out the frail Ambato, calming them all. 'He's right . . .'

There was a long silence then and when Ambato closed his eyes Tervicz thought that he was going to slip away, he seemed so light upon the ground, his ribs showing through his old fur, the weals and gouges of his wounds on face and shoulder, and down his haunch, seeming more substantial than he was. Why would Klimt not let the female go to him? What did he know?

'Why did you journey here if you knew it was not the place Wulf had shown you?' asked Klimt matter-of-factly.

Ambato stirred, almost irritably, and said, 'Because . . .

because . . . *you* were here. From the north you came, and him . . . *he's* here too.'

Ambato waved a weak paw towards Tervicz.

'You know who we are?'

'Not your names, no, but I know who you are. For a millennium there have been wolves who knew you would come, and when you told those murderous ones yesterday that you were of the Wolves of Time, I knew why I had come here . . .'

'Tell us, wolf, tell us.'

Ambato looked at Tervicz and signalled him nearer.

'You're of the Bukov pack, you must be . . .'

'He is not, but I am!' said Tervicz in wonderment.

'And you . . . ?'

Klimt did not reply, so Ambato frowned and tried to think, but it would not come easily. Then finally he said, '*You're* of the north, that I know now, remembering. Once I knew more, once I knew your name, and the stars in whose constellation you were born . . .'

'I am Klimt of Tornesdal,' said Klimt softly. 'To the south of us were once the Storuman and Östersund, while to the north were the many Lappish packs and . . .'

'. . . And thence of Onega, Russian-born and wanderers over the ice . . . Yesss . . . oh yes!'

'You know such things?' said Klimt, his voice touched with excitement for once. 'Why, in far distant times, my forefathers came over the ice from Onega, and theirs before them travelled the ways from Pechora itself!'

'Pechora, birthplace of the God of War . . . Kobrin. Has *he* come?'

'Not quite . . .' said Klimt before his voice faltered and he added, 'but those tales have been lost from our pack for generations now, and knowledge of the wolfways lost as well . . .'

'The knowledge of most wolfways has been lost, for how

can wolves remember them who have never known them through the generations? The Mennen destroyed our ways and all our memory except a few tidbits that by themselves are nothing but an old wolf's wanderings.'

'Not quite all, old wolf,' said Klimt, 'for always the importance of the Heartland and Tatra has been known, that at least has been taught by parents to their offspring . . .'

'To Tatra, yes,' concurred Ambato softly, the excitement of sharing these common teachings with Klimt having put a little life into him for a time, but a life that was now fast ebbing away once more. 'And perhaps it was wolves' temporal Heartland once, but more than that . . .'

'More?' said Klimt. 'Was the dream that Wulf put into you of a different place?'

'Yes!' said Ambato fiercely, reaching a paw towards Klimt. 'Yes it was! Nearby perhaps, but different. I knew it when I led us here to find you. Hereabout may be a territory of sorts, as ancient as any we're ever likely to find, with wolfways of the kind that Mann found last night. For what is the Heartland heartland of?'

'You wonder that too!' said Klimt with surprise.

'I can scent such things across a vale!' laughed Ambato, a little bitterly. 'How else do you think just an old wolf like me, and my companion, could have made the trek so far? By star and by scent a wolf must travel over alien land. Then, too, my forefathers trekked those ways in lifetimes past to get to where I was born, and left a residual memory buried in my heart. Just so, in yours, there'll be a memory of the difficult ways to Onega, and to Pechora, and yet further on. You'll find your home at last!'

Klimt almost wept at that, for he had never in his life heard such comforting words.

Ambato coughed, and wheezed, tried to eat and failed, coughed up blood, swore, and went to sleep. Klimt stayed by his side; Tervicz, muttering to himself, checked the territory about, his hackles rising only once at some alien lupine scent which was too fresh for his liking, but there were no other signs than that. Elhana stayed as near to Ambato as Klimt allowed, easier now, and seeming to slumber until her father stirred or made a sound, at which she would be instantly alert.

Sometimes he muttered of stars and dreams, and once even tried to rise as if to get to that place which he desired so much to find, and as dusk set in two things seemed obvious to all of them: first, that he was striving to make one last effort to talk to Klimt and second, that as the light was fading away, so was his life.

Klimt moved away from him for a time and Elhana took the opportunity to take his place. These two had not spoken directly at all, and barely exchanged a glance, but though there was a stiffness in Klimt's Nordic formality in his contact with the female, and an awkward and unconvincing deference in Elhana's attitude to him thus far, yet there was as well the sense of a bond made now in the shared experience of Ambato's struggle and suffering. While Elhana plainly suffered with Ambato, Klimt equally plainly respected him in a way that leaders rarely respected dying males to whom they owed no loyalty.

Twilight was upon them when Ambato spoke again, and when he did he signalled that it was to Klimt he wished to address his words, and Elhana now gave up her place to him willingly enough.

'Klimt of Tornesdal,' he began, 'you can see I am near my end. Yesterday you had not met me, or my companion whose name you know, from what I have said, to be Elhana, Elhana of the Benevento. Once she was its ledrene. Now she is a vagrant like myself. I cannot speak for her and nor will I. But for myself I have no desire to die a vagrant. A wolf who thinks only of himself thinks of nothing at all. Only in the pack, in sharing with others, does a wolf find that thing which can properly be called himself. Therefore, Klimt of Tornesdal, though you know me not, and I can be of no service to you now, I ask that you accept me into your pack . . .'

Klimt was still as ice as the twilight deepened about them all.

Then he said, 'Ambato of the Benevento, when, yesterday, Tervicz and myself came to your aid we did so because we heard an ancient call, one to which we may have responded in other lives, but then without success. Wulf granted that yesterday we came to you in time and here you are, near death perhaps, but living still. I have no other members of my pack than Tervicz here, though in him are many wolves alive and more power and strength than he himself knows. It would be an honour to me if you consented to run with us . . .'

'In sickness and in health . . .' whispered Ambato ironically.

'Just so,' responded Klimt.

How strong Klimt seemed, how alive as he stood over the ailing Benevento wolf; but how gentle and respectful too in posture, even if his words were careful to observe the niceties.

'What is your command?' said Ambato. 'What may I do for thee?'

'Will you obey and never be disloyal?'

'I will!'

'Will you ever put the pack before yourself, and the pack before me?'

'Always!'

'Will you protect our females and our young before the Mennen and the wanderers?'

'For ever, now and in all lives to come!'

'Is Wulf your God?'

'And Wulfin too . . .'

'Then it will be an honour if you run with us . . . Speak out the name of your adoptive pack.'

'You are . . . *we* are . . . the Wolves of Time.'

'Of what territory are we?'

'We are outcast of all the territories of wolves but one, which is . . . which is . . .'

'Speak its name, Ambato.'

'It is . . .'

'Tell us the name of the place which you have spent your life trying to find!'

'I know not its name. We are outcast of all places, all . . . but where the gods were born, where Wulf took his first steps, where Wulfin became his mate, where the rocks rise into mists and mystery and no mortal wolf may go, that place . . . that hallowed place . . . might be the territory of the Wolves of Time, for the gods have lost it now, and we shall have as our territory all that land and the cliffs that bound it wherein the WulfRock rises. That is the territory we must win and hold against the day that Wulf returns.'

His voice failed him and he began to choke. Elhana went to him, and nuzzled at him, the tears on her face like the stars that were beginning to show on the eastern horizon across the fell.

'Klimt, I can say no more of it for it was but a dream I had once, long ago. Command me in anything else, but this is not mine to speak of further. Command me in another way!'

These were brave words spoken by a wolf whose time seemed almost to have come, and Tervicz took them as no more than that, whilst Elhana, grief-stricken and silent could surely have thought no differently.

But Klimt! He stood above them all, strong and proud, like some mountain seen far-off, and his presence seemed to defy even death itself, which having circled so close all day seemed now to be creeping up to them with the shadows of the night to take Ambato's life away.

'You shall obey my command, whatever it may be?'

'I shall try,' said Ambato.

'Then listen, wolf, and listen well, for I am not in the habit of giving commands twice over. In this pack, as Tervicz knows, once should always be enough.'

The hard edge of purposeful command was indeed in his voice now.

'You are the oldest amongst us, Ambato. From what little you have said so far it seems you have knowledge of lore that none of us have. If you die, who will teach us the things that only you know? You have lived alone far longer than any of us, and know the strengths and dangers of such living better than we. If you die, who can help us to avoid those dangers, and learn those strengths, better than you yourself?

'You have heard Wulf's whispers, and known his dreams, and you believe that there is a place you have never reached but which exists somewhere, if only at present in your heart. If you die, wolf, who will take us there?'

He spoke slowly and clearly and in a voice that was a leader's, though not any leader's any of them had ever known before. This was not a wolf who led by force alone, or even by temperament, this was one who thought about the pack's needs and sought a way to make its members give their help towards their shared fulfilment. More than that, he found a way to make members believe they could, they *must* do far more than they thought they could.

Listening now, Tervicz began to see how it had been that he had gained a belief in himself since he had been with Klimt; now he saw how Klimt was putting purpose into Ambato's heart, and belief in his mind, and he held his breath at the audacity of it: for Ambato was so near death what purpose could he have?

'I cannot do much for your . . . for our pack,' whispered Ambato, 'except in wish and spirit, for I . . .'

'There is one thing you can do.'

'Name it, wolf,' said Ambato weakly.

'One thing only that I command . . .'

'Name it, Klimt of Tornesdal, my leader now.'

'You can live,' said Klimt very quietly. 'Live for me and live for all of us. Live as the Wolves of Time have lived.'

'But . . . !' began Ambato in blank astonishment.

'You will *not* die and take from the pack what it has only just discovered it might have; you *must* not!' said Klimt savagely, those last three words a snarl.

'But he is near death, for Wulf's sake!' cried Elhana suddenly, her passions and grief, held in check all day, suddenly breaking free. She stood snout to snout with Klimt like ledrene to leader, and her eyes were fierce. So fierce, indeed, so full of fiery light in the dusk, that Tervicz, unused to such passion, wished he might almost sink into the ground for fear of what would happen. It felt as if the elements themselves had broken loose.

It felt, too, as if an important moment in the pack's young life had come, and that its leader was being challenged in the way that only ledrenes can, not in body but in spirit. Tervicz had never felt the presence of a powerful female so much as he did now. He looked away in apprehension, but waited, listening.

'No, wolf,' replied Klimt calmly. 'He *thinks* he is near death, and you think he is near death. Why else have I kept you from him most of this day? Your conviction that he is dying would weaken him still more. His wounds are grievous, yet he is still alive, and listening, it seems. I have granted him membership of our pack not that he might become a dead memory the day he joins us but that he might be a living example for some time to come!'

He stared on at Elhana and, finally, her tail restless with

irritation, she backed away, muttering rather in the way Ambato had that morning.

'Well, then, Ambato,' said Klimt more lightly, 'you had better choose, for we are travelling on now that dusk has come. I do not wish to linger here much longer. There is danger here, and little food. I command you to follow us. As for you . . .' he went on addressing Elhana coldly, 'you have not asked to join our pack, and nor have we asked you. This wolf might still be unwounded if you had not let him lead you this far.'

'But . . .' protested Elhana, glaring at him, '. . . what wolf do you think you . . .'

'Perhaps you will follow us, who knows?' said Klimt non-committally.

'But I *came* with him,' said Elhana.

Klimt shrugged and said, 'And now, if he follows my command, he comes with us. Perhaps *you* can make yourself useful to us, perhaps you can't. But do not get too near. Nordic wolves bite! Come Tervicz, and you Ambato, let us be on our way . . .'

Tervicz dared look up again and taking a position behind Ambato waited until the old wolf, struggling, muttering, not believing what he did, rose up at last, and began a slow limping progress behind Klimt, who set off at a slow pace among the rocky outcrops and out into the fell. While at a distance, sometimes off to one side, sometimes trailing behind, Elhana followed the other three.

She had at first been angry at Klimt's seeming indifference to her and unhappy too, for after so long travelling with Ambato she did not like settling down to rest alone, even if the others were not so far away. But she felt awed at Ambato's apparent recovery and, too, by the daunting power she felt in Klimt's presence. It seemed to her that he was a cold wolf, a distant one – one quite unlike any of the males she had known among the Benevento, and yet

. . . again and again she remembered that brief glance they had shared when he had first come to rescue them, in which she too had glimpsed part of a life she had somehow lost centuries before. A life, perhaps, long since left behind in the wolfways of time but one to which the journeyings of Wulf knows how many successive lives had brought her back.

'Perhaps,' she mused to herself as she rested hours later, licking her paws and listening to the soft chatter of the other three a little way to the north of where she lay, 'perhaps he is afraid of what it really means, as I am. In that look we shared there was more than recognition: there was doubt and fear as well.'

She mused some more on that, until her thoughts drifted to better things, less certain things, like dreams and wishes: and Elhana settled down more comfortably still and reflected that, thus far at least, she was the only female on the outskirts of a pack of males – if pack it could be called that had no female yet! More than that, she was at the beginning of the pack's formation and whatever Klimt might have meant by the 'Wolves of Time', it was purposeful and important and more than mere legend, and she wished to be part of it.

Night came. As it did and with the others nearby, and the sense that it was now Klimt's looming presence that dominated them all, Elhana slept more deeply than she had for months past. Whilst Klimt, sleepless, taking the watch, came and stared at her from the shadows and wondered what wolf she was, and what wolf she might one day become.

IV

THE BROKEN HEARTLAND

*In which, as the dark millennium begins
to end, wolfkind and the Mennen fight each other
and themselves as they seek a way
out of eternal strife*

CHAPTER TWENTY-ONE

*A leader and ledrene fail to find harmony
and we meet the Huntermann*

TEN DAYS LATER, after much covert wandering by the group across the Southern Fell, Elhana became aware that other wolves were loitering about. She took this as a welcome opportunity to talk to Klimt directly, for she could not tell if he had seen them.

'We know,' he said curtly. 'While you slept last night, Tervicz and I went to watch them. No doubt they have scented you.'

He smiled coldly and then added, 'Why did you think I have continued to make you trek separately from us, if not to flush out other wolves?'

She retreated, feeling annoyed and rejected. So she was simply a decoy . . . a wolf to use.

'And he is so distant and dismissive!' she told herself. 'I would not wish to be ledrene with him as leader! But at least . . . at least Ambato looks as if he has regained something of his former strength.'

Something, but not all. Her father had recovered but he was thinner now, and not only was his face more lined, but his fur seemed greyer and faded. He did not have so long to live. Not more than a season or so.

After this brief and unsatisfactory encounter with Klimt, Elhana retreated to the shadows once more and gave herself up to the pleasurable contemplation of the wolves who loitered nearby. There were two of them, or possibly three: all males who kept well clear of where Klimt and the others were. She glimpsed them occasionally and guessed them to be vagrants, though of what tribe she could not tell for she was unfamiliar with their combination of stocky build, stiff-legged gait and rufous-coloured fur.

'They're certainly after me,' she decided, with some anticipation. It was a good few years since a male had dared show such open interest in her as these did – apart from the Magyar leader Hassler – and her only regret about Ambato was that such things had never seemed to cross his mind on their long journey to the Tatras: not that she wanted her father, though such a thought did not repel her: wolves must where wolves can, as her mother told her once with a wry smile. But she would have liked the opportunity of saying no.

Such thoughts as these were persistent, but they did not dominate. Like the need for food and its satisfaction, memories afterwards were general rather than specific. What impressed her far more during those days of exploration, and Ambato too, as she found when they had a chance to talk from time to time, was the scale and nature of the territory they were in.

The dark rises towards the Tatra Mountains seemed to dominate every view, though in fact the valleys of the rivers that wound their way up from east and west were deep enough that when they entered into them the mountains might be lost for days at a time. The 'Southern Fell', as Klimt and Tervicz called it, was really an area of undulating pasture and forest lands which formed the watershed of the rivers that dissected the ground to east, west and south.

At its southern extremity the fell dropped down to lower ground, and from the top of the last escarpment they could see the great vale of the Danube River stretching southwestwards, and on crystal-clear days, usually after rain, they could make out the huge mass of the Alps, whose eastward length Elhana and Ambato had travelled, rising up and away into mists and clouds.

The gully up which Klimt had led them immediately after rescuing them from the Magyars, and where they had rested that first night, was at the south-westward end of the fell lands, and to Elhana, as to the others, it felt like their true base. Klimt led them in great loops of exploration out from it, each time covering new ground, and familiarizing them with what they already knew.

It was in this period that they began to understand something of the run of the deer herds, and to see how they used the more inaccessible stands of trees above the streams and rivers for cover, and a few chosen routes to reach the wilder waters and high lakes to drink and mate.

East of this territory the centre of the Magyar territory lay, in the heads of river valleys there, which gave them access not only to the fell, but northward to the Tatras and the Carpathians, and west down to lower ground. These areas Klimt and his small pack usually avoided, travelling into them only for purposes of reconnaissance, to understand the general lie of the land, and the context of the fells which they were beginning to hope they might make their own. It was more marginal land, exposed to the weather, the prey more scarce, and unpleasantly waterlogged in parts with surface water of stagnant pools and lakes which ranged outward in every direction but north. Barren land, a barren part of the Heartland, over which the northern scarps loomed uninvitingly.

The male visitors lingered on, daily getting nearer, watching. Sometimes Klimt let them help with a hunt, and share some food. But none were allowed to talk to Elhana.

If she had been without the others near, and remembering the ferocity of the Magyars' attack on them, she might have been more concerned. But she was not so old that she had forgotten the scent of a questing male when she came across it, and it was March now and spring was not so far away. She had wanted to mate for weeks past.

She might even have been tempted to wander off by herself in the hope that one of the males might find her but that, sensing competition (as *she* had hoped) Klimt himself had come by one day and stood staring at her. She liked that more and had stared back at him for long enough to show that at least she was not indifferent, before, head high, she turned off into undergrowth and circled about the place to go back to where he had been and stand for a time and enjoy the lingering of his presence: dark, strange, potent, brooding, formidable. . . She *liked* that and it made her tremble.

All of which was enough to encourage her to keep her distance from her unseen admirers, though she lingered behind Klimt's group enough for the visitors to have space to get closer still. Then one afternoon, one dared come into full view: Slavic for certain, young, his fur rough as yet, without the sleekness of maturity and confidence. Shy as well; uncertain. She let him hang about until dusk and then chased him off, making enough noise doing so that Klimt might hear. She wanted him to. She wanted . . .

When the wolf had gone, Klimt was there, staring, silent, expressionless. For the first time Elhana felt she wanted him or, if not him, then what he might give her. Wolves like the one she had just chased off would stand no chance against him. It was, she said to herself, a matter of power, not affection or love. No, it was the power of being ledrene to a leader who could hold a pack and mould it to his will that she wanted. To such a wolf she could give much in return.

306

'*Much* . . .' she said to herself fiercely, surprised at the passion in what she felt, and the sudden excitement that thrilled through her. Love had been her obsession, but having met Klimt she was beginning to give up hope of it; power, and the protection of one so strong, began to seem more potent still.

The following day the wolf that she had seen off reappeared, and showed himself off. But she was unimpressed by the speed with which he disappeared downslope and away the moment a more solid threat appeared: a large and stocky male of uncertain pedigree, one of the other two who had been following. Having done no more than stare at the other to make him flee, the new wolf did not hesitate: he came straight over to Elhana, snouted at her, and made his desires, if not quite his intentions, plain.

She growled fiercely, the more so because he was an intimidating wolf and though probably no match for Klimt himself and indeed the Magyar leader Hassler, yet he was not likely to give way without a fight. By comparison to the Benevento males those that appeared to inhabit these parts were impressive indeed.

She snarled at him and the wolf ritually backed off, his neck fur ruffling up in a pleasing way, and Elhana growled more loudly still, hoping that Klimt would come by once more. He did not, though she supposed he might be nearby downwind, for she would not have scented him among the gorse bushes there. She waited, and it was not long before the male came nearer again and settled down in ground he scent-marked, looking large and confident. His face was lined and pitted with scars, and his shoulder fur patchy in places. Was Klimt really going to let him be? Could he? Elhana began an uncertain wait, and what she imagined might well be a long one.

But it was not, or did not seem so. Certainly it was not yet midday before the third vagrant appeared. In size he

was not much smaller than the one who had made himself
at such ease before Elhana, but less muscular, and yet . . .
more lithe perhaps, younger too. Elhana allowed herself a
smile.

The two seemed to know one another, for the larger did
not move at all but glowered at the new arrival and said,
'Where the hell did *you* come from?'

'The same place as you, Wulfin rest our mother's soul!'
replied the other, grinning mischievously and nonchalantly
walking straight past him and up to Elhana.

'Madam, you are I hear, a stranger in these parts, and
alone. Or alone-ish. The vagrant lupine world of the fell-
lands of Tatra waits to see if that murderous and, if I may
say so, impressive wolf who saved your skin some days ago,
Klimt of Tornesdal, will ask you to join his pack. We need
hardly ask in what capacity it will be if he does. However
. . . he appears to me a mite slow off the mark in matters
of mating and so forth. Nordic you see. They're like that.
It's the cold summers. Brrr! Does nothing for the loins.
Ha!'

He laughed, and Elhana smiled.

'Meanwhile certain others of us, and myself in particular,
wish to advance our claims to you and as it were . . . My
name is Stry.'

But then Stry, with a most weary glance at Elhana and
a confidential wink as if to say, 'Sorry for the interruption
– I'll be back shortly', leapt sideways and sideways again
as with an enormous bound, followed by a ferocious charge,
the other wolf went straight for him. He missed, and the
force of his charge combined with his bulk carried him a
good deal further on before he was able to stop and turn,
by which time Stry was settled back comfortably where the
first had been.

'Meet my elder and better, Morten,' said Stry with a
grin.

Morten glowered and taking a few steps towards Elhana settled down again to watch. Elhana noticed that in addition to the scars his face had pleasing lines of patience, and even good humour.

Elhana shifted, got up, and judiciously took up a place about the same distance from each of them, from where she could see both of them easily and, in addition, the cover from which she hoped Klimt might eventually emerge. Surely he was near . . .

'A nuisance, all this,' said Stry wryly. 'Rather tedious in some ways. Yet the world goes round and round! In our case forever.'

'You know each other?' asked Elhana politely.

'Like a river knows its bank,' said Stry cheerfully, 'me being the river, and a particularly beautiful and bountiful one, and Morten being the bank, an especially dull one.'

'Like leaders know runts,' observed Morten coolly, 'he being the runt.'

'Ah! Now there's an interesting view of things, Elhana – we may call you Elhana I presume?'

'How do you know . . . ?'

'Creeping, listening, lurking in the night, that's us local wolves.'

'Magyars?'

'Slavic in fact, not the same as Magyars, that's all you need to know,' said Stry confidentially, moving a little nearer. 'Don't mix them up or the whole region will be down on you . . . but, yes we do know each other which is hardly surprising since we have the same mother *and* the same father *and* were born in the same place.'

Morten heaved a weary sigh and said, 'I'll give you the short version to save you getting the longer one from *him*. It is true we are brothers. There were three of us, two males and a female: he was the runt. Mennen got our parents, Mennen got our sister. We survived. We crossed the Tatra and enjoy avoiding the Magyars. That's all you need to know about us . . .'

'Is it?' said Elhana, turning to Stry. Morten had spoken calmly but she suspected his voice belied a deeper story.

Stry said, 'I'll tell you the truth: no it's not. The Mennen would have killed me but he saved me as close as that Klimt saved *you*. He dragged me to safety.'

'Dragged him all the bloody way to a place called Stry and then I said, "You can make your own way from here or not at all!"'

'That's why he called me Stry, he says it's where I started.'

'Do you remember your parents?' asked Elhana.

'I remember a big wolf, and hiding against him; I remember my mother stopping me shaking; I remember them dragging me, I remember . . .'

Stry was staring at Morten, who in turn was staring at the ground. It seemed plain enough what mother and what father Stry remembered, and the love and loyalty which he freely gave his brother, for all his teasing and mischief.

'And now . . . ?'

'He's stronger, bigger, *heavier*. . . but I'm more lithe, and faster, and *lighter*,' said Stry, laughing. 'He catches me sometimes and I fool him sometimes and today, here and now and him being impressive but relatively inarticulate, and me being less impressive and relatively more articulate, you have a hard choice to make, Elhana of the Benevento. Oh, tell us of your journey here, of the territories you crossed, or the places you saw. Tell us of the southern sun, and mountains so hot that snow never falls, tell us . . .'

As Stry drifted off into this ironic appeal and his brother looked far more ill-tempered than he probably was, Elhana told herself that it was not just the way in which Stry presented himself and his brother that made her smile, but the fact that it was a very long time since she had enjoyed this kind of conversation. Not in fact since the distant days when she was still ledrene of the Beneventos and it was one of those summer days with plenty of food and a cool wind.

'Well, Madam, we . . .' began the indefatigable Stry once more.

'Stry . . .' said Morten in a low voice, sufficiently filled with warning that Elhana at least looked up in alarm, and then about the clearing where they talked.

'It's all right, I'm not . . .' continued Stry, thinking perhaps that Morten's warning tone concerned him overdoing his overtures to Elhana.

But it was not that at all that had Elhana rising to her paws as Morten had.

For out of the cover behind where Stry squatted Klimt had come, huge and angry-looking, yet silent as death, so much so that none of them had heard him at all. Then, before any of them could move Klimt bounded across the clear ground and was on Stry, tumbling him expertly, his mouth poised above his throat, his eyes on Morten, challenging.

'Oh dear!' said Stry with surprising composure. 'Caught napping!'

His brother was advancing menacingly towards Klimt, head ever lower, eyes ever more intent, his thick, rugged head with an awful, formidable life of its own, his jaws a little open.

Klimt put a paw on Stry's belly and, with the gentlest of shoves, rolled him away in a magnificent gesture of power rather than superiority. There was no snapping at the beaten wolf, no after-fight punishment, but, rather, the calm assurance of a wolf who in a few brief moments had shown that he could dominate the other and had no need to do more. Stry knew his place and moved away willingly enough, stood up, backed off from the other two and shaking himself, stood watching.

Klimt turned to Morten, and the two faced each other, growling. Their front paws fretted at the ground, each watching for the other's first move.

Stry, nothing daunted, and to his credit perhaps, said lightly to Elhana, 'Well I don't know, but at a time like this I always think that there must be a better way.'

To Elhana's great surprise, though without once taking his eyes off his foe, the normally taciturn Morten growled, 'Tell me when you've found out what it is, meanwhile shut up!'

There was a certain rueful irony in his voice which she had not expected. There were other things, too, which she would not have known had she not seen the two wolves facing each other as they now were. One was that contrary to all she would have said until that moment, it was the Slav who was the bigger wolf, not Klimt, who gave the impression of size, she now realized, by the force of his dark and silent personality.

It was plain enough which was the more hungry of the two for power: Klimt. He moved with a more ruthless purpose, stared with more focus and concentration, and as he now advanced one paw after another slowly and carefully on the ground he seemed somehow more there, more absolute. The rock against which the heaviest sea would break.

However, Morten did not flinch or show any fear at all, but stood his ground warily, shifting his weight from one front paw to another, readying himself for whatever action would be needed. Watching him, it seemed to Elhana that Morten had a quality she had not seen before. It was more than strength and courage, and certainly more than simple male pride.

There was . . . there was in him . . . he seemed . . .

'Searching,' whispered Elhana to herself, 'and hoping that he will find . . . Why, he's *testing* Klimt!'

Some test! For as Elhana told herself that this must be what Morten was doing, Klimt lunged suddenly forward and Morten reared up to meet him, his two front paws rising off the ground. Klimt continued forward, swerved, ducked, and bit his opponent painfully on the shoulder as he passed him by. The latter grunted in pain and turned too late to catch his foe.

The two faced each other once more, panting, a trickle of blood on Morten's shoulder now, catching their breath . . .

Klimt went in again, straight now, and brutally hard, his paws entangling briefly with Morten's and then clamping tight and locking. Klimt was faster and more resolute, Morten slower but more powerful, so that when he jerked his head, or swung it one way or another, it was Klimt's paws that struggled to keep their hold on the ground, not his own.

Klimt, nearly over-balanced, turned again, twisted, and broke free, snarling and ferocious and then, quite suddenly, still.

Morten stared in astonishment, himself panting and gasping with the struggle, glad of the moment's rest, intimidated by Klimt's sudden self-control and calm.

Klimt turned his head slowly to stare at Elhana, his eyes impassive and ungiving as he caught her gaze and stilled her too. It seemed that the whole world had been brought to silence by Klimt, and that all things waited on him now to move again: the clouds in the sky, the watching wolves, and even the wind in the grass about them, and the trees beyond. She felt stunned inside, and not *as if* she stared at her own destiny, but *knowing* she did.

She had dreamed of a mate to match her longing and sense of destiny, she had so often ached with the loneliness of one who believes that life has begun to pass them by before destiny has been fulfilled, and true companionship found. Now, lost and numb before Klimt's gaze, she saw that dreams and destiny are one thing, their reality another – less safe, less comfortable, and revealing ways forward that might prove too hard. In those moments Elhana was stirred by the thrill of discovered hopes and the chill of the insight that their fulfilment might ask more of her than she had to give, and give her less comfort than she had hoped.

Then, as sudden and shocking as the stillness, Klimt moved. One moment he was staring at her and the next he had turned back to Morten, shivered very slightly, and surged forward upon him, awesome and unstoppable. From somewhere he had found a power and strength he seemed not quite to have in the first phase of their fight; from somewhere, it seemed, the light of the grace of leadership was on him, in his fur, in the glint of his eyes, in the purpose of his paws; and in the commanding thrust and gape of his muzzle grip on Morten's left shoulder.

The bigger wolf was stopped in his response, he was turned, and then with a ripping of flesh he was turned again and thrown, the muscles of his haunches flexing and straining to stop his over-toppling before, giving up, he rolled away in a welter of paws and grunts.

Klimt bounded after him, stood over him, and there was no doubt that if Morten did not yield, and fast, he would grind in to inflict real injury.

'No!' whispered Stry, who stood off to one side, shocked and miserable, frightened for his brother.

'Noooo,' growled Morten deeply. 'No . . .'

He turned where he lay, his paws rose off the ground, and he submitted himself to the Nordic wolf.

'Yes,' said Klimt, his voice as harshly gentle as the hiss of wind over ice on the fjells above Tornesdal. 'Oh yes . . .'

His tail flicked, his eyes softened, and proud, daring any

314

to question him, he stared about the clearing, and then at the beaten Morten.

Then down he went and nipped Morten's other flank, hard enough to produce a grunt of pain, hard enough to shift the great wolf's body when he raised his head before opening his mouth to let Morten free; enough to master yet not quite humiliate; enough for Morten and any other who saw, never to forget.

Then Klimt turned away and went straight to Elhana, the blank savagery and purposefulness of the fight in his eyes and on his face.

'Come!' he commanded. 'Now!'

She went with him, closer to the trees and not quite out of sight, herself proud, proud and wanting; wanting and shaking with the suddenness of it.

He scented her, back and forth, and she him. He nudged her, he pawed her and then disregarding the others close by he turned hard upon her, mounted her, and took her until her hind legs shook with strain, and her neck hurt and ached where his teeth raked and ravaged her to match the sweet fire between her legs.

Out of the Nordic wastes he had come, and she from the sun-beaten south, his cold and blizzard touch to her warmth and passion.

She sighed into the pleasure and pain of it; and he, Klimt of Tornesdal, publicly took what he had fairly won that others might know and honour him, and her, and know that he was leader, and she ledrene. Know and honour, that was what they would do.

But even as he shuddered to completion inside her, she knew something more the others could not: the wolf who in mastering them had mastered her, had not released his all into her but withheld something vital of his heart, something of himself, from her. It felt to her that he had left it behind in the icy Nordic wastes from which he had come.

As she felt him lose all but that inside her, she knew that the wolf who moved away from her was a stranger still, yet one she yearned now to know, to open up. She began to twist and turn away from him, frustrated and unhappy. She found herself staring across to the clearing, and into the eyes of Ambato; who stared, and looked so old, and seemed to smile with eyes that said, 'For you, too, it begins now, for you as well . . .'

Elhana yearned then, as she never had before, for the warm sun of the south where hearts and passions were open and wild, and wolves carried no icy burdens from out of the north. She yearned . . .

Then, as suddenly as Klimt had taken her, he startled up, ears forward, as from his muzzle came a low, throaty, almost inaudible growl which brought them all to attention, all else forgotten.

'What is it?' whispered Tervicz, moving to Klimt's flank.

Klimt was looking diagonally upslope towards a cluster of low, shrubby trees that lay above a jut of rock, a good long way away.

He said one word only before he turned and led them away as fast as shadows out of sight. One word, and the place they had been was emptied of wolf.

'Mennen,' he said.

Huntermann lay on heather and grass, his right eye to the rifle's scope whose sighting lines made a grid of the place the wolves had been.

He lay marvelling.

He was a kilometre off at least, probably a little more, and he had not moved in an hour, and still they had sensed him there.

'Wolves,' he muttered, the way he spoke the word full of

resonance: respect, fear, bloodlust, sensuality, love, absolute hatred: wolves!

'Wolves,' *he said, softly this time, pleasurably, like a voyeur who enjoys even more in recall what he has only just covertly watched.*

For a long thirty minutes he had held one or other of the six wolves he watched in his sights. He might have shot any he wished, and as the mating took place he had been tempted to shoot the female out from under the male.

'That would have fucked him,' *Huntermann laughed to himself.* 'The first recorded instance of a necrophiliac wolf!'

The Mann's face grimaced in a kind of laugh, but he made no sound.

'I could have shot any of them,' *he told himself with satisfaction.*

He felt hot and, the excitement of the stalk and watch over with and the wolves well gone across the fell, he broke a rule and took off one of his gloves. He wiped his forehead of sweat, he licked at the palm of his hand to taste himself, then pushed himself slowly up to a squat position, checked his gear and slid away, animal-like, barely visible; a shadow shifting out of sight.

Huntermann did not stand upright for two hundred and fifty metres, only when he reached a track. Then he was upright and stretching. He sighed happily and began a long and almost silent trek down to the road three kilometres away. He was large, and dressed in camouflage-fatigues, his face khaki and black with grease. Now and then he paused and crouched to examine tracks and spoors; once he took off his glove again to finger some hairs caught on the point of a spear thistle stem. He scented at the hairs.

Then he was up and on down the track, quite rapidly, but without giving the impression of speed. A Mann utterly at home with where he was and what he did. A carnivore.

Three hundred metres from the road he went off the path

and stalked his own vehicle. He studied it and the area around through binoculars. He checked out some wires set above the ground. Then, whistling very softly, he emerged and went down to the vehicle itself. He checked around it once more, opened the passenger door, took off his gloves, unloaded his gear, and then methodically packed away his rifle. Everything was neat and orderly. The handgun he produced from under his jacket he looked at, checked, and put back where it had been.

He cleared the ground about his vehicle of the lines he had laid, and demobilized an alarm beneath the vehicle.

He went round to the driver's side and seemed about to get in before he turned suddenly away from the vehicle, a bulking, khaki shadow by the roadside. He unbuttoned himself and eased out his penis. It was fatter than the ball of his thumb, longer than his fingers, and he was uncircumcised. He played with himself for a moment or two before a flush of urine arced down into the grass. He let his penis go as, hands on hips he both urinated and enjoyed the view. Then, finished, he retracted his foreskin and shook himself as dry as he could. A driblet of urine flecked onto the back of his hand and he wiped it on his thigh. The shiny pink-purple head of his penis caught the sky for a moment, the only colour about him, and then it was gone, pushed back within his clothes.

He climbed into the vehicle and accelerated slowly, orderly, measured, organized.

Then he was gone, and where he had been bubbles of urine died away into the grass, and exhaust fumes dispersed into the evening air.

Two hours, and a hundred and twenty kilometres later . . .

  'Huntermann?'

  'Yes.'

'They're ready.'

'You got what you needed?'

A short laugh, hard and dismissive.

'There's nothing left to get.'

'Fifteen minutes.'

'I'll tell them.'

This time they both laughed, laughs which rose up out of traditions of torture, centuries of internecine death.

'Fifteen minutes then.'

Huntermann finished his drink, which was water, and went to stand at the door of his daughter's room.

'Story,' she said sleepily.

'If you're still awake when I get back I'll tell you one.'

He turned back downstairs, said a word to his wife who barely looked up, and was gone outside, to his second car, a black Mercedes, three years old. As solid in build as he was.

He drove for ten minutes, a route he knew so well he barely seemed to look at the road. He got out of his vehicle into an atmosphere odorous with chemical waste which Huntermann breathed in with the same satisfaction he breathed in the air of the fell. One was income, the other was escape. To Huntermann both represented aspects of his liberty, and to him the stench of money was as fragrant as the scents of nature.

Huntermann had parked by a gate above which a hoarding bore his name: Huntermann Chemical Engineering. A man at the gate let him in, giving him a small salute as he passed by.

'They're ready, sir.'

'C18?'

'Yes.'

He made his way through the shadows of unlit warehouses and smaller square units, past a couple of embayments holding raw materials. All was neat, ordered. All was quiet.

He turned a corner, came to an apparently unlit building, and a door opened for him.

'Lock it,' he ordered.

Down some worn concrete steps, round a corner, through two more doors, and into a room that stank of disinfectant. It was large and well-lit and five men, naked, hung over a concrete pit of the sort used to service machinery from below. Each of them was attached to a metal beam above by new blue nylon ropes, so that their heads were at about shoulder height to the floor. Two moaned. Three were limp. Where one of them had had eyes, was congealed blood and flesh. One of them had thighs down which blood had spurted and run, and then dried. He was never going to pee by the side of a road, for he had nothing left to pee with. He turned where he hung. He turned more and his eyes, still there, stared in terror out of hell.

Another, unharmed except for the unnatural stretch in his arm from which he had been hung, stared out of living eyes, black and smouldering.

Huntermann looked at them briefly, and then talked to one of the men who stood nearby. The man wore a western suit and had a face that seemed all the more ruddy for the pallor of the victims.

'All right?' said Huntermann finally.

'That one's mine,' said the one who seemed to think he was more important than any other there. 'He said he was the people's man. He said he would fight corruption by the state and me. Me! Yes, that one's mine.'

'That one's yours,' he said slowly, and the eyes of the guard who had locked the door glanced impassively at the man who had said, foolishly, 'That one's mine.' He knew menace in Huntermann's voice when he heard it.

'Over here,' said the guard.

The others joined him while Huntermann stood his ground. At the far end of the warehouse, near huge doors, an open lorry waited. He produced his handgun and moved to one side, so that his line of fire was clear of the lorry. He raised his gun and took aim at one of them, stock-still.

He lowered the gun and said over his shoulder to the guard: 'Get them moving.'

The guard went to the nearest of the line of hanging, tortured, men, went to half a cabinet of the duly elect, a nation's hopes, and pulled one of them back and then heaved him suddenly forward into the next one. The men swung into each other, swinging and swaying, and some of them moved their legs, some their free arms, back and forth, up and down, grotesque. One screamed quite suddenly, and another wept.

Huntermann raised his gun again, took aim, and began to fire rapidly. Movement, blood, slumping death, and the screaming of one man. Silence finally, but for a bubbling and a fart, and the sudden, nervous laugh of one of the watchers.

'Didn't know that dead men fart.'

A door opened beyond steam and vats, acid vats, their sides encrusted by processes that made metal shine, and men's flesh and bones dissolve to sludge. Pulleys worked, wheels ran through thick oil, bodies swung, and blanched and tortured feet poised before being lowered into the vats, where the acrid liquid welcomed them with a hiss.

Huntermann turned from the swinging, dropping, dissolving bodies without a word and said, with his back to them, 'Keep one for the wolves, but disfigure it so it cannot be identified. Just one . . .'

Then he was gone the way he came, out of the building and back to his car.

He sat there for a long time, planning. From the far side of the warehouse a sluice opened and thick gunge began to flow, loosened by the black water that fed into it. It flowed

*and gathered pace, off beneath another building, round
past piles of crude metal bars, past three abandoned containers and thence, free at last, beneath a leaning metal
perimeter fence, across a field of poppies fluttering in the
breeze and finally slurping and sliding through a pipe to
plunge into the waters of a stream, frothing with pollution,
but flowing on and on, a vile mix of Wulf knows what,
westward, eastward, northward, and to the south, a flow
of gunge and filth, poison and pollution made of men by
Mennen, across a land whose final boundary was not even
sea: for beyond that, beyond the furthest horizon, where
the sky rose up to night, were stars and ancient wolfways,
and there and only there the atmosphere was clear, and
light was pure.*

*Down on the polluted earth Huntermann turned the key
in his car, revved up, reversed, and drove home to his wife,
and the love of his daughter-child.*

Klimt remained uneasy long after the others had fallen
asleep, and then on into the early morning. Then, taking
Tervicz with him, he began to quarter the ground beyond
where he thought he had sensed the Mann, finally picking
up the scent of saliva and sweat on a patch of rock and
heather. They found a weak scent away from the spot and
trailed it cautiously downslope. A long way, and only when
mid-morning was long past, did they reach its end, where
it was subsumed by the oily scents of a vehicle.

They padded about and Tervicz picked up the smell of
the Mann's urine. Acrid where the grass was still damp at
the root, subtler higher up: unpleasant finally.

'One to remember,' said Klimt, and they swung round
back the way they had come, and left the Mann's scent to
die into the ground, and be gone. They summoned the
others to witness what they had found.

Morten scented the Mann's marking and summoned Stry who did the same.

'Well?'

There was fear in Stry's eyes.

'It is the scent of Huntermann,' he said.

Huntermann was the Mann who had killed their sister with a single shot. He came silently, he shot, he pissed, he left.

Was he one or many? wondered Klimt. One like the Mann who was benign, or many like the Mennen who were not. Stry did not know anything beyond the fear and dread he felt scenting Huntermann.

That night, an hour to the south, they found a Mann's corpse, white and swollen under the stars. Magyars were about. They scented it, and Klimt simply said, 'Not the Huntermann.'

He meant the scent they had found earlier; but as he said it he remembered the other Mann, the Mann whose scent was benign, the Mann he suddenly feared the corpse might be.

He scented it again, relieved and curious.

'Leave it untouched . . .' he began, turning away. But then he changed his mind and turned back to stand over the corpse. Strangely, his eyes look less bleak than they sometimes did. There was compassion in them, and sadness.

The others had kept some distance away, as if to go near the dead white thing, which glistened with night-dew, and stank sweet and sour, might bring them ill-luck. Klimt stood so still, so impressive, that they grouped a little nearer.

'It is ancient lore that we do not kill the Mennen,' he began. 'It was thought that for each one of them we might kill, they would return to kill a thousand of us. But . . .' and now his voice dropped to almost a whisper, and his head hunched over the corpse almost possessively,

'. . . once, not so long ago, I had reason to kill a Mann.'

They gasped, astonished and horrified, except for Tervicz who had long since known this, and that the Mann had tortured one of Klimt's cubs.

Klimt continued: 'It gave me no pleasure and nor did I have to do it. It was for punishment I did it. But . . . know this. I did not die as a result, though Wulf knows I was harried almost to death. Nor did a thousand wolves die as we might have feared. A Mann did what he should not do and I killed him. For centuries, for a whole millennium, Mennen have done what they should not do, to us, and to all creatures, and to the land as well. They have gone unpunished. Now . . . I do not know if we should kill them . . . I do not know. I know only that I no longer fear to think of it, and nor should the day come again will I fear to do it.

'As for *eating* Mennen, well then . . .' and here he half-smiled and shook his head. 'Do they smell like good food to you? No, unless the circumstances be special no wolf under my command shall ever do such a thing. Mennen are tainted in spirit and therefore they will be tainted in body. Smell it!'

He nodded his head at their disgust and disquiet.

'But wolves, you shall touch it. Yes, you *shall* . . .' and he growled threateningly as some of them sought to move away.

'Touch it so that you shall remember not to fear something that is only flesh and blood and bones like us. Touch it to be free of lore that we may need to change. Touch it *now*.'

One by one they did so, some nervously, some with curiosity; some with snout and some with paw. Touched, examined and scented at the flesh and the wounds and the orifices of something each had been raised to fear and now would never look on in the same way again.

Then they moved off a little way; but that was not quite the end of their knowledge of that corpse. A little while later they heard the slink and run of alien wolves, and then they scented them. Magyars. A bark, a soft howl of pleasure, and Klimt sent Tervicz to find out what he could.

He came back grim-faced.

'Come and see for yourselves,' he said with disgust, 'and don't worry even if they *are* Magyars: they are too absorbed in what they are doing to bother with keeping watch.'

They crept forward once more and saw, by the light of star and moon, Magyars feasting on Mennen flesh. Their heads and maws shiny with the grease and flesh of their foul toil, the corpse shifting and rising as if alive again, as one pulled its limbs away from another, and one sought to win the softest flesh, while a third tussled at the head.

'Magyars!' said Tervicz, and that said it all.

Then Klimt led them away as one, closer now, grimmer, shadows disappearing into the deep and future night.

CHAPTER TWENTY-TWO

*Klimt and his pack prudently choose to flee
the Magyars; while Ambato dares to journey alone to where
he hears the gods call his name*

I T WAS IN LATE APRIL that a new urgency overtook
the pack's search for a territory. It was Ambato who
knew why first, and Klimt only second: of the others,
Morten and Stry guessed why soon enough. Tervicz, most
innocent of them all in the ways of families and new life,
did not guess at all until he was told.

'Our ledrene's got herself with cub,' said Stry laconically
one morning. 'Why else do you think our worthy leader is
restless as dry birch leaves in a breeze?'

But for all his irony he sounded pleased, and his eyes
could not keep from glancing with respect at Elhana, who
lay dozing near a tree, and with excitement at Klimt.

'Within a few days Klimt's finally going to have to decide
where we're going to stop and establish ourselves, or
Elhana will do it for him. Once her cubs start moving inside
she'll not want to be wandering about all over the Tatra,
she'll insist on a place to call her own.'

'As far from the Eastern Rivers as possible, if she's got any
sense,' added Spry. They now called the valley headlands to
the east where the Magyars had their stronghold the 'Eastern Rivers'.

'Oh,' said Tervicz, to whom all this talk was as nothing
compared to the knowledge that if they were right then

Klimt would become true leader of them all, and he, Tervicz, member of a pack with young, which meant . . .

'Which *means*,' he said a little later to Klimt whom he had joined where he stood at a vantage point he had found, surveying the landscape to the west, 'that we're going to have our work cut out watching over her and *them*.'

His voice expressed not only his excitement, but real concern as well, for all he could remember of his own cubhood was the way his father led him and his siblings from one hide to another, harried by the Magyar wolves, never able to rest or to settle. To Tervicz it felt that the pattern must repeat itself, only this time he was one of those charged with the task of protection.

'You are right to feel worried, Tervicz, as I know only too well,' said Klimt.

There was something in his voice, some strain of bitterness and loss, that Tervicz caught. Klimt had told him a little about how he had fathered young before, but of the circumstances of their loss he had spoken once only, and his friend had not inquired further. Klimt was not a wolf who spoke so personally, nor one another dared ask to talk about such things more than he cared to.

So Tervicz glanced at where Klimt stood in profile, and observed the loss in his eyes without comment.

'We shall find a worthy place to raise the young, I expect,' he said. 'Perhaps . . .' —

Klimt turned to look at him and then nodded curtly, which was his way of telling another that on this occasion he could express a view.

'. . . I was going to say that perhaps you will decide that since things have now changed we shall retreat from the area the Magyars control, to find a safe haven where the pack can rear and raise the young without interference. After all, if the Magyars learn . . .'

'They will have guessed by now where we are,' said Klimt.

'. . . then if they think about it long enough, they will re-double their efforts to get rid of us, *especially* an alien wolf's young.'

'Hmmph!' said Klimt noncommittally, still staring at Tervicz, though in that blank, cold way he adopted when he was thinking hard. Tervicz stayed where he was, and finally settled down, scenting at the air, enjoying the sounds of late spring, of the chattering and warning calls of birds, the touch of fresh, green growth that was coming now to grass and shrub, and to the early-leafing trees.

But Klimt seemed to be enjoying none of this at all, lost as he was with his thoughts.

In the old days (as Tervicz now thought of that time when he and Klimt had first met and journeyed to the fells) Klimt might have talked of what it was that worried him. But now, leader as he was, his decisions were more lonely ones, for a leader who consults too widely is too often a leader confused. Yet Tervicz guessed that today at least his presence nearby was some kind of help.

'We must never forget the reason why we came here, each one of us from a different place, each one to help form our pack. But the pack is not yet complete, Tervicz.'

'It will be when the young are born.'

Klimt shook his head.

'Oh no, there are others to come yet. Do you think we are the only Wolves of Time? No, I shall know when we are complete. Our young shall be our purpose, not our completion. I worry that she is with cub before the others who are coming have found us. We cannot leave the Heartland now. We must stay for a while in the hope that others will come. Though for the sake of our coming young I would prefer to find a place further from the Magyar threat, but for the pack . . . we must stay.'

'There, the decision is made,' thought Tervicz not liking it at all. Nor did the others like it, not one bit, and they grumbled as they followed Klimt on across the territory of the Heartland in search of a place to make their own. Sites that could be defended, approaches that could be watched, a choice of prey, water . . . and freedom from harassment at the paws of the Magyars. That was all they asked for!

'He'll not find anything *this* way,' grumbled Stry as they went, 'for it's still too near the Eastern Rivers. Anyway, Mennen come here for the snow in winter as their structures show, and it's a job to avoid them camped out on the ground away from the roads in the summer . . .'

If Klimt heard it, he ignored it. They had a good few days yet before they really needed to find somewhere to settle down, and he had long since decided that if all else failed they *would* retreat, back to the ancient gully down which he and Tervicz had first run to rescue Elhana. The gully was as good a place as any to raise young, and Morten and Stry, now accepted by the others, confirmed it to be on the very edge of the Magyars' general territory and, as such, it was not quite beyond the limits of where he was prepared to stay.

Meanwhile they must press on, learning all they could, not always believing what Morten and Stry said, for they saw this landscape with over-familiar eyes, and a leader, whilst he must always listen, must always see as much for himself as he can.

So, grumbling still, discontented as all wolves are when their grouping is not yet quite a pack, and they have no place to call their own, they carried on for another day, and then another . . .

Until, on the third day after Klimt's brief conversation with Tervicz, the Magyars suddenly appeared in force once more.

This time there was nothing surreptitious about their coming. They were simply there, spread out across the rising trail among the rocks and trees beyond which mountains rose.

At their head now was one of the wolves Klimt had injured in his rescue of Elhana.

'Well at least our friend Hassler isn't here,' breathed Stry, grouping with the others tight enough to defend each other, loose enough for the enemy not to be able to focus on one part of them for attack.

'I'm going to have *you*,' said the leading Magyar to Elhana immediately with an unpleasant smile. Then he looked insolently at Klimt and said, 'You'd better get out of the Heartland while you can. Stay here and you'll be dead, and all this lot with you except for *her*, and she'll *wish* she was once Hassler has his way with her. Which he will! He will . . .'

As their leader of the moment, the wolf did not quite have the authority to be taken seriously, and nor did those around him carry themselves with anything more than the mob style of younger breakaways from a bigger pack. The wolf looked round for support to his friends, who sniggered appeciatively at his words.

They waited then for a response from Klimt, who gave them none at all, but stared, and waited in his turn. His own wolves gathered closer in, with Elhana in their midst, her own eyes searching out for any females amongst those that opposed them but finding only one. She was a thin, weak-looking thing and not as bold as the others tried to be. She looked merely tired, and abused.

Thus far, in all their wanderings, Klimt's wolves had not met a single female other than Elhana herself, and so there had never been any challenge to Elhana's role as ledrene. How she might fare against another none could know, though if this was the only female opposition she was likely to meet hereabouts then Elhana would be ledrene of all she surveyed for many a season yet.

The two packs, or nearly-packs, stood off one from the other, stiff-legged and restless, while Klimt remained much where he had been, proud and too formidable for the Magyars to risk challenging him. But unease was in the air, and the possibility that any moment now other Magyars might arrive and change the balance of things.

'It's what they like to do, you see,' whispered Morten. 'They go out in parties from the main den-ground, keeping an eye on things, seeking out food, ready to spy out aliens and warn off the less interesting ones. Then, if they find an alien or two they alert the leader and do as he commands. Chances are he's about somewhere, though in this location it would be hard for him and any others to take us much by surprise. But then they have probably never had a pack try to form itself in their midst before, nor wolves that neither flee nor challenge. They will be confused.'

Klimt turned at last from facing out the Magyars, honour satisfied for now and called Tervicz over to him, glancing westward where the ground fell away to one of the many valleys that dissected those parts. Tervicz nodded and was gone, but southward, the way they had come, and not at all in the way Klimt had looked.

'So tell me, Morten,' asked Klimt loudly, 'is this the kind of rabble the Magyars normally produce?'

Morten grinned, enjoying the rage on the Magyars' faces.

But his reply was serious and quiet enough that the Magyars did not hear: 'Don't be in any doubt, Klimt: there'll be others nearby. Is that why you've sent Tervicz off? To find a route away?'

'Maybe,' said Klimt, turning back towards the enemy.

Tervicz's sudden disappearance had caused interest and movement among them, though not at all as Klimt might have expected. True, there was nothing surprising in the fact that one of the Magyars loped off after Tervicz, taking an elliptical course well clear of the aliens before speeding off to keep an eye on his quarry. But what was unexpected was that the other Magyars now began to whisper to the bedraggled-looking female in their midst who, at first, tried to ignore them, and then to shift her ground away from them, though not outside their orbit.

But at last she could prevaricate no more and was forced to listen, with lowered head, to whatever it was the Magyar in charge was instructing her to do. As he talked urgently she glanced up occasionally towards Elhana who, aware suddenly that she was now the target of the others' interest sat up attentively, her ears forward, her front paws firming on the ground.

All of them became restive, tails jerking, ears flicking, each glancing at each other, uneasy, ready for action, ready to panic. The Magyar female rose and moved forward through her own pack, eyes narrowing on Elhana. This told the others that this was a matter for females – a challenge perhaps, a test probably, a trap just possibly. In such matters between females, males did not ever interfere unless there was a threat to the pack as a whole – but it paid to stay watchful, and anyway, it was a matter of some interest to see what happened. What else was there to do so long as the leaders of the two groups were willing to let the day pass sitting it out?

Elhana watched, apparently with indifference, but in fact her mind was racing, assessing, and finally deciding. Her years as ledrene of the Benevento pack had taught her much, and most of all that the best actions struck a balance between thought and instinct, and were best put in a general context before they were decided on.

This context was made up of several elements, all of which she had been thinking about for most of the time she had been sitting 'doing nothing'. For one thing it was plain that a general attack was in the offing, and probably from more than just the wolves who dallied across the ground above them. Klimt had sent Tervicz off to reconnoitre, so that there was a known escape route if he needed it – or rather two, for they could always go back the way they had come.

Then there was the fact that thus far, because there had been no other females in their group, Elhana had not had a chance to show her fighting skills and ability to dominate. To do so now, before she got too heavy with young, might well be prudent, and she wished to establish her strengths in the males' minds at least. Males were gossips and would warn arriving females what they might expect . . . A fight is best won if it is never fought.

Then there was instinct, and the sense that this female who approached her now was discontented and dismayed: she seemed a wolf constrained by circumstance. Such wolves, once beaten, often became allies. They needed another female in their ranks . . .

'And *finally* . . .' Elhana told herself as she readied herself for the move she must make, 'Tervicz is coming back upslope towards us and a diversion will give him time to report to Klimt, and time for our retreat to begin, for retreat it must be. We are in no position to fight pack to pack . . .'

It was not the grace with which Elhana then rose and moved swiftly forward, nor even the general speed of it, though that was impressive enough, no . . . it was the ferocity and skill with which she crowded her opponent back and to the side of the group of Magyars, to their west side, just where Klimt would wish her to be if they retreated.

Her front paws biffed and buffeted, her jaws snapped yet avoided drawing blood, her more powerful shoulders heaved, twisted and shoved the female down.

It was fast, furious and effective, and when the Magyar female made a final twist to try to get away, which failed,

Elhana stood over her and gazed down into her eyes before they had turned away, and as her flanks heaved with the stress of it, her throat lay open, vulnerable, and she was beaten.

Elhana had seen enough in those eyes to know what it was the wolf wished to say but could not.

'The answer,' whispered Elhana into her ear, 'is that "yes" you may join us, if the others will have you, but never forget what wolf it was first permitted it. Loyalty I reward, treachery, weakness, deceit all sicken me. I have seen enough of them.'

'Yes, ledrene,' whispered the wolf in muffled reply, and then, almost eagerly, 'yes . . .'

'And your name?'

'Jicin,' she replied.

As Elhana moved away to let the beaten female rise and rejoin her own it seemed that a shadow fell across them all. She herself backed way immediately into the midst of her friends, who had regrouped around Klimt and Tervicz. There was a new and different air about the place now, the very trees seemed to have darkened, the ground to have become chill and hard and such spring colour as there had been in the shrubs and fields, even in the sky, was gone.

Two wolves emerged from shadows beyond the Magyars and stared. Leader and ledrene had arrived.

'Hassler,' breathed Morten.

'And his mate,' said Tervicz, of the hag of a wolf that crouched behind him.

'Dendrine,' said Stry, and something chilled in Tervicz's heart: for though he could scarcely believe it, and did not know what she looked like for he was too young when she had left, he looked upon the female who had killed his mother. He shuddered and felt ill, for in her features he saw something of the cast of his sister Szaba's face.

The two stood above the rest, with the others backing

and ranging about them, males and the female, all staring implacably at Klimt.

Hassler was vast, his head huge and rough, his jaws almost misshapen in their muscular strength, his shoulders torn and scarred with years of fighting and of dominance.

His mate, Dendrine, rose up from crouching behind him, slighter and grubbier, without the kind of grace or obvious strength that made Elhana so plainly meant to be ledrene. Her face seemed almost to smile, her eyes to glitter, but they were the smiles and glitters of an intelligent cruelty, and the smug confidence of one who knows she is most powerful, ledrene, mother, tormentor, torturer of any who might seek to disobey her, murderer of any who displeased her, destroyer of any who might even think to displace her in the affections of her brute lord.

One other thing was plain, to Elhana at least. From the same gaunt flanks, the same haggard fur, and her frightened glances, it was surely now clear that Jicin was Dendrine's unhappy daughter. By comparison, Jicin seemed a gentle forlorn thing; and all the frightful years of bullying, of deprivation and of lovelessness there must have been from mother to daughter seemed to be there before them now.

'Our friends have come then, for a closer look!' said Hassler in the mocking, confident way he had. 'Eh Dendrine? And what do we make of them?'

'We make puke of them,' said Dendrine, scratching herself and grinning slyly to reveal her yellow teeth. 'We make shit of them. We make everything but friends with them, lord.'

This 'lord' was spoken in a ghastly sing-song way, and contained strange elements of irony and subjugation which seemed quite at odds with each other. It was as if one flank of Dendrine was almost mocking her mocking mate, while the other flank was opening itself with masochistic enjoyment to whatever pleasures he might care to take with her.

Then Hassler moved so fast that those around him startled and then froze. He moved his head to grasp at a young male that stood nearby, take his neck fur in his teeth, yank him over and down onto the ground, before he said, 'Vollutt, see where the aliens stand?'

'I do, father,' said the subjugated Vollutt, striving not to get grit and humus in his mouth, whilst also seeking to look at what his father bade him see.

'What have they come for then?'

'Things that should not concern them,' said Vollutt hopefully.

It seemed that such ritual humiliation by public interrogation was something he was used to.

'*That's* certainly true,' said Hassler, flicking Vollutt away from him with almost no movement at all, so that one moment his son was lying on the ground, and the next he was up on his paws again, 'but *then* . . .'

He seemed about to turn to another one of the wolves, probably another of his sons indeed, to mete out the same treatment, as a way no doubt of instilling in Klimt and the others the same fear and dread that he appeared to have imposed upon his brood of followers. In which he had partially succeeded, for certainly Morten and Spry, and Tervicz too, were staring in consternation at him.

The more so because as he spoke the wolves around him seemed to shift and paw the ground in a curious regular way, moving a little nearer to each other all the time they did so. Hassler's talk, his smooth brutality, and Dendrine's lascivious, mocking words and her movements at his flank, all conspired to make quite unmistakeable that very shortly the whole foul pack of Magyars were going to attack.

'So *you* are the guardians of the Heartland?' said Klimt suddenly.

He said it coldly and with a strong hint of disbelief.

Hassler frowned, puzzled perhaps by facing one who

feared him not; Dendrine's eyes narrowed and grew more interested in Klimt, and then in Elhana who stood just a little way behind him and Tervicz. Then she peered closely at Tervicz and said dismissively, 'What's *he*?'

'I am . . .' began Tervicz, hating her, wanting to tell her what he was to her, wanting to declare that he was of Bukov, as she was.

'You are disobedient,' said Klimt, shutting him up. 'Well?' he continued, unabashed. 'And are you guardians whose task is to keep all away? Or did Wulf appoint you guardians until others come who may know what to make of the Heartland when the dark millennium ends?'

Hassler blinked and shook his head in wonder, as if some puny, youthful male had dared to challenge him and he could not quite work out why. Suddenly he smiled benevolently. 'None may enter the sanctuary of the WulfRock,' intoned his son Vollutt suddenly, almost comically, as if it was a phrase learned and repeated through previous generations so many times that its original meaning was quite lost and it might now serve to ease an awkward situation.

Klimt heard it, and felt a shiver down his spine at this first mention by the Magyars of the sacred place. If they spoke of it in this way then they must know where it was.

'None visit it?' said Klimt. 'None except the Wolves of Time!'

Hassler blinked once more, uncomprehending. The Magyars, who fancied themselves the greatest pack of all, and as such had been charged with the holiest and most difficult of tasks, seemed to have declined into a world of ignorance.

Meanwhile Dendrine had shifted her attention from Tervicz to Elhana.

'Such a handsome thing, such pretty eyes,' she muttered.

Klimt turned from them quite suddenly and nodded at

Tervicz, who moved quickly past the others to the edge of the slope to the west.

'This way,' purred Tervicz, grinning. 'Let us leave the guardians to guard.'

'What!' roared Hassler.

Then Tervicz was gone and the others after him, swift as the shadows of driven clouds across a valley floor on a sunny day.

'*You!*' roared Hassler, ordering Klimt to stop.

This was to Klimt who watched over the others as they left smoothly, until he himself was last; then, with a final forbidding stare he too was gone, leaving behind him an astonished gathering of wolves which, looking to Hassler for guidance, erupted in curses and recriminations as Hassler himself roared after them.

While Dendrine cried, 'Follow the filth that was here! *Follow it!*'

There was a certain exhilaration in the chase downslope from the spot where they had had their confrontation. For one thing Tervicz chose a clever route – steep and dangerous, but easy enough to follow for any who were led, as he led them now. For another they had the advantage of surprise and leadership from Klimt behind.

With the Magyars left in temporary disarray the surprise was everything, and down Klimt's wolves charged one after another, down and down by way of crumbling screes and clumps of precarious grass that disintegrated under their paws leaving behind no grip as good as the one their quarry had had.

At the bottom of the drop at last, gathered together for a last gleeful stare back up the steep face towards the Slavs, Tervicz broke through their glee with a cry of alarm.

'Where's Ambato?'

It was the most shocking of moments, and one which of them all Klimt felt most sear his soul. Somewhere, somehow, Ambato had been lost. Not at the top of the slope, for several had seen him start on down, nor at the bottom, for Tervicz had been first down and was sure he had not come down with the others: somewhere coming down he had been lost.

Above them they could hear the shouts and curses of the descending Magyars coming ever nearer, and see now at the head the furious form of Hassler himself, leaping from point to point on the descent, urging his followers on, coming ever nearer.

Klimt looked up, looked around, and said, 'Did anyone see Ambato fall?'

No.

'Did any see him diverge from the rest of us?'

No, not even Stry in front of whom Ambato had been.

'I saw him ahead, I slowed, I paused, and then he was not there. I guessed he had gone down a little faster than me.'

'How far down were you when you last saw him?' asked Tervicz urgently.

'Halfway up,' said Stry.

'We cannot go back,' said Klimt firmly. 'Any wolf climbing up towards that rabble of Magyars will be caught and killed. It would be impossible to fight back upslope. At least their descent does not appear to have been interrupted by discovery of Ambato, as surely it would have been if they had found him. If he fell he is lying low and unseen. If he took a different route then he may be safer than any of us, for the Magyars are following us and not him. We shall continue on and later, when we are safe, we shall consider ways to find him again. Ambato may be old, but he is a wolf of great experience . . . Come!'

He turned to lead them on and away towards the shore

of a lake that lay a little below and whose far fringes of forest would offer them a clean escape.

'Elhana, come.'

She alone had delayed, to stare in shock and disbelief that so swiftly she might have lost her father. But Klimt's voice of command was harsh, cold, and spoken not to the mate that carried the future of the pack within her now, but to an individual who now threatened its safety.

'Come, wolf,' he roared at her, nipping at her flanks and drawing blood. 'Obey!'

Even then she thought, too, of Jicin, wondering if she might have been able to escape the Magyars and join Klimt's group. It seemed that now it could not be.

'Elhana!' Klimt roared one last time.

Then he turned, knowing she must follow or be abandoned, and led them down towards the lake, and then around its rocky edge until they reached the safety of more trees. There they turned and looked back to see the last of the Magyars reaching the bottom of the steep descent and assembling around Hassler before they continued the chase.

'They're not going to give up easily,' said Klimt regretfully. Had they done so then he and the others could have lain low a while until the way back was clear, and then gone in search of Ambato. As it was they must journey on, and each hour travelled one way put three hours between them and the one they had lost: an hour to return, an hour to catch up to where he had been, and an hour to where he might have gone.

'Come on . . . !' and they followed Klimt once more in close single file, heads low, tails sunk, angry with themselves and with their leader.

'Come *on*!' roared Klimt, snapping at the one behind. And they had to go.

*   *   *

Ambato stared ruefully down the steep scree slope at the last of the Magyars as they stumbled and swore in the chase to catch up with Klimt and his fellow fugitives. He stared and ached, watched and winced, peered about for others still to come and nuzzled at his legs and flanks to see if it was more than bruising and abrasions that he had suffered in his lunging fall.

He remembered the void ahead of him, he remembered desperately pulling off to one side to avoid it and find a paw-hold, *any* paw-hold, that would save him from tilting forward, turning scrabbling in the air, thumping down and down and down hard again, stars in his eyes of a most unwelcome kind, dust and grit in his mouth, a world turning away from him which he could not control, and then . . . then a dim memory of knowing he must crouch and hide, pulling himself into shadow.

He had regained consciousness to find the huge, malevolent shape of Hassler almost within reach of the shadowed ledge under which he hid, standing there, shouting commands, to wolves above and wolves below. Then he turned and was gone.

Ambato saw it all: the arrival of Klimt at the bottom, their evident distress at seeing he was not there, their discussion about the wisdom of climbing back up to find him. 'Don't even try,' he urged them silently. 'Don't risk yourselves for one who is past his prime and has brought danger to you by his clumsiness.' And then Klimt's sharp and audible command to all of them, especially Elhana, to follow him.

Ambato watched his friends set off around the lake and then disappear into scrub near the forest trees. Beyond that, and looming above, the hillside rose steeply once more into a different and darker rock, cleft with gullies, places to hide. Then he watched with some respect at how Hassler gathered his pack about him and began to impose order and purpose upon them after Klimt's well-planned escape. Perhaps they were not used to resistance and so had been slow to respond to it, but now they recovered themselves before Ambato's eyes and set off in pursuit of Klimt.

Guessing that some wolves might have stayed behind and still be above him – 'That Dendrine for one!' thought Ambato with a shudder – he decided to stay where he was and not move at all. None could see him, though a troublesome raven, which scented the blood from his cuts and grazes hovered about and drew attention to where he was.

'I'll move at dusk,' he told himself, hoping to sleep away his pain. 'I'll set off to find Klimt and the others then.'

When he woke it was night, and a murky one, for there was a drizzle of rain from the clouds that obscured moon and stars. His pains were worse and he knew in his heart that he was badly hurt somewhere inside, somewhere deep where an old wolf begins to die. He hardly wanted to move at all.

'Yet . . .'

Ambato heaved himself up, scented at the miserable air, and began to contour his way along the steep slope, doing his best not to disturb rocks and soil, able to keep his height by reference to the pale shine of the lake below, and the stolid rise of the mountains ahead. He knew it was no good trying to find Klimt for now. All he could do was to get away to somewhere safe where he might rest up for a few days and recover.

Soon each step was painful to his flanks, each twist seemed to reach into his gut and stab it with broken rock, each moment to slide away from the one before and the one ahead in dull agony of not knowing where he was, where he was going . . .

'Wulf, guide me, guide me . . .' he whispered brokenly,

for the night was dreadful and long and he could find no place to rest, or hope for any wolf to help. Ambato wept with pain.

'Help me, great Wulf, show me to a place of rest and respite. Do not let me die without knowing the journey of my life held the purpose which I had faith I would one day find. Help me now.'

Dawn came and with it a wolf unable to move more. He scraped a place and slept, watching as rain swept across the trees below, and dripped from the rocks above that gave him shelter. A day of clinging on to memories to stop drowning in the sea of pain.

'Lauria, my dear, our daughter has the light of grace. Lauria, be proud. Lauria, you were the only one I loved. Lauria . . .'

Ambato lay broken all that long day, his memory of the wolf he had loved for so long his only comfort; the life of their daughter, his only hope. By nightfall he could not move his left hind leg, nor feel any more the pain in his gut. Just cold, cold, a cold that beckoned him to sleep some more . . .

Fighting that dangerous temptation he staggered up, dragging his stiff limb, stumbling for a time in the gloom before, finding the semblance of a way between ancient boulders and the rising cliffs and gullies beyond the plateau he found himself upon, he set off once more. He knew that if he stopped he might well sleep and die, but what he hoped to find ahead to save him from a fate that seemed increasingly appealing to him now, he did not know.

He mumbled and groaned in his pain; he swore; he scowled into the night and dared the darkness to take shape and form and attack him now. He did not care. The shapes of cliffs loomed above him, the thrusts and overhangs of rock stooped down at him, the jags of shattered rock across which he went tore at his paws, but Ambato cared not now.

He dared such dangers and shadows to take him. He dared because he did not care.

Then suddenly he fell, not far, but far enough to rip his flank open and feel the hot blood of his wound before it grew sticky and congealed down his thin fur. He laughed the cracked laugh of madness and of age, and clambered back up to the way from which he had fallen, and swore at it that it made him fall. He carried on, and on into the dawn; and on into the morning, head low, knowing he must not stop.

'Ambato!'

Was it Wulf who called his name? Was it Wulf who loomed down at him from the grey shadows out of which he awoke?

'Ambato, wolf of faith, awake, awake . . .'

He knew her voice just as he had heard it before, many times before, as many times as he had had previous lives. He knew, or now remembered that he knew, the way he had been on.

'Ambato, follow me,' he thought he heard Wulfin say.

Not daring to look up, yet knowing all, even where he must put his torn paws if he was to survive, he followed the voice of Wulfin, mate of Wulf, saviour of the faithful fallen.

'Ambato . . .'

Her voice, like her paws, echoed away ahead of him, and she laughed softly, to tell him he had done well, and was safe, and must go no further.

'Ambato . . .' he said, speaking his own name to wake himself, 'sleep now, wolf!'

He opened his eyes and knew for the moment before sleep closed them again to where he had come. The light that was so gentle and yet so bright told him. The peace the place offered told him.

The rise of dark rock about him higher and higher, and

in front, across the bright green sward, over which lay the bleached bones and skulls of rabbit and of deer, like stars, the way rose up and was lost among gullies he must not yet ascend but where, hidden now, but waiting for the Wolves who would one day dare to go that way, must be the WulfRock itself.

But where he was would give him succour and respite, here where prey would come and he might feed unseen; here where the clear waters of healing dripped and ran from the sheer cliffs above; here where the grass was so green, that it seemed to him to verge towards blue, into blue, the blue of a sky into which he could fall, and sleep, and sleep . . . Ambato had almost come home to the place he had been lost to since the very beginning of time.

'Great Wulfin, receive me now,' he whispered, wanting death.

'No wolf,' she said gently above him, all around him, holding him, 'not yet, my dear . . .'

Then Ambato knew the blessed darkness of a sleep that would heal him, and a She-wolf who would guide him from danger back to safety, and thence back into the light of day.

CHAPTER TWENTY THREE

*Ambato discovers that he is not yet immortal,
and Jicin, Dendrine's daughter, speaks of the WulfRock*

DAYS LATER, AMBATO AWOKE, convinced that his journey to the stars was complete, and the gods themselves had found him.

Muttering by a silvery lake, a lake that was not unlike the one around which he had watched Klimt and the others race away from the Magyars, he sat up, and stared about himself in confusion. He was certain of one thing only, and that was that he must find Klimt and tell him what he had so nearly found . . .

Oh, but he was beset by sorrow at the peace he had left behind.

He rose to his paws once more, conscious with sudden delight that he was without pain.

His sorrow to have left it all behind and come back to this world once again was mixed with the sense of duty that he felt that where he had been, or nearly been, the others must go. Wulfin would guide them there, and Wulf would be beyond the Rock itself, within the Rock, which was eternity.

'He's there, and she is waiting and I . . . I must find . . . must . . .'

'Old wolf, be still, you are safe with us.'

Then Ambato's vision cleared of the sorrows and compulsions that confused him and he saw the waters of the lake, and the trees on the far side, and the gods who stood staring at him.

'You,' he said, head swimming, the ripple of water in his ears, the breeze cool and pleasant at his fur, and colder where his wounds were, soothing.

They were not gods but wolves, and neither of them seemed like Magyar wolves. One was long of leg and gangly, with shining eyes and a look that seemed to see beyond his own. The other had fur that caught the sun and if ever a wolf carried the light of grace it was he. Strong, certain, his four paws upon the ground as sure as the roots of a graceful tree, he stared curiously at Ambato, and with sympathy.

'We have watched over you for two days past, wolf. We saved you from Magyar wolves out hunting by dragging you back and forth among the rocks. Wulf knows why they did not find your scent. But then, *we* could not find your scent. Only the scent of grass and light and water pure as stars. So, what's your name wolf?'

'Ambato of the Benevento, traveller, seeker, old wolf now. I am with . . . I was with . . . my leader is Klimt of Tornesdal. And your names?'

'Aragon of the Cabrera pack,' said one.

'Lounel, last of the Auvergne,' said the other, stranger one.

'Where are you going?' asked the wolf, Aragon.

'Better to ask me where I have come from. But if I am now to go anywhere, it is to Klimt,' said Ambato, his voice sounding far away.

The wolf Lounel said, 'Well then, Ambato of the Benevento, where *have* you come from?'

'I do not quite know,' whispered Ambato, faltering. 'I cannot quite tell . . .'

He wept for loss of the place he had been.

Only when he was ready did Aragon say, 'Ambato, we'll

travel with you to meet this Klimt. Perhaps he is the wolf we seek.'

'Or if he is not, perhaps it is he who will lead us to where we must go.'

It was Lounel who spoke, but his words seemed to come down from the cliffs and gullies of the scarpland beyond the wide plateau above, and from the grass at their feet, and out of the clear water of the lake.

'Come then,' said Aragon gently, and together they went in the direction in which Klimt and the others had fled – hours before, days ago, or weeks perhaps. Ambato had no idea . . .

Hassler was not a wolf to give up readily, nor one to let those he ruled give up at all. His pack might have been taken by surprise by Klimt's decision to let Tervicz lead them helter-skelter down a broken mountainside, but once in pursuit he knew what to do. What was more, he and his fellow Magyars knew the ground better than Klimt could know it. Yet not so well as Stry and Morten, whose knowledge of this part of the Heartland now proved invaluable to Klimt and the others as they set off to escape the Magyar wolves.

Born on the northern side of the Tatra, vagrants as they had been for years upon its southern slopes, between them the two knew the terrain well, and where they were not sure of it they could read its geology and vegetation and guess where an escape route, or good hiding, might be found.

Klimt was content to let them guide the pack on, not just to escape, but to give them rest and respite as well, especially Elhana.

'We'll climb up into those gullied hills first,' said Morten, who relished such a chase as this.

'. . . and then down to those streams over to the east where there are pools, and the bears taught us to fish. Remember?' said Stry.

'I remember!'

Off they went, upslope for a few days, downslope to feed along a river bank a few days later.

But always the Magyars came on, first one sighting them, and then his call bringing the others to his flanks, ready for attack.

'I've heard that the way the Magyars do it, and always have, the cunning bastards, is by fanning out across a territory once they've lost the scent of whatever they're chasing. One of them is sure to pick it up before too long and then he howls the others to him, or reports back double quick. There are rewards for those who find the quarry, and punishments for those who don't.'

'Rewards?' wondered Tervicz, as they lolled upon a river bank having eaten their fill of trout. 'Punishments?'

'Hassler gives out the reward, and Dendrine metes out the punishments. It might be simple praise, which coming from him is so rare as to seem as if Wulf himself has spoken to you. It may be a promised punishment deferred. In special cases, very special mind, he'll give a male some time with the current sterile female . . . Which I would say is the female we briefly saw with their pack . . .'

'Jicin,' murmured Elhana.

'Never!' said Stry, without the usual irony. 'But Morten and I met a lone Magyar who told us she's Dendrine's daughter, one of the few allowed to reach maturity. They've turned her into fodder for the younger males.'

Tervicz looked shocked at this, yet wanted to know more.

'Go on,' said Klimt.

It gave Morten no pleasure to talk about such things, and he did so now as briefly and dispassionately as he could.

He told how Hassler had devised his way of keeping his subordinate males' loyalty by the promise of a coupling with some addled and over-used female or other. It was generally Dendrine's pleasure that it was one of her daughters, one, usually, that she did not like. She let Hassler abuse these females first for a time and then, if she was sterile, let others take her after her lord had finished with her.

'She likes to call him "lord"!' explained Morten heavily. 'Flatters him and gives her strange pleasure. She purrs the word. Wulfin help those put-upon females if they got with cub! That happened just the once before we made good our escape. Naturally Dendrine saw that the female concerned was outcast, her cubs killed.'

'The "female concerned", as he puts it, was Jicin,' interjected Stry quietly.

'Almost ripped them from her daughter's belly she did,' said Morten savagely, 'and killed them even as they tried to take their first breath. After that, Jicin was taken into the pack again and none ever spoke of it, except in whispers. She never got with cub again, just with disease. She's got the pox all right, and fleas. But . . . well, a male that wants it enough will have it with almost anything!'

Then he turned to Stry: 'You wouldn't think it was the same wolf, would you?'

Stry shook his head sadly and said nothing.

The mood of the wolves after the initial flight proved successful and the chase was reduced to occasional harassment was good.

But now, a pall of gloom hung about them. Ambato had gone missing, probably badly injured, and as each day went by without his re-appearance, or any hope of them finding any sign of him, Elhana seemed to grow grimmer and quieter, beset by sorrow even as she daily grew a little bigger and slower with her young.

It cannot be said that Klimt was much comfort. The responsibility of leading the pack weighed heavily on him, and put into his face and eyes the bleak chill of the Nordic wastes where he was raised. Try though Elhana sometimes did to get him to relax and be warmer and more natural, he did not soften. It was hard to wring from him the warmth a mate might normally give his ledrene, or the kindness, or hoped-for signs of care that came more naturally to others there. For each in his own way gave Elhana the comfort that Klimt could not give: Tervicz with his chatter, and his wonder at the mystery of the coming cubs. Stry by his laugher and self-deprecating irony, and most comforting of all, his conviction that Ambato would turn up safe and well; Morten by the fact of his rough presence, and the easy way he would sometimes put his flank to Elhana's, to warm her when her heart felt cold, and her faith was growing weak.

But never once did Klimt take time out from leadership to talk to her and ease her mind. Truly, he was a wolf others could respect and fear, but not a wolf any would ever find it easy to love, least of all his mate.

Yet there was little time for such reflection. Two days might go by, three at most, before the Magyars were on their trail again and the tell-tale scent of their tracks and spoor along the way were picked up, or they detected some movement and staring eyes among the rocks above the trail, or far below it, to tell that they were observed.

The one thing that Klimt had not been able to do was to lead them back to the lake near which they had lost Ambato. The Magyars had put a cordon across that route, and short of going up into the scarplands and the Tatras and circling around, which might have taken months by the time the journey was complete, there was no easy way through. So it was that, chased and harried, Klimt and the others slowly beat a retreat to the west, and then down to the south towards the area near the gully where they had first entered the Heartland. But at least one thing was in their favour – this far from the Heartland's centre the Magyars seemed to be less concerned by their presence, and perhaps Hassler was losing interest in prolonged pursuit.

'Maybe Dendrine's with young just as Elhana is,' said Stry. 'She's old, but she's been a good breeder of males, I'll give her that. Most of the Magyar packs are led by her sons, one way or another there's probably kin of her and Hassler right down the Carpathians. I've heard it said that if Hassler calls for their help he expects them to come – and they will, for they were surely drilled in obedience from the time they were cubs. So he's more than just a leader of the Magyars round the Heartland, and in that respect he's like Kobrin of all the Russias.'

It was a reference they all understood, knowing the story of how centuries before Kobrin had been a wolf who, having fought his way up to head the greatest of the Russian packs when he was barely mature, went on to dominate many others. After that, the Russian wolves were said to have a Kobrin in each generation, to whom loyalty took precedence over loyalty to the local pack leader.

Such legends had appeal, and Elhana was glad to hear of them, for they were not part of her tradition. These days none knew if there were still Kobrins any more, for since the ascendancy of the Mennen, the Russian wolves had been cut off. Maybe their isolation marked the true beginning of the decline of wolfdom. What wolf knew?

One day, after a long and all too typical period of silence, Klimt summoned them all together and announced: 'When summer comes and our cubs are long born and nurtured to safety, I'm going to send one or two of you off to search across the Magyars' territory. That way we may begin to concentrate on finding the WulfRock itself, and, perhaps find what happened to Ambato.'

This promise of action to come and the prospect of exploration and adventure in high summer after that had great appeal. It was . . .

'What's that?'

It was Tervicz who heard the sound amidst the grass and rocks above their heads, and Stry who, with a practised leap and swerve was above where the sound was heard, then pouncing down upon the shadows whence it came.

She emerged cowering, weak and bloodied, the female Jicin, daughter of Dendrine and Hassler. She came shivering into their midst where Klimt turned from her proudly, the other males feigned indifference, and only Elhana went near and looked hard into her eyes. Jicin immediately swung her tail down between her legs and lowered her head before half-lowering her body, whining her submission most pathetically.

'Well?' growled Elhana.

'I've left them . . .'

Stry snorted and snarled.

'You don't leave wolves like your parents, not alive anyway and not unless they let you. You were sent . . .'

Stry went for her, not hard but painfully enough, and she squealed and fell.

'You've still got fleas!'

Klimt turned and stared impassively.

'Leave her to Elhana,' he said. 'Tervicz, you watch her while they talk. The rest of you follow me.' At moments like that Klimt spoke with such authority that the others fell silent and did his bidding. As ever, he led them quietly away.

In fact, Klimt liked Jicin's coming no more than Stry did, but it was his policy to let every wolf have their chance, and even if it proved to be a trick of some kind, which he

353

was inclined to believe was likely, then something might still be learned from it. Another female in the pack might prove useful in the future, as any leader knows . . . But then they did not want to needlessly aggravate Hassler and Dendrine, or provoke new interest in following them just when it seemed to have declined.

Elhana and Jicin talked in low voices for a long time, one certain of herself and kindly, the other high-pitched and afraid. It had to be said that if it *was* a trick it was a dangerous one: the chances of such a wolf surviving in such a situation if she were found out were low. But what had *she* to offer *them*?

'She can wander with the pack at a distance,' decreed Elhana at last, 'but if any seek to mate with her I shall kill her myself – and maybe them as well . . .'

As ledrene this was her right – to draw such boundaries of behaviour – and her status could only be enhanced by the presence of another female wolf.

'It's more than just having another female about the place, Klimt,' she began to say that same evening, when Jicin was lingering some way off chewing at a bone which was all they granted her to eat, 'for I think there's something about her I do not dislike, something that can be nurtured in her, as goodness and courage can be nurtured in a cub. Such a wolf can teach us much about the Heartland and, if we gain her trust, about the Magyars as well.'

Klimt nodded his agreement, secretly pleased and quite impressed: he had not thought of Elhana, or any females come to that, as being capable of strategy. He betrayed nothing, but from that day Elhana gained respect in his eyes.

Reluctant though he was to be alone with Elhana in this way, there were times, usually at dusk when the loss in his eyes of a past he still tried to forget might not be seen by others, when he wished he could find the words to tell how much Elhana meant to him. She was proving to be . . . a wise ledrene. He wished he might have told her himself she was a wolf he could love, but . . . 'but, I loved and lost another and shall never risk love again.'

So he had told himself – and Tervicz in that moment of confidence months before – and so he intended it should remain.

Some movement Jicin made caught his eye, and he glanced over at her where she lurked, dowdy and forlorn, with only a look of pathetic gratitude in her eyes not to have been driven off, as she might have expected, or killed, as she probably feared.

'Yes, I suppose we need one like her around us. But we shall tell her nothing for now. We shall use her to learn from. You understand?'

Elhana nodded, knowing he was right, but feeling he was harsh. Yet perhaps a leader had to be. Still, did he always have to be so cold and so calculating? She longed sometimes for the southern sun, for dry dust on her paws, for the hum of insects and the rising fussing buzz of honey bees. For love . . .

'She will have her uses,' concurred Elhana quietly.

Elhana was right about Jicin helping to make the pack bond more closely – having her constantly on their periphery, now to the side, now behind, occasionally in front, just as Elhana herself had once been, daily confirmed their own grouping, and gradually they grew used to her. Her very exclusion made them feel more united so that, paradoxically, she began to have a role. At the same time, she grew confident in her subordination, and dared to test her boundaries by coming in closer to feed, or on a lazy day when they felt secure from the harrying Magyars, she drifted nearer and lazed with them.

At such times they would deign to ask her questions that she was pleased to try to answer, though at first her answers had been no more than, 'Really, I don't know,' or 'I couldn't say much about that,' or 'That I was never privileged to be told.'

They wanted to know about Hassler's intentions, but soon gave up on that. Such a wolf as him, as Stry and Morten had already warned, never confided in any but his mate. Then they wanted to know about where they might be safe from the Magyar for a time — so that they could decide where Elhana might safely have her young.

'Far away from Dendrine, that's the best place,' offered Jicin. 'I think that's the best. I . . . I . . .'

'Yes,, wolf?' asked Elhana, speaking more gently than the others. It was to her that Jicin spoke most.

'I mean to say, will your cubs be born soon?'

'Not long now. They grow daily and I grow more uncomfortable.'

'You've cubbed before?'

Elhana laughed and said that indeed she had, several times.

'I did once,' said Jicin miserably.

Nothing could be as bleak as the way she said 'once'. As if the once was the only time, the only time she *ever* would.

'Hmmph!' said Elhana, some instinct telling her it was better not to encourage Jicin to talk of that.

The pack asked her, too, about the WulfRock, and where it might be. Had she seen it? Had she been near?

'Near?' she whispered frowning. 'It has been near us. It is nearby *us*.'

'What do you mean?' asked Klimt, swinging round to her.

'I . . . I don't know what I mean. I didn't mean anything. I mean . . .'

'Well, do you know where it is or not?' asked Klimt, impatient.

Elhana frowned at him. That was not the way to get a timid broken female to talk, and she was right. Jicin slunk away silently, and lay down out of reach, utterly miserable.

'What *did* you mean?' Elhana asked her later.

'Magyars have been guardians of the WulfRock since the beginning of time,' murmured Jicin, 'though our lore says we must not talk of it, or ask of it, or seek to find it. But . . .'

'But what, my dear?' whispered Elhana.

'I think . . . I think perhaps . . . I . . .'

'Mmm?' murmured Elhana.

'I think it's lonely now.'

Elhana stayed silent at this, and saddened. What could she mean: 'lonely'? How could the WulfRock be lonely? Jicin was just a wolf trying to make sense of things. A wolf born in the wrong place, to the wrong parents. It was *she* who was lonely.

Like all of us in a way, added Elhana to herself. Or, at least, *like wolves born in the wrong time*.

Who was Jicin to provoke such thoughts?

'Has any living wolf been there?' asked Elhana impulsively.

'Don't know, mustn't know, can't know,' said Jicin suddenly terrified. 'Don't tell. Never tell.'

'Tell what?'

How long was Jicin's silence then! As long as all the stars took to cloud over from east to west, from north to far south. As long as it took the others to fall into deep sleep. As long as it took for stars to begin to show themselves again.

Still Elhana waited.

'I had a brother once who went away,' whispered Jicin, shivering.

'Where did he go?'

'His name is Vollutt. You saw him. My mother Dendrine used her evil arts to steal his brotherhood from me.'

'And you from him,' said Elhana, a thought that seemed never to have occurred to the humble Jicin.

'I had four cubs who went away,' she continued suddenly.

'Where did they go, my dear?'

There were stars of a kind on Jicin's dark face, and they trickled down towards dawn.

'I had a grandfather who went away.'

'To where, my love, to where?' Elhana knew that poor Jicin had named the only wolves she had ever been able to love. All, it seemed, taken from her.

'Mother said it was to keep the WulfRock company that she killed them and sent them there. I think.'

'Is it near where we have been?' asked Elhana.

Jicin nodded in the night and said, 'Oh yes, and they'll be waiting for me there. That's what I think. Wolfkind will be waiting for us all there.'

'And who are we?'

It was not Elhana's voice that spoke then. It was a voice that was deep and gentle in the night. The voice of a wolf who had known real pain and loss. The voice of one who needed darkness to hide *his* trickling, starlit tears.

The voice was Klimt's, who stood there, unthreatening now, stars on his face as well, listening.

And who are we?

'After he first saw you my father said you are the Wolves of Time. I've come because I thought you could show me where to find the ones my mother Dendrine sent away. I was scared to come. I'm scared now. But I've come because I'll find my cubs at the WulfRock where they wait. Things wait for you if you have faith they'll still be there. They wait forever until you're ready to come. They do! It's what my grandfather said before he went. It's what the Ratgeb . . .'

She did not finish this strange word but rushed ahead to say, 'It's true! At least . . . I think it is.'

Klimt stared at her for a time, and then at Elhana, and his eyes were as gentle for a moment as his voice had been.

'Sleep wolves,' he said, 'and when the time is right we shall guide each other to the WulfRock and find what we have all lost there and what waits for each of us. Sleep now, and when the morning comes, Jicin of the Magyar, you will run with us for we shall accept you to our pack. Sleep now . . .' and he turned from them, huge, strong, watchful, protective, beginning to be wise; and, in their different ways, knowing he was there and guarding them, they found that sleep was easy to find, and had been waiting patiently for each of them.

CHAPTER TWENTY-FOUR

The Magyars finally track down the Wolves of Time,
whose strength begins to fail

IT WAS A FEW DAYS after this that the Magyars began an assault upon them once more, one that soon turned serious. It was no longer a question of being harried from time to time, but became a continual attack through night and day, and then by night again by two or three of the Magyars at a time.

It began with an attack on Tervicz who had always been one to wander off, though he got back to the safety of the pack with only a buffeting and some scratches that time, and it continued with an attempt to isolate Stry and do him real injury.

After that they stayed grouped closer together, and even Jicin, as a mark perhaps that they valued her, was ordered by Klimt to stay nearby. There was no sign of Hassler himself, nor Dendrine, and while some of the others they had seen before, others were strangers to all of them, including Jicin.

'It looks as if Hassler's summoned wolves in from more distant parts, though why they do not come altogether and make a proper go of it I can't think.'

'Klimt's put fear in them,' said Morten.

'He puts fear into *me*,' said Stry, glancing at their leader as he went ahead of them, seemingly always with more energy, always with less sleep.

They had reached what Morten said was the western boundary of the Magyars' territory, beyond which, had they ventured on, Hassler would probably have given up following them, feeling they had been properly beaten and driven away. But Klimt, being Klimt, had listened, nodded, and said, 'We'll turn south then, back towards where our journey into the Heartland truly began. Eh, Tervicz?'

Tervicz grinned, suspecting that Klimt had always meant to head back for the fell above the gully down whose wolfway they had first run to save Elhana and Ambato. It made sense. They knew it, and liked it, and so far as anywhere had felt like home since they had first come to these parts, the gully was it. The gully was defensible and it was not quite within the Heartland, nor yet without it. There the honour of Hassler and Klimt might be well satisfied, the one having driven the other out, the other having not quite been driven out at all . . .

'Provided we keep on moving until we get there they'll not stop us,' Tervicz said on the grey afternoon two days after the attack began when, for a few hours, the Magyars stopped coming at them.

'The gully's not that far off, but there *is* something that will stop us moving . . .'

He glanced at Elhana for whose sake they had paused. Her time was near, for the cubbing could not be more than two or three days away, four at most.

She had looked at Klimt, and he at her, when he decreed they move south and all she had done was nod wearily with eyes that said, 'But not too far Klimt, not too far further now.'

Klimt knew why she obeyed so readily. What Jicin had told her about Dendrine had put real fear in her: she did not want her cubs to go the way of those wolves Jicin had loved, and be told that they would be waiting for her at the WulfRock.

So now they moved south with stolid urgency, each taking turns to run at Elhana's flank, not to hurry her yet not to let her lag. Each was ready now to defend her to the death though among them all she would have been the first to acknowledge that it was not for her they would die but for the future that she carried.

'How far now?' asked Morten suddenly two days later. 'I think she's . . .'

'More than a day she told me just now,' said Tervicz worriedly, 'and the Magyars . . .'

They came attacking again, from the left flank this time, and Morten automatically went for them, while Klimt backed up to Elhana and watched the right flank and the back. One thing about the Magyars: their tactics were predictable. He summoned Jicin closer, he checked Stry's position, and when the Magyars *did* come from the right, he went hard at them, vicious and unpleasant, impatient with their play. Wulf knows what damage he caused to the wolves he sent squealing, but there was blood on his face and down his front, and utter ruthlessness in his eyes. The Magyars would have to see them all dead before they got close enough to Elhana to harm a hair on her flank.

The Magyars retreated once more, but just as the wolves began to relax and get ready to retreat they saw movement across the vale out of a dark rise of pines. Hassler had come once more.

He stood there staring, implacable and still, as around him came others, more than twelve – nearly twenty counting those that had been involved in the latest attack. Klimt's heart beat faster and he knew fear then, though he did not show it.

'If we can only keep moving,' Tervicz had said and he was right. If only they could . . .

'Klimt,' whispered Elhana. 'Klimt my dear . . .' and they

knew, all of them, that her time was near now and they would not be able to move far.

'You wait,' commanded Klimt turning on her. 'You *wait*!'

It was like the cold, sheer face of rock rising before a storm: rock to wind, death to life, the darkness of night trying to hold back the dawn.

'Come!'

As they turned and left they were relieved to see that Hassler did not move but watched them go, impassive. Perhaps he did not know how near the gully they were, or if he did, that it was so defensible. Nor could he know that Elhana was so near her time.

'He's going to wait until we're so bloody tired we can't lift a paw to save her,' said Morten. 'That's his game. He knows we'll fight to kill and that we've got more to lose, so he's exhausting us.'

'Come!' commanded Klimt again, and they knew that this time there would be no halting until they reached their destination, unless the halting was for birth, and for death beneath Magyar teeth and claws.

Running desperate, afternoon to dusk. Dusk to twilight. Twilight towards night, each paw-step sore, each moving limb an ache, and for every moan they heard from Elhana they heard an answering crack of twig, the brush of low branches on enemy flanks, the dash of enemy paws, and the howling signals of Magyars following in the night.

Pause.

Klimt scented the air. Then on in a new direction, the ground more familiar as the fell they knew before came back to them; the hags of peat and heather beneath their paws as they trotted swiftly among its shallow pools and lakes which reflected the dying sky.

Klimt paused again.

Scented this way and that. Summoned Tervicz. They conferred and Klimt nodded, calm, decisive.

'You lead this last stretch, wolf. I am tired and I may make a mistake. Anyway, they are close behind and it is from there or at our flanks that they will attack. Best for me to be where I can see. Show us the way to our home now . . .'

Not the words of one who leads always from the front, and yet every wolf who heard them felt reassured.

They turned as one after Tervicz, and began to run for their lives, and the lives of the cubs Elhana carried.

A howling bark to one side, harsh in the night. A signal to approach. Then another to the other flank. Howls they knew were the signals for a final attack. Then the plash of paws from across the pool-laden fell, to right-flank and left, and from behind.

Only ahead was safe. Ahead where the gully waited. Ahead now, one after the other, each as tired as the next as from out of the darkness on either side ran the Magyar wolves, fresher, teeth glinting in the night light, eyes narrowed for the coming kills; and a barking command behind, deep, confident, mocking.

Hassler. His heavier paws sounding on the ground.

Run, Tervicz, run. . . run now, wolf, run . . .

Klimt slowed down now to let all others pass that he might be ready to turn and hold the Magyars back for a time and so let the others escape into the gully when they reached it.

Tervicz ran, searching the way ahead by scent and sight, searching and perplexed. Shapes of rocks he knew, but the pool he passed was different, smaller, dried by summer winds . . .

Near here now, off to the left, and there . . . there . . .

The hairs on his back began to rise and he to slow, for he had crossed the scent of alien wolf and it had been *ahead*.

Behind, to right, to left, all that in the dark and bloody

night was bad enough, but *ahead*, waiting for them, it was too much, too . . .

The scent again, alien and strange. Fresh. Fresh and . . .

'Come *on!*' he called. 'It's not far now! Come *on!*'

Fresh and *familiar* was that scent.

He knew the scent, or part of it.

He knew that Wulf was with them now, Wulf running with them, and he knew that he, Tervicz, last of the Bukov pack, was showing that he could route-find for others, which was his ancient task. He knew this place, this run, and he saw the eyes and teeth and heard the panting, brutal patter of the ones who chased, the same sound that wolves who were pursued had heard down the routeways of time. He knew where and what he was, and where the danger went. He had fled so many times before, through so many lives, and now he fled through a final life, a last one, and he must use all the skills he had ever learnt.

'*On!*' he cried, for ahead were the shadows of the shrubland into which the gully rose, or from which it dropped towards the quarry. Rising here and there as they approached were the great beshadowed rocks where he and Klimt had been before.

He dared to turn for a moment. Stry just behind. Elhana next, desperate and limping now and longing to stop and rest.

Morten just behind, urging her. Then Jicin almost dead on her feet, eyes wild, mouth gulping at the air as her head went from side to side in the final stages before collapse.

Behind *her*, Klimt.

Formidable and solid still, snarling to right and left at the Magyars who were almost on them now, snapping at his flanks to bring him down, their throats filled with that foul sound of blood-lust as yet unsatisfied.

Behind these the most formidable of them all: Hassler, running heavily but with ease, shoving his own wolves out of his way as he sensed that Klimt was failing and that it might be pleasant if it was he himself who brought him down and ripped the life from out of him.

While above them all, tearing across the face of the moon, the clouds of a high storm, now lit, now dark, swirling into the darkness that loomed past them all. A moon that itself seemed to rise, yellow and distorted, like the single eye of a mad, corrupted enemy.

Tervicz pulled himself back from nightmare and cried out, 'There's the entrance!'

He swerved to his left towards the entrance to the gully, the ground before it dark and light with the racing moon.

'Through here with me *now!*' he cried.

The scent ahead was strong now, part familiar and part strange, but a risk they must take, for there was no other way forward.

As they slowed to take the last steps down into the defile, the Magyars, thinking they could go no further, slowed as well and bayed in triumph.

Hassler roared, 'Kill the bastards!' and Klimt, not quite reaching safety, turned to fight them to the death.

Somewhere a Magyar laughed hysterically, the laugh of one who has been given liberty to maim and kill and knows there is nothing now to stop him indulging his vile lusts.

Nothing?

Tervicz saw it first and was forced to swerve out of the way. Then Stry saw, and gasped, and Elhana who felt nothing but the pains of coming birth; then Morten saw the alien wolf.

And last of all Klimt, as he feinted at Hassler's first advance, turned to divert him, the teeth of Hassler sliding at his back, Klimt saw the wolf rear out of the shadows of the gully's mouth, he saw and swerved, and turned and roared, and knew exactly what he must do.

He ran straight past into the gully's darkness, and let the wolf who stood there stand for them all.

The wolf advanced, spectral in the night, seeming larger than Hassler himself, his fur haloed by the moon's changing, fearful light. Behind him the others turned and grouped and stared, as surprised as the Magyars, as dumbstruck as Hassler.

He stopped, the Magyars retreated muttering and angry, superstitious and afraid. Then the wolf that stood there solid in the night, a wolf of stars and moon, a stranger to them all, moved forward.

'Aragon is my name,' he said, his voice a strange, shouting whisper in the night, 'and this my pack's territory; and *this* the leader of my pack.'

He moved to one side, graceful as a young male in prime, and glanced back at Klimt who came forward to stand along-flank with him, and then he said, 'There are many more of us below, in the shadows, and at peace. Shall I summon them to war?'

Some of the Magyars might well have fled, so frightening was his appearance and his voice. But Hassler stood firm.

'You . . . shall . . . die . . .' he said, uncertain of himself before the Wolves of Time.

Aragon smiled and then, glancing at Klimt as if to ask permission for what he was about to do, he stepped forward and shook his head.

'No, no, *I* shall not die. Not tonight at any rate, and nor at your minions' paws . . .'

As Hassler started forward, Aragon, laughing, leapt to one side and onto the little knoll above and to one side of the entrance down. All was shaken with moonlight where he stood, and the entrance to the gully below seemed no more than a cave. Perhaps the Magyars thought that Klimt's wolves were trapped. Perhaps there was magic in the illusion Aragon now made.

'But why not try to kill me? Now!' mocked Aragon. 'Set four of your best upon me and I shall kill *them* . . .'

Hassler growled, 'Three will do,' and barked out three names. Three of his largest followers came forward.

'Kill him now and then we shall take these others to our teeth. They have led us far enough. Now we'll show them a short route to death.'

The three stared for a moment up at where Aragon stood. He smiled and shrugged and said, 'I await my death at the teeth and claws of Magyars. Come . . .'

This last word he spoke as alluringly as a mother to a mewing cub who seeks the comfort of her teat.

'Come!' he purred teasingly.

The first leapt up to where he stood on the edge of shadows, and the second was already on his way as Aragon stepped back into darkness, laughing.

'Kill the bugger!' roared Hassler, hating to be mocked.

The third leapt into shadow as the first followed Aragon out of sight. Then the second was gone, and the third after them. Four wolves gone.

A groan in the night; the sound of tussling, swearing, and then the first of three screams, long and hopeless, out into the night, and depth. Then nothing. Except . . .

And now the Magyars did back away, and even Hassler showed his fear.

For there was the soft pad of a lone wolf's paws on rock, the pull of his weight from a ledge, a sad laugh and a sigh, and out into the light once more came Aragon, the more terrifying for the look in his eyes that told of three wolves' deaths. Hassler's best were gone, Wulf knew where, to death certainly, over a cliff's edge, while above them all, in the same place in the sky, the misshapen moon raced on.

Klimt roared and came forward out of the gully's mouth, below where Aragon stood poised, and he charged at Hassler powerfully.

For a brief moment it seemed that the Magyars still might make a fight of it, before first one and then another turned and ran, terrified. Then Hassler, unsupported now, with Klimt almost upon him and Aragon ready to leap, and all those other alien wolves readying to attack from out of the mouth of darkness . . . Hassler lost his nerve, turned, and fled across the benighted fell.

CHAPTER TWENTY FIVE

We learn of maternal love and loss,
while the foul Dendrine demonstrates maternal hate

EVEN BEFORE ARAGON had appeared to help Klimt see off the Magyars, Elhana had begun the first movements of birthing, so there was no time for more than a token acknowledgement that from out of the darkling hell of the past weeks, Ambato had come back; and that with him were two other, extraordinary, wolves.

Who *they* were she cared not: it was Ambato alone she wanted near her now, he whose touch was all that in this cold and dangerous place reminded her of the south she missed, and the sun into which she would have liked to bring forth her young. The warm southern sun. Wulf had taken Ambato away for a time, but surely it was Wulfin who had sent him back.

As the others fought and growled, postured and did as packs and males must do, she felt the waves of pain of birth and struggled to find ease and comfort to help her cubs into the world. It was night, and cold, and, and . . .

'Oooh . . . !'

In a moment of respite from pain, Ambato helped her down to the middle recesses of the gully where, in the murk, and now beginning to drag her hinder parts, she sniffed about and found a place that would have to do.

Above her in shadows of the defile, and below in its

steep depths, with the Magyars now in retreat, the other members of the pack settled down to watch and wait.

'*Father!*'

The pains came and went and came again. Between them she rose and fretted at the soil and roots that marked out the place she had chosen. She muzzled some leaf-litter against its wall, she tore away smaller roots with her teeth and settled them with her paws.

The pains came strong now and, gasping at their enormity, she sank to her haunches and then into a birthing position. A lull, and she saw Jicin creep nearer, her eyes staring down at where Elhana lay. Elhana snarled, her space invaded, and Jicin slunk away, forlorn.

She let only Ambato stay close by, acting as guard and silent comfort, just occasionally their eyes meeting, each in their own way desperately tired.

'Ambato,' she whispered again and again: 'Father.' She wanted to ask where he had been and what had happened, but the birthing prevented her.

Ambato smiled and yawned, wide mouth open and up to the swirling night sky. There would be time to tell his daughter the mystery he had come so near.

He sighed and dozed, and it was while he dozed deep in the night that quite suddenly the first of three cubs was born from out of a climax pain and then the blessed searing relief of birth itself. Out into a warm, moist, dark world it came, defined entirely by Elhana's belly and her circling legs, its only point of orientation her teats, which would be its only purpose for a time, but which the cub could not yet even try to find. She licked it, sucked at it, tried to clean it.

A pause, mounting pain, and then the second one was born.

Ambato nodded into wakefulness, looked over into the murk where Elhana lay, heard no sound, thought that nothing had yet happened, muttered, 'You all right?' and then drifted into sleep once more.

Tiredness, fatigue, an aching pain within her now; and dread. The mother's primordial dread of malformation and death at birth. She struggled to help the third one out. She felt its turn. She felt its difficulties. She felt its weakening. She felt . . .

'Fa . . .'

No.

'*Mother!*' she screamed, the cry for help eternal.

The third and final cub was born, not quite alive. Elhana worked at it, licking it, goading it, chiding it for being still and floppy, pulling it from where the other two blindly scrabbled out a way, tried to save it, but she was so tired, and it . . . it was not right. It lay, still and wet, joined soon by the afterbirth. Elhana scented it, licked that as well, and ate it down, noisy and gulping in the night.

She pushed the third cub to one side, for it was dead and she must tend the two that lived. In the night she could see its face, perfect, eyes that never opened, a muzzle that had tried to breathe in life and failed.

Elhana's face was sticky with blood and muck; her eyes tired now, and lit black-grey by a lurid, troubled sky. She moved her legs, and the living cubs scrabbled weakly to her warmth, the dead thing lying beyond them on the ground, beyond the circle of protection, half-forgotten now, without hope, its moment passed for ever, its life ending as it tried to begin.

'Wulfin, take this one back to your womb and let him live again,' intoned Elhana, speaking the prayer for those still-born. 'Great Wulfin . . .'

Ambato, startled awake by the momentary flash of what he thought was distant lightning, but was really the brief shoot and shine of an end-of-winter shooting star, a flash that caught in its light the fleeting run of a female wolf who was sniffing and snouting at the forgotten cub. A flicking tongue, Jicin's mouth opening, the snarling rising form of Elhana, Ambato caught in a star's fading light as he came forward to prevent Jicin taking it.

'Leave her: it's dead,' said Elhana weakly. 'Let her take it.'

Jicin poised with the cub dangling from her jaws, a morsel of dead life, no more substantial than the star that had already died. She stared, desperate and terrified. Wolves turned from above and from below.

'Leave her . . .' sighed Elhana, turning back to what lived. 'Leave her with her dead.'

Jicin slunk up through the gully with her prize and then, almost out onto the fell, hurried past Tervicz and Klimt, the first of whom snapped at her, disgusted, and the second who turned slowly and stared, and remembered his dead young.

'Leave her be,' he echoed, with the patience of one who is discovering late that his own load of loss is not unique. 'Let her be now . . .'

'You've got two living cubs,' said Ambato who, having followed Jicin, and talked briefly to Tervicz, now stopped at Klimt's flank.

'Have we?' said Klimt blankly. Again, the 'we' was not personal to him, but to the pack. One was enough, two was better, three . . . another time perhaps. Now this was done there were other things to plan, and he was so tired. Tomorrow was already here.

'You've a tale to tell, Ambato, about where you've been, I can see it in your face. And these other two you have brought back with you . . .' he said it slowly, and he meant, 'You can tell it to me when I've had a sleep.'

Ambato smiled wearily and said, 'The bold one's called Aragon; the other, the gangly one, he's Lounel. They'll introduce themselves to you. They're good additions to the

373

pack, perhaps more than that. You can sleep deeply, leader.'

'You survived.'

'I did more than that,' said Ambato. 'I came back with news.'

'Of what?' asked Klimt reluctantly, for truly he needed rest. Yet as leader he must ask.

'I found a place, a place that I felt might be near the WulfRock.'

Klimt trembled with excitement but sank to his haunches in utter fatigue. 'Tell me,' he began wearily.

Which Ambato began to do for a moment until he saw that Klimt was exhausted.

'In the morning, Klimt, I'll tell you then.'

'In the morning tell me of the WulfRock,' muttered Klimt, 'yes . . .'

Nodding, smiling, Ambato turned back to the gully to be near Elhana again, but found Lounel standing there, staring at the stars and racing moon.

'So this is Klimt of Tornesdal of whom you told me,' he said, still looking at the stars.

'Yes,' said Ambato.

'He had so many shadows in his eyes when he was awake, and now he sleeps the shadows remain across his face.'

'He's kept the pack together for days past, Tervicz says. *We* had an easy run of it, probably because *he* drew the Magyars away from the route we took. *You'd* have shadows in your eyes if you'd done what he has.'

'Hmmph!' said Lounel. 'You all need sleep.'

'But not you Lounel, eh?'

Ambato had grown used to Lounel's strange ways and irregular habits over the days of their journey.

'He sleeps and wakes to his own time,' Aragon had explained. 'He's not like other wolves. He knows things.'

'What things?' the practical Ambato had asked.

'What's coming, what's been, what is. He's *here* when a wolf like me is wandering along behind, or rushing on ahead. I don't know quite what I mean by it when I say it, but he's *here*.'

But slowly, Ambato had began to understand what Aragon might mean. He watched as Lounel moved out of the gully past Klimt, his rough, fair fur lighter than the leader's, his inelegant gait like some creature uneasy with a world he knew too well, knew better than any of them.

'Lounel . . . !' he called, but Lounel did not turn back. Instead he went on into the night where Jicin had gone with her surrogate cub. Ambato shook his head, and went back down to Elhana, nodded and smiled at her, peered at his kin-cubs and, feeling afraid for them, settled down to watch out the night.

'Jicin . . . ? Are you the one they call Jicin?' asked Lounel of the female who sought to cuddle the dead cub back to life.

She stared at him, abject and pleading that this at least would not be taken from her. He knew the loneliness in her eyes; he knew the look of one who has almost forgotten who she is.

'That one you hold . . .'

'He's mine,' whispered Jicin.

Lounel shook his head.

'He's Wulfin's now. Did you not see the star that showed his life journeying across the sky back to her? Did you . . .'

'He's mine!' said Jicin vehemently, grasping the dead thing tighter.

'Others will need a wolf like you, not him,' said Lounel sombrely. 'And others after them. One of them will need you most of all. Let go of that one you hold now, for he has died and gone on before us. He will be there, Jicin, waiting for us, and for you. Let him go from you that you may see him better when the time comes.'

Lounel moved slowly towards her, from what deep instinct he did not know himself, or even question, but his paws went on an ancient wolfway then, and it was gentle and it led to where Jicin crouched, with all that she sought to hold on to and could not; it led to all her past and more. He went in a few short, quiet steps, and even as she whispered, 'No! Let me keep him! He is mine . . . this one is mine . . .' Lounel bent down and took the cub from her, so gently it must have been with love, or as he himself had once been picked up by those who had loved him.

'He's mine!' wept Jicin, half-rising now and cubless, watching Lounel take the cub out into the dangerous night.

A racing moon, a sky that never ceased to be angry all the night; wolves who lay asleep in a gully that lay on the very edge of the Heartland boundary, and pools of water across the fell where Lounel went, weeping for all he too had lost, weeping for what else would soon be lost, weeping tears from out of the swirling clouds above, down into the pools that lightened with the dawning of the sky, and began to turn as red as blood.

Somewhere there, Lounel laid the cub to rest. He had seen its face. He knew it was a god that had returned to Wulfin's womb, this time too early: next time would be soon enough.

'Take him, Wulf!' cried out Lounel, and felt the enormous numbing emptiness of the sky. He knew then, for the first time, knew with certainty, that Wulf was not there. The god that had been great *had* fallen into mortality and become transitory, which is something worse than nothing: a speck of dust blown on contrary winds over indifferent lands and seas to settle Wulf knew . . . no, *none* knew, where.

'Wulfin . . .' Lounel whispered, and knew then whose

tears he had wept and what wolf he himself might be a part of . . .

Lounel dared to face what wolves spend lives, generations, millennia choosing not to see: Wulf is not there to pray to; he may have lived but now is dead. Wolves bore him and he died, as the cub that lay in the night heather had died, eyes never open to the world that is, breath never breathed in the world that is.

Lounel faced into the void that is wolves' hearts and minds and wept for the impossibility he felt of filling it.

'Guide me, Wulfin,' he whispered at last, 'and teach me to teach them the hardest things I learn. Guide me . . .' he said, staring at where the dawn rose now in the bloody pools, and wondering how such wolves as these, with all they must confront, could find a way to say 'forgiveness' in such terrible times.

A new-born cub lay dead, and Lounel dared to wonder how, and when, and where, and *if*, he might be born again, that wolves might find a way beyond the void that crippled them and Mennen too.

He came just after dawn, Huntermann. Led by a female Magyar wolf.

She took him silently into the quarry into which the gully led, she put her tracks in the puddled mud on the quarry floor, directing them up towards where the gully began.

Then Dendrine waited for him to come, slow and stinking, as she had before. She was tired, and fat with her own latest brood of cubs, yet not so tired that she could not finish off what Hassler had left incomplete.

'Left them?' she had screamed, tearing and clawing at him. 'Left the Wolves of Time *alive*?'

'There was a wolf, not one we've seen before.'

'You superstitious no-good bastard! Can kill wolves not

worth killing. Can put the fear of Wulf into every wolf but the ones with strength. You're shit!'

'Dendrine . . .'

'Shit-face! Bastard! Weak . . . !' Spittle ran down one side of her mouth as she began to shout out far worse invective at him than this, as she always did when she got in a rage.

That day, when he had returned to their den-ground with three less wolves and having failed to subdue the incursive pack, Hassler felt like killing her. He would have gone for her *seriously* then and there if she had not been with young. But then he knew, she only got this bad when she *was* with young. It happened every time. Getting with cub changed her into something vile and foul . . . but then, he knew, she liked him for his strength in taking it. Liked him for his indifference. Liked him when he got angry too.

'Silly bitch!' he roared. 'Fuck off. Shit off. Piss . . . piss down your own legs . . .'

They raged and roared and tore at each other about the dark and filthy place they liked to call the Heartland of their home. It was their joke, their way of raging at the fate that put them where they were, so near and so far. Guardians of the WulfRock they must not go near.

The WulfRock that blinded you if you dared to gaze on it.

It turned you to stone.

It took you in its clefts and fissures and there it crushed you.

It was the lie they could not tell.

It made your teeth rot. It made your head ache.

It was not a rock at all but a place that sank down into a pit without a single star.

It was a mass which could not be ascended.

It was all they feared, the WulfRock, and they were its guardians and its prisoners.

'Shit, fuck, eat crap, vomit your own shit . . .'

She had the final word or two, she always did, able as she was to descend far lower than he ever could. Then, when their argument was exhausted, she left to do some mischief somewhere or other. To kill a wolf. To find the Huntermann who was their friend, the Huntermann who left out carrion of Mennen, the Huntermann she liked and who liked her.

Hassler followed her, and she knew he did. She liked that. She might turn back and rage at him, or she might not. He liked that as well. Not knowing, all uncertain, wild and violent and crude as murder.

That night she did not turn back but let him tag along because she scented birthing in the air; that female she had seen was due which was all the more reason for being angry at her lord for failing in his task. Only she, Dendrine, was allowed to have cubs that could stay alive. Just her in the Heartland and no other wolf. Her alone. That alien bitch, smug and fat with young.

'Fuck birth,' she swore as she went along, laughing foully at the thought. 'Fuck *them*!'

Dendrine had her black ways of cleaving the Huntermann to her. To make it follow. To lead it. To lead Huntermann to whom she was bonded like a toad unto its mate, tight and expressionless, inseparable. The Huntermann she led from time to time, and he used skills so like a wolf's that they did not scent him as one of the Mennen, or hear him as more than another natural sound – a falling twig perhaps, the passage of time between the trees, often quite unseen, not known until the crack of gunshot in the ears that came at the same time as tumbling pain or blackness, and the long fall into death.

He, whose walls bore the heads of those he slew.

He, the Huntermann, whose fingers scented of oil and shit, and her own sex scent where she let him play.

He, whose fingers she suckled when she was young, and were the only living teats she ever knew. Sometimes the moon would rise and take her to its maddened heights and then she would be driven to find the Huntermann again, to kiss his hands, to know the exquisite fear she felt in his dangerous presence; to scent his fear.

'Come,' her kisses usually said finally, for this was his reward afterwards, when they ambled through the night, wolf and Huntermann. 'Come, for I have creatures you may wish to take.'

Sometimes the Huntermann shot them, sometimes he did not. She liked the uncertainty. She liked submitting to his choice.

By night she led him, pausing along the way that he might catch her up, marvelling that one of the Mennen at least could be so silent, though so slow, pleased at the grey glint of dawn that shone on the gun he carried; pleased and filled with anticipation that his choice would be a killing one.

By the dawn he was there in the quarry, ready for what she led him to, her tracks deliberately clear as the dawning day in the puddled places until he reached the gully mouth, and Dendrine slipped away into shadows of her own.

The pains in her womb were beginning; new fodder for her maternal hatred on the way; new cubs to mould into distorted shapes. But this final birthing could wait. She wanted to see the Huntermann take death up into the gully. She wanted to see them try to flee. She wanted to watch them crawl away. She wanted to hear and see and smell them die . . .

But then her too-familiar, far too comfortable journey along the wolfways of hate was stopped short as violently and horribly as if having helped a stag to fall, preparatory to feeding off its head, that same head reared, turned, stared and bit her in the face.

What stopped the foul Dendrine absolutely short, and sent her spinning away from her endless round of cruel thoughts was that there, upon the scree beneath the gully's vertical cliffs, their teeth catching light, their eyes glazed dull, their femurs burst through broken skin and fur, their backs broken into the angles and clefts of the rocks on which they fell, three wolves lay.

It was not death that shocked her, nor the violence of these deaths, but rather, this: each was a son of hers.

Each only *she* had a right to kill.

Each, then, had failed her.

Almost immediately she was back on a wolfway of abusive hate.

'Failed me long ago,' she rasped at them, scenting them, no pity in her angry gaze for the wolves her womb had produced.

Dendrine turned from her dead brood of sons, turned to stare back at the Huntermann, who stared at her. She snarled at him and settled for a moment down among their bloody heads, in obscene and ironic semblance of a suckling mother.

Her belly stirred. Her thin and wrinkled teats quivered. She felt internal pain. The tight skin moved, fleas jumped, and inside her something tried to bite its way out, or so she hoped. Twisting down and round to look upon herself she watched the jubbing movement of the cub slide along the inside of her belly before it faded back to amniotic anonymity.

Something had woken briefly in her.

Something was getting ready to come out.

Athwart her trio of dead sons, Dendrine licked and nuzzled at herself and pondered names. Or one name. The others, they would not last and would remain anonymous to her. But *this* one would live and live.

'Come my sweet, come out of me,' she purred, nibbling

at her flank as if to return his brief internal bites. Then she heaved her horrid, raddled body upslope through the undergrowth by the gully's entrance, there to watch the Huntermann go past, from there to follow him and see the bloody end to the alien wolves that he must make. Huntermann approached, wolflike, scenting more of wolves than of Mennen, peering at the ground, scenting ahead, feeling out which way to go to find the creatures she had led him to.

He looked about, knowing that his lupine love was watching near, and slipped inside the gully's lower shadows.

Stry startled at the sound below him, and a subtle scent of oil and shit he could not place. He stared into the murky shadows, his ears pricked forward and his breath stopped as he slowly turned his head to glance upslope to where Jicin lay. She was asleep and had not stirred at all.

Stry waited and watched, narrowing his eyes as he stared down the gully, and listened.

Nothing in the dense dark of night.

Nothing but the sense that there was *something*, the scent of a female wolf, and something more . . . Then it was gone and the gully's scents of ferns and damp soil prevailed once more.

Stry grew bored and dozed again, enough to miss the slide of hand on rock, the pull of human muscles and the rise of human head; the peer of eye, camouflaged by mud encrusted onto face, and the slow raising of black circles to those eyes as they peered through binoculars and began to examine every shadow in the gully stretching above.

Stry startled again, peered cursorily, and settled down once more, but the eyes ignored him, moving instead first to the tail and right hind leg of Morten beyond him, which was all that was visible, and then upslope once more to an older wolf: Ambato.

The secret search went on before the binoculars were dropped back and Huntermann stayed still, pondering. Then questing fingers found a small rock, pebble-sized, among the detritus where he hid. He pulled out a wire catapult from a pocket, placed the rock in the leather holder, eyed the cliffs above, pulled the rubber not too far, aimed, and lobbed the stone up and away to the far top side of the gully, somewhere above the restless wolf's head.

The rock flew, hit more rock, and rattled down upon scree and through vegetation. As the wolves started up and stared that way Huntermann, unseen, swung himself up the gully-side to the ledge above his head and fell still once more.

Dawn lit its gradual way up the gully as he watched, his binoculared gaze on the shadowed place that lay to the old wolf's left flank. Movement. Nothing. Nothing. Nothing.

Huntermann stayed unutterably, horribly, obsessively still.

Movement, but not his.

Elhana shifted, stretched, came out to the old wolf, yawned, exchanged a touch with him and turned.

Teats. The shaggy belly of a female who had cubbed. Not his lupine love, his mistress of the night, not her at all. Another, who dared to bear young, who must suffer and die for her arrogance. So this was why he had been led here, this his task.

The human rock sighed and the encrustations on the face strained and cracked with the stress of the brief hard smile beneath.

Cubs then. New birth. In at the beginning.

What keeps Mennen so achingly still so long?

Obsession.

What drives Mennen to track wolves with a wolf's skill?

Obsession.

What makes Mennen such as the Huntermann want to hunt with seeming love, and kill with evident hate?

Obsession.

What set *this* Huntermann, this pursuer of wolves, apart from Mennen who sought to do the same?

Complete obsession, total skill, and the desire to be powerful and in control: of wolves, of men, of earth, of sky, of everything.

The cubbed female emerges once more, but briefly, and the cubs remain unseen. Huntermann shifts, eases into a minute stretch, winces with weariness, doubts his endurance for a moment, settles down to wait some more. Blessed numbness is setting in.

Day came. Hours passed. Wolves hardly shifted at all. Huntermann thought that he had heard . . .

He swung down, hunched for a moment, and then slipped away as slowly and as gently as the whispered, unseen breeze that shifts stiff grass upon a cliff before it stills. Down, away, he went, out into the quarry, and then beyond, unseen by wolves or Mennen, before straightening up and stretching, and looking back through trees to where he hoped to get his prize.

'Sooner than later,' he said, his fingers slipping to the stock of his gun, and settled down to wait.

Three days later, Lounel, on one of his nocturnal walkabouts, thought he saw a wolf. Well, he *did* see one. Female, haggard, horrible . . . Dendrine.

After three days sniffing about across the fell, watching and listening, Dendrine decided that the Huntermann had failed her, and that her time was coming now.

He, her next-born, was bidding to emerge. *He* was nudging his snout and his paw at the threshold of life. He was pushing and shoving and urging himself to be born into a new millennium.

'And I shall be your mother, your first love, your everything you'll need, your world into which the rest, the growing massive rest you'll dominate and change, will be but a part. I . . .'

She groaned in pre-natal pain, and sighed the pleasurable sigh of one who knows that their journey to a destination they have longed for, for so long, is within reach.

Then she slipped away out onto the fell, over towards the plateau by way of the lake and then towards the scarplands. There she would ascend until she found the den she had decided to use this time, a den she had never used before, a den in a high dark place where the rocks cleft up above and back into forbidden places no wolf had visited for a thousand years, as she thought. Of Ambato's journey to those parts she did not know.

Her grandfather had once showed her that place saying, 'My dear, when the time comes that you feel sure that it is to *him* you shall give birth then there is a place here, a holy place they call it, where you must have him. Here let him be born.'

Oh, she sighed, remembering her grandfather's words: 'For you are of the Bukov tribe, and yours is the secret.'

Her good grandfather – Dendrine always spoke the word 'good' with ironic contempt, for good was weak, and good was ever to be perverted, good was *bad* – had always said that a great wolf would be born who would help wolfkind. In old age, mad old age so far as Dendrine was concerned, her grandfather seemed to think that Dendrine would be holy mother of the coming saviour wolf.

What else could he think? Her grandmother could cub no more and her favourite daughter, Dendrine's mother, had been killed by the Huntermann when he stole her cubs – a threesome which include Dendrine herself and her sister. Her sister escaped one day, and she much later, after the Huntermann had taught her not to fear him. Taught her to kill.

Her brother she ate, he taught her that.

Her sister she knew she would kill one day, and had! Then she 'escaped' the Magyar and Hassler, but she had never escaped the Huntermann. Later, she had become stronger by far than any other female there, and cleverer and more ruthless, so much so that she had become ledrene.

An old male, falling back on silly hopes, told secrets to his granddaughter, and showed her the place where, so it was said, a great wolf would one day be born.

'Ours, my dear,' cooed grandfather.

'Mine, you silly bastard,' hissed Dendrine to herself, smiling at him gently. That was the day before she left the silly old fool to die, and watched the raven pecking at the wound she made, and the old idiot crawling away across the grass, blinded, lost; calling, of all things, for Dendrine to help . . .

Instead, Dendrine summoned the Huntermann and he came, to the creature she provided: her dying grandfather.

Dendrine and the Huntermann watched him crawl to death, each fascinated at their own calm; Dendrine marvelling at the bliss of feeling nothing at all.

'The bastard,' she said finally, 'is dead.'

The Huntermann took Grandpa away to hang his raddled, blinded head upon a wall. Good riddance.

Now Dendrine did not have to wait much longer. He was bidding to come out and she must journey now to the secret place and let him be born . . .

She turned from the fell and went cursing Huntermann for having failed to kill the alien wolves she was growing to fear and hate, as she thought.

* * *

Of all the Wolves of Time, only Lounel knew that she had been out there through those first nights and days after the cubs' birth in the gully. He had never seen her clearly, of course, but then he did not need to. He knew when evil was about, and he knew it was across the fell, for he had smelt it from down there about the quarry mouth.

Not that Klimt would listen to his urging to move on.

'We cannot, wolf, not with cubs that are so young.'

'It would be wise to take the risk. There are more than evil wolves about. There are Mennen.'

'There are always Mennen, always have been, always will be,' said Klimt, a shade impatiently.

'Not always, either in the past or in the future. Their time was the dark millennium which now ends, and ours began before they were, and will be after they have become insignificant once more.'

'Hmmph!' said Klimt, turning away, discussion over.

Lounel stared at him and knew everything, and most of all, this: that Klimt was shocked by what he had said, and yet had not dismissed it. He was thinking.

'He's *like* that,' said Tervicz. 'He does not like to talk things through.'

'But does he *think* them through?' asked Lounel quietly.

'In time,' said Tervicz ruefully.

'Then that will be his greatness, that he can learn.'

'He's not learned to listen to you, Lounel, has he now?' said Aragon, joining in and eyeing Tervicz with a smile. Thus far the two were equal, circling each other for status.

'You should all listen to Lounel,' Aragon told Tervicz later. 'He *knows* . . .'

But not even Lounel knew when.

'When' was four nights later, sudden as thunder from behind a rise of rock, dangerous as lightning from out of riven cloud.

Noise out upon the fell, unease, but not quite enough to

investigate. Noise later from down below in the quarry,
Mennen probably. But nothing much, probably nothing
at all.

But then, suddenly, 'when' came. More than anything it
proved that dangerous is as Mennen does; and that
Mennen, and Huntermann particularly, had the mindless
patience of eternity.

Four days after the cubs' birth, eternity reached its end.

CHAPTER TWENTY-SIX

A Mann of his time, namely the Huntermann,
takes time out from a disintegrating world; and Jicin finds
herself alone once more

THE HUNTERMANN SHOT at Stry first, but not to kill him. It was the panic that pain brings that he wanted to create.

So, a searing, shocking pain came with a quiet 'phutt!' out of the dusk somewhere just inside the quarry entrance to the gully, and Stry fell. He struggled up, began to scrabble upslope and cry out a warning at the same time, and then, as blood began to flow, he fell again.

Morten was the first to respond and Huntermann, a furrow of calm concentration on his brow, shot him, too, smoothly, and by chance less painfully: a graze across his shoulder that served only to make Morten angry. He helped Stry up to the safety of a clump of holly and ferns, and barked a further quick warning to the pack above in the shadows of the gully. Get away, get out fast, escape. Then he turned to face the direction of the enemy.

Klimt was out of sleep immediately, and after commanding Lounel to ready Elhana and the others to escape up onto the fell, he went straight down the gully to Morten and Stry. Neither was so badly injured they could not move, and Klimt rapidly decided they must all try to get upslope away from the Huntermann below, out to the open fell. The gully, which had been a haven, had become a trap.

Though he knew Mennen work when he saw it, and what sights and scents he was looking for, he saw nothing and scented only . . . fresh mud, too fresh, and oil and . . . something foul. He thought rapidly: Lounel's warning had come true, and now its nature was known. Definitely Mennen, even if they could not be seen. There was no fighting *them*, not here. Best to retreat, and *now*. There were no Mennen at the top of the gully, and it would surely be easy to evade them across the fell. And there were the cubs . . . Retreat then, and away out of the Heartland territory.

'We cannot fight both Magyars and Mennen,' he told himself.

All this had taken but moments, a time during which he had crouched calmly, peering out of the cover of ferns, not knowing how much his sure presence had taken the panic out of the others, who now waited on his further command.

He turned back.

'We move *now*. Elhana, take one cub; you, Jicin, the other. I shall lead and you, Tervicz, shall take the rear with Morten, if he can manage it. Stry, can you run with us?'

'Hmmph!' exclaimed Stry, wincing with pain. 'I'm not staying here to die.'

'They are too young to be moved like this,' began Elhana, wretched with it all. From the first this seemed to have been a fated cubbing.

'We must move them all the same,' said Klimt decisively. 'It is my command. Now, follow me . . .'

He led them off in close formation without further discussion, but checking them with backward glances again and again. Elhana had signalled to Jicin which cub to take, insisting that she go first so that she could keep an eye on both. Upslope, between the rugged sides of the gully, with its gnarled old trees growing out of the rock, was the gap onto the fell. Klimt ordered Aragon forward to check out what dangers lay ahead. He was back in a moment:

there were no obvious ones, but nothing felt quite right.

'The breeze is up-gully, so there's little chance of scenting danger ahead,' he warned.

They moved on, their nervousness calmed by Klimt's coolness. He did not hurry. For one thing Elhana was slow and Stry clearly in pain, for another, it seemed to him that they were going where an enemy might expect them to go.

Aragon went back up, and then came down suddenly, Lounel behind him.

'There's a Mann there. He came over the top, silent as snow in the night. Lounel saw him.'

Lounel nodded, looking uneasily about him. He was a southern wolf who liked limestone and southern vegetation. These dark, forbidding gully walls and looming yews, were not to his taste, which was why he had preferred to stay out on the fell whenever he could.

Klimt said nothing, considering what to do. He and Tervicz had long since checked out other routes from the gully, and the best they had found rose just off to their left flank. There were others, but they led to dangerous drops back down into the quarry, or out onto the fells at points where, if an enemy had guessed their intentions, he would have them at his mercy. There might be other Mennen than the one Lounel had seen. They could always retreat back downslope but then there might be a similar trap at the bottom end of the gully.

He called Tervicz to him and they consulted.

'Stry will find the last part difficult because of its steepness, but I'll be right behind him,' said Tervicz. 'Morten seems all right – his wound's not serious.'

'Right then, you stay right at the rear,' Klimt ordered Tervicz. 'Aragon, you're the stronger one, you help Stry if he has difficulties. And all of you . . . stay within sight of each other, and especially the two females with the cubs . . .'

He had to pause for, dangling from Jicin's mouth, the cub she held waggled its paws in the air, vainly trying to gain a grasp of something. Then it opened its mouth and bleated softly, helpless and vulnerable. The cub that Elhana held seemed only limp, as if the move and rush was too much for him and he chose not to struggle at all.

'Right,' said Klimt more gently, 'let's get out of here.'

They climbed up the steep, winding route, each of them trying not to dislodge stones and earth as they went. Only once did Elhana slip, falling sideways to protect her cub. But Stry struggled all the way up, falling three times and twice needing the nudging and support of Aragon behind because his damaged hind leg had lost most of its strength. Behind *them* Morten watched anxiously, cursing that he could not help his brother, irritated with the stinging wound he himself had suffered and which sent blood dripping sometimes down his side.

'We're a sorry lot, we are!' he kept muttering to himself, the first seeds of doubt about the wisdom of their joining Klimt's group now sown within him. Vagrancy was surely better than this!

They clambered on up the narrow way, anxious to get out onto clearer ground. The route flattened into an amphitheatre of rock, the final climb on top of the fell at its far side. Klimt and Lounel stopped to allow them to re-group and give the weaker and wounded ones time to catch their breath.

They came into view one by one: Ambato, Jicin with one cub, Elhana with the other, Stry limping badly now, with Aragon behind and Lounel; then Morten, fitter now it seemed than when he set off, and finally Tervicz, cool, cocky, a source of strength and good cheer.

'Ten with the two cubs, eleven including myself,' thought Klimt. 'Now . . .'

But Elhana had put down the cub she had been carrying

and was tending to it, licking it, for all was not right. It did not move at all. Jicin went over to her, the other hanging safely from her muzzle, and stared. Then, not letting go of the one she had for a single moment, she moved away to take a position by Klimt.

'We must move on,' said Klimt. 'Same order as before. Stry, we'll try to get to a place of safety as fast as we can so you can rest. But we'll need to cross to the north-west corner of the fell first. After that we should find scrubland away from the Mennen and outside the Heartland territory where we can lose ourselves . . .'

It was clear and to the point, and told all of them what to do, and what to expect. As for Elhana's cub, priorities were shifting in Klimt's mind. It looked worse than poorly, which would leave just one, but one was better than none and, before even that one, the pack itself was paramount.

Klimt led them off across the open space of the amphitheatre and up at last to the cool breeze of the fell and its open spaces. The others soon joined him and as they did it was tragically all too plain that the cub Elhana carried had died.

She laid it down, tended to it some more, and looked about, disconsolate. Ambato came nearer, but not too near. Best to keep clear of a ledrene at such a moment. While Jicin, no doubt thinking she must now yield up the one she carried to her ledrene, slunk back to Klimt's flank. The pack circled on itself, uncertain, vulnerable, feeling they must wait upon Elhana, yet knowing they must move on; *now*.

Elhana, too, knew this was the case and turned decisively from the cub who had died of the strain of being carried too soon, and lunged purposefully towards Jicin, as if rather than helping her she had stolen the last cub.

Klimt sighed and moved away, knowing that in such matters a leader does well to let the females sort things out

themselves. But even as he turned, there was a warning
bark from Tervicz, and a slight odd movement up amongst
some rocks and vegetation to his right. There was a hiss, a
spatter of turf and rock dust, the phutt!, again, of a gun
from the direction of the movement, and all was immediate
danger once more. A Huntermann must be here.

'Run with me!' ordered Klimt. 'Run for your lives.'

Even that was not enough, for as they shot up the last
defile before the fell there, across their way, was a
schranke,* its hanging confusions an obstacle Klimt had
been shown when young.

'See! It is nothing!' his father had said. 'A wolf could
jump it . . .'

'. . . or run though it!' the young Klimt had replied.

Now, as the pack fell back in confusion Klimt snouted at
the barrier, knew for certain what it was, and cried, 'Charge
it! Jump it! *Go through it. Now!*'

Of them all, it was Aragon who understood best what to
do. He had seen *schranken* before.

He charged low, disappeared beyond, and then turned
back to show what he had done. To the others it seemed a
miracle.

'Follow him!' commanded Klimt, running along the back
of the line, nipping and snarling at each in turn, forcing
them to follow Aragon's lead.

One by one they did so, astonished that what seemed so
solid was as insubstantial as mist. Through it they went,

---

* *Schranke* is the old wolf-word for the man-made barrier, which some
packs call *Vorhang*, literally a curtain. *Schranken* are multi-coloured hang-
ings of strips of cloth, hung from a horizontal line a metre or so above the
ground. Incredible as it may seem, though they could easily pass through
them, wolves very rarely do so. After flushing wolves out of cover with
noise and dogs, hunters, who would otherwise find it nearly impossible
to track wolves down, use *schranken* to divert and contain them. Once
in the open wolves can be easily seen, and shot.

puzzling at the Mennen-scented fronds that slid over them as they did so.

'Now scatter across the fell! Run and scatter!' cried Klimt, for nothing else seemed safe, and already the Huntermann was shooting again and the turf was flying about them. And . . .

'Run!' he cried, as he felt a stinging in his cheek and knew that death had all but taken him then and there: 'Scatter now!'

An hour later they began to straggle in on the far side of the fell, one by one. Two hours later, all were there but Jicin, and the cub she had been carrying. Elhana had not quite reached her in time to take it before the shooting had begun.

Elhana, exhausted and quite lost.

Ambato, so tired, so very tired.

Stry, weak with the loss of blood.

Lounel, staring back across the fell, and wondering.

Morten, angry with the irritation of his wound, and with their circumstances.

Aragon, angry, frowning, uncertain what to do.

Tervicz, inclined like Morten to set off back over the fell and search for Jicin and the cub.

Klimt, dark and brooding, ready to attack any there that dared say the wrong thing. This was not a time for doubt or weakness. They had lost much, but they had not lost themselves. It could have been much worse.

'You were right, we should have moved earlier,' muttered Klimt at last, speaking only to Lounel.

'But you have led us well, wolf. We might none of us be alive had you not done so. Let us thank Wulf for small mercies . . .'

Klimt growled his frustration and general displeasure and

then said so that all could hear: 'We wait until dark and then some of us will search for Jicin and the cub. If we find nothing then we shall head to the west and out of the Heartland for a time to strengthen ourselves. We shall be back . . .'

Night came over the fell, and somewhere across it, hidden and shivering, Jicin skulked, alone. She had done as the wolf, Klimt, had bid, and scattered. But then, seeing the others all gone, finding herself alone, she had panicked. Uncertain which way to go, the cub bleating noisily in her mouth, unable to quiet it, she must have turned back on her tracks. She was not sure . . .

But suddenly she blundered into that moving wall of fronds, the *schranke*, and all confusion was before her and she knew she had done wrong. She had lain down the cub for a moment in a place of safety, shushed it, and gone forward to investigate. Through the wall she went, saw that she was back where she had started, turned hurriedly to go back, heard a noise, pushed through the wall and there he was, the Huntermann. The one her mother loved.

He stood stinking there. In his white hands the cub, alive and bleating.

Jicin had not flinched, not for a second, nor even felt much fear. The cub was her charge now and she would defend it to the death. With a low and terrible growl, as if the earth itself was angry, she charged Huntermann.

Huntermann growled too, like a wolf.

There was movement, there was darkness in the air swinging down on her, there was a bang, there was a clouding darkness about her head and stars, stars flying into red and the red melding into darkness, and oblivion.

* * *

Huntermann stared down at the thin female he might have killed, squatted at her side, ran the back of his hand down her throat. Might have, but had not.

The manoeuvre was a dangerous one and he knew it. Many animals feign death, many recover fast, and a frightened wolf, loomed over by a man, might easily bite before it fled. There was, after all, rabies to fear. This one, especially, since it was protecting young was dangerous. But this was not the mother: the teats were dry.

Yet he squatted down and touched her, liking the dance with injury and death. His blow with the gun had concussed her. She would not bite.

'Shut up,' he purred affectionately to the bleating cub, contemplating whether or not to shoot the adult then and there. Had it been human he would have cut its throat. But since it was wolf, and he was pleased to have gained a cub, he decided to be benevolent.

He backed off, rifle ready, the cub in a canvas bag. Only days old, but he had the skill to make sure that it survived. Days old, that was all his she-wolf had been. Now he had another . . .

For she . . . she was leaving him forever. She had a last brood coming, a final one to give all the love she had to so there would be none left for him. He knew it and he feared it. That was why she had made the offering of this alien pack to kill, this cub to take. The other dead upon the ground . . . he left it. He had seen no more.

Huntermann lay down on the furthest horizon before the drop down back to the quarry and placed the bumpy, soft bag on the ground at his side. He aimed at the unconscious adult and waited. If she came his way he would kill her; if she set off across the fell he would let her go.

Huntermann sighed. Was this foray his last alone for a time, or ever? They had wanted to send four bodyguards with him. The boss man had gone too far, been too weak, *shown fear, shown no respect. Tonight they would take him; soon, but not too soon, they would kill him and Huntermann would be . . .*

'*No longer free. Power but less liberty.*'

Hence the bodyguards.

'*What happens to us if something happens to you, Huntermann? Eh?*'

'*Just one more time, one last time. I need a memory of wolves . . .*'

'*One more time, then, brother. But where do you go, what do you do . . . ?*'

Huntermann smiled and said nothing. That silence, that secret place in which he out-wolved wolves was his liberty.

So now, ultimate power in his grasp, liberty threatened, he was taking home more than memory: he was taking a new wolf, so young it was more likely to die than live. Like their party. Like their corrupt purpose.

Huntermann waited, alone on the fell, alone with wolves, alone with the solitary skylark that sang and drifted high overhead; and the wind whispered at his face, and the stiff, dry grass trembled before his eyes.

Then . . .

'*Fuck it!*' *he said, rising, impatient for the future, and he raised the rifle to his hip one-handed and fired at the prone wolf. And missed. He laughed, bagged up the schranke, picked up the bag, and dropped away from view.*

Jicin had woken at dusk, aching and in pain, and known at once that Huntermann was gone, and the cub as well. She tried to scent about, to follow him to know . . . to carry on the fight. But the scents were confusing – oil, a cub, faecal odour foul as bile. She turned at last into the darkness of the night confused, and utterly distraught.

'I have failed a second time,' was all she could think to herself. Failure, utter failure, and the desire to curl up and die.

She wandered over the fell, by hag and by pool, wandered aimlessly.

She found a scrape and dozed.

She woke to the soft call of her name and never knew real fear until then. It sounded like Lounel. There were others with him. They had come to kill her. They had come to show contempt for her because she had failed to save their last cub.

Jicin slipped into the dark chill of a pool and stayed there, only her eyes and muzzle above the water.

Shadows passed by and scented about.

'Jicin!' came the whisper of her name. 'Jicin.'

Then, at last, they were gone.

Come shivering dawn she decided it was best to go and find them and headed to the north-west where Klimt had said they would be going.

She found where they had been and following their trail was able to see them at last, in a vale far below, one following the other, leaving her behind. She could not follow them because she knew they would not want her. She wanted to howl. She wanted to cry. She wanted to die.

Jicin had done her best when she joined the pack and she had failed it utterly. What was entrusted to her was destroyed. They would have her back only to kill her; now the Wolves of Time had passed her by forever and left her nowhere, in no time.

Alone, desperate, unguided, Jicin turned back across the fell and was lost once more among its hummocks, and its cold, cruel pools.

* * *

White fingers at the dawn, and the muzzle of a cub, questing out a teat. White, pale fingers that scented of things the cub knew no name for, having no words.

'Can I look, Daddy?'

'No, not even that. It's a wild animal, not a pet. It must remain that way.'

'Will you tell me a story?'

'I've people to see, meetings to attend. And there's a wolf man coming to see me later this evening. But if you're awake when I've finished, then . . .'

'Yes, Daddy,' Huntermann's daughter said, fading towards sleep.

He looked down at her.

She was eighteen, and she was still his little girl. Eighteen, and the world was full of dangerous men. Eighteen, and he knew what he would do to them.

In just eighteen years the world had grown old and grey and needed men like him now.

'I'll never let anyone harm you, girl, never,' he whispered. He was trembling and mad at all the dangers that loomed so near, that threatened him and his, that were burgeoning in the world through which he stalked, in which he must now kill, and keep on killing, or be killed. Muslims. Christians. Social Democrats. Social Democrats! Ha ha ha.

'None will harm you, my dear. Ever,' he whispered, looking at where she lay and the shape of her.

Except, of course, himself. He felt a final surge of anger, having had the thought that she might betray him, she might be disloyal . . .

'I'd kill you, girl,' he whispered sadly. And he would.

He pulled the door to, but not quite closed. She had never liked the door shut. She was afraid of the dark, but felt safe if he was near.

'That man's come,' his wife said from the top of the stairs.

'Shit,' hissed Huntermann.

Oh yes, a Mann had come, and one who had been to Helsingborg, and wept tears before a wolf of the High Auvergne, and who, Huntermann had been told, might know more about wolves than he did. Huntermann did not like that. The Mann was German. Mmm.

'He's early,' apologized his wife.

Huntermann stared at his watch, stared at time. Time used to tick when he was a child but now it did not, it flew instead.

'Too early,' said Huntermann, disliking the Mann immediately. 'It's because he's a fucking German.'

His wife smiled a shade bleakly. Somewhere in her far past there had been a German. He never came too early . . . Ha ha ha. In their lost and horrid world there was still room for mirth, even if it was silent and unshared.

'I sat him down with a drink and said you might be a little time . . .'

Huntermann smiled. He liked the obedience in his wife. His hand slid down her shoulder and then her back, sensual not affectionate. It was the thought of his daughter made him fancy his wife, and she he was touching, her rump his hand settled on. But then his hand was the enemy's, the alien's, the shadows that loomed behind whom he and his men would kill.

'You do things well,' he said.

'Yes, I think I do, my dear, and I understand. Is she asleep? Yes? Good . . . Now . . .'

'As he's early we've got time . . .'

Huntermann's wife smiled compliantly and took his hand to slow it, to gentle it, to make more time. He took her as if she was his daughter; she took him as if he was the Mann.

The Mann waited, unsuspecting, down below in a room which had an old stuffed she-wolf's head on the wall. A trophy. He tried not to dislike Huntermann even before he had met him. He needed this dangerous politician's help. Few knew wolves better than he. So he waited, sipping schnapps. While above, no more than a creak in the ceiling, Huntermann's wife did things well.

CHAPTER TWENTY-SEVEN

*Dendrine spawns a cub or two, and Ambato,
old now, sets off to find the WulfRock*

GROANING IN THE DAWN.
Far, far away, where cliffs rose high, and clefts split them deep, there in the unnumbered, uncharted caves and overhangs below the Tatra, near the Heartland's heart, too near for the comfort of the good, a haggard evil female gave birth, and that was the groaning and the panting in the dawn.

One for pain.

One for tiredness.

But the last, the huge distorted last . . . The last whose head was already bigger than the bodies of its hapless siblings.

The last for joy, this especial cub being born, and the present took a turn for the worse.

'You, my dear, are the one for whom we have waited a whole millennium,' cooed Dendrine. 'You shall be my pride and joy. They thought the darkness would end. But you shall turn the dark to black impenetrable, and in that blackness wolfkind will slide to oblivion.'

Just then, from the fell below there came a howl of loss and misery, gyring up and outwards for all to hear.

Klimt's pack heard it; the Magyars heard it, wherever they lay and skulked; and Dendrine too, where she nursed her cubs in the forbidden, secret, holy place.

Jicin's howl was heard even by her newest and vilest brother, for he turned his blind, misshapen head at its sound and, dribbling milk and spittle from his clumsy muzzle, seemed to try to peer out towards the light of the world beyond his mother's teats and the cave's entrance.

'Not so fast, my little sweetling,' Dendrine purred in a honeyed mimic voice that, coming from her, was like the pink flowers of eglantine growing out of crawling dung. 'But do not fear, it shall not be so long before the whole world shall be thine. Be patient my love.'

One of the cub's two hapless siblings made the mistake of getting in his path on his way back to Dendrine's teats and even worse, of resisting his already savage attempts to get him out of the way. Dendrine watched this early sibling battle and lunged savagely at its victim.

She nipped him, drew blood, and, ignoring his pathetic squeals, said to him whom she now served, 'There my dear, don't let *him* upset you. You shall always be first and all others last. Yes, yes, feed my dear; sup; drink; take my goodness into you for you shall grow more powerful than all of us in time. As for *him* . . .' and here Dendrine pushed the bleating, bleeding sibling out of the circle of her belly and paws, 'he is banished for a time. Let him crawl away and die for trying to hurt you.'

The cub did not crawl away and die but stayed nearby and shivered until the night, when, with mother, favourite cub, and second cub all fast asleep, it crawled back towards the scent of milk and fed as best it could, until, the others stirring, it was buffeted out of the way once more.

Thus did Dendrine begin to raise her last litter of cubs, nurturing the one at the expense of all else, teaching it by example what its position in the coming world would be: first before all others.

*　　*　　*

For now and for such others, enshadowment came not from fresh-born evil in the form of a malformed cub, but from simple loss.

No pack likes to lose its young, least of all a pack to whom the lost young were their first. An old pack may survive such a loss well enough, living off the memory of former successes until another litter comes their way and their loss may be forgotten in the new purpose and excitement of raising young.

But a new-formed pack, whose fragile bonds may have been formed only from a temporary need for companionship, or to resist a common threat, is unlikely to last long after a whole litter is lost, as Klimt and Elhana's had now been. Even more so when they have been brought together by the insubstantial dreams of a nearly-forgotten WulfRock, of whose whereabouts they are unsure, and whose role is undefined. This is not much to keep a pack together, especially when the cubs are lost and the Heartland seems to have fled.

But the pack's break-up looked set to be accelerated by the taciturn unpredictability of Klimt in the days following their departure from the gully. They had followed him willingly enough, too shocked to think of doing anything else, and well aware that Stry's serious injury, and Morten's hurt, coupled with Ambato's age and almost visible slowing down as the days went by, meant that it was best they stayed together.

But Stry began to recover, and Morten's wound to heal, while even Ambato, though more visibly saddened by the loss of the young than any but Elhana herself, began to assume once more a certain southern cheer. Then they began to question, first individually and then together, whether Klimt was now leading them where they should go, and to what purpose. Certainly there seemed no pattern to the route he took, nor clear reason for the sometimes lengthy stops he insisted upon. Indeed, his leadership now seemed arbitrary and unjust – he would attack one or other of them for no good reason, or insist on leading them up some steep and mountainous way which the older and weaker ones found almost too hard to climb.

Sometimes he would take them, quite deliberately it appeared, by way of some dangerous mountain stream which it was surely far too risky to cross, and savagely insist, for no good reason they could see, that they crossed it. Then again, for three whole days, he was determined that they live off carrion along a busy Mennen road down in the valley below the mountains and fells, where, at any moment, they might have been seen.

Soon disgruntlement set in. It got worse when Klimt savaged Tervicz again and again, a wolf whom all knew was weaker in combat than he, and one as well who was more loyal than any of them.

'Leave, wolf, if you will!' roared Klimt. 'But if you wish to stay then start behaving like a wolf should, like a wolf *should*.'

'It would help,' said Stry a day or two later when several of them were idling about and Klimt had gone off somewhere without saying where or why, 'if *he* behaved like a *leader* should.'

There was a murmur of agreement from, among others, Morten and Ambato, and it was notable that Elhana, who was within hearing distance, sighed and did not disagree.

Of the others Lounel said nothing, and gave nothing away, licking and toothing at his paws and then extending his head along them to doze; Tervicz, torn and bloody from Klimt's attacks lay some way off, silent, and miserable. Aragon had moved off beyond where Elhana lay, to sit in the shadow of a rock, always unwilling to be drawn into discussions such as these. Indeed, had a vagrant happened by and seen the pack distributed as they now were he might well have concluded that it was a complete pack, and Aragon its leader.

Aragon! A wolf who enjoyed more influence on the pack the more Klimt seemed to lose it – the more so because he never made any attempt to challenge Klimt or be disloyal to him. Nor, most noticeable of all, did Klimt threaten him, preferring, it seemed, to ask for and get token obeisance, never more than that.

More significant still, the day before the conversation about Klimt's leadership took place, Klimt had let Aragon feed off a deer they found injured along the way for far longer than, by rights, a leader should have done.

'If you ask me,' murmured Morten, who had no special liking for Klimt and did not like a leader who did not assert himself, 'there's a wolf among us could take him on and win . . .'

Stry and Ambato nodded their heads and Ambato said, 'He might *now*, it's true, but I'm not sure any wolf could have defeated Klimt the day he rescued Elhana and myself from the Magyar pack. I've never seen anything like it in my life . . . But now he seems to have lost the will to lead.'

'You've not seen a lot of leading in your life, Ambato, eh?' said Morten, mock-snarling at him. 'You've been a vagrant for most of it from what Elhana said in the days before she got so miserable that she stopped talking to us . . .'

They all cast glances in Elhana's direction and, perhaps because their voices had dropped to that conspiratorial whisper which wolves adopt when they are talking disloyally of their leader they all happened to catch something none of them had ever noticed before.

It was as subtle as it was fleeting, and gone the moment Elhana caught them staring, and perhaps it was just a chance stare they saw, nothing more. But as they looked at her, they saw she was staring at Aragon, and he at her, a long stare as it seemed, expressionless as it appeared, and yet . . . one that had something potent to it as well.

'Uh uh!' said Stry.

'Dangerous,' observed Morten quietly.

'The perfect Aragon has imperfect thoughts it seems,' said Ambato with cheerful irony.

Such things happened, and provided they stayed as 'imperfect thoughts' (though even then it was best the leader did not know about them, or turned a blind eye) no one suffered. Certainly no lore is clearer than this: the leader and the ledrene are as one, where cubbing is concerned, and when they are not, the pack will fall apart until a new leader, more willing or more able to impose the lore, wins ascendancy. But then, just as certain is the fact that a wolf will enjoy thinking about what is forbidden as much as what is allowable.

Not that dalliance *as such* matters too much: the play of young males and females is but the dance of life, and life has its storms, its calms, and its climaxes. It is unwise lore that tries to stop life from being its organic self. So therefore . . . ledrenes may flirt if they like, and if behind a rock, below in the vale, above in the fell, a male should find a chance and mutual willingness, none is going to break up a pack for that.

Leaders may flirt as well, and have their way with younger females if they can get away with it, but privily, unflauntingly. The lore does not allow it to be public and when it is, then it must be fought over until honour is satisfied, or a new balance found.

Such thoughts, or something like them, went through the minds of all three wolves who saw that impassioned stare between a grieving ledrene, and a wolf who until that moment had given no cause for his leader to doubt his loyalty.

But then, these days, Klimt did not generally need a cause to confront any one of them –

Meanwhile, for one of them, the future was rapidly running out. Ambato was often tired now, the escape from the gully and the loss of the cubs seeming to drain him of his last resources. He was slower, somehow more lined and grey, and when they travelled, he was always the one who was left behind. Worse, he seemed in no special hurry to catch them up, as if he knew his time was coming and that to be lost out in the wilderness of the mountains, to be taken by the rough, cold waters of some river he was trying to cross, or to miss his step above a windy void and fall on to rocks below, where the ravens could take him, would not now be so bad.

He had, at least, almost reached the heart of the Heartland once, which was a satisfaction. Then too he felt he had glimpsed a small part of a vision of the future. It gave him satisfaction that Elhana was in it, as was the pack, so far shadowy in form and uncertain in purpose, the pack which Klimt had called the Wolves of Time.

These were comforts, the fact that he was in no pain for so old a wolf – none of the agonies of aching, rotting teeth which had beset his father, nor the painful wasting away that had made one of his brother's young life such hell before he died. Only weariness now, and sight that was getting less clear; and sometimes plain boredom.

He could see the coming struggle between Klimt and Aragon all too plainly, and the fact that whichever of them won it, the others would be loyal to him – provided they were still around. *That* was more the problem, for increasingly detached as he was, he could see that the pack was in danger of disintegration. There were other things as well . . . Elhana and Aragon for one, *that* was predictable. Oh, well, but did it matter, did it . . . ?

When his mind turned and turned on such things and

grew tired, he had recourse to a memory that gave him greater comfort than all else, and a recent one too. It was of the mysterious place up in the mountains where Wulf had led him after he had become separated from the others, before Aragon and Lounel found him. That high, mysterious, wonderful place, with green, lush grass, cropped by rabbits, overflown by the dark ravens, which led up and up to a place of light and rocks, and where he knew, he *knew* the WulfRock rose.

Of that place he had said almost nothing, for Klimt had never mentioned it again after he had spoken of it the first night they reached the gully; nor had Lounel, to whom he had told much during the journey to the gully. But now Ambato knew he was growing weaker by the day he thought anew of that place, and wondered why he had not tried to climb up to it, to see with his own eyes and discover with his heart, the truth of the WulfRock, of which he had dreamed all his life.

But then . . . had he really been to where he remembered being, and even if he had, how could he find his way back to it? So long a way, so dangerous a route, and he so tired now, so near his end . . .

'Wolf, wolf . . . *Ambato*! . . . you must not linger here. The others have gone on far ahead.'

It was Lounel, smiling down at where he had settled down to doze and think, the pack having seemed to go so far ahead that he was not sure he wanted to bother following them. Here had seemed as good as anywhere.

'Lounel!' he exclaimed with pleasure and some apology, 'I am sorry, I was . . .'

'Dreaming?'

Lounel always looked at him with such clear eyes, as if he saw everything, and more.

'No, not dreaming, not quite that. You remember how you and Aragon found me . . . well, I was just wondering. I was asking myself whether it would be possible to find that place again. I was just wondering.'

'Where had you been, before we found you?'

'I think you know where I *thought* I had been. I think I said.'

Lounel nodded and looked north-eastward, as if to see the place they talked about.

'You almost said. You almost said that you had nearly seen what might have been the place where the WulfRock rises.'

'I did,' agreed Ambato sombrely.

'And you want to return there, to see if you were right?'

'I think that I do. I am near my end, Lounel, and all my life I wanted to know if the oldest legend of all was the truest.'

'Have you strength to go back?'

'If Wulf grants it me, I have. If not . . . I tried. But it is so far and I am so tired. Why, I can hardly stay with the pack these days. When I was young and saw wolves as old as I am now struggling to keep up, I felt pity for them. But now I understand there comes a time, if one is lucky, when one might wish to linger so long that the pack cannot be caught up. For each of us there is only one wolfway to the stars. We shall surely be alone when we find it. But . . .'

Ambato raised his old head a little and stared the way Lounel had and went on, 'But I *am* curious about that place I thought I went to, and what lay above and beyond the part of it I reached.'

'And so am I, Ambato,' said Lounel calmly. 'Very curious. There is no time like the present. As for goodbyes, well, they are superfluous. We turn finally, and we go, that is all. Those we loved will always know we loved them, whether we say goodbye or not; those we loved will not benefit much from a long goodbye . . .'

'You are . . .' began Ambato, not sure what Lounel was at all. More than a wolf. Not quite a wolf. Sometimes when Lounel spoke, his eyes held the light of stars, as they did now. Ambato found his heart was thumping, and he knew he had been confronted by his own doubt, and offered the fulfilment of his own wishes. He knew he could not say no, yet Lounel had not quite said yes.

'I am . . .' tried Ambato, and failing once more.

'Stay here,' said Lounel gently, 'for I must speak with Klimt. I shall not be long. He is . . . not such a bad leader when all is said and done. He may be what we need. I hope he will understand. Stay here, wolf, and rest, for you and I have a long way to go.'

'I will,' said Ambato faintly, feeling that all strain was leaving him, all pressure. He had no need, then, to keep up with the pack. That race was run.

'Elhana!' he called after Lounel, who was already loping in his clumsy way up the path the others had taken. 'Tell her . . . *tell* her.' Lounel turned for a moment, smiled, nodded, and was gone.

'Tell her what?' muttered Ambato, settling down to await Lounel's return. She knew he loved her. She knew Lauria loved her. It was all, finally, he had to give Elhana. Then he found himself thinking that he hoped that Lounel would stay at Klimt's side, to advise him, to love him, to be the wise counsel and comfort his bleak Nordic heart needed . . .

Later, how much later Ambato did not know, Elhana came and settled by him.

'So . . .'

'So . . .' he agreed. Yes, he was going now and glad that Lounel would accompany him.

'Father . . .'

'My dear?'

'My mother . . . your . . .'

'My what?'

His eyes were clear and untroubled as they looked into hers, and his smile was full of love.

'You never said that . . . you never . . .'

'In my day, Elhana, we did not speak of such things, however deeply they were felt. And anyway, she was ledrene and I of lower rank . . .'

'It doesn't matter,' said Elhana passionately.

'It does,' he said.

His head trembled a little now, and in places his skin had lost all fur. He was so thin, so frail. Her father was suddenly so old.

'Well, then . . .' she said, rather miserably.

'Your mother . . . my Lauria . . . was beautiful, and she shared my dreams and understood them. Her faith made real what had felt so insubstantial; her love gave me strength to leave; and your coming gave me strength to continue the journey to its end.'

'Its end?'

Ambato nodded slowly, looking eastward for a moment before the movement of Lounel making his way towards them caught his eye.

'I have missed your mother ever since I left the Benevento, missed her every day, every hour of every day, every moment. Your coming brought her back to me, but I missed her still. Did I never tell you . . . did I . . . my dear . . .'

'No father, you never told me.'

'I love your mother, my dear, as true as the sunrise, as deeply as oceans, as powerfully as the strongest storm. In my old and frail body sun and ocean, ocean and storm, storm and sun again, exist together, always, now, even now . . .'

Slow tears coursed down his face then and Elhana went

to him, nuzzled him, her strength the support of his weakness, and the love of Lauria their comfort.

'I am going to find the WulfRock now and she shall be there waiting for me, she shall be there . . .'

'Will she, father?' whispered Elhana.

'She will, my love, she will . . .'

Lounel returned and waited until their farewell was over.

'Come, wolf, let us go,' he said at last.

'Has he the strength for so great a journey,' whispered Ambato, 'who can hardly rise to his old legs?'

Out of the shadows they came silently, the others of the pack. Tervicz, Stry, Morten and Aragon. And finally Klimt.

'Has he the strength, he asks!' said Lounel with a smile.

'He has!' said the others.

'And you Klimt, my chosen leader, have you a last command for me?'

'I bade you once to live for all of us, and you did,' said Klimt. 'Now wolf . . . I bid you go before us all. Be the first of us to find the WulfRock. Wait for us. Watch over us, for we shall need your care and love.'

'Love?' said Ambato, rising. 'Love does not die . . .'

He nodded to Lounel, touched Elhana a final time, and turned from them all, a Wolf of Time, seeking out a place so hard to find, so very hard, that others might in due time find the journey there a little easier, knowing he had gone before.

'Farewell,' whispered Klimt, 'farewell.'

Two wolves travelling slowly through the high summer, one old now and very slow; the other no stranger to route-finding in high places, nor to travelling unseen. In all his life Ambato had never felt so safe as he did following Lounel, nor so sure that the destination he sought was right, even if they might not find it.

But there came a day when they reached the top of a rise and, looking down, saw the lake where Klimt and the others had finally fled the Magyars, and where, later, Ambato had been found by Lounel and Aragon. Down there they lingered, for Lounel said it was now for Ambato to decide which way to go.

'It will come to you if you let it,' said Lounel patiently.

'Or death will,' said Ambato. 'Trouble is I have an unpleasant feeling that the way I should go is up there . . .'

He pointed at the steepest slope away from the lake, which lay to the north over a wide plateau and then towards dark, sheer faces of rock, and crags and clefts, where ravens hung and where, at night, they sometimes heard the spattering of falling stones, and the far-off roar of rock.

'You must decide, not I,' said Lounel. 'You alone. I have led you here, now you must lead me until . . .'

'Until what, for Wulf's sake?' said Ambato sharply. Sometimes Lounel's unfinished sentences left frightening voids into which a wolf might easily fall. But then again, sometimes Lounel seemed as vulnerable as a cub.

'I don't know where you will lead me, I really don't,' said Lounel.

They finally set off that early evening with the sun dying down their backs, climbing slowly through rough, pitted ground, resting frequently and then climbing on. The lake below grew ever smaller, the crags and cliffs above more and more huge. Until, before they eventually stopped, the cliffs were as russet as old bracken, and then they began to grow dark.

Dawn and more climbing. No food, just a lick at the rivulets of water that ran down here and there, and a suck at some damp moss in a dark place. Above them, where the cliffs met the slope, there seemed no way forward, but then shadows and fissures hide many things. They climbed on, the way ahead strewn with the fresh shards and fragments of broken rock where it had smashed down from above; the heights above sonorous, and echoing with the racking caws of ravens, and the shrill call of solitary eagle, unseen.

'There!' said Ambato, stopping and panting and indicating an abutment of rock off to their left, beyond which there might well be a cleft. Beneath it, the scree was stained with rocks of a different colour, and red soil.

They climbed on slowly, the sun turning some corner of the mountainous horizon and beating down on them so that they felt thirsty, and their sweat dried and caked in their fur. Above them, the cleft seemed like a sanctuary.

They reached it, peered inside, saw a rocky path climb up brokenly and picked their way between its walls. Moss, green as newts; grass, green and lush. The route eased, the walls above them were lower and the sheer cliffs that had seemed so impenetrable and huge gave way and were as nothing. In moist shadows, near where rabbits grazed, they rested, and surveyed the vast terrace into which they had climbed. Looming over it, was another cliff, which looked as substantial as the first and yet might, if they had faith, offer a route beyond.

On they went, the cliffs rising ever before them, to right and to left, the grass strewn with the bones and skulls of rabbits, the sky touched sometimes by the turn and caw of ravens; the caves and overhangs above them, far and near, echoing sometimes with eagles' cries. And they, alone, on virgin grass, picking their way to the very stars.

Dusk. Night. The cliffs were alive about them, and the rocks shifting, moving, thundering, threatening now. Deep night and a vast shot of lightning through the sky, and sudden, fearful, rain. The lightning so bright, the rain so fierce, that they saw a rabbit plump and trembling before them, unable to move. The gods had given them food.

They tore and ate the offering, and they slept. And next

day, or perhaps the one after, they moved on, but very, very slowly now, for Ambato was so tired.

'Lounel . . .' he whispered, 'where do we go? To where?'

'You must lead, wolf, not I,' said Lounel, 'you alone.'

'Lounel, to there we'll go, to there . . .'

And on he went, on by the shining grassy ways, on between strange-shaped looming rocks, wolves petrified, grey-white amidst the luminescent green, on faster than he should, faster than Lounel could follow, on to the shade of a huge boulder beyond which was another cleft . . . beyond which the sky lightened, the storm all gone.

'Lounel!' cried Ambato from the shadows of the cleft above, his voice beginning to echo like a god's.

Unable to climb more, unutterably spent, marvelling at the old wolf's fortitude, Lounel squinted his eyes the better to see where Ambato stood, and saw him turn and go on once more.

Lounel summoned the last strength he had and climbed on, up and up to a place that seemed so far, calling, muttering, 'Ambato! Ambato!'

He reached the boulder and then the cleft and saw the rocky defile go on up, floored with lush grass, and far off, as it seemed, he saw a wolf upon whom, from some place or thing out of sight, a light shone bright, a light which made his worn body seemed young, and his fur seem smooth, and his old paws strong once more.

'Ambato!' whispered Lounel, too tired to travel more. 'Ambato!'

And he heard an old wolf laugh the laugh of youthful dreams fulfilled and hopes discovered, and he heard the patter of paws on loose rock which echoed like sparkles of light about him and seemed to form a wolfway to the stars.

'Ambato!' Lounel then seemed to hear another call, a female's voice, filled with love, a voice so beautiful that Lounel knew the name of she whose voice it was. The light shone bright and the first of the Wolves of Time made his way at last to that place of which once he had only dreamed, but which now was his. And where he had been was the rising of rocks, too awesome for Lounel to look full on, and the WulfRock, whose light and shade and waiting destiny he had not yet eyes to see.

CHAPTER TWENTY-EIGHT

*The Wolves of Time, waiting for Lounel's return,
grow irritable, and forbidden love joins the pack*

SUMMER CAME and the days were long and often
hot. In the weeks that followed the first hint that
there might be an attraction between Elhana and
Aragon, the foothills of the Tatra were at their most beautiful. The grass still held the verdant greens of spring and
the rocky places, so dead and bleak in winter, were alive
now with towering fern and dew-decked alpine mantle,
with the buzz of mountain honeybee and the crawl of shining beetle, and seemed to hold all the sounds and colours
of the summer sky.

Where water oozed from the crevices of rocks, moss
shone out its green luminescence; where pools of water lay
across the fell the high shifting cumulus clouds above
seemed to swirl and turn, and waterfowl, which had kept
away down south, or in lower vales for so long, flew straight
to them, to land as if they knew they had been there waiting
for a thousand years.

Curlew called, and ravens rasped out their croak about
the crags and flipped over on their backs on updraughts of
wind, their blue-black shine as fleeting as it was mysterious,
and were gone.

Meanwhile, ponderous, smelly, loud, the Mennen sped
along the road that skirted round the fell and rushed on up
into the mountains. Sometimes they stopped, their vehicles

falling silent but for creaks and the soft farts of fumes. These were not like Huntermann. They got out timorously, and stood on the edge of their known world and peered, or ate, and hurled their rubbish.

Where Mennen ventured forth and walked all creatures lay low, not in homage but in fear, and the waterfowl scurried out of sight, while only the ravens in their high places turned and stared and blinked their white lids, not in surprise or fear but weariness, for Mennen come, and Mennen go, and the corvids, to whom the world is carrion or not, hover and drop, snatch and tear, and fly up and away.

That summer, Mennen or no, the wolves the taciturn Klimt still led kept by day up among the forest trees watching out from the seeming darkness where they hid and lazed, though usually lying out in some sunny glade hidden deep among the trees which, for days or even weeks at a time, became their rendezvous. By night, sometimes, they roamed abroad together and took what ailing deer there were, or lesser creatures that they found. But come the dawn they crept back one by one to the safety of the forest.

Ambato's departure to find a different wolfway had surprised none of them, for he had been in decline since they had known him, and a wise wolf chooses the time of his last journey for himself alone and none other. He was an old wolf who bore himself with dignity and who had had a dream which, so far as any of them knew, may not have quite been fulfilled but almost so. Well, that was as much as a pack could hope – though most of them privately hoped for rather more: that he had done Klimt's bidding, and reached the very heart of the Heartland. They had been surprised but pleased at Lounel's unusual decision to travel with him.

'Ambato believed that he had come near the WulfRock before Lounel and Aragon found him and I granted permission for Lounel to go with him that he might find out the truth of what old Ambato had seen,' explained Klimt.

'And be company for Ambato as well,' suggested Aragon.

'Yes, and that,' said Klimt brusquely. 'That as well.'

So the sadness of Ambato's departure was overlain with a certain apprehension concerning Lounel's safety, and yet excitement too, for if he brought back a clue to the whereabouts of the WulfRock then they might have a goal to aim for at last.

'*If* Lounel gets back to us alive to tell us,' said Stry uneasily.

However, the dignity of Ambato's departure, combined with the shared interest in Lounel's return, was enough to keep the pack together a while longer, and for a time to divert the mounting irritation with Klimt's leadership, and the general sense of disaffection.

Then, too, so long as Aragon made no bid for leadership, but continued to build up the loyalty of the others to him, the pack would want to stay and see the outcome. The very fact that he maintained a commendable silence upon the subject of Klimt as leader, and never once expressed the doubts the others did, further gained their liking and respect.

While – and this might have been the dark side of the same rising moon of change – Klimt continued to do nothing much at all, least of all inform the others of his thoughts, and thereby he continued to lose their respect. Lost now in his own silence, capable still of sudden attacks on any of them, fearsome when angry, his general attitude seemed to be made up of indifference, silence, absence in spirit and, increasingly in body. He chose too often now, as the days warmed into full summer, not to be there, but to wander off by himself, communing alone with Wulf knows what part of his Nordic bleakness and memory.

Which being so, none was surprised that the once insubstantial passion between Elhana and Aragon seemed now to begin to grow into something more. Still discreet certainly, but certainly it was more than glances now. When, as often happened in those slow balmy days, they had eaten well and were resting, and Klimt had disappeared once more, Aragon would sometimes be induced to talk about his strange birth into the Cabrera pack, the epic traditions of his forebears, and the call of the gods, as he imagined it, which had summoned him eastward to the Heartland.

He spoke modestly, making light of the many escapes and moments of courage needed to enable him to journey in safety further than any of them there. And he spoke lightly too, with a passion and a poetry that contrasted utterly with Klimt's ungiving, taciturn way.

'It was Lounel who saved my life,' he began one day, 'a wolf like no other I have ever met or expect to meet. As my mother Jimena would have said, I met in Lounel a "wolf of dreams" . . .'

'The way Lounel told it,' said Morten, easing his bulky frame a little as he generally did before he spoke, as if (unlike his brother Stry) he found speaking in a group embarrassing, 'you saved his life . . .'

There was respect and liking in Morten's voice, and it was obvious he had no doubt that Aragon had done as Lounel said.

Aragon smiled in his darkly handsome way, his eyes warm, and said, 'Well, then, let us say we saved each other. He would not have left the Auvergne without support, and I would not have wished to go beyond it without company.'

'You're always going on about your mother, Aragon,' interrupted Stry whose hind leg was sufficiently healed now for him to be pacing restlessly among them to stretch his muscles and curse a bit, 'but you've not ever said much about her in my hearing. I mean Jimena's a funny sort of name for a start . . .'

Aragon's eyes flashed a little, for if he had a fault it was

that he was touchy if there seemed a threat to his honour
– and his honour appeared to be bound up closely with
Jimena. When Stry said in his rough and friendly way
'you're always going on about your mother' Aragon's eyes
grew cold for a few moments, and a different-seeming wolf
showed through. But the moment passed and his eyes lit
up with affection, and he said, 'Jimena's a beautiful name,
and an ancient one too. You see, my mother was the last
of the Segundera . . .

> Out of this dry land
> This wolf will be great
> A leader of leaders
> A maker of gods . . .'

He spoke the words of the Segundera's ancient epic prophecy, softly, but with feeling and a sense of history that
carried them far beyond where they sat and lay in their
safe glade, beyond even the trees around them, to the cliffs
beyond the forest, and the wide fell beneath.

'My mother escaped the Mennen's assault on the last of
her pack and made her way to the Cabrera's territory,
whose pack was altogether different, rougher, tougher perhaps, than her own. I believe Jimena was beautiful . . .
and the eyes of males followed her wherever she went.

'Naturally the ledrene of the pack she joined was jealous
of her, and naturally, too, the leader, Baillo by name and
as rough, crude and unthinking a wolf as my mother was
beautiful, took a fancy to her. These things happen do they
not . . . ?'

He smiled, lightly, and glanced at Elhana who could not
help laughing, which made the others smile and grin as
well. Aragon was a wolf who played with words and whose
words gave others pleasure and delight. That he could make
sad Elhana laugh was comfort to them all, for it was taking

time for her to recover from the loss of all her cubs.

'So Baillo and my mother . . . well, that spring was a lovely one and the ledrene was fat with young, and what happened was but a brief thing, a moment's passing.'

'And the result?' asked Stry.

'You are looking at the result, Stry. I am their son, their sole cub. And my mother, liking memories of the past as she did, chose to call me Aragon after the most famous of all the Spanish packs with which, on her father's side, she claimed ancient connection. Unfortunately Baillo's mate, the ledrene Ameria, had herself wished to use the name Aragon for one of *her* cubs. My mother should have let her do so and found a different name for me but she did not . . . There is a strain of stubbornness and pride that runs very deep in my family. She had chosen my name and she claimed her maternal right to name me as she wished, a right supported by Baillo.

'Ameria exacted a terrible revenge: she took my mother's good looks from her, ripping her face apart and nearly blinding her, but letting her live that she might suckle me.'

Elhana sighed with pain at the thought of it. It was the kind of thing some ledrenes did, though it would never have been her way.

'My mother lived,' continued Aragon in a quieter voice, 'though after that she was the lowest in the female order in our pack. She survived that I might survive . . . and she taught me the stories of the old Iberian packs which her mother Sainfoin taught her.

'Of the Epic Age of Wulf she told, and of how the Iberian packs were formed by wolves outcast from the Heartland many centuries ago, after the scourge of the Mennen truly began.

None shall aid him
None give him support

He shall be a stranger
In the territory he shall end in;
None knows his name
By deed
By sight
By any word or thought . . .
He shall be outcast
From the Heartland gone forever
And death shall be his punishment

If ever his paws or those of any descendant
Try to touch again the hallowed Heartland's soil . . .'

Aragon's voice seemed to flow like a full river with the tale
his mother had taught him, which was of how his own
namesake, Aragon, was banished by one of the five Dark
Wolves of Carpathia, and outcast to wolfless Iberia, there
to form a pack that would in time find glory all across that
distant peninsula.

'And did any of his descendants come back to the Heartland?' wondered Stry, struck still by Aragon's tale.

Aragon shrugged and smiled.

'You must understand the Iberian temperament to
understand that tale. We are romantics, and romantics are
liars, and liars tell tales for pleasure, and to hide things.
My mother never believed there *were* "five Dark Wolves
of Carpathia". No, no, she preferred another, older tale,
which I doubt that any of you have ever heard, being as it
was in Castilian and in a language no wolves speak these
days, including myself. My mother told it me once, in
whispers.'

'What tale was that?' asked Stry.

'About a wolf called Harbesch. Now he *was* of the
Heartland . . .'

'*She*,' said Tervicz quietly. 'Harbesch was a female of the

425

Bukov tribe. She it was sent out the Wolves of Time. Maybe this first wolf of whom Aragon speaks, this *first* Aragon, was the one of that last pack who made it to Iberia . . .'

Tervicz looked at Aragon and felt no doubt at all that what he heard was the remnant of that ancient tale.

Aragon stared at his paws, frowning and evidently not liking that Tervicz knew more of Harbesch than he did. Then he said, 'Well, whatever, my mother Jimena long ago decided that one of us should go back to the Heartland, so here we are! *I* came back, as you did, Elhana, and Tervicz over there . . . All of us . . .

'Are we not all the ancestors of outcasts seeking to return now to the Heartland? That is what keeps us together and gives us a sense of purpose, even if we are not yet sure why we are here.'

The sun was warm on his fur, and bright in his eyes, and he spoke of dreams and things of which it would have been better that Klimt himself spoke. For now in Elhana's eyes was a longing, and in all their eyes was the glimmering of a hope, that Aragon might one day lead them.

While in the shadows, unseen, was a wolf who saw and heard these things and did nothing: Klimt. Watching to see how things were, biding his time perhaps before he sought to crush the upstart Aragon, who, despite not seeming to try, was stealing not only his ledrene but his pack as well.

So Klimt watched, listened, and retreated back into the shadows, doing nothing. Instead he climbed the crumbly heights above the tree-line, seemingly to forget what he heard, forget what he felt, and stare instead over the fell at how the shadows of the clouds drove across the Heartland fells, and on among the cleft mountains beyond. He stared that way because it was somewhere there that Ambato believed he had come close to the WulfRock. It was somewhere there, too, that Lounel must now be, searching as

Klimt had commanded him, finding what he could before he came back.

In truth, the pack did Klimt an injustice, for lost though he might often be in morose thoughts and uncertainty, he did not forget Lounel. He had incurred the wrath of others, Stry especially, and even Elhana on one occasion, for refusing to go back into the Heartland to seek out Lounel and give him the help he might need in his journey back through Magyar territory.

But Klimt was adamant, and ferocious in his determination that members of the pack should not set off eastward on what he described as an unnecessarily dangerous chase. It was an issue on which Aragon, Lounel's closest friend, might have chosen to pick an argument over the leadership with Klimt but strangely did not.

But what the pack did not know, because he chose not to tell them, was that Lounel had insisted that he be allowed to make his own way back, and in this Aragon's judgement of his friend was right.

'Klimt, you know me little yet, but in time you will get to know me better,' Lounel had said, that day he had asked for permission to accompany Ambato. 'I was trained by the last of my kin to travel alone and it is no hardship for me. In a pack I am but a clumsy wolf, my limbs do not run so smoothly as those of a wolf such as you, or like Aragon. I am not made that way. But when I am alone the stars are my companions, and the trees my friends, and the very rock and soil and waters of the streams and lakes talk to me. They shall warn me of danger, they shall direct me back and forth. I can hear them better when I am alone. So I ask only that you wait for me in this safe place, and that you watch for me, and listen for my call, for who knows what condition I may be in? Not I! Only that it is in the last part of a long journey, in the final descent, that we are at our most vulnerable. Watch out for me.'

'I shall, Lounel,' Klimt had replied, easier with Lounel than all the others but Tervicz.

'Klimt,' Lounel had said softly.

'Wolf?' growled Klimt.

'These wolves that are together with you, vagrant wolves from east and west and south, they will take time now to become a pack. The loss of the cubs has set you back. But . . .'

'Well?'

'On the night the cubs were born I saw a star shoot across the sky on that first cub's death . . .'

'And I,' said Klimt softly.

'A cub born too soon becomes a star to be born again, so the lore of the Auvergnois says.'

'And Nordic lore as well.'

'Well then, why do you think I wish to journey with Ambato? To find the WulfRock or to find a wolf?'

Klimt stared at him, saying nothing.

'Therefore Klimt of Tornesdal, who shall be our leader yet, strive to keep this unhappy pack together. Beware of Aragon for he has more power than he knows and he is too proud, too personal. Learn before he does what your weaknesses may be.'

'I thought you and Aragon were friends!'

Lounel laughed in the free and simple way he sometimes did.

'We are! But friends know each other's strengths and weaknesses, and what follies and what dreams drive each one along. I love Aragon as if he were my brother. Why, Klimt, he *is* my brother in a sense. But you . . .'

'I?' muttered Klimt, unused to such direct talk, for the others were too in awe of him to speak like this, even Tervicz.

'You are my brother too. Not an easy one, I fear. But in you I sense different strengths, which one day we shall all need. You shall be our leader yet.'

So Lounel had gone, leaving Klimt with the certainty that he would come back and that they should watch and listen for him when he did. Leaving, as well, much to ponder, for why should he have said not once but twice, 'You shall be leader *yet*?' Was he not already leader? Perhaps, after all he was not. Perhaps Lounel meant . . . Klimt might have many weaknesses but, as Lounel himself had already understood, he had one great strength: he was a wolf who thought, who grew.

So, still silent most of the time, still irritable, still inclined to lunge at one or other of them and assert his leadership, Klimt used that waiting time to think, and think more; and as the days passed, and he began to think that Lounel might soon return, he took to watching out over the fell, and seeing to it that when he did not, others did so in his place.

'For what?' they asked.

'For sound or sight, hint or sign of Lounel, wolf.'

July came and Klimt had been as good as his word: he had watched and he had kept the pack in the same broad territory up in the forests that rose west of the fells. Sometime then there came to all of them the sense that over in the Heartland things were happening and Lounel might be part of it, or might simply be coming back. None could say quite why they knew it, but they did, and it troubled them.

'Let us go out over the fell to try to find him,' said Stry many times.

'No.'

'But even you can surely sense he's out there?' said Morten, losing patience.

'*Even* I?' said Klimt affronted, and threatening.

'I did not mean . . .'

'No,' growled Klimt, 'you did not mean.'

'But we might at least discuss what we can do,' said

Elhana, easier now the summer had advanced, and better at talking to Klimt without provoking him back to silence, or into threat. Truly, the pall of loss had lifted from her, leaving only occasional shadows behind.

'We might discuss many things I suppose,' he replied, 'but this we have no need to. It is safer that we stay where we are. It is what Lounel himself suggested.'

'You did not say that before.'

'I said nothing before,' said Klimt, almost pleasantly.

'Klimt, you are *difficult*,' said Elhana, not without some bitterness.

'I am from the north, Elhana, and you are from the south. My eyes saw the clean icy wastes of the Baltic before they saw the sun. Your body knew the sun before ever it felt cold. We each have a long way to travel before we can meet. It is *we* who are difficult, not I, or you.'

Elhana was stunned by this unexpected speech, which seemed to her almost more words together than Klimt had spoken for weeks. More than that, what he said suggested he had thought about things she had long since concluded he never thought about at all.

'Klimt . . .' she said softly, for he was her leader and in some things she wished to be led.

'Yes, wolf?' he said, his eyes grey and steady on her, giving nothing more away. She longed for a smile in his eyes, and for the sun to soften them but she knew as well that as he looked at her he too longed for something he had once had, and had lost.

'Klimt, I am glad you spoke to me,' was what she finally said.

'Yes,' he said, not knowing how easy it would have been to say just a little more, and how much it would have meant to his ledrene.

'Klimt! Leader!' Tervicz cried, bringing their strange moment of bleak intimacy to an end. 'Look!'

For a moment Klimt's heart lifted, for Tervicz had been watching the fell, and he thought it might be Lounel he saw. But it was not. Where Tervicz pointed and where Klimt and the others within earshot now crept and looked was across the fell to the south of them. It was a Mann, far off and solitary and coming not on the road but from out of the low hills across from it. There was no vehicle with him. He was a Mann alone.

But Klimt immediately suspected more. It was *the* Mann come back.

'Very strange,' said Tervicz.

'Strange-ish,' said Stry. 'Where Morten and I came from there were such Mennen occasionally, but they were rarely alone and most came in vehicles. But this one – where he comes from there are no vehicles at all.'

They watched the Mann's slow progress with little apprehension, for he was far across the fell and well below them. It would be a good few hours before he reached them at such a pace and by then they would have slipped away, higher into the forest. But he did not come so far. Rather he stopped and started, and then stopped again, sometimes for long periods. Until at last, dusk coming, he stopped altogether and made a dark shape, greener than the peat grasses around him, and was lost within it.

'Seen that before,' said Stry. 'Eh, Morten?'

'Food,' said Morten. 'If the wind shifts we'll scent food from his direction. Sweet as honey, Mennen food. If the wind *doesn't* shift then maybe we should go and investigate!'

A short while later Klimt gave his assent to this and, when night fell, the two wolves set off. They were gone for fully two hours.

'He's there all right, the wind playing about the green den he's made, whining in its wires,' reported Morten. 'But there's little scent.'

'No food?' said Tervicz.

431

'None.'

'We found his tracks and followed them back across the road and could have gone much further,' said Stry. 'He's come from the direction of the Heartland.'

'He's no danger to us,' said Klimt. 'Not down there. We'll watch over him, tomorrow.'

'He'll move tomorrow, they usually do,' said Morten.

Three days later the Mann had not moved at all, and had barely shown himself beyond his mottled green den. Indeed the wolves had the greatest difficulty seeing where it was, for the Mann put vegetation over it, and his scentlessness did not help.

'"He'll move tomorrow", eh?' said Tervicz, mocking Morten once again.

'Most unusual,' said Morten grumpily. 'Most irregular.'

Tervicz laughed and said: 'The Mennen *are* irregular!'

That same evening Klimt himself went down to investigate, ducking between the hummocks on the fell, enjoying the twilight scents of summer. He went alone, knowing well enough that the others were up at the forest edge, overwatching the fell. They would see nothing of him, and even less of the camouflaged Mann, but they would be watching nonetheless.

He sensed no danger at all, rather the opposite in fact, but he circled the site carefully, pausing frequently to listen, and to scent at the air. Once he heard a cough, just slight; once he caught the touch of a scent among the cotton-grass.

It was the first shock of the night, for the scent, though faint, reminded him of Lounel's. No, it *was* Lounel's! He had come back, or rather he had come near. Klimt tracked back and picked up the scent again.

'He has been following the Mann!' he said, surprised and pleased. 'He's a *wolf* is Lounel! Now, why would he follow the Mann?'

He tracked nearer and nearer to where the Mann was, the scent of the Mann beginning to subsume that of Lounel, both being three or four days old. Then Lounel's slid away to the right and for the first time Klimt caught the Mann's scent unmixed with another.

Oh yes, he knew that scent, he knew it well. In Helsingborg there was a Mann who scented thus. And when he and Tervicz saved Elhana and Ambato from the Magyars, this was the scent of the Mann they saw.

'He is benign,' Klimt told himself in wonder. 'He *is* benign. Mann, what are you? You are not the Huntermann, that's not what you are.'

Klimt was nearer the truth than he could know.

How long he stayed there wondering he did not know, but he felt safe out there on the fell, the Mann silent nearby. He felt at one with the ground that was beneath them both, and the wind that whined in the grass and at the Mann's den, and at one with the stars that shone down upon them both.

A cough in the night and Klimt felt no fear. The turn of a body, and Klimt stayed easy; the coming of cloud and light rain, and its patter on the den, different and more hollow than rain falling on natural things. Klimt wanted to stay for a while.

A bark in the night, questioning. Tervicz. Klimt had been too long.

Tervicz: and Klimt remembered how it had been when they had first met, and wondered about the darkness he had felt, and the bleakness that followed the death of those cubs.

Rain on his face, and tears in his eyes. He remembered with a stab in his heart the pleasure he had felt when he first got to know Tervicz. Would such pleasure ever be his again?

The bark again and, silently, vainly wishing his tears would dry, Klimt rose and slipped the long way round and made his way to where he thought Tervicz was waiting and listening out for him with growing concern.

'Tervicz!'

'Ah!' said Tervicz, nervous, not knowing how Klimt would react to his coming looking for him.

'I am glad to see you, wolf,' said Klimt.

Glad was not a word Klimt often used.

'Tervicz?'

'Yes?' whispered his friend.

'I . . . there will be changes, wolf. We have much to learn. Have faith in me and I shall repay it many times. Have faith.'

'Master . . .' began Tervicz, using the Carpathian form he had used before with Klimt, though never in the hearing of the others, 'I know there must be a reason for your harshness to me through these weeks past and that perhaps you cannot say what it is. But I promised always to be loyal to you, always, and I shall be.'

'I am glad of it, Tervicz, more glad than you know. Whatever happens, do as I say and trust me, for I shall not fail you or the Wolves of Time. But . . .'

'Yes, master?'

'It . . . is . . . hard. If I could tell you more I would, but I know hardly anything myself of what I do, or why I do it. Wulf is hard on those who love him best.'

'He is.'

There was silence between them and the rain fell harder.

'The Mann is benign,' said Klimt.

'And the Mann is *wet*,' said Tervicz, grinning in the dark and feeling more content than he had for many a long day past.

'Come, friend,' said Klimt, 'or the others will fret for you as you fretted for me . . . I am glad we have talked.'

'And I.'

Morning brought a drifting, rainy mist across the fell which did not clear until the afternoon, and then but briefly.

Where the Mann's den had been was nothing now.

'The Mann has gone!' declared Stry, surprised. They had heard nothing at all though the wind had favoured them.

'The Mann moves like a fox,' said Morten with some admiration.

'The Mann moves as well as Huntermann,' said Stry.

Klimt heard them but his eyes were on the fell, though not where the Mann had been. They were fixed on a spot much nearer and there was a glint in his eyes as he decided what it was he thought he saw. A glint, and the glimmer of a smile. The Mann was not the only fox upon the fell.

The mist rolled in again and the rain, sweeping from left to right across their view, now a wall of white, now a shifting rising thing that revealed the fell behind. It thickened and Klimt stood up, ears pricked, pretending to have sighted something fierce and terrible.

'For Wulf's sake!' began Stry, starting up. 'What is it?'

'A monster,' whispered Klimt, eyes narrowing.

'I see only mist,' said Morten.

'And I,' whispered Tervicz.

'And I,' breathed the others, staring hard where Klimt did. The pack was grouping before the common threat.

The mist shifted and moved and out of it, coming nearer perhaps, or simply revealed there came what certainly looked like a monster wolf. Tall, spectral, silent, staring.

'Lounel!' cried Aragon, recognizing him at last with relief in his voice and running out to him, buffeting him, welcoming him, 'Lounel . . .'

Lounel smiled and Klimt bounded out to him as well, his happiness and relief revealing for the first time the deep fear he must have felt for his friend.

Then they all came out, and circled and scrapped, laughing and barking in the mist.

It was Tervicz who started the howl, their first group howl for a long time. Up it went, to be picked up by Stry and then led on by Aragon until at last all their howls were one, and Klimt's soaring above them all. Up into mist and sky they howled, howled for loss suffered, grief survived, a friend returned, and hopes still living in their hearts.

'And did you find the WulfRock, wolf?' said Aragon later, lightly.

It was to Klimt that Lounel replied.

'I think Ambato may have done . . .'

Then, the mist clearing and the sun coming out once more, they went up into the shelter of the forest, found the warmest, driest place they could, ate, slept, listened and, when twilight came, settled down to hear all that Lounel would tell them, and wonder at the parts where he fell silent . . .

'. . . Then I grew weak and could go on no further, but Ambato, he had strength, Wulf gave him strength, and he went on, he journeyed on . . .'

Elhana listened and felt joy. Her father had found the wolfway he had always sought. He had gone ahead of all of them, and one day, if Wulf and Wulfin favoured them, they, or . . . or their cubs . . . would find a way to follow.

Then Elhana began to howl her sorrow for what they had lost, her sorrow for what each of them had lost at different times, and the pack howled with her, and somewhere in that new howl, somewhere in that night, the Wolves of Time began to be a pack.

One day in high summer Elhana rose slowly, carefully, and picked her way out of the main area where the wolves lay out through the day to find a place down by the river to drink. Chill water on her mouth, and the lights of a thousand minute darting suns freckling her face; and the shadow of a wolf behind.

'Elhana.'

She turned at his voice and stared up at him, breathless before him, knowing he would be there.

'Aragon.'

Fatally he stepped nearer, into that circle from which wolves find it hard to pull back, where words matter not one bit, and the heart thumps so strongly it feels as if the whole world might know.

'I thought . . .'

It mattered not what Aragon thought.

He was near enough that she could scent him well, and want much more.

He drank the waters she had drunk.

She was close enough that he could hear the jerk and stop-start of her breathing, and see where the water she had drunk was shiny in the matted fur of her muzzle. And her eyes, waiting.

Above them the trees rose darkly into the bright sky, and by them the river flowed, strong and chill; where they moved, their paws beginning to stumble they were so close, their bodies beginning to pattern together, he one way, she another, the air was warm and close, and beyond it, the trees and the river were beginning to fade.

'Elhana, I should not be here, not now, with you. You are ledrene . . .'

He said it not as she might have feared, diffidently and with a question in his voice hoping to pass the decision to her, but matter-of-factly, even a little ruefully.

'No,' she agreed, 'you should not.'

There was a long silence between them in which they hardly moved at all. Elhana felt his sympathy, his sense of ease.

'Is it true that Ambato was your father? You said so once and he did not disagree . . .'

'It is. I think. Who can tell such things? It was a long time ago and my mother . . .'

'Her name?'

'Lauria. My mother . . .'

'Was she as beautiful as you?'

'More so. My mother . . .'

'And as fair?'

He smiled, their voices conspiratorial, yet light-hearted. It was a game between wolves who were discovering that they might play and laugh and mean nothing more by it than . . .

'Fairer. She . . .'

'Was in love?'

'She was, wolf, and improperly so. He was not the leader of the pack.'

'Aah . . .' sighed Aragon. He lay down, and as he did so his flank touched hers and she knew, she knew as certain as the trees that rose up and the river that flowed on, that one day, one day there would be, between them, nothing. They would be one. One day, and perhaps no more than that . . .

The dust of trees and soil hung in the shafts of sunlight that angled down amidst them, and the soaring wings of hover-flies, caught by the light, hung, soared, hung again, and were gone.

They talked, the close, continual talk of wolves who, for

now, would be only friends, but in whose shared secrets and histories, tales of mothers and memories of fears and losses, discoveries of places, and insights gained, there was a sudden growing intimacy and passion that was deeper than any snatched physical union might have been that day. Neither dared think of the love that might be, but both felt and desired it, and could think of nothing else.

V

RIVALRY AND WAR

In which feuds divide the Wolves of Time in their struggle against Wulf's enemies and Kobrin suggests a new kind of war

CHAPTER TWENTY NINE

*Klimt breaks his long silence and, taking the pack
into his confidence, surprises them all*

LATER THAT SAME DAY, as twilight settled down
into night, Klimt appeared in the group's clearing,
sombre and tired. If he knew that the balance of
his world had shifted as a result of a meeting between
Elhana and Aragon he did not betray it. Certainly Tervicz,
who did suspect, saw no sign of jealousy or anger in Klimt's
face, and he knew him best of all.

'Tomorrow we move on,' announced Klimt.

'Where to?' growled Morten. It was a challenge of a sort.
Its tone said, '*You* may wish to move on but *we* need per-
suading, so persuade us.'

Klimt slowly rose up, frowning. He looked at Tervicz
and for a moment seemed to consider attacking him; then
he stared hard at Morten, whom he had fought once and
looked now quite willing to fight again. Then at Stry, dismissively. Then over towards Elhana, at whom he gazed
for a time as if he might brutally mate her, and then he
seemed to dismiss that idea as well. Finally he went straight
over to where Aragon lay in his usually calm and easy way,
and stared down at him. Aragon dropped his gaze, and
moved his tail just enough to show subordination; but only
just enough. Challenges were in the air.

It said much for the power of Klimt's presence that he
could convey all this without a word said, and it left them

443

all restive, all on edge. All a little afraid. Behind Klimt the trees rose up darkly, shifting one beyond another, and beyond them, the harsh faces of the cliffs and abutments of the mountains rose, one above the other, up and up until they reached the sky.

Against it all Klimt seemed suddenly small, and their challenges smaller and themselves more puny still: they were, after all, just a small untried pack of wolves, with a history of problems behind them, and an uncertain future ahead. Klimt moved forward, his eyes tired, and his body seeming thinner, less bulky, than before. As if to accentuate all this he began to speak to them with a strange weariness and wisdom that made them feel that whatever it was he was going to say he had thought long and hard about. Suddenly the moment and its context, and Klimt's lonely gravitas, made it seem that history was in his words, and a future that might be more shifting and uncertain than any forest tree, and harsher than any mountain face.

'I have been silent to you all these weeks and months past, and silent for the most part to my ledrene. Through this time I have had little way with words, which I think you know. But in these most recent weeks I have found it hard to find any words at all, though once, Elhana, I think you and I spoke in a way that one day we might find we can do again.'

He looked over to her and she nodded her agreement.

'Well then, now, as best I can, I wish to speak to all of you. We are not yet quite a pack. Nor should we yet use such words as "Wolves of Time" to describe ourselves, though it was I myself who told the Magyars that that was our name. I now think it was presumptuous. I am learning, and I am finding that the wolfway on which I am set, upon which we all are set, is hard and fraught with difficulty.'

They were all still and silent, and only the trees beyond Klimt offered any sound or movement at all: the whisper of wind through leaves and branches, and the shift and sway of life itself.

'We lost our cubs,' said Klimt, the first time he had publicly acknowledged it. 'In that my ledrene lost something of her soul forever, and for that, as your leader, I hold myself responsible. I say "lost" because we cannot yet be sure they are all dead. One was still-born, and one died as Elhana held her. But the last, the one Jicin took, may still be alive. We cannot know. I believe that Jicin would have done all she could to save him. I think that wolf was one I would trust with my own life, for despite all she had suffered she had courage to seek us out, and entrust her life to our pack. I do not know why she became separated and did not find us later – but then, we might have done more to seek *her* . . .'

'We did search for her,' said Tervicz.

'Do we still search for her?' said Klimt. He shook his head and added, 'We should have done, we should do, we must do, for our strength as a pack can only be measured by the way we look after our individual members. I think my ledrene will agree with my judgement of Jicin . . .'

For the second time he had appealed to her, and for the second time she nodded her head in agreement, this time looking over to him, acknowledging him. She did not, could not, love him: he was so stiff, so bleak, so much of him was tight and unavailable, but as he spoke, or tried to speak, she could feel how hard he was trying to reveal his heart, how much he wanted to be a leader who served them as much as they served him. A rush of respect and admiration came to her, and if not love, then sympathy, and the insight that this was a great wolf chosen by the gods for a great task, and he was struggling to find the wolfway which would lead to its achievement.

'And I too, I too,' he said suddenly, his voice breaking,

'I lost something of my soul when our cubs died and the last living one was lost . . .'

'Oh Klimt,' whispered Elhana, going to his flank as a ledrene should, and not minding that others saw the tears she should have wept long before. Stiff and impersonal he might be, but he somehow briefly managed to put a paw to hers, and if he did not quite weep himself, it was some time before he began to speak again. In those hard moments, when no words were said of the suffering and loss all felt, the pack was at one in sharing its grief.

'But now,' continued Klimt at last, 'we must put that behind us and have faith that ahead of us, waiting for our coming, will be challenges and triumphs that will alleviate our memories of loss.

'The time. . .'

Klimt's voice had faltered for a while, but now it deepened, and slowed. The trees seem to grow darker, the mountains more lowering.

'The time has come for us to return to the Heartland and to seek out the WulfRock. I do not wish to have a war with the Magyar wolves but if we must we must. How or when I do not know. They will resist our return and they will seek to destroy us. There can be no second retreat. But what are seven against so many? What is a group that is not quite a pack, against one of the most ancient packs of wolfdom, one indeed that is formed of many packs across the Carpathians whose true strength we have not yet seen?

'The answer is: I do not know. But I have a vision and I want to share it with you, as perhaps I should have done before. We know that wolfkind is very near its end. The Mennen brought us down, and our own weaknesses and loss of memory and lore are finally finishing us off.

'My ledrene, Elhana, came from a pack which, from what she says, was but a rump of what it must once have been. Her father Ambato foresaw its decline, and saw as well, as in different ways we all have done, that if there was a future for wolfkind at all it must lie where all began: in the Heartland, in the shadow of the fabled WulfRock.

'You, Tervicz, you too come from a pack that has all but disappeared. And you Lounel, are the very last of your kind. Wolves run no more upon the high causses of France's Massif Central. Of Aragon's history we have all now heard, and how he, like myself, answered the summons of Wulf, whose voice comes upon the wind, or in the rumble of a fall of rock, and whose eyes are in the light across the waters.

'As for you, Morten, and your brother, Stry, born nearer here than any of us, dismissive of the Magyar wolves, willing to follow whatever poor lead I have so far given, well . . . you know as much about decline as any of us.

'Of my own history, I will say only this. My mother's kin were originally of Pechora in northern Russia; my father was a Lappish wolf. Both came from communities of wolves that have suffered as all have suffered at the hands and guns of Mennen, for many generations past. Out of that suffering, as out of the Nordic landscape, comes silence not words; thought before action; too little, perhaps, of what most in a pack desire. But so it is, so it is, that is what I am.'

He looked at them seriously, seeming somehow aged by his own words, as wolfkind had aged and bowed before the hard, slow centuries that were the heritage of each of their packs and tribes. They were all still and silent, each making of his words what their histories and their inclinations wished them to.

Elhana was most still and silent of them all, her eyes expressing something of the surprise she felt the more he spoke, for behind his silences she had thought there was a cold mind and an unkind heart. Now the more he spoke, the more clearly she saw there was a courage she had not understood, as well as the obsessive drive that she sensed, and a sensitivity to the past which gave Klimt a clarity of purpose for the future. It was the present he had problems with! A trace of a smile warmed her eyes, she glanced at Aragon who, she found, was looking at her, and she looked quickly away again. Had he seen the smile, and did he understand it? Yet in that moment her heart beat faster and was in confusion: respect and admiration for one, love and desire for the other . . . oh, Aragon, a wolf of wild Iberia, and sun, and epic dreams, and an alluring pride . . .

Oh, Klimt, my lawful leader. Respect but no love. Duty but no joy. Purpose but no . . . She was thinking 'passion' but that would be unfair. He felt passion all right, a grim Nordic passion that was so alien to the wilder warmer passions of wolves like her, and like Aragon too, from the sunnier drier lands of the south.

Had she really the strength to be ledrene to such a wolf as he? She shivered with apprehension and wished there was another female here who might take the mantle from her. But even then she felt doubt about what it might be that Klimt was going to want from them.

Klimt frowned and was silent for a time, suddenly forbidding. It was summer but there was ice in his eyes.

'You know, because you have heard him talk of it, that Lounel believes he came close to the WulfRock. Ambato, perhaps, went on to see it. We cannot know. The location is somewhere above the lake where we successfully evaded the Magyars when we first confronted Hassler and Dendrine and the rest.

'But it is important for what I have decided you shall do next that you are all clear what it was that Lounel thought he saw, and about other matters he has only spoken of to me. Lounel . . .'

He turned to Lounel to speak, but one or two of them – Aragon perhaps, Tervicz certainly, and Lounel himself –

were thinking that whatever it was that Klimt was leading to might be something they could never have predicted. In saying 'I have decided *you* shall do . . .' he seemed not to include himself. Could that possibly be his intention? No, it was not possible . . .

'Lounel . . .' he said again, cutting right across such thoughts.

Lounel sighed, for he did not like addressing a group. He liked to look into a wolf's eyes when he spoke and a group did not have one pair of eyes, nor one heart, and nor one mind.

So he sighed, and said, 'It is true that I may have got close to the WulfRock, and it is also true I did not try to venture on and see it. This surprises some of you I know. If we return to that high place wherein the WulfRock may rise you may try to make your own ways there, and you will understand my difficulty. Some places are harder to reach the nearer you get; or if not, they are not worth visiting! But know this: there is a wolf living in those parts already. Perhaps more than one.'

There was a murmur of excitement at his words for he had said nothing of this before.

Lounel nodded and continued, 'Indeed, it is so. There were the carcasses and tatters of rabbits as evidence, and the prints of wolf's paws in the slurried scree below broken cliffs in whose overhangs a vagrant might well hide. Or a nursing mother . . .'

There were more murmurs at this revelation. Lounel was never a wolf to say such things for effect.

'I did not investigate my suspicions, which will disappoint some of you. I thought it unwise. A wolf would choose to hide in those parts for very good reasons of their own. There were shadows about the paw-prints that I saw, and there was darkness amongst the rocks to which they led. I judged it best to leave well alone.

'But that broken place, through which Ambato led me as if he had been there many times before, is but a prelude to the WulfRock. Into it I have no doubt many wolves have been and gone. It is a place touched by the light and dark of Wulf's own life, and Wulfin's too.

'One thing I know. It is a place easily overwatched and therefore easily defended. It is a place well provided with food, though rabbits can be dull. The ravens overfly it, which speaks well of it and suggests its holiness, for my mother used to say that ravens are the shadows of Wulf and Wulfin's wishes: mysterious, beyond our reach, changing, disturbing, before and after the lives of wolves.

'But should wolves go there? I think they should. Do wolves risk something doing so? I think they do. The Magyar wolves have had all the dark millennium to go there, and they have not; now the time has come for other wolves to try.

'Are we those wolves? You Stry, and you, Morten? All of us? Was Ambato?'

Lounel twisted and turned his head as if to seek the answer somewhere in the air, then shrugged, turned, turned again, and finally sighed.

'I know this: the gods led Ambato there and afterwards he wanted to go back. Ambato led me there and I want to go back. I shall lead you there and you will want I know not what. Ambato, Lounel . . . and that wolf who lingers in the dark heights there. These are individuals. But *us*, we are something else. A pack created through time. Eh, Klimt? Is that what we are? Beset by time?'

He had finished talking, but he had not finished thinking. Lounel followed his words with a strange muttered silence, in which he sank to his haunches among them, nibbled at his paws as if they needed cleansing of some filth he had walked through. Which was in a way quite true. For what Lounel then remembered, but what he did not speak of, was that he had seen more than shadows in the heights: he had seen two wolves.

One was the haggard Dendrine, ledrene of the Magyars, standing above him as still as death, except for her rotten fur which was tugged this way and that by updraughts of wind, like the matted hair of sheep at the end of summer.

The other was a well-grown wolf cub – well-grown but malformed. This creature stared down at Lounel dispassionately, its milky blue eyes not the least of its entire anatomy that was hideous and strange. Legs too long, fur awry, haunches thick, tail thicker, head like molten rock gone skew where it had set. Mouth open. But the eyes . . . frightening in their blue directness.

Lounel knew evil when he saw it, and he knew good, and he knew that in those two he saw evil. The wolf-cub had turned from where it looked down on him, barked an order strangely brutal in one so young, and Lounel saw, or thought he saw, another cub, thin and weedy as a sapling blocked in by bigger trees. This cub, this poor thing, dragged itself across Lounel's view, its back an open sore, its gait expressive of deep suffering. Why was he permitted to see such a thing? Lounel did not know, except that evil shows nothing without intent, and since evil thrives on fear, the creation of fear was probably its purpose.

These things Lounel had seen, but he did not speak of them to Klimt, or any other wolf. He thought of them, and worried over them, and nibbled and fretted at his paws to pry out a meaning for them yet again, and failed. He looked up, realized that he had forgotten where he was, and with a cough and an apology, got up and loped away to the pack's far edge, saying nothing more.

Thus, while Klimt had intimidated them, Lounel left them much disturbed, aware of the shadows and the threats which his spoken words left inarticulate. After that, no one spoke for a long time, and all were restless and uneasy.

None caught the gaze of others, all found that they strove to see things they could not describe.

'So . . .' continued Klimt finally, 'I think the time has come to move back into the Heartland. Back to try to occupy the place where Lounel has already been. But, do not presume that our destination is the WulfRock itself, or that I should be your leader . . .'

At this there was a ripple of reaction. *Not the leader?* What leader would say such a thing?

'Presume nothing. We are not yet what I judge to be a pack. This is the time of our coming and it may be that we are not all here yet. We are a pack in the making with a destiny we cannot yet describe. Ambato came and showed us the way we might go. Others will show us how to get nearer still. And we, gathered here, uneasy, uncertain, more familiar so far with failure and escape, with nothing yet to show but doubts and dreams, we . . . are . . . not . . . a pack.

'As for myself, I think it best I do not travel on with you for now . . .'

There was sudden protest at this, a course which he had already hinted at. He raised a paw to quieten them.

'No, no, I must not. I am not unaware that in this pack, as in any I suppose, there are tensions and unfulfilled desires. Nor am I certain that I am the right leader, or Elhana the right ledrene. We came together by chance, and I have assumed leadership over you by right of precedence. True, Morten, you did me the honour of fighting with me for Elhana, but . . . things have changed.'

He looked at Aragon, and then, with meaning, at Elhana. He half-smiled, a little ruefully perhaps and then half-shook his head.

'I do not know if a leader and ledrene should love one another. I do know that my mother loved my father, and that in their love was the heartland of our small pack. I

452

know too, that there have been successful packs without love between the two who led them – packs indeed that were better without such love.

'But for myself, I am used to love. Now, I do not say I do not feel it for Elhana, far from it . . . but I know what she feels for me, and what she might feel for another. What I do not know is what is best for the Wolves of Time. Love? Duty? Old lore? New? *I do not know*.

'Therefore, I have decided to cede leadership and spend time alone. My last order to you as your leader is to follow through what I have advised: seek out the place that Ambato found for us and make it your own. Choose a new leader. Discover love or loves if they exist. Do these things without deceit.

'I shall travel alone for a time, and I shall seek what guidance I can find in earth and stars, lake and running water, and in the whispering wind. Then, too, I shall be free to do what I should have done the night we fled the gully: as a leader I had to lead the pack to safety. As a father and nothing more I can now go back and try to find my cub, and Jicin too. We accepted her into the haven of our pack. We failed to protect her.'

'But Klimt, leader . . .' began Morten.

Klimt slowly shook his head.

'This I must do alone. I shall try to find the truth of what happened, try to find the cub and Jicin and whatever else I can. Alone I prefer to do it. You shall find out the truth of those other things I talked about.

'But know this: if, when my thinking and my search are done I deem it wise to return, then I shall do so. And if I deem it wise to challenge for the leadership, I shall do that too. And doing it, and succeeding in it, there shall be no more talk or thought, covert glances or hidden desires, or love forbidden. Whichever female is ledrene when I return, if Wulf grants that I can wrest the leadership back, that female I shall serve and expect to serve me with loyalty, with duty, with care, and finally with all the love Wulfin grants, until the day I die, or yield up my leadership. This I vow. For truly, the pack I wish to lead should have a leader and ledrene as devoted to each other as my father and my mother were.

'One more thing: I am not so sure who our enemy is . . .'

'The Magyar!' said Stry.

'The Mennen!' said Morten.

'Not ourselves?' whispered Klimt. 'Well, I do not know. So now I must journey for a time without you, in no great expectation that I shall see you again. I see shadows that make me afraid. When I was young and I saw my first blizzard sweep towards me across the flat plain north of the Baltic I was afraid as well, mortally afraid, though my father stood at my flank.

'"You're shivering, wolf," he said. "What are you afraid of?"

'"I don't know," I replied, "I don't know."

'Now I am afraid once more and I don't know why, but I cannot turn away from what I see coming. Nor understand why I think it might be that it is *we* who are coming. I am afraid and will not pretend otherwise. I pray that I may find the cub we lost and I abandoned. I pray that you Elhana, my ledrene until now, find the love you yearn for, and the leadership you seek. I pray for all of us, us Wolves of Time.'

How he had done it they did not know but the wolves listening to Klimt saw before them then not the huge, forbidding wolf they had begun to grow to dislike, and whom they had wished to desert, but a wolf who was no more than a cub, who stood with only the shadow of a father for protection, and who now, whatever they decided, had summoned up the courage to advance towards the coming blizzard, alone. More than that, they saw a wolf of truth, worthy to be leader of them all.

They wanted to say much in different ways, but Klimt had forestalled them all. He turned to face the fell and then, with only the briefest of glances back at them, picked his way slowly downslope among the heather and the peat hags. As lonely, as courageous and as noble a wolf as any of them had ever seen.

But more than that . . .

When he was gone, Lounel saw the first thing Elhana did, and Aragon as well. It was to glance at each other, a covert glance, a glance of love and opportunity.

Then Lounel knew for certain what he had long since guessed, that as well as being noble and courageous, Klimt of Tornesdal was wise as well.

'Return,' whispered Lounel to the wind, '*return to us when you have discovered what it is you seek . . .*'

CHAPTER THIRTY

*The pack begins an uneasy journey in the Heartland
and finds that replacing Klimt is not an easy task*

THE WOLVES FOUND that the fells were much
changed since they had fled from the Magyars across
them earlier in the year, and then, after the loss of
their cubs, right out of the Heartland.

Then, spring was only just ending and all had been fresh
and vibrant with new life. Above the fells and valley sides
the snipe had tumbled in the sky, drumming their mating
sounds; and the stags, nervous for their hinds, had led their
harems up and away into the high screes, and bellowed
their anger and lust from the headland vales.

Now, months later, the skylark, trilling on a bright wind
against a blue sky, had replaced the snipe, and the herds
of deer, their stags easier, ran in larger flocks, their coats
a warm bracken-colour, and their young, once hidden,
nimble now, and foolish in the balmy breeze.

High summer had come, and with it the vegetation had
grown blowsy – the cotton-grass was white and swaying,
while here and there the grasses and sedges were already
fading into the dry and duller greens that would turn yellow
and pale beige when September came. The grass, now
matted and untidy, would soon thin out over the dry soil
and rock, while beetles and ants and solitary bees began
to die or burrow towards sleep, their spring and summer
work all done, their life continued in new generations

as they grew old and ready to turn back to the soil that bore them.

For now, the only indications of this drying out, this coming autumnal decline, was the way the grass stalks whispered and rattled together in the breeze, and that the alpine flowers had mostly gone, though the air hung sometimes with their floating seeds, warm and balmy still.

It was across this different landscape that the wolves began their journey, uneasy since Klimt's departure. They took their time, moving by way of the best cover they could find, and pausing often in the gullies and hollows which they found along the way; or resting out of the light of brighter days until duller dusk set in, or the first hours after dawn gave them new liberty.

Given half a chance a male will try to fulfil his dream of leading others, and the pack now had at least two males – Morten and Aragon – who harboured such hopes.

In these early days of their journey therefore they were skirmishing for power which, the pack recognizing the importance of deciding the issue, meant they went slowly and with prudence. Best to sort out who was going to lead before they run into trouble with the Magyars.

In these circumstances it was Lounel who assumed the role of route-finder and guide while the others sorted themselves out, which made sense given that he had journeyed back from the lake which, by now, all knew to be the key to finding the territory of the WulfRock itself. He was quite content to lie down and rest away from the other males while they bickered and quarrelled, and Aragon and Morten sized each other up, tussled and nipped a bit, and began to try to find a way to determine who should lead.

'Well, I must admit,' confessed Tervicz to Lounel one lazy afternoon, 'that this is getting tedious. If only one or

other of them would go for it, but . . . well . . . they're
evenly matched.'

'Who are?'

'Aragon and Morten. We all know who Elhana wants as
leader but . . . what a ledrene wants isn't always what she
gets, as Klimt proved . . . It's a pity he's gone. You don't
think he'd be mucking about with wrangles and tussles like
this do you?'

Lounel smiled.

'And who do you want as leader?'

'Of those two? Aragon!' said Tervicz promptly. 'First
because if Morten takes over I'll suffer more than most. He
won't be able to talk to me as he usually does. I'll lose a
friend, just as I lost a friend in Klimt when the pack
expanded and he became its leader . . .'

Lounel saw nostalgia mixed with unhappiness in
Tervicz's eyes.

'And second?' prompted Lounel.

'I don't like saying it, but I think Aragon offers the pack
a better chance as leader. He always gave me the feeling
of holding back in deference to Klimt. Morten, on the
other hand, had his chance and Klimt defeated him.
The thing about Morten is the pack can rely on him as a
follower because he's loyal and tough and can use his initiative. But as a leader . . . well, he might not be flexible
enough.'

'You've given this some thought,' said Lounel slowly.

'You've got to remember that I was brought up by a
true leader, even if I didn't always like him. My father
Zcale . . .'

Lounel nodded. Tervicz had told the story of his upbring-
ing, and spoken of Zcale frequently with much loving
respect.

'. . . and then again, I served Klimt for a good few
months before you others came along, and I learnt a lot

from him about what a leader could and could not be. It is not an easy task leading a pack.'

'And what do you think of Klimt now that he has left us?'

'I am confused and disappointed. I thought he was a better leader than that, but . . . but . . .'

'But what, wolf?'

'Maybe . . .'

'Maybe what?'

The moment passed, and Tervicz was not going to speak his thought, though Lounel did not miss the way he glanced around where Aragon stood stiff and staring aggressively at Morten, and then at Elhana. They both understood why Klimt had left, and how wise he might have been to let things take their course now, when it mattered less, rather than later, when it might be ruinous to the pack's well-being. Love, Klimt might hope, thinking of Aragon and Elhana, had a shorter life than duty, thinking of himself and the demands such a leader as he might in time be forced to make upon both his ledrene and his pack. In his absence love – and lust – could run its course all the faster.

'But you think he will come back?'

'I hope he will, Lounel,' said Tervicz fervently.

They travelled generally north-eastward, and might have made better time but for the need to hunt for food, and the fact that early on they picked up Magyar trails and recent scent markings.

As Stry put it: 'Given half a chance, and even if he's pursued by a dozen enemies, a Magyar will pee on a rock as he rushes by it, just to say that he's been there . . .'

They came upon such tracks and markings several times, and those of a couple of lone wolves, too. As well as that, the pack was shadowed by a wolf they saw only in the distance, but who escaped their pursuit. A clever wolf, dark and large, seen best of all when he was forced by a clever manoeuvre by Morten and Stry to cross a patch of snow on his way to escape over a col.

'Huge,' said Aragon looking at the paw marks, himself no small wolf.

'Large enough,' conceded the wiry Tervicz. 'It is a pity he avoids us.'

'We have males enough, Tervicz,' said Aragon who, with the issue of leadership unresolved, did not wish to complicate matters.

'If we're going to survive against the Magyar, we shall need all the help we can get. And anyway . . .' he added mischievously, 'he looked like leadership material to me!'

'We're lacking females just as much as males', said Elhana, who had overheard their talk. 'That is why the loss of Jicin was a real one. But then, perhaps, the better way to add to our numbers, whether male or female, is through breeding. Cubs bring a pack together. Lack or loss of them is divisive . . .'

The others could not help but see the way she glanced at Aragon once or twice as she spoke. Nor be unaware of the extra incentive towards taking leadership it seemed to give him. There was an almost smouldering passion about the way he carried himself now, and he was going to be hard to beat.

So all continued to be tense, all close, like the heaviness of the humidity that precedes a summer thunderstorm; and the burden of it was becoming unbearable.

Perhaps sensing what she had done – perhaps, indeed, intending to have done it, for Elhana was emerging as a skilled and experienced ledrene who knew how to get her own way – she added, 'We should proceed rather more like a pack seeking our own territory, and less like one chasing its own tail!'

'And you think that territory hereabouts lies fallow, waiting for the Wolves of Time to turn up and occupy it like rabbits taking over badger setts?' said Tervicz. 'Anyway we are not looking just for territory – but for territory near the WulfRock.'

'I think that Wulf and Wulfin will direct us to the right place,' Elhana said safely. She had no stomach yet for outright argument.

'Perhaps the gods will so direct us,' said Tervicz, 'and perhaps they won't. Meanwhile, now we are back in the Heartland, and knowing what we do about the Magyars, it is surely a matter of time before we are located and attacked. All I was trying to say was that once that happens then I am sure we will wish that that brute of a vagrant we saw earlier was on our side.'

They saw the same large wolf several times more, and once Stry came face to face with him – across the roar of a mountain stream. Even then he was hard to see clearly for he did not show all of himself, but he *was* 'huge', as Aragon had put it, and rough as well, and heavily scarred about the face.

'I do not say that he was ugly, nor even especially threatening, but then perhaps he was doing his best to smile!' reported Stry in the off-hand way he had. 'He seemed as curious of me as I of him, but cautious, for I only had to blink and he was gone. Where he went I have no idea, for the only cover was where he had been in. Impressive. One for our pack, that's what Tervicz said before, and now I agree with him. Meanwhile . . .'

'Meanwhile?' said Lounel quietly.

'Meanwhile, I am glad there was a stream between myself and our brutal-looking friend,' said Stry with a self-deprecating grin.

That particular vagrant might have made an even greater impression than he did had there not been several others to occupy their conversation. Most were younger and skirmished on the periphery of the pack before losing their courage and moving off.

One, a young Magyar vagrant almost certainly, engaged with Stry and got a mauling for his impudence before running off.

Stry was glad of the encounter, for since he had been wounded by the Mann he had lost a little of his fighting confidence. Now it had returned. He seemed to have a nose for scenting out where aliens might be.

'Still, it was a shame he scarpered, for surely such wolves as those return to their pack and gain respect for having sighted a pack such as ours. Perhaps Hassler has sent such wolves off as scouts to gain information.'

But Morten shook his head. 'He may have done, but remember it is high summer. Cubs have been reared, old wolves have died, prey is plentiful, and it is the time when vagrants roam forth. Did we not begin our own climb through the passes of the Tatras at this time of year, Stry?'

But there were other incidents to think about as well. One night there came a howling out of part of the fell they had travelled through during the day, when they had all been sure a wolf had followed them. For that reason they had been on the alert, and set a double watch, but the howling was only that of a lone female, and one they had heard distantly before but which they could never quite track down. That night it was as if she howled not to draw wolves to her and make contact, but rather as a sign that *she* knew they were there but chose to go her own way.

As it was, the expected attack came two weeks or so after they had set off on their slow meandering journey to find the lake, and the moment that it did they all wished they had resolved the issue of leadership long since. But sometimes it takes a crisis to clear the air, and make wolves see sense.

The Magyar ambush was brilliantly managed. For two

days past the fells had been beset by the last of the high summer heat and while the distant hills and mountains shimmered in the haze, the lake edges, exposed as the water receded, buzzed with flies and wasps seeking moisture, and a cool haven. The wolves felt no different and, still leaderless, were less strict about keeping watch than Klimt would have insisted had he been there.

Whatever the cause, whoever deserved to take the blame, Morten suddenly found himself confronted by an apparently solitary Magyar some little distance from where the main pack lazed. He had no chance to retreat before the wolf engaged with him ferociously, biting and tumbling him and drawing him away rather than towards the safety of the others.

So not only was time lost before he was able to send out a warning bark, but he found himself further away than he should have been without a clear line of retreat. This being so, when warning came, the others could not quite see what was wrong and instead of responding in a measured way, being cautious about what they did, Stry and Tervicz rose up and crested the depression in which the lake lay, searched the hazy fell for where Morten was, and set off towards him without any further thought than to reach him and lend their aid as quickly as they could.

Nor can it be said that Aragon did any more than to follow them from the lake, leaving Lounel and Elhana at its edge, see what they were doing and decide not to follow, as all it must be was another vagrant who needed warning off. Surely three could manage him, and he therefore turned back to join the others. Only after he had done so did he hear shouts and the sounds of fighting from the direction in which Morten and the others had gone, and turned back once more to get a better look.

If luck plays a part in deciding who leads whom, luck was now on Aragon's side, for from the slightly elevated position he was the only one among them able to see the situation they had unwittingly got themselves into, and that it was serious.

Below him near the lake, and advancing through the dry heather with grim resolution on Lounel and Elhana, were three large wolves *they* had not yet seen. Aragon immediately lowered himself, thinking that perhaps they thought he had gone on over the edge of the depression to help out the others, and he did not yet bark out a warning. The slow and careful advance of the Magyars on the two by the lake gave him a few moments' grace.

He turned back towards the others, still keeping out of sight. The fewer Magyars who saw him the better. But what *he* now saw more than alarmed him: as Tervicz and Stry approached to give aid to Morten, three more Magyars rose from a hollow ahead of them, beyond which Morten had been lured, whilst a motley bunch of other wolves were advancing on them all from either flank. Three by the lake, three confronting the other two, one or two now with Morten: that made eight plus three or four more approaching, twelve to their six.

Not only had the pack been outnumbered, but they had been outmanoeuvred too, so that their small group had been split into three parts, each isolated and under attack, except for he himself. He turned back to see how Lounel and Elhana were faring, and already they were engaged in fighting, a task which Lounel was singularly ill-equipped for. But at least there were no other Magyars joining in this part of the fray.

Still keeping out of sight, Aragon looked back and forth once more and decided it was the two by the lake who could be most effectively helped. More than that, even as he began a low advance through the heather so that he was not seen until the last moment, he saw that there might be a way of routing the Magyars at this point and joining forces with the others. He remembered Tervicz's graphic account of how Klimt had sent the Magyars packing the last time they attacked Elhana, and decided to go in hard himself.

The nearest he could get to the fighting was by taking ground cover nearly to the lake itself, so that when he finally emerged into the open the quickest advance on the three Magyars was across open water. Fortunately he knew its depth, for he had cooled himself in it the day before, so now he did not hesitate.

He gave no warning roar, but instead fixed on the nearest of the three wolves, who after their first assault were now advancing one by one in little darts on Lounel and Elhana, and he bounded forward in great leaps and splashes across the water towards him. The effect must have been frightening; it was certainly dramatic: for all the wolves saw, including the two under attack, were sprays and cascades of sun-filled water, and what seemed like a whole pack of wolves advancing on them out of the confusion.

'There's more coming,' roared Aragon, working the time-honoured bluff which, combined with surprise, often disconcerts an attacking force, and panics them into fleeing. To give them less time to think, Aragon did not bother with preliminaries but grabbed the haunch of the nearest wolf, tore and ripped at him and bowled him over, leaving Elhana to continue the attack as he rose up from the fallen wolf and advanced hugely on the next in line.

Even as Aragon decided that the bluff could not possibly work, the other two Magyars faltered and then fled, too shocked and frightened by Aragon's arrival to have the courage or mettle to go to their fallen comrade's aid. That wolf, bleeding now at front and rear, rose up, whining, saw a gap between Lounel and the lake, and dashed past, tail between his legs. This part of the fight, at least, was won.

'Now, follow me you two,' commanded Aragon, 'and both of you keep down as low as you can. And Lounel – *try* to look fierce!'

This was something almost impossible for Lounel to do, but there was a certain wildness about his clumsy gait and abstracted expression that Aragon hoped an enemy might find intimidating.

Aragon's aim now was to go to the aid of Stry and Tervicz, for if he and the others could join with them then a force of five might very well break through to Morten and, depending on his condition, that would make six. They heard the fight before they dared break cover to see it, but finally with no cover left, they upped and charged, each going hard for a wolf designated by Aragon. This time the Magyars did not retreat so readily but at least their numbers were not as great as Aragon had feared, there being only five of them, one of whom was already wounded, and another who was young and nervous.

Again Aragon did not hesitate and he was surprised how useful his experience as a young wolf with the rough Cabrera pack now came in, ducking and feinting, backing off and then, when the opportunity arose, going in hard at an opponent's vulnerable points, and drawing blood. By the time they arrived Stry and Tervicz had been driven back to back, both weary with the struggle which had been prolonged by the Magyars' mistaken assumption that since they could easily defeat the aliens they might as well taunt and provoke them first. Had they been more ruthless from the start, Aragon might not have been in time to save either of them from serious injury.

As it was, his arrival with Lounel and Elhana gave the other two new life, and it was not long before the Magyars retreated, growling, and finally gave up. Meanwhile, further across the fell, where Morten had been fighting, there was nothing to be seen at all but a crippled Magyar, whining and swearing. His leg was bleeding and broken and he could hardly move.

'Where is the wolf you attacked?' demanded Stry of this hapless wolf.

'Fled, for Wulf's sake. Across the fell. We were . . .'

'Shut up,' said Stry, listening.

All was suddenly silent, but for the heavy breathing of the listening wolves, and as the wounded Magyar crawled away others of his pack stood off uncertainly, watching the aliens one moment and looking out after their friends another. The fight was over.

Stry relaxed and said, 'We could follow his trail but I wouldn't advise it. Morten's very good at giving wolves the miss. If he's run then he'll not be badly wounded, otherwise he would have stood his ground. He was probably hoping to draw them away to make it easier for us.'

'He's succeeded,' said Aragon. 'If he's good at losing wolves chasing him, he'll be good at making his own way back. We'll retreat so that these Magyars think that we too have fled, then they are less likely to come after us. But we'll not go so far that Morten won't find us . . .'

It was a command, not a suggestion, and the wolves accepted it, following the lead Aragon now gave. They moved one way and the Magyars drifted another and the hours passed. There was little conversation, for each of them ached, and some had suffered gashes and bruises, but nothing too serious. What preoccupied them was Morten's return, not only because they wanted to be sure that he was safe, but because now there must be a confrontation over leadership, and all knew that Aragon would not easily give up the leadership the fight had allowed him to assume.

They were right. It was late afternoon when Morten showed, and from his limp and the swelling about his face it was obvious that he had not had an easy time.

'Well . . .' he began laconically, but the smile left his

face as he saw what the others were thinking, and the way they looked at Aragon.

'Yes,' said Aragon, and he did not hesitate, for he knew he might be lost if he did.

The fight, if that was what it was, was over in moments, with Morten dropping his tail in submission, and opening up his guard so that if Aragon had wished to he might easily have crippled him, or worse. In truth, Morten was too tired to fight, Aragon too filled with the taste of leadership not to.

'Shit,' said Morten, giving in, 'you can lead the whole bloody lot of us if you like, for I don't have the stomach for it any more. Don't worry, wolf, you can count on my loyalty.'

'And I,' said Tervicz, 'until one more worthy takes your place.'

These were the Bukovians' traditional words for ceding power to a new leader, but Aragon, being an Iberian wolf and easily insulted took them the wrong way and charged Tervicz too.

'More worthy?' he snarled.

Tervicz stared into Aragon's eyes and though his expression said 'oh yes, wolf, more worthy', the words he spoke were, 'I shall be loyal so long as you are leader.'

Honour was satisfied, but Tervicz could not help thinking that there was more to leading a pack than gaining such satisfaction as that, while Aragon knew he had begun badly with Tervicz, but was not sure why. So soon may there be hints of what is yet to come. Autumn comes before winter, clouds before the rain.

Irritated, Aragon went over to Stry who calmly said, 'It's all right, wolf, I will give you my loyalty!'

Then turning to his brother Morten, Stry added by way of apology and explanation, 'He saved our lives – or at least, made sure that the Magyars did not damage us too much!'

'And I . . .' said Elhana in the ritual way ledrenes must say such things, 'I shall be ledrene to your leadership.'

Thus the pack had its leader, and the leader had his pack.

'It is well,' said Aragon, staring down on each in turn and surprised at how tired, burdened and lonely he suddenly felt. 'It is well. We shall press on and find a place to rest for a day or two and then decide how we can deal with the Magyars when they next attack. For they will, they will . . .'

Yet Morten had not quite finished with it all.

'Do you know what saved my life?' he said quietly, before they moved off. 'I was chased by four Magyars and though normally they would not have posed a problem, the battering I had received slowed me down. I came to a deep stream course on the edge of the fell and they were close behind and I thought they had me trapped. Then that brute of a wolf who's been following us appeared from Wulf knows where. He stood his ground with me and the Magyars faded away at the sight of us both.

'"These aliens will give us no more trouble," he said by way of excuse.

'All that wolf would say when I thanked him and tried to get him to talk was, "Magyars are all show, so how did you get separated by that lot from your pack? Eh? Very foolish!" Then with a look of disgust he was gone. But he's about here somewhere, Aragon, and he may be useful to us.'

'Then let us hope he finally makes himself known to us,' said Aragon shortly. With that he led them on in silence.

Klimt's shadow still fell across their path, and now those of the Magyars and vagrants as well. They had a leader, yet they still felt adrift in a sea of uncertainty.

CHAPTER THIRTY-ONE

Tervicz and Morten return to the lake,
and sense more than they can see

THE AREA TO WHICH Aragon led them was the broken country that formed a slanting wedge between the Southern Fell, the Tatras to the north, and the valley heads that drained off eastward, and where the Magyar had their so-far-unvisited stronghold. It was rough, indifferent ground, its rises and dips and strips of shattered soil and rock all evidence that this was glacial moraine country, made even more confused by the fans of outwash material brought down by floodwater from the scarps above.

In this poor area Aragon found a place that was nondescript, well-masked by shrub, and a good place to hide. So good indeed that he very soon began to harbour the thought that here they might already have found the territory they were looking for. It might be hard to find better.

'You know where we are?' asked Stry, who had a pretty good idea.

What was the matter with Aragon since he had taken over the leadership? His grace and smile seemed to have deserted him, and brusque rudeness had taken their place, as if he thought that that was the only and best way to lead wolves. Plainly, he was not sure he *did* know the place they had come to, but he was not willing to admit it outright.

'Well, wolf, you seem to!' he replied. 'So what have you to say about it?'

Stry shrugged off Aragon's gracelessness. He had seen worse. A leader needs to settle in and they must give this one time. The Aragon they had known was dead; long live the new . . .

'When we escaped the Magyars before, by following Tervicz's lead down to the lake near where we lost Ambato, there was a plateau above it that led up to these same scarplands that rise above us now. We kept lower down and took a route through forest and rough shrub and then south onto the Southern Fell. But if instead of coming lower we had kept going westward we would have come into these moraine lands and, no doubt, made our way to this hidden place in time.'

Stry turned eastward, and pointed. 'The lake cannot be so far over there. Eh Lounel?'

Lounel nodded.

Aragon pondered. He was thinking still that the country they had reached was safe, and the levels of prey probably high enough to sustain them all without much effort. The disadvantages – the difficulty of communication in such broken country, and the sense of being loomed over by the scarps, he preferred to ignore. They were safe for now and here they could stay. And anyway . . .

He glanced at Elhana and she at him. They had waited a long time to be leader and ledrene together and they had done so honourably. Aragon had earned what was coming to him and so had she. He had no wish to move on, not yet. The pack needed to be reminded in more ways than one who was dominant.

As he hesitated, he enjoyed the sense of power that came with them waiting on his words, and suddenly felt good. Very good. Why, Klimt had mastered the art of silence so well that he hardly said a thing, and look how in awe of him they had all been.

Aragon brooded, thinking, really thinking, but it was

tactics that preoccupied him, not strategy, and what weighed most with him was his own need – his lust for Elhana indeed, his need to consolidate – not the pack's need.

'What of it?' he growled to himself, 'I've earned it.' And in one sense, he had.

'Some of us are wounded, all of us are tired,' he said at last. 'This area seems safe enough, though Wulf knows I shall impose strict watches from now on after our near-defeat by the Magyars. If we had had a proper rota of watches before they would not have caught us out so easily. I do not intend that it should happen again. So . . . we will rest and feed for a day or two and then I shall send the fittest of you forth to find out the best route to the lake . . . agreed?'

He was assured enough, and his plan was hard to fault – hard, that is, had they been an ordinary pack in any ordinary place in ordinary times. Aragon seemed to have forgotten that they hoped for something more. But leadership is no easy thing, and the route to its summit can be as treacherous as raw clay on a slope after rain.

'Tervicz, you will take the first watch, and Morten, you the second. I shall take the third.'

His look softened: 'And you, Elhana,' he said, his voice a shade lower, a shade more vibrant, his eyes a touch more alight, 'my ledrene . . . a word with you if you please . . .'

The pack watched Elhana move towards him and she was awkward with the consciousness that they were watching, awkward in her own eagerness to be with him now, but eager, very eager. Some were indifferent to all this, some relieved that what was happening was open and without guile, and some . . .

Tervicz turned away, urinated in disgust, squatted down, stared up at the dark and looming scarps above them, and thought of Klimt.

'Master,' he told himself, 'may Wulf send you back to us soon, and may he help me understand why you went away. Klimt . . .' And he remembered the wolf who had saved his life, with whom he had travelled to the Heartland, and in whom he had begun to see made flesh the first forms and shapes of the Wolves of Time. But . . . they were coming, they were forming, but they were not yet here, not as they should be, not as they would need to be. *This* was not how it should be.

'It is one thing to howl down a dream, another to help transform it to reality.'

'What, wolf?' said Lounel.

Had he spoken aloud, or did Lounel know so much of others that he could read their thoughts?

'I was thinking.'

'You were mumbling, Tervicz,' said Lounel with a smile.

'What will happen to us?' said Tervicz.

'For now,' said Lounel a little wearily, 'I expect that what will happen is much what Klimt thought *would* happen. Time does not travel quite as regularly as night and day, or winter and summer or as wolves think. Time sometimes slows and sometimes speeds. For now it has slowed a little, that things may work themselves through while it does not much matter.'

'You're a strange wolf, Lounel!'

'I have a strange past, wolf. Let me tell you a little about it . . . after all, *we* have nothing better to do.'

He gave a smile so wry, so charming, so full of unspoken understanding of what was going on, that Tervicz could not but smile back and boldly ask, 'Have *you* ever mated, Lounel?'

Lounel laughed outright, in acknowledgement that Tervicz had read his own thoughts and guessed about what their worthy leader and ledrene were up to, and something else as well: 'Me? Females *frighten* me. It is the flaw in

my character. I look at Elhana and I shiver at the thought
of . . . of . . .'

'Mating? You surely know how . . .' Could so wise a wolf
know so little about something so important?

Lounel shook his head in mock horror and said, 'Spare me
the details. I can imagine them. Females . . . worry me.'

'Well, well!' said Tervicz, much amused. 'If even you
have so much to learn, then our budding pack certainly has
far to go. Now, you were going to tell me . . .'

Alone at last: not so far from the pack that they could not be
alerted in moments, yet not in a place where others could
surprise them, Aragon and Elhana stood flank to flank,
pressing, swaying, taking in each other's scent as if it were
the fragrance of eglantine on an evening, warm and still.

'It *is* evening,' he said.

'It *is* warm and still,' she replied.

'And as good as eglantine is what it seems to be,' one or
other of them said, nuzzling, sliding closer, and then pulling apart once more.

Elhana's eyes were closed, her mouth open, his touch
more sure and gentle than any of the males had ever been
with her, and in that secret vale to which he took her there
was only dappled sunshine, and no shadow that made the
form of Klimt. Here, now, where they began to explore
their pleasure, was nothing else. Here was everything.

For Aragon was not Klimt at all, not cold in what he did,
never brutal in what he took, ever gracious in what he gave;
where love was concerned. The love-words he had learned
from his mother, the rest from his ancient, epic heritage
in which wolves travelled vast wolfways to make love to the
one who was theirs, and were true to their vow of celibacy
for long years of parting.

Yet they did not yet mate.

This was . . . preliminary.

This was . . . play.

These were the preparations for something the prospect of which left Elhana wanting so much more, and Aragon feeling that he stood balanced before a field of pleasure whose joy would be the greater and all the more consuming for waiting a little.

'Not yet,' he sighed at last, pulling away, smiling, teasing her with just a little more. 'Not quite yet, Elhana. In a day or two, perhaps.'

'A day . . . or two?' she said. 'Perhaps! No, my dear, now . . .'

'Not yet,' he laughed, twisting and turning from her grasp, in this art at least a leader born.

Where they were was more than dappled sun, more than evening fragrance. Where they played was light, love and humour, and if wolves dream of love, are not their dreams like this?

'Soon,' he sighed, and Elhana thought he had never looked as good, as true, as whole as he did then. And she was right.

'Duty then, for a day or two,' she conceded, herself pulling away. Mating has its own time, its right beginning, its modulations, and its endings. For now . . .

'No more,' he whispered, going to her one last time, teasing her, playing with her, pulling her back into the world they were leaving. Making her sigh and close her eyes, making her hope he had given in. Until, opening her eyes once more, his strong touch still so much upon her that she thought that he was still right there, she saw that he had let her go and was leaving. And that the afternoon had fled before the night.

'It is time for my watch,' he said and, for now, it was.

* * *

Two days later Aragon ordered Tervicz and Morten, as the fittest there, to reconnoitre the route to the lake, and the environs of the lake itself. Not that he was yet convinced that that was the way they should go to find a territory – the moraines were proving more than adequate. What influenced Aragon most was Elhana's view that they *should* explore further – a view she had been happy to press, if only for the pleasure it gave her to find that with Aragon she had a leader who would listen to what she had to say. Klimt had never seemed to do that.

Klimt . . .

What Aragon missed in Elhana's argument in favour of further exploration was what she missed as well: that somewhere in her heart she desired at least to know what had become of Klimt, and that he was . . . safe. Tervicz could be trusted to find such a thing out if any wolf could. As for Morten, he would give Tervicz the physical support the two might need if Magyars confronted them, and Aragon was happy to see his main rival out of the way, at least until he had finally consummated his leadership with his ledrene. That was a pleasure that would be all the greater for the absence of Morten, and Tervicz as well.

The two followed the moraines east and, cutting south towards the fell, once more made their way across the track they had taken during their flight west in the late spring. They covered the ground quickly, for this was not a task over which they should dally. Two days at most was needed to find out what they must. Then back again with what information they had gathered, and Aragon could be left to make the decision about the pack's future movements.

When they crested the last rise before the lake itself, they did so circumspectly, through forest trees from the north-west and well off any obvious tracks, and they knew immediately it was the lake they sought. It lay below them, oval but for a break in its curve where rock jutted out into the water. The level of the water was lower than they remembered it, there having been little rain for a month or two, and they could see the mark of darker, exposed rock where the lake-sides were steepest. Elsewhere the banks shaded down into the water, and muddy stones and shingle were revealed, bleached by wind and sun.

The lake seemed little visited by Mennen, there being no road to it except a narrow track on the southern side, zig-zagging its way through scree and rock, and more noticeable than a path any animal might make, except sheep, of which they had unfortunately seen none about at all. Northward, beyond an extensive grass and rock plateau, rose the succession of scarps that led up into mountains.

The plateau itself was unremarkable, and ideal deer country, and its only feature was a jagged and ugly channel that crossed from the scarps to the lake and which, though not quite dry, looked like its only source of water.

'I can't remember crossing any flow of water when we were here before,' said Morten.

'We were running for our lives if you remember,' murmured Tervicz, keeping low. 'But I do remember the feel and roar of water. It must run under that last ridge, through the moraine and on into the lake.'

They gazed about and took in the topography and other details. Mennen were not near, but they were not so far either. They knew from their early and separate explorations of the fells that at night, off to the south, they occasionally saw the lights of vehicles shining up into the sky, and with the right wind, they sometimes heard their sound, and even got the scent of their fumes. But at least the road itself did not come near.

As for the lake, there was something awesome about it, something old and sonorous, though Tervicz felt it more than Morten did. To him there was something distantly familiar about the place, and to one who believed as a

Bukov wolf must, in the power of past lives and incarnations, he could not but conclude that in some former time, on a wolfway now too far away in time for him to travel back along in memory, he had known this place before.

Lying low, watching, the two wolves soon worked out the pattern of life around the lake. Rabbits first, in the soft moraine ground immediately below them and over to the south; and, too, a smaller warren among rocks that drifted up onto the steeper slopes to the north, which lay to their left.

'Where rabbits bob, foxes lope,' muttered Morten, repeating an old saying of his Polish forebears, and here was no exception. The ground was routinely quartered by two foxes, not a pair, one of which came up from the south, the other coming from the east. The lake marked a shared boundary, but prudence seemed to dictate they did their hunting when the other was not about.

The two wolves had long since decided to keep to their cover and so for food and drink they retreated back the way they had come, taking a hare or two well out of sight of the lake, and drinking at one of the many streamlets that came off the steep slopes to their left.

The temptation to go down to the lake itself was great, the more so because on the second evening the weather grew oppressively dry and warm, while the lake below them looked invitingly cool. But it was as well that they stayed out of sight. As dusk settled on the second evening they heard the picking steps of a herd of deer come down through the screes of the scarplands above, and then saw them come out onto the plateau, taking their time to cross it towards the lake. The deer scented at the air and pricked their ears until, satisfied that the lake was safe, they came down to its edge to drink.

Neither wolf had seen so appealing a sight for many months past, and they lay together, hidden among the rocks above, watching, filled with the lusts of hunger and the hunt, and the rigours of thirst as well, as the herd drank and grazed its way along the lake's edge, some watching out while the heads of others bobbed up and down at water and tufts of grass, and nosed among the stones.

As the sun lowered the line of its last light moved across the surface of the water and up its banks, leaving them in shade. Then it rose to touch the crags across the plateau to their left and turned them to fire. Tervicz saw movement on the far side of the vale, and breathed, 'There!'

Two, no, three forms, visible in the dull light only when they moved, which they did in stops and starts as they contoured the lake, and began to drop down towards the deer. Wolves. Well-rehearsed and more than vagrants: Magyar wolves.

'Oops! Clumsy!' said Tervicz.

One of them had set a rock running loose and it scuttered for a moment before falling still. A rook rose up out of a mountain ash and flew slowly across the far side of the lake. The three forms had frozen and even to the watching wolves, were now almost invisible.

The Magyars began moving once more and the deer, already startled and made alert by the falling stone, were stock-still before one turned. The sun having left the lake-side, the deer's russet coats were now dull brown and grey. There was a moment's hesitation, then the stalking wolves broke cover and ran, and those of the herd in the water wheeled with splashes out of it, joining their fellows on shore, and then took off upslope, faster and faster, barely more than fleet shadows in the poor light, straight up towards where Tervicz and Morten lay.

'Shit!' said Tervicz, less used to such a situation than Morten, who, laughing, pulled Tervicz down with him, as the herd tore and leapt its way upslope straight to them. The deer came in great running bounds, the hooves of one or other of them scrabbling at the rocky pebbly ground as they swerved this way and that, tried to keep their foothold and then leapt on, some of them almost on the two wolves themselves, the others a little further off.

'It is a pity we cannot show ourselves or else we could take one with ease,' said Morten.

One of the deer must have seen the two wolves, or scented them at least, for at its lead they all veered off to the right and a new urgency came into the whole herd's stride. With wheezy pants, the clatter of hooves, and a final rush, they were gone past the two wolves and on up the slopes above, where they twisted and turned among larger rocks out onto the plateau itself, and were suddenly gone.

Meanwhile, below them, the Magyar wolves had reached the lake and given up the chase. They circled about, peering up the way the deer had gone, watching out perhaps for a weaker one whom they could more easily pick off. But failing that, and unwilling to begin the steep ascent for prey that would be long gone, they circled about a little more and then drank their fill of water, just as the deer had done.

Tervicz and Morten assessed them silently, unimpressed by the way they alerted the deer and by their unwillingness to pursue, and studied the distant slope where they had first appeared for sign of others there, but they saw none. But the evening light was weakening and it was hard to make out much across the valley.

Below them, the wolves were easier to see. There were two younger ones, a male and a female, and an older tough-looking male. They were still there when darkness finally fell. Tervicz and Morten stayed absolutely quiet and were relieved to hear the ones below them barking to each other that they were moving off back the way they had come. Later there was a howl followed by another, but nothing much. Just bored wolves in the night unable to sleep.

'They're watchers, probably,' said Morten. 'We'll wait until dawn and see if they are still about.'

'Watching for what, that's what I'd like to know.'

Morten shrugged indifferently.

Tervicz said, 'Let's retreat for a while well out of earshot and all possibility of being scented. There's still some carrion over by that stream where we left it if the rats haven't been at it. The sight and scent of deer makes a wolf hungry.'

'The sight and scent of us scared them shitless,' said Morten laughing. 'Did you see how they veered off and got going up that slope after they realized we were here? It was as if the whole lot had been stung by hornets.'

Tervicz suddenly remembered his father with a pang, and the way he would have thought about such things.

'Shouldn't have let them know we were here, not even by scent,' he muttered. 'If the Magyars had their wits about them they would have seen that veer in the herd and guessed we were here.'

'Well they didn't,' said Morten, and Tervicz found himself thinking of Klimt once more, and missing him. *He* would have guessed that they were here.

Ghosts of wolves who had been. Spirits of the past. Wolfways out of time and into it. Tervicz looked down at the lake and saw that it was beginning to reflect the reddening of the sky, and he began to have a sense, still distant, still inarticulate, of what lake this might well be. So strange was it, so vivid, that his hackles began to rise.

'Come on, Tervicz, let's get that food. We'll come back before dawn in time to see if our friends are still about. We have work to do tomorrow before we turn back to find Aragon again. He'll want to know how many Magyar watchers there are, what their disposition is, and why we think they are here.'

'Right,' said Tervicz, and they slid away together in the night.

*　　*　　*

481

The two had a good night, each sleeping deeply through the period of the other's watch, as wolves do who trust one another. With the coming of pre-dawn both were awake. They moved back to the lake and Morten said, 'Once the sun rises we will be exposed here as it will be on us long before the Magyars. Let's contour round to get into a better position . . .'

He had no need to finish for Tervicz understood immediately what was needed, and himself took the lead on the careful journey round above the lake. Not for the first time Morten was impressed by Tervicz's skill and coolness, and the easy way he managed that most risky of manoeuvres – breaking cover to cross a gap between rocks or vegetation. He always studied the terrain ahead carefully before beginning, he never made a sudden move, and however sparse the cover might be – a slight dip in the ground, or a thin patch of grass, he went behind it if he could; and he never stopped until he was in safe hiding again.

By the time Tervicz judged they were in good position again they were higher above the lake than they had been, the day had grown sufficiently hot for prickles of sweat to darken and spike their neck fur, and they could look back to where they had spent the night and watch the sun rise steadily, flooding it with light. A couple of rabbits came out to graze, sniffing about uneasily where they had been, probably picking up their scent.

'Look!' whispered Morten, pointing at an angle downslope.

They could see the Magyar watchers quite clearly, or two of them at least: the young male and female, and both awake. Then an older third wolf ambled into view, stretched and yawned, and the two males mock fought for a few moments before the female took up a scrap of bone one of the others had been chewing, and carried it off out of sight.

'To rest, probably,' said Morten.

They watched over the position in silence, each noting all they could about it, for they knew that when they came back to the site with the others they would need as much information as possible about lines of sight, and the likely time it might take for any Magyar watchers to reach alien wolves on the far side of the lake.

Eventually they conferred in whispers, agreeing the obvious points, and debating some doubtful ones – the most problematic of which was why the Magyars had taken a position so high above the lake if their purpose was to watch over it and be able to attack any creatures that came to water, or travelled through on the easy east-west terrain.

All this time the mountains that lay off to the north, above the plateau on whose lower flanks they had spent the night, were shrouded in cloud beneath a dark sky, and there were sweeps of rain along the far edge of the plateau.

'They may have chosen to be where they are so that they can get away all the more quickly out onto the fells that we know lie west of here – which they can do unseen,' said Tervicz. 'This is a position for observation rather than attack.'

Morten nodded slowly, not entirely convinced.

'Also, from where they are, a howling would be much more easily heard eastward, further into their core territory in the Heartland, whereas if they were lower down inside the cirque itself howling might be less easily heard, and its echoes the more confused . . .'

As Tervicz spoke, the sky to the north began to lighten and both looked that way, in the hope of being able to get their first good view of the range of mountains there. Their patience was rewarded, for the mountains now began to be slowly revealed. Not that the swirling clouds were any less thick, but in that quarter they seemed to have become uneasy and strange, now lifting mist in one place, now bringing it down once more in another, so that no overall pattern or shape to the range was discernible for a long time, though its brooding mass was all too plain to see.

What was clear, however, was that below the rise of the main range was a high plateau of grass which looked bright green against the dark swirl of mists and rock-faces above it. Its lushness was evidence of the streams that flowed down from the heights above and the rich sediments the waters brought, while its cropped shortness told them that this was part of the grazing range of deer, some of which they had already seen.

Beyond the plateau the mists across the scarp faces continued to shift and rise, revealing more and more of the great cliffs above. As well as vertical, white gashes of waterfalls, higher still, deep in dark recesses of clefts and gullied rock, were pockets of snow, some of which appeared to be sources for the waterfalls. Occasionally some wind-shift or other along the great face made the mists fade and flow, slipping behind formations along the sheer faces to reveal isolated pinnacles that stood clear of the line of the main cliffs.

The wind now began to fret and strain near where they lay watching, though still the sky directly above them was blue, and the lake sun-filled. But what they saw in the distance was that this was a storm coming, and a strange one, for the winds seemed troubled and disturbed.

It was difficult for Tervicz and Morten to make out the detailed shape of the massive formations above them, or even to judge how near or far they were. Their scale was such, their changing shape so confusing, that they could only stare in wonder. But one thing began to become clear to each of them: the hard edge of the rock-faces' high parts, broken as they were by the deep incisions of gullies great and small, did not mark the highest part of the range itself. They were, rather, a further edge to a higher plateau still, and what lay beyond that dark and mazy place, difficult and dangerous to penetrate no doubt, none could judge from so far below.

'One thing's plain at least,' said Morten. 'We can now see what it is that these Magyars may be watching over . . . From where they are they can not only see the lake below and the routes of which it is the focus, but also the plateau above, and the rock-faces beyond.'

'Yes, but . . . but why?' asked Tervicz in a quiet voice, thinking as he asked it that somewhere inside himself he knew the answer. The sense of awe about the lake, and the feeling that he had been here before was increasing, doubling and redoubling in his heart and mind and body, like the great roiling clouds that mounted now over the mountains, and across the sky towards them.

So caught with the question and the sense that its answer was imminent and within him, if he could only grasp it, was Tervicz, that he quite forgot himself and broke cover to cry out aloud, *'Why?'*

'For Wulf's sake and ours as well *get down, Tervicz* . . . !' hissed Morten, pulling him down.

He looked across at the Magyars and sure enough their attention had been caught by Tervicz's voice and movement, though Morten had got Tervicz back out of sight fast enough for them not to be sure where it came from. They paced about, uneasy, ready to investigate if they heard anything more.

'Right,' said Morten resolutely, 'that's it! We've seen enough and we're getting out before they find us.'

'No!' said Tervicz in a low, growling voice which was quite unlike him.

'What do you mean, "No"?' said Morten, astonished. It had never been put to the test, but in terms of strength and power he was stronger than Tervicz, which meant that in such a situation as this he took command.

'We haven't seen the most important thing. We haven't seen *why* it is we have travelled so long to get here.'

'What do you mean "the most important thing"? How do you know anything more is going to happen than what we've already seen? As for travelling a long way, it's hardly been . . .'

'Morten – this lake, don't you feel anything special here? Can't you hear the patter of wolves' paws down the wolf-ways of time? I can feel it and I can hear it because I have been here before.'

'Yes, you have, you were . . .'

'No, not when we fled through this place from the Magyars in spring. Long before that, long before I was born into this life . . .'

'We're going,' said Morten firmly.

'We're not,' said Tervicz, turning calmly from him and settling down, knowing that to make him go, Morten would have to draw attention to them both.

'Shit, shit, shit!' said Morten, settling down.

'Look!' said Tervicz.

The sweep of rain that travelled across the distant scarp faces now was strange and formidable. Stranger because, by some trick of cloud formation, the sun shone down onto the black sheer faces of the broken scarp, and was bright where the rain swept past. More than that, it caught at the thin lines of white waterfalls that they could see delineated for the first time, the source of the roaring they had heard in the night; and then, as they watched, they saw more of these falls appear, more gushing of water, tumbling down to be lost in the screes below.

Where they were the sun was only now beginning to fade before the building thunderclouds, and for now the rocks and soil and vegetation all about were warm, and dry as dust. Unnaturally so.

'Shit,' said Morten again, but even he seemed caught

up in the power of what was approaching from out of the mountains, and the sense that something was happening, and they were its ordained witnesses, with the Magyars – and Wulf knows what other wolves might be here, ghosts or otherwise.

'And there *are* others here,' whispered Tervicz. 'I know it . . .'

The Magyars certainly seemed to sense it, for they were up and restless, peering about, and then staring in the direction Morten had suggested they might be watching, which was across the plateau. What had they seen?

Tervicz and Morten followed their gaze. Out of the swirling mists and shafts of rain a herd of deer ran towards the lower clearer ground, followed as it seemed by a wall of approaching rain, which overtook them and poured down from the lowering clouds above, so hard, so brutal, that the herd stopped and stood with bowed heads until the weaker ones among them faltered, and even the stags went down upon their knees and haunches.

'If it *is* the rain they're fleeing from,' whispered Tervicz, the clouds of lost memory in his own head clearing, the sense of what it might be that was imminent now, thrusting itself into his unwilling consciousness.

'*For I am a Bukov wolf, and centuries ago, before the dark millennium, my tribe was given the secret of the way back to the WulfRock,*' he intoned.

'Shut up!' growled Morten, his eyes wide with apprehension. But the wolf was right, something was there, something that made deer flee, and storms broil and break, and put fear into him such as he had never felt, without even showing its face.

Something terrible was coming from the scarps, and it was as ancient as it was new, and it threatened all of them, and all wolfkind.

CHAPTER THIRTY-TWO

Dendrine weans her last-born son of milk;
and Aragon begins to understand the nature of leadership

U P ALONG THE ROCK-FACE, within one of the
gullies that time had weathered back into the cliff
and up to the hidden ground behind, beneath an
overhang . . .

Creatures. Secret and cruel bondings. Evil.

Around that overhang the rush of turbulent winds, the
roar of racing water.

Beneath that overhang, dry and safe, Dendrine and her
loathsome cub.

The winds wild, the waterfalls roaring all about, as Dendrine laughed and pushed her sweetling away. 'No, no, my
little love, you know my dugs are dry, and you need more
than milk. Flesh is what you need and it is meet you get
it . . .'

She cackled at her pun, her teats – the sacky, hanging
things she liked to call her dugs – shaking with her mirth,
all worn from overuse and age, all puckered up and spent
from a final suckling, though white-green milk dribbled
from one of them.

Her cub stared with malevolent eyes at the empty things
that had once given him sustenance, angry to be denied.
He was hovering now between the comfort of milk and an
alluring bloodlust for torn meat.

'Now, where is our larder?'

Her eyes still mirthful with bad jokes and blind with mother love, Dendrine reached her curling, untended claws into the murk behind. There a thing moved. There eyes stared. There living food awaited the savage attentions of the beloved cub.

Dendrine got a grip and pulled, and out it came, not struggling now, but not yet dead, though it had given up on life.

The thing she brought forth as her maternal offering was the cub's sole surviving sibling, the thing kept too long alive that it might be the flesh and blood to which its brother could be weaned. It was half his size, yet not so small that where its haunches had been stripped of skin and half the flesh, there was not still more flesh to find. A cub, even a malevolent one, does not eat much at first. A mouthful or two a day will do.

'No, no, no, no!' said mother lovingly. 'Don't tear him there. You'll *kill* him.'

Big brother had hold of little brother's face and was trying to rip it off. Little brother's eyes were wide enough, and his scream loud enough, to suggest he still felt pain, and still knew he was not dead.

'Try *here* . . .' said Dendrine, and expertly explored the smaller cub's half-eaten haunch, raw red, with bone and muscle showing, and parts already black and foul where gangrene was setting in.

She found a healthy morsel, toothed and loosened it to yet more cries of pain from one and salivating anticipation from the other.

'Shut up, you,' she hissed between clenched teeth, ripping the flesh some more, yet not so much that big brother would not have a little work to do.

She lifted her head away and let go the part she had, watching it flop and pull back to where it had been, and signalled to her son to have a go.

He did, placing his front paws upon his smaller brother's

body, to get a better purchase, and pulled the loose meat off, ignoring the screams; and chomped, half-choking in his eagerness, ignoring both his mother's adoration, and his brother's terror and deep pain.

'Look!' said Dendrine, pointing out across the plateau as she pushed the torn and now writhing body back into the shadows until the next meal-time.

'That is the plateau, and it will be where you learn to hunt. Deer live there especially for you. Rain falls so you may drink it. Sun shines so you can lie in it. Snow and ice come to harden your body and ready your heart. Oh my best beloved, for you we have waited so long, so many centuries now, and I shall prepare you for the great trial that shall be your life. You are my god and I worship you; all who love you and serve you shall be saved. All who reject you shall soon die.'

The cub stared, his head as jagged and askew as split rock, his eyes black as night, his expression greedy.

'Milk,' he said in a harsh rasping voice. 'Dug?'

'No no, nooooo,' cooed Dendrine, putting her head close to his, 'not out there, not when you are grown. You shall learn to like flesh. You shall enjoy whole tribes of wolves whose weakness you shall feed off.'

Behind them, unseen, eyes stared out of hopeless terror, and the knowledge, unspoken and primordial, that the feeding off others had already begun.

'Look, the rain has stopped: the sun is coming out. Shall we go out into its warmth? Shall I show you to the world? Perhaps the wolves of the lake who wait to serve you will glimpse you. How happy they should be!'

Dendrine pushed the cub out of the shadows of the over-hang, and it ventured a few steps towards a drift of snow, wet now with the rain that had been and would soon come back, softer too. Black against the white, the cub ripped and tore at the snow with soft growls that pleased its mother, and made her prattle more. Its paws were too big for its body yet, its tail unsure how to balance itself. But its movements were sure enough for a cub, and the way it killed the pure white of the snow was as deadly as pushing helpless prey over a cliff, and as ruthless, and as fast. Yet not fast enough it seemed, for the cub raged at the snow, and tried to kill it more.

'Patience,' purred Dendrine, going to her cub.

All around them was the roar of rushing water from the rains.

Then, 'No, nooooo, not me, not milk. If you want food you know where you can get it. But look, the rain sweeps over us once more . . .'

The cub raised its head as more rain began to fall, stared back towards the overhang and then lolloped back beneath it once again, to enter the shadows, and play with his raw red sibling, and make merry with his cries.

'Just listen to the running waters roar,' sighed Dendrine, stretching still in the brief snatch of sun, blissful in her moment's rest.

Black dots on a patch of snow was all the watchers saw, but it was enough to have them still and staring past the rain, over the top of the abject herd of deer who had fled from something horrible.

Dots which might have been a wolf, though a small one, Tervicz said. A distant thing all black, fleeting for a moment and then gone, but which sent a shiver of horror through the clouds and brought forth a flash of lightning on the scarps above, and the roll of answering thunder to tremble through the rocks.

But it was not till the wolves, watchers and aliens alike, saw something more, that Tervicz knew why the lake they had come back to held such ancient resonance, and what had happened there long before.

No more than a ripping roar at first, no more than what seemed a curl of mist below the screes on the far side of the plateau. Then the abject herd raised its communal head, listened, heard, and was gone, sudden sun glancing off their backs. The roaring increased, the curl of mist took form, mounting forward, and they saw it was the white spray at the head of a surge of water.

Across the plateau it came, pushing all before it, following as yet no defined path yet drawn like carnivore to prey towards the dry and waterless gulley that led down into the lake, the same gully Tervicz and Morten had noticed when they first came.

'Just look at that!' said Morten, a paw reaching out to Tervicz, as if in trepidation that the mounting torrent of water, whose front rolled and surged across the grass and rock with a force that roared out ahead of it, would reach up and tear them down, even where they lay.

How long it took to reach the first part of the gully they did not know; no more than a few seconds, no more than that. And when it did it slowed for a moment or two, filling the deepest part before mounting up again, to begin its forward push once more.

Huge now, rushing, a great wave of water, down the last part of the plateau, bursting at the banks that time had carved, and pushing dust and rocks before it. Then it poised and fell, a rushing, crushing torrent of water, down in a surge to the lake itself, surging out across it, huge and fierce, the placid dried-up lake suddenly suffused with . . .

For the power of it was not all. For the torrent's spray was not white, nor its waters green or grey. No, no . . . from somewhere along its course, touched by some ancient stratum formed in lakes dried by desert sun aeons before, the water was stained red, murky horrid red, the red of drying blood.

But where the sun shone down upon its flow, where it

arced and tumbled down into the lake itself, its colour was that of fresh blood, and the lake was changing to an open, unhealed wound.

'Here,' whispered Tervicz, the awe of ancient memory upon his face, '*here* was where the Bukov wolf first formed the pack that became the Wolves of Time. From here, Morten, they left that they might hold fast to ancient lore; to here we are returning that the lore may be set aright once more. Here the Wolves grieved for the loss of their gods; here the Mennen's triumph began.

'To here that wolf that shall be god will come again, and Mennen shall worship him. Here, Morten, *here* . . .'

His voice was no more than a whisper against the torrent's red and roaring sound, but Morten heard it well. He saw, too, what Tervicz now proposed to do, but this time he did not try to stop him.

For Tervicz stepped boldly forth, not caring if a Magyar saw, and raised his head and howled the joy of his discovery, that the Wolves of Time were coming home.

'But this time,' he howled, 'this time it will be to the WulfRock and Wulf himself they go, not to far and distant lands to await their time. Their time has come and they are coming home.'

Then, more quietly still, '*We* are coming home.'

He turned to Morten and said, 'We have seen what we were sent to see, and discovered what we had to. Come . . .'

And then they left, even as the Magyar saw where they were and shaken by all they had seen, and all they had heard, began their stumbling and failed pursuit.

Though their paws ran ever so fast on the wolfway to get back to Aragon and the others again and report what they had seen, they could never run as fast as the tide of passion that had already overtaken Elhana and Aragon, and swept them both along in its turbulent wake.

With a place as safe as the moraines for their home, and Tervicz's and Morten's departure to find the lake leaving them free of memory of Klimt and rivalry, there was no hindrance left. Not that Aragon entirely ignored his responsibility to the pack: rather, he used it to his lustful need.

The territorial boundaries were paced and marked, the watches organized, and food of a trivial rabbit kind was found. For the rest, Aragon made plain that he wished to be left alone with his ledrene. Let Stry or Lounel disturb them if they must but . . . there had better be good reason for it.

'You don't think we should take this opportunity of exploring up into the scarps above this area of moraine?' Stry wondered more than once.

Aragon shook his head as patiently as he could and said, 'No point until we know what the others find out.'

'Or perhaps we could . . . well, talk about what it is we shall be aiming to do once we have found a territory?' tried Lounel.

'I think not,' said Aragon, eyeing his consort, wanting to get back to her.

'But, wolf,' continued Lounel, 'when we were travelling to the Heartland you often talked about the great and epic things an Iberian wolf would do. You said . . .'

'No doubt I said many things,' growled Aragon irritably, 'but that was before . . .' and again he eyed Elhana while she eyed nothing in particular, thought of nothing much, except that he was taking time on trivia when they could be . . . together. Private. Dancing in that place they had discovered to which no other wolves need ever come. She looked over at him impatiently.

'. . . before I sent Tervicz and Morten off to do a job. They are taking too long over it. They are holding us up.'

It was all nonsense, and Lounel knew it. The difficulty was that Aragon did not. He believed the half-truths he told. Lounel turned from him wearily, though quite without the contempt that Aragon seemed to think that he implied.

Aragon rushed up to his friend, nipped him without warning in the haunch, tumbled him, humiliated him.

'Aragon!' snarled Stry.

'You mean "Leader",' said Aragon calmly, turned from Lounel whom he was now unable to look in the eye, and went straight over to Stry, of whom he had the measure.

'Leader,' conceded Stry reluctantly.

'We shall wait until their return before we do anything. Until then, rest and do nothing. You, come!'

This last was to Elhana, and it sought to be masterly, and to her it was.

'I don't know what's come over them,' grumbled Stry when they had gone.

'Lust,' said Lounel matter-of-factly, licking where Aragon had drawn blood. 'I thought you knew more of that than me.'

'Hmmph!'

'Don't you think you were too hard on them?' said Elhana when they were alone.

And then, as he came to her, pushing her, wanting his actions to speak louder than words, for he could not find any that could justify assaulting Lounel or refusing to listen to Stry, he scented and licked roughly at her.

'Don't . . . you . . .' she tried again, giving way to his pushing and touching, yielding in the way he made her yield.

'Who cares when we have . . . this,' he said, his voice thick, his eyes closed to the world, his need shifting and sliding from the general to the particular, and from the particular to the very particular, which was with him somewhere inside her.

'But . . .' she said, not meaning *but* at all.

'But nothing,' he said, knowing by now her invitation when he heard it, and still feeling irritated with the others, and so taking her all the harder.

'But?' he rasped, biting at her back and neck as he mounted and entered her.

'But nothing, Aragon, but everything, but only do it, but but but b-u-tttttt!'

She held onto the sigh as long as she could and then when it came it was a gasp and a cry.

'They are so irritating sometimes,' he said afterwards, in the lazy sun, limbs entwined, their need satisfied, their spent lust no more now than the dry grass that swayed near their faces and the daytime moth that fluttered out of sight to lose itself in shade.

'My love, my love,' she said, 'you are their leader and must listen to them . . .'

'Not you, Elhana,' he said impatiently. 'No, no not you as well . . .'

'Not me,' she sighed, easing her rump into him, stirring him, wanting him . . .

'Already?'

'Nearly ready.'

They laughed and talked of nothing for an hour or maybe three.

Stry and Lounel who waited out of earshot, not thought of at all; Tervicz and Morten, and their quest, forgotten completely.

'We could . . .' she began after he had mounted her again and taken her until it almost hurt, and he was so tired he slept, 'we could do what Stry suggested.'

'What did he suggest?'

'Explore the scarp.'

Aragon groaned.

'Just a little way.' She pulled away from him, suddenly needing space. Suddenly quite bored. 'I'm thirsty,' she lied, the first lie she told. Lust-love has its season and like a moth's life it is short.

'Mmmm,' he groaned, and together they rose and paced off into the undergrowth and thence upslope.

'Where are you going?'

It was Lounel, further upslope, though whether he was watching and what he was thinking they did not much care.

'Exploring,' said Elhana.

'Reconnaissance,' said Aragon, looking him boldly in the eye, but with shame.

'Beware,' said Lounel quietly, and with a soft smile, as if it was almost a joke that he made.

'We will!' responded Elhana playfully, but Lounel did not laugh and nor did Aragon.

They journeyed up the slope towards the screes that skirted the scarp face itself, and they got thirstier as they climbed. Nearer to, the cliff was steeper, and the scree was loose and difficult, a place of dried-up, dislodged plants, the smell of dust, and the spoor of deer along old tracks that formed terracettes whose only life so late in summer was the scurry of faded wagtail, and the stirring of the fallen feathers of the ravens who lived in the cliffs above.

'Nothing,' muttered Aragon.

'No way through,' said Elhana craning her neck to look up and along for some way forward.

'Why should there be?' said Aragon.

'It feels as if there should be.'

'There's always a way for us, though not on a slope as steep as this,' he said. He looked suddenly young, suddenly alien, and Elhana felt old, and a little tired. There was not a fleck of grey in his fine fur, unlike her own, nor any scar on his face, and he was strong and young.

Standing there, the cliff above, the fells stretching far away before them, and the area of the moraines all rough and scrubby just below, she saw him as he was, not as she thought he was: she saw a wolf too young to lead, a wolf too full of lust and love, a wolf not yet quite wise.

'A wolf I am foolish to like and love, yet love him I do,' she told herself.

She smiled at the way he stared about, and the way he stared down at her, wondering what she was thinking. He was what she had dreamed of in a mate when she had passed through the Dolomites with her father Ambato. He made her laugh, and he irritated her just a little; and she was afraid for him. She had met him too late, and he had found her far too soon.

'What are you thinking?' he asked, as she knew he would.

'That I hope time changes things for the better,' she said, 'and that I love you, Aragon. I love you.'

'And I you,' he said, coming to her but not understanding her passion or the depth of what she said at all. 'What do we need with time when we have each other?'

He pushed against her, they slipped and fell, they laughed, and though she did not care to think of past or future, she found herself saying, 'There is no way through for us up here.'

The scarp face seemed so bleak and dark yet she was drawn to it, though Aragon sought to make her think of something else. She looked up at it as he took her yet again, and she lost herself in its fissures and faces, voids and juts, rises and overhangs, in all its complexity.

Then Elhana knew there must be a way through, and she thought of Klimt, and knew that *he* would find a way through here or anywhere. She thought of Klimt and his courage and his hurt, his coldness and his vulnerability, and as her young wolf made love to her, she knew why it was she wept.

That same day, when Lounel had watched them climb beyond the tree-line and out of sight across the steep slopes above, Stry went wandering too.

'Can't stand to do nothing, so I'll do something. I'll – I'll go and find some prey.'

'With care,' said Lounel who seemed in a warning mood that day. He lay down and dozed. On late summer days like that there is little a wolf can do to hurry the days on to cooler weather and the changes that must come. Best snooze and wait; cock an ear, half open an eye, and listen to the world spinning the day by, and the distant whisper of the coming stars.

Stry was in the mood to find prey, to stalk it, and maybe even catch it. Never easy and he was tired of rabbits, which made the chances even less.

The sun bore down, and finally he lazed too, drawn to a trickle of a stream, cooling his paws in a dribble of water, staring up at the hazy faces of the escarpment, waiting for Morten and Tervicz to return.

The scent of blood, the rustle and limping of a young doe, Mennen-wounded; dying.

'Shit!' he said, staying just where he was until she stretched her neck towards the water and he took her as easy as blinking. The brief struggle, the cry, the shiver, and the flow of blood, and there she lay, her stomach breathing in and out, in and out, then in, and that was all. Her legs trembled after she had died, one eye slowly closed. Where she had been shot were flies. Killed by Mennen for pleasure, or just inefficiently?

'Who cares! Wulf be praised she's mine, that's all!' he muttered, and dug in, incising the skin, giving up and taking on the wound, ripping the skin some more, and muzzling into the red flesh of the shoulder and beginning a leisurely feast. 'Best thing all summer,' he mumbled, panting and greedy. 'Best thing for years.'

He rested, dozed a little, flicked away flies and a dozy bumble bee, and muzzled in once more, deep into the bloody hole he had made.

The sky blacked out as he came up for air.

'*Shit*!' he swore again, rising, snarling, but guarding what he had got.

He knew the wolf at once. Last time he saw it had been by just such a stream. Did it use streams as routes then, exploiting the noise, the breezes that water creates, and the shifting scents? It seemed it did.

'Greetings,' said the huge gruff wolf, calm as anything.

'Yes,' said Stry, frowning and debating his chances. Not great he would think. But then he had fed well. Or reasonably well.

He took another bite without taking his eyes off the new arrival who stood, rather grandly as it seemed to Stry, right in the middle of the stream.

Stry decided he did not stand a chance and rapidly tore some more while he still could. The wolf advanced one step and then another, its broad and furrowed face holding eyes that stared at the food with cheerful appreciation, and at Stry with comparative indifference.

Stry took another bite and wisely retreated, sitting down a little to one side and licking his paws and then using them to clean his face fur.

The wolf tucked in, making tears and bites that were bigger than Stry's had been, and with considerably more power. He ate without looking up, without covering the ground, a wolf of confidence.

'Yet, not aggression,' thought Stry thankfully.

Then he said, 'My name is Stry. I come from the Polish Tatra.'

The wolf paused and then chomped on, belching once or twice, pausing, looking up at Stry as if to make sure he was still there.

Finally he said, 'And I am of the Russias.'

'A Russian wolf!' repeated Stry excitedly.

The wolf's face darkened and Stry understood that that was not a subject he wished to talk about.

'Tell me about the pack you travel with,' said the wolf at last, beginning to clean his paws as Stry had done, but by going down to the stream and standing his front paws in it before dipping his head a bit and then drinking. This position made him quite exposed and vulnerable but he showed no fear of Stry at all.

Remembering his conversation with the others about how they could do with a wolf like this in the pack, even if he was getting on a bit, Stry answered the question by extolling the virtues of the wolves he travelled with, though giving little else away. He said nothing about the fact that they had all come from different places, or about recent changes in the pack, or even . . .

The wolf drew back from the water, settled down some way off from the deer carcass so that Stry could have a second go without constraint and, nodding a little with impatience, said, 'Yes, yes, well I daresay they are all fine wolves individually. But it's the pack and its purpose I asked about.'

The wolf's gaze was sharp and shrewd and Stry had no doubt that he had been a leader of his own pack in the past. Age, injury, defeat, all or one could have helped displace him.

'Our pack?' he said, playing for time.

The wolf sighed wearily and said: 'Where's your leader gone, for example? Or, if you have any, what are your pack's objectives? Or, if that's too much to tell one you hardly know, how about this: what are the strengths and weakness of your pack?'

'That's a lot of questions,' said Stry.

'If you want others to add their strength to yours, you need to satisfy them that you have something to offer, don't you? You need a wolf like me.'

'Er, yes, I suppose we do,' said Stry, unused to such questioning, and the more discomfited for sensing that his inquisitor was very used to it indeed.

'You asked about Klimt. But how did you know . . . ?'

'I have been watching and listening in these parts for some months past: you and the Magyars, deciding which to join. Why, you saw me before yourself.'

'I did.'

'So . . . Where did the leader who has just left the pack come from?'

This time the question was quite sharp, almost a command.

'He is a Nordic wolf.'

'How come he was ousted?'

'He left of his own accord, worse luck,' said Stry.

'Tell me all about it,' said the stranger, and very soon Stry found he was doing so, feeling that this was a wolf he could trust, and there was no way such a wolf would join their pack unless he was satisfied it was worth his while.

It was late afternoon by the time their conversation was over, and each had eaten well. The wolf had said hardly anything at all about himself, but that he had been a vagrant for more than a year, had travelled distances Stry could only dream of, and knew so much about the way a pack worked that if he had not been the leader of one, then he must certainly have been a member of one that was well and openly led.

The wolf got up to go.

'You can come and meet . . .'

The wolf shook his head.

'I am not ready yet, and I think it is time I spoke to this wolf Klimt, if I can find him. As for meeting Aragon, it sounds as if he might see me as a threat, which would be tedious.'

'But you're not . . .'

'Weak leaders, especially young ones, see threats in everything. I have enjoyed talking with you, Stry, and I shall look forward to meeting you again.'

'You will . . . ?'

'Probably, yes. Winter is coming and there is change in the air hereabouts. Much change. It is to help nudge it in the right direction that I have come.'

'Who are you, wolf?' asked Stry, his voice suddenly urgent. He felt they should not lose this wolf.

'Ask rather what part of your pack I might be. There is only one thing I can give, or one best thing at any rate . . . or so it seems to me. But then a wolf does not always know his own strengths, nor his own weaknesses. And in any case . . .'

'In any case?' asked Stry.

The wolf came forward and spoke some more about the nature of packs, with such seriousness and intensity that all Stry could do was listen. Then, with a smile, and before Stry recovered himself enough to say another word, he nodded a thank you for the food, and splashed away down the stream, to keep cool no doubt, and leave no scent that others could follow.

'And so what did he say when you asked him what he meant by "in any case"?' asked Lounel later, when Stry told him about his meeting with the wolf.

'Well, what I think he said was – and by then we had talked a good long time, or rather he asked questions and I found myself answering them – that . . . that . . .'

'Well, wolf?' said Lounel a shade impatiently.

'That he had known many packs in his time and without exception their collective strengths and weaknesses were never the same as those of the individuals who comprised them. And then he said something like, "There's never yet been a pack that realized its full collective strength, and when there is the world will change. That's the pack I'm looking for, wolf. Is it the pack you're a member of?" It all sounded very impressive, Lounel, but I'm not sure what he meant by it.'

'He meant that he was sounding us out.'

'Well obviously he was. I know that!'

'He meant that he takes rather more seriously what we are about than perhaps our pack presently does. But then Aragon and Elhana needed time. And so did Klimt.'

'Well they've had it, haven't they?'

'I hope so,' said Lounel, 'because I think our time is running out.'

Morten and Tervicz, full of their news and discoveries, finally came back the following morning, only to find Aragon and Elhana were not with the others.

'"Taking time off," was the way he put it,' said Stry heavily. 'Told us to "rest a bit" until you got back and although we see them from time to time, well, you know . . . I expect they'll drift in later in the day.'

'Hmmph!' said Morten. 'What we've got to report ought to be to the leader and ledrene of the pack, but if they're not here . . . well, we'll wait I suppose.'

They waited until evening, but when Aragon came he seemed tired and distracted, and was unwilling to talk.

The morning would do, he suggested. Elhana was more interested, and had Aragon not insisted that it wait until the morning, she would have had the two wolves tell her then and there what they had found out.

She seemed more irritated than distracted, and leader and ledrene barely said a word to each other before Aragon took up a place in their clearing they were using from where he could watch them all, and glower. For Tervicz and Morten it was a depressing return.

But the night passed, day came, food was eaten, ablutions completed and Aragon was affable enough in his listening and thorough with his questions about all that had happened by the lake. Affable, but not much affected; listening, but not too interested.

Tervicz tried to describe what they had seen, and the sense of change and destiny, and that up there by the scarp was a wolf the watchers waited for, and it was coming and would bring with it a tide of blood.

'Yes, yes, yes . . . Tervicz!' said Aragon finally. 'You said that just now one way and then in another and now you're going on about it a third time. We all know you Bukov wolves have vivid imaginations!'

He laughed and looked around at the others to join in. None did, though Elhana managed a weak loyal smile.

'Don't misunderstand me,' he continued more thoughtfully, retreating now from outright mockery. 'I take seriously what you say, and trust your combined judgement that what you sensed coming might be dangerous. But, in truth you saw little but a gully flood, and as for blood, well, where I come from in Iberia such flash-floods occur once in a while, and they stain the lakes they flow into with the colour of whatever soil and loose rock they pass through. As it happens, it is often red. So . . .

'As for the watchers, it sounds as if the Magyars are doing what any prudent tribe would do in summer when vagrants are about – and they know we're likely to come back. It seems to me therefore that we should do something a little different, a little unexpected . . .'

He had made a poor start, but now it sounded as if Aragon was finally going to come up with a strategy. They drew closer to him.

'In the last few days I and my ledrene have been exploring hereabout a little . . .' he hesitated only fractionally, as if to gather force, though it gave Stry long enough to glance over and see the expression on Elhana's face. Faint surprise is what he saw.

'. . . and we have come to the conclusion that there may be a way through the scarps above us which will get us to the same place finally as the overwatched route above the lake we now know about. Isn't that so, Elhana?'

Reluctantly Elhana nodded her agreement, but she could not bring herself to actually say so, a fact that Stry noted. Meanwhile, a distant and far-away look had come to Lounel's eyes, which, though fixed upon the great scar of the scarp above them, and its inhospitable length, seemingly wandered somewhere else entirely, where there were routes beyond, and better ways to find them.

'The moraines have proved a good and safe home to us,' continued Aragon, 'so I see no point in hurrying on from here. We shall explore slowly and then in a month or two perhaps . . .'

'But Aragon . . .' began Tervicz.

'Well?'

'There was a sense of urgency about what we witnessed by the lake, a need to take the moment. I do not think we can afford to "explore slowly" as you . . .'

'You do not think? You doubt me? Certainly you do not think of the time I have spent these past days putting my mind to the pack's need. You have no thought . . .'

It was bravado, and it was nonsense, and it was a shame

there was no wolf there with the will and strength to challenge him outright. But when a leader has newly taken over, and his ledrene stays loyal, it is hard to dislodge him. Anyway, would another of them have done better? The problem was that Aragon was not listening, and the others, even Lounel it seemed, did not have the will or desire to guide him towards something better. The strange wolf had been right: a pack's strength might very well be more than its individuals' strengths, but its weakness might be more as well.

'Certainly we seem safe enough here,' said Morten slowly, thinking perhaps that if they were going to mess about chasing shadows, seeking wolfways that probably did not exist, best to do it somewhere safe. Aragon would see sense before long, and they must hope it was not too late to confront the nameless thing that he and Tervicz had sensed was coming. How much easier it would have been if they had seen an enemy! But there was nothing, nothing but a pervading feeling of doom.

'Perhaps you would come to the lake yourself,' he said, thinking suddenly that if he was actually there and sensed what they had Aragon might change his mind.

'I doubt that I would see something you did not,' said Aragon, 'and I have no wish to risk letting the Magyars know where we are . . . So, there it is then, decision made. In a day or two we'll decide how we shall start exploring the scarp above us . . .'

But it was four days before they finally began, days in which each of them became more restless and unhappy. While between Aragon and Elhana, as lust began to die, there was less talk of love, and each put the blame for everything upon an ungrateful pack . . .

CHAPTER THIRTY-THREE

Klimt makes the acquaintance of three wolves;
the first being himself; the second being one afraid of him
and the third being afraid of no wolf at all

WHEN KLIMT HAD BEGUN his farewell speech to the pack he had not intended it as such at all. Rather the opposite: he had hoped to open his heart to them, bond Elhana closer, and motivate them to want to go back into the Heartland to establish a territory.

It had not worked out that way. So unused was he to talking personally – so unused indeed to *thinking* personally – that when he tried, he found himself quite startled and overtaken by his thoughts. Always an honest wolf, always one with high ideals and a purpose which had little to do with his own need and a great deal to do with that of the pack, he had talked himself into abdication. For the more he found himself talking, the more that seemed the only honourable course, and the pain of giving up leadership was only equalled, and genuinely so, by his growing understanding that as leader he had failed his ledrene: she was unhappy with him, and with what dreadful pangs did he see from her gaze, and the mood of the pack, that she might be happy with another.

Though he used the word 'love' he did not yet know what it meant, except if it be love of a parent, or the love he had felt for Elsinor, which had been young, vibrant, naive, romantic, and like most such loves, finally doomed. Abiding love grows through an open heart and careful thought for the other, it is not found by chance along the way like a drift of snow, or a random fall of leaves. Love, the solid, sure love between a leader and ledrene on which a pack may thrive and depend, and which sends that pack's wolves out into the unsure world with hearts and minds healthy with inner confidence, is never merely 'found'. It is the product of hard work.

This Klimt did not then know. He had lost his first 'love', his first cubs, his first pack, most terribly, and he felt not only pain but guilt, and could not risk giving his heart to another, as Elhana wished. But there was more to Klimt's decision to leave than that: there was a certain common-sense as well, as Lounel had been the first to recognize.

For Klimt understood that a struggle with Aragon over Elhana's loyalty, in which her love for one would battle with her duty to another, was a struggle he could not win. Or rather (and here his intelligence and cunning showed itself) it was not something he could win by direct confrontation. The more he tried to dominate Aragon and the more he succeeded, the more Elhana would resent him; and if he went so far as to kill or banish Aragon, the battle for her heart and love would be forever lost. Much better to let Aragon have liberty to show his faults. If he showed his strength instead, well then, Klimt could have the satisfaction of knowing he had served his pack best by leaving it.

Such were the reasons for his departure, and wolves who know more of life than Klimt then did, might well conclude that though they might be sound enough, they were not everything. Much else could happen, other factors come into play and, whatever else might be said, with such complex and weighty matters as love and leadership, packs and individuals, journeys to the Heartland and the establishing of territory, the unexpected *always* happens. It is in how they deal with this that wolves reveal their worthiness, or otherwise.

When challenges are successfully met and change gives way to stasis, a wolf's perspective on the world alters, and past decisions, whether impulsive at the time, or made with difficulty, may seem suddenly absurd, unreal, or weak. For some it seems too late, and crippling regret sets in; for others, and these are the greater wolves, the ones who grow, new perspectives offer new challenges: the past is over, regrets are a waste of time and all *can* be regained, and much much more . . .

The least of Klimt's concerns when he left the pack and set off across the Southern Fell was his own safety. Indeed, having left so peremptorily he worried more about running across the pack again the next day, or the day after that. He decided therefore to set off for a place he knew, and think for a while, and so it was that before very long he found himself back at the gully, which had been his starting point into the Heartland before, and now could be again.

The gully held no fears for Klimt, nor any special memories – he regretted the loss of the cubs but . . . somehow their coming had been inauspicious and too soon. There was some evidence that Mennen had been there recently, and wolves as well, though who they were he had no real idea.

Yet there were clues that gave him pause for thought. The first of these he found stretched out and desiccated above the gully, in that small area of ground where he and the others had briefly been trapped. It was the skin and bones of an infant wolf, and he had no doubt it was the one that died in Elhana's muzzle as she tried vainly to carry it to safety. His son.

But he gazed at it dispassionately, for if a cub is so weak

when it is born that it struggles to survive, it is better left to die. His face hardened as he looked at it, his eyes grew chilly once again. Klimt had far to travel before he opened his heart to compassion, and to simple sadness. He turned away to think of other things, and the life that had been and now was gone forever lay forlorn and broken, its lifeless parts frayed by the weather, sinking without trace into the earth; a shadow in its mother's heart, but not even that within its father's.

The other clue was smaller but more substantial, for it spoke of life: paw-prints in the gully, and of a huge and formidable kind. Then, when Klimt tracked them down out into the quarry below there they were again in puddled mud, clearer still. So big that for a time he wondered if they were the tracks of some huge mongrel dog, until he put his own paws in them and saw them for what they were – simply bigger, and with a stride to match.

He examined them with interest, and with some trepidation, for a wolf like this, even though a vagrant, was not one another liked to meet unexpectedly. The tracks yielded two further clues than size: the first was that the claws were thick and worn, which spoke of an ageing wolf; the second that the right back paw was damaged in some way, though whether a part of it was lost, or the wolf was partially crippled in that leg, Klimt could not tell.

There was a third part to his sense of this mystery wolf, and it was most strange – the wolf, though so far unseen, felt benign. That he had been in the gully, and as Klimt later worked out, had stayed some time there, suggested one who like himself appreciated the place's age and sonority. From then on, Klimt kept an eye open for the wolf or his tracks, and determined if he could to make contact with it.

But finally it was not this wolf at all that he first met – apart from a few vagrants he had seen or scented about

before, Magyars mainly and of little consequence. He kept
clear of these.

No, the first he met was one he heard howling one night
upon the open fell, and who he tracked two full days and
nights. A female from the howl, familiar from the scent,
and her identity correctly guessed by him a good day before
he confronted her.

'Jicin?' he growled out of the shadows of some larches
one morning, and never had a wolf started so violently, nor
been so full of fear. She lay outstretched beneath the
shadow of fissured rock which seemed at once her home
and comfort. Discovered, she withered before his eyes,
shivering, sweating, her snout growing pale, her eyes quite
dreadful in their fear.

So extreme was her reaction to his unexpected appearance in a place in which she presumably felt herself to be
quite safe, that Klimt almost thought he must have brought
monsters with him, and he glanced behind himself to make
sure that he had not. But no, the monsters were all inside
her head.

It was an hour before she spoke any word, and the only
sounds she made were moans and sobs and whines whose
sum, it seemed to him, was a jumble much like this:
'Killmequickly Ididmybest anddid notmean anythingatall,
didn't. WhatIlostwas meandall ofmine I would preferto
bedeadthanhereand . . . now! Please do it quickly!' When
finally she understood that he was not going to kill her for
'losing' the cub that Elhana had borne, she was silent for
an hour more – and this was as horrid to behold as her
earlier abject terror – before she suddenly decided that it
was mating he must want instead of murder.

'IfyouwantityoucanhaveittakemenowmatemeandIlikeit-
whentheydo. Ilikeyoupleasejusttakemeand . . .' As she

proffered herself to him in such an obscene way, his earlier pity for her gave way to anger. Torn between attacking her and leaving her where she was to go on alone, he simply turned away until, finally, after more attempts to win with words and movement, she fell silent, whimpering.

'What do you want then?' she asked at last, so much later that dusk had come and he was half-asleep.

What did he want? He had no idea, not then, and so stayed silent, thinking. Why did he feel better here than when he had been alone?

The company.

This company?

Some is better than none.

'Conversation,' he said aloud. 'Wouldn't mind that.'

He spoke it with a certain wonder in his voice, for so simple a thought and need as this had never occurred to him before.

'Oh,' she said, falling silent immediately.

Then, eventually and rather timidly, she said, 'That's a hard thing, that is.'

Hard? What was hard about it? It was . . . it *was*.

'You're right, it is hard,' Klimt finally conceded. 'Tell me what happened after we others left the gully.'

She tried several times, but her voice shook and she was close to tears. Klimt did not see this: he was still turned from her, his eyes half-shut against the night, and a certain weary patience overtaking him. Let her take her time, that was all he could think to do.

Eventually what she said seemed so odd to him that he thought he might have misheard.

'Did you say that?' she said.

'I said, "Tell me what happ . . ."'

'No, before that.'

'I said . . .' he began trying to remember what he had said.

'You said, "You're right, it *is* hard".'

513

'Well?'

'Welll!' she said. 'You're not going to mate with me and you're not going to kill me and you think me right. So what are you going to do with me?'

'With you, nothing. I'm going to sleep. I'm tired. You can keep watch. Only wake me if you need to.'

'Oh!' she said again, surprised, and her surprise was the last thing he remembered before he woke next day into daylight.

Jicin did not sleep. She lay quite still, wondering what she should do to watch out for another, for another had never asked her to do such a thing before.

So, wondering, she did nothing at all at first, but listen, and hear sounds, and start up in alarm, and wonder not once but a thousand times if she should wake him.

'Only wake me if you need to,' he had said, and that perplexed her. At first the sounds seemed so ominous, the cracking of the larch wood indicative of dangerous life and dark intent.

Three times she nearly woke him.

The first quite soon, because she was sure a whole pack of wolves was about to attack them.

The second because the pack had reduced itself to one, but that had come nearer still, and was cracking twigs, and breathing breaths that were as . . . as . . . that were no more than the night wind.

The third because . . . because she was lonely and wanted . . . wanted . . . conversation; company.

She stared down at his huge form, as it seemed to her, and at his still face, his closed eyes, and suddenly his sleeping ease and trust in her, relaxed and stilled her paw before she touched him.

So then she simply looked at him, and settled down, and knew what she had never known, which is the simple peace of knowing another is *here*, solid as the earth and as sure.

How long Jicin stared at him and watched over him, she did not care to know. Like pure, cold water it was, to one who has thirsted too long; like food to one whose hunger seemed that it would never end.

But perhaps she slept a little, for certainly dawn woke her from a waking dream, which was no dream, for it had been about him lying there, and there he was.

Food.

She fetched it for him and it was awaiting him when he awoke.

Water.

She led him to it, fearful that he would not follow, though he did.

Peace.

They found it slowly in the days that followed, the one from the burden of leading a pack; the other from the burden of never knowing that another demanded nothing of her but that she was herself.

And conversation. Which, when it started, flowed between them as easily as the little stream from which they drank flowed from somewhere they could not see, to somewhere else they did not yet care to find. Now fast, now slow, now dark and deep, now filled with sun and rippling, easy, without strain. To each of them it was quite inexplicable, but neither could deny that it was so.

Klimt talked of Tornesdal, she of Dendrine. Klimt talked of cubs he lost, she of cubs she surely yet would find. He of duty, she of love; he of puzzlement, and she of suffering and hope.

'You need some weight on you,' he said.

'And you need none.'

'*I* need time . . .'

'There isn't much of that . . .'

'No . . .'

Their silences were as full of words as their words were

resonant with meaning far beyond what they tried to say. But most of all, most puzzling, most strange, neither felt any fear of what the other might say, or do, or think.

'Klimt? Do I look strange?'

'Yes.'

That was the first time she laughed.

'And I?' he wondered.

'Oh, definitely!'

That was the first time he smiled so simply and so at ease with himself, and her, that all his lines seemed gone.

The place he had found her in, and where they stayed, was a patch of scrubby trees, Mennen-planted, by a stream in terrain so rough and undulating that wolves might hide there for a year and not be seen by fellow wolves, or even by Mennen searching for them. To those two wolves it was far more than years that passed in those few days of interchange. Neither threatened the other. Neither asked for much. Each was content that they were needed, and each was witness to the other's change.

Jicin gained a little weight, as Klimt had suggested that she should, and the hunted look that she had had was gone. Nothing could erase the sense of loss and guilt that accompanied the horror of Dendrine's destruction of her cubs, but some wolves are born with hope, and she was one of them. It was not much, but then a seed that survives a fire in a vale may bloom into rose bay willow-herb, or ragwort, or an oak that may in time grow to be ancient, and wise, able to protect others from the rains and driving blizzards that life brings. Hope is not always in vain; miracles occur. Such is the power of the gods whose names to Jicin were Wulf and Wulfin, and to others of their kind.

Klimt, so long driven by a sense of duty and purpose, and crippled with guilt as Jicin had been, discovered that he could live at ease; he could talk of uneasy things and the world would not fall apart. He could not yet laugh too loud, nor weep, but so far as he was able he could be a little nearer the wolf others might have wished him to be. With Jicin, at least, with her alone.

They mated perfunctorily once or twice and gave it up, laughing, giggling, unlike a leader, unlike Jicin. As yet it was not consequential. They preferred to talk, and be at ease, and, having eaten or talked or stared out across the fells, lying flank to flank and listening to the buzz of late-summer flies and bees that were slowing down was infinitely more preferable than the sudden thrusting act they thought they should engage in. Finally it was of no consequence.

A colder day came, Klimt grew restless, and Jicin said, 'Well?'

'Time to move on.'

'Where to?'

She did not doubt for one moment that she would go with him, nor that where they went and what they found, might be difficult. But both knew, for they had talked of it, that what they hoped for was something far beyond either of their lives. The WulfRock, that was where they were going. And the Wolves of Time, that was the pack that Klimt would lead, a little more wisely now, and with her as part of it, they knew that all of it would be hard.

The territory too, they had discussed that and she had told him much that few others could have spoken of.

'Beyond the Red Lake, as we Magyars call it . . .'

'Why "Red"?'

'Peat. Rock stain. No one knows for sure. It happens when it rains . . . well, up there beyond the scarp face you can see . . .'

'We saw it when we fled from Hassler . . .'

'Yes, you would have done. Beyond that, and I've only ever seen the beginning of it, is what Magyars call the ever seen the beginning of it, is what Magyars call the Scarpfeld, where few ever go, and when they do they are not allowed to go far in there. Anyway it's too dangerous, so they say.'

'Why?'

Jicin shrugged and said, 'My grandfather claimed it was all nonsense, but then he would. *He* said there was no place in the world better for rabbits, and that the grass was so green and lush it was almost blue! Dendrine's been up there. She bears her young up there. She bore *me* somewhere up there.'

Was this the wolf who had trembled before him such a short time before?

'Jicin, where did you . . . I mean, *how* did you survive?'

He meant to say, survive and be intelligent; survive and be able to talk normally and still to feel awe and faith that there was something up there beyond the Scarpfeld worth guarding all these centuries past, despite the evil of the guardians.

'The Magyars aren't all bad you know. My grandfather was not, and nor was Hassler until Dendrine got her claws deep into him, so I've been told. He was brutal all right, but it was she who turned and twisted his mind to order others to do evil things. It's Dendrine's fault.'

Klimt smiled and said, 'It takes others to make a Dendrine . . .'

'Anyway, she's a Bukov wolf, originally, like Tervicz. Did he know her? Did he tell you? I never dared open my mouth long enough in your pack to ask, but I often wondered.'

Klimt remembered his early journey with Tervicz and all he had been told. The conversation was not one to share with others, not even Jicin now. He knew more than he needed to tell.

'Perhaps he did, perhaps not.'

'You're being careful, Klimt.'

'I'm being discreet.'

She looked serious.

'You were going to say where we were going . . .'

'South and east, to find out what we can about the strength and disposition of your friendly tribe, beyond what you've already told me.'

'If they catch me . . .'

She was afraid, but not so much that it would stop her travelling with him.

'I'll see that they won't. I'm cautious by nature.'

'Yes, I think you are.'

He stared out over the fell, debating which route to take, and as he did so, she looked at him fondly. He had given her a sense of pride and though she wasn't much, not compared to wolves like Elhana or even, in a very different way to her own mother Dendrine, at least she was *something* now, and had a memory that no wolf would ever take from her. She suspected she would never be ledrene to his leadership, she had not the strength, nor even the desire for such a role. But then, whatever ledrene he did find, even if it was Elhana again, would never know the small secrets they had shared in talk and in silence through the days of summer that were now drawing to an end.

'Shall we go?' she said, suddenly restless. 'I don't want to stay here any longer. Not one moment more.'

She did not look back, though Klimt did, wondering if he would ever see the little, anonymous patch of a place again.

'There's nothing remarkable about it at all,' he called after her, half-hoping she might turn back and share his brief reverie.

'Just the fissured rock in whose shadow you found me, Klimt, over by the larch trees: that's remarkable to me.'

She did turn round then and nodded towards where the

rock rose in the lee of the trees through which he had first crept to find her. The sun was on it now, and it was no more remarkable than ten thousand other small outcrops.

When they had journeyed on a little they would not be able to make it out at all.

'But I'll never forget the place,' he said.

'Nor I.'

Only a few days passed before they became aware that they were trailed by a wolf, and Klimt was not slow to discover which it was. The tracks by a river in a vale south of the fells told him that, though, as Klimt said, such a wolf was unlikely to leave tracks he did not expect others to find.

That night they risked a howl, the first they had made together, and it told of two vagrants who meant no harm and would not mind contact with one similar.

'He'll come,' said Klimt after a further day, 'and when he does you'll wonder how we missed him!'

So, finally, he did, out of a misty morning of the kind that now beset the lower ground before the start of the day. The year was a topsy-turvy one: the first hints of autumn change were across the lower ground, and already the heather was purple and the grass and sedges burnished by September sun and winds. Autumn had come to the lower ground first.

The wolf loomed finally out of the mist near where they fed, stood still for a time, came forward a little more, and suddenly there he was, no less solid than the rock that had given Jicin protection, nor his fur much less black. Jicin fell back, Klimt went forward, hackles rising, his stance ready for attack, but his eyes calm. He knew the wolf at once, and what he saw confirmed his belief that he was benign.

The wolf was a shade older than Klimt had expected, though there was little trace of grey in his fur, and he was a shade thicker of build. But in bulk he was not quite so large as his paw-size had implied, though Wulf knows how formidable and frightening he must have seemed when he was younger. No, he was like a mountain that had weathered down, its edges softer, its cliffs less steep, but its structure showing quite plainly how impressive it would have been when first it rose out of the ground, and before time softened it.

'You are the wolf Klimt,' the wolf said. His voice was deep, accented and rich, and it was slow. There was nothing about him weak at all, least of all his gaze, which Klimt saw now was keen and not lacking in good humour. Indeed the wolf might almost have been called benevolent, so sure of his strength that he needed to express no aggression at all; like a great bear that sits and stares and feels no fear. Klimt felt instinctive liking for the wolf, though Jicin, less sure of herself, and much smaller too, had retreated so much behind Klimt that she was hardly visible.

'Indeed, I am Klimt of Tornesdal,' said Klimt, wondering how the wolf had got his name.

'My name is Kobrin,' said the wolf.

No words can easily convey the grave sense of authority this simple statement conveyed, though perhaps it was helped by the fact that Klimt knew very well what the name 'Kobrin' meant – from his mother, whose ancestry went back to the Pechora wolves of north-east Russia, and from the legends Tervicz told.

But surely, no wolf would be *the* Kobrin, who is leader of leaders of the Russian packs; a wolf of wolves. Kobrins *are*, and then they die, and another takes their place. And anyway, this wolf, impressive though he was, surely had not once had so much power that he ruled over so many packs . . .

'Kobrin?' repeated Klimt, ruminatively. 'Not really once the Kobrin of the Russian packs . . .'

The wolf nodded wearily, as if he had half-expected such a response and though he knew he must explain himself yet he had better things to do.

'The same. They are not all legends. They do not all die. This one survived and is alive.'

'But . . .' began Klimt, and then thought better of it. The wolf was benign and in his view posed no threat. Plainly he was not Magyar, nor any kind of spy. A wolf must trust his judgement or waste much time affirming it.

'. . . forgive me,' Klimt continued, 'but yours is a famous and impressive name.'

'And I am not now an impressive wolf?'

The two smiled at each other and Klimt shrugged and said, 'Perhaps less impressive than you were?'

'Perhaps,' agreed the wolf, chuckling. 'No, definitely less impressive now, most definitely. Now, your friend . . .'

'Jicin of . . . of the Scarpfeld,' said Klimt, pulling her forward.

If words would have failed earlier to describe the gravitas that went with Kobrin's name, they failed utterly now to convey the rough good nature of his charm.

He came forward, looked down at Jicin as if he proposed to hug her close, and said, 'You have changed for the better since I saw you some months back. That's very good . . .'

'Oh!' stuttered Jicin, much confused to be hemmed in by two such large and gently formidable males. 'Am I?'

'She is,' said Kobrin, firmly turning back to Klimt. 'Now, Klimt of Tornesdal, before we say anything more you had better tell me how you came to be ousted from your pack . . .'

'He wasn't ousted,' said Jicin. 'He left them.'

'Even more interesting and strange,' said Kobrin. 'Especially as the pack you left is having some difficulties at the moment and seems not to know, as the Poles put it, their arse from their face.'

'There was a problem with them which I judged it best they sort out without my help. Sometimes leaders do best to let events take their course and not interfere.'

'Strong leaders, yes,' agreed Kobrin eyeing Klimt appraisingly and seeming to like what he saw.

'And you?' said Klimt. 'Why would the Kobrin of all the Russias choose to leave not only his packs, but all his territories? Were *you* ousted, as you put it. Injured perhaps?' Klimt gestured towards Kobrin's back right leg which he had rightly guessed from his tracks had been broken in the past and was now stiff and lame.

'Injured yes, ousted no. An ousted Kobrin dies and I was never defeated. I never have been. I was injured, and then I came in search of something, and these months past I have begun to think I might be near to finding it.'

'In search of what?' said Klimt.

'A wolf to follow,' said Kobrin quietly.

Klimt stared at him, expressionless, and Jicin looked from one to another, overawed again. She could see something beyond them they did not see. It was the first rising scarp that led to the Scarpfeld, and across it the drift of clouds alternated with the warmth of sun. Then more shadows came.

'To follow . . . ?' doubted Klimt.

'To follow and to offer advice,' said Kobrin.

'About what?'

'The coming war.'

'Against the Magyars?' whispered Klimt.

Clouds shifted once again; summer was ending, the scarps that Jicin could see were plunged into shadows once more, and above them, where the Scarpfeld lay but could not be seen, the sky was black as fear.

'No, no . . .' growled Kobrin, 'not the Magyars. It is a war against the Mennen that the pack I join will have to wage.'

'The *Mennen*?!' exclaimed Klimt and looked at Jicin, thinking that what they had found together seemed suddenly so frail and so long ago, and as if it might never be again. Before what Kobrin represented, even memory began to feel as if it was slipping away.

'Come then,' said Klimt resolutely, for the journey must always go forward if they were to stay alive spiritually, never backward to what had been. 'We three shall talk. You for hope, Jicin; I for leadership; and Kobrin of war. But all of us shall finally talk as one, for however long our journeys to the Heartland have been, and however hard our wanderings on the wolfways yet shall prove, it is together and with other like-minded wolves that we shall be seekers of the stars.'

As Klimt led them off, and Jicin followed, there was in Kobrin's eyes a look of grave excitement, as of one who has found a wolf and a way he had been seeking so long that he had despaired he would ever succeed in his quest. Now, the wolf who had once been the Kobrin of all the Russias, who had never followed another wolf, followed Klimt.

CHAPTER THIRTY-FOUR

Aragon discovers what Klimt already knows:
that love and leadership do not easily mix

B Y MID-SEPTEMBER summer had fled before an
easterly onslaught of wet autumnal weather, and
by October the deer were moving down to lower
ground.

The moraines, so dry when the pack had first arrived,
now roared and rilled to the sound of running water, and
here and there along the escarpment, waterfalls which had
been sleeping trickles all summer had woken up again.
Overhead, by day and night, the bird migrations continued
on and on – the wheeze and whir of unseen geese passing
at dawn, and sometimes, on the downdraught of the wind,
the squeaking cries of smaller passerines were heard from
beyond the lowering cloud, as they took the south-
westward route and sought to reach their breeding grounds
in Africa.

For them, the world below meant nothing at all, a bleak,
black mass of rock perhaps, an undulating fell or two, a
place from where a raptor gyred up, before it stooped back
down to kill weaker, errant birds struggling below. Wise
wolves remember that to other creatures, living other lives,
the whole of wolfdom may be but a passing thing, mysterious perhaps, but of no consequence at all.

Such thoughts occurred to each of them in different ways
as October carried on the downfall of summer that Sep-

tember began, and warned of winter's coming, and decline, and death.

November came with darkening days and the last leaves in the valley trees clung on before they scattered downslope or were battered from branch to trunk, from trunk and out onto quarry face. As the skies began to glimmer lurid sometimes with coming snow, the days shortened, and the deer lowered their heads and stepped carefully down to lower ground and leas.

The pack had given up its search for ways out above. Not that their search had entirely failed, for Tervicz, determined to get them out of the area of the moraines, had tirelessly searched the steep slopes to east and west and found places where the escarpment weakened into gullies, and there was the promise of ways up, out and beyond.

But Aragon was slow to follow up these leads, confirming himself to be, as yet, more a wolf of style than substance: one who might dream of great things to come but was overwhelmed by how uncertain things began to seem when there was a decision to be made. For such pack leaders venturing forth is less appealing than playing safe, and all kinds of excuses can be found for doing nothing but stay safely where they are.

So it was that Aragon initially argued that they should take advantage of the safety of where they were, and then later, when Stry injured his left front leg, that they had best stay on lower ground; and finally, when Stry was better, he argued that the coming of the deer offered them a chance of food it would be folly to reject.

'But we should go higher while we can, before the snows begin,' said one of them. 'There may be better ground . . .'

'What's so wrong with where we are? If we're waiting for "something to happen" as you others seem to think, Wulf is as likely to make it happen here as somewhere up there . . .'

'But nothing might happen here at all,' said Stry, who was as anxious to get on as the others were.

'You've been injured, wolf,' said Aragon, 'and we could hardly have moved before. Now . . . well, you're still weak when you trek upslope . . .'

'I won't get strong staying on the level!' responded Stry stoutly, not wanting his injury to be used as the excuse for the delay.

'Well, anyway . . .' said Aragon vaguely, 'I may have other plans now, something that will help us to achieve what we want more safely than charging up into territory that remains unknown to us.'

'What plans?' said Tervicz and Morten almost together, and equally dubiously. They doubted that Aragon had any plans at all, and suspected that if he did, they would not be good ones.

Aragon smiled blandly and said that he would reveal his plans when it seemed prudent to do so. Meanwhile, did they not have a good safe territory? Yes! Was there plenty of food? Yes! Had there been a repetition of the attack by the notorious Magyar wolves? No there had not!

Aragon smiled again and dismissed his discontented pack, much less concerned about their doubts than he would have been three months before. He had learned many things in the months past, the most important of which was that he did not have to fight a wolf every time he disagreed with something he had said, or with an order given. An occasional show of strength did not hurt, but he was wiser now with the when and the where. There were easier ways than force of keeping a pack in control. He had discovered that it is in the nature of power that other wolves agree to most things without serious objection – so he smiled noncommittally, he was bland, he made sure they were safe and well-fed.

'He lacks all inspiration,' grumbled Stry to Morten. 'I

mean, I never liked Klimt much, but you felt you were going somewhere with him . . .'

'Did you?' queried his brother. 'I seem to remember months of indecision.'

'That was after the cubs were lost,' interjected Tervicz, always ready to defend Klimt.

'And whose fault was that?' wondered Stry, lowering his voice because Elhana had appeared nearby. She gazed at them thoughtfully and then wandered away again.

'Well?'

'It was the fault of all of us,' said Tervicz, 'and none of us. The Huntermann came, and we know what happened . . . no leader, no pack can foretell what the Huntermann will do. If he wished he could wipe us all out across the Heartland. At least Klimt led us off to safety. Can we be so sure that our new leader would have done the same?'

'Hmmph!' muttered Morten, after a moment's thought. 'That kind of situation might be what Aragon's best at. He saved the day when the Magyars attacked us on the fells, and which of us will ever forget how he dealt with the Magyars when we arrived back at the gully after being chased for so long? Eh?'

'Well . . . all I'm saying is that we could do with a bit of inspiration around here. Meanwhile, "Wolves of Time", my arse!'

They laughed, even Lounel, who on such grumbling occasions kept silent out of loyalty to Aragon. Then they talked of other things until Stry remembered it was his time to take over watch from Aragon himself.

'One thing you can say is that he's prudent. I've never known a leader be so strict about watches as him . . .'

Stry went scuttling away to do his watch and the pack settled down, gossiped, scratched, shrank back into the lee of tree and rock to avoid the withering November wind . . .

Aragon strolled in among them, causing each to stir a little as he passed by, out of a desire to show respect. Finally he settled down near Lounel, the only one among them who remained himself when Aragon came near, and did not stir at all.

'All well?' said Lounel.

'All well,' said Aragon, surveying the pack, and the rough ground of the moraines, and how the scarp above them was already darkening and losing colour towards black, though it was only mid-afternoon.

All *was* well, Aragon told himself, but it would be better still if his ledrene could get with cub. November, December, January . . . and then, or nearly then, Elhana's time would be right.

Then, or nearly then, the pack would have a purpose once again: cubs were unity; cubs were loyalty; cubs made a leader strong. The truth was that if he had a plan at all, that was what it was.

Meanwhile winter was coming, and he was pleased. No pack wants to climb too high in winter. Already the prey was coming down. The pack's grumbling about moving on to better territory would falter at the first powdering of snow; and they would cease moaning altogether with the first heavy fall.

'Come on, time,' Aragon muttered to himself, but he did not offer it as a prayer to Wulf. Aragon's gaze darkened. Let the pack consolidate, let his leadership be more certain yet, let Elhana have some cubs, let a new year lengthen and summer come once more and then, only then, would he turn his attention back to Wulf, to the WulfRock, and to holy territory, or whatever it was that Wolves of Time should be in possession of. Wolves of Time – the words crumbled and broke up in his mind. Wolves . . .

'What are you thinking, Lounel?' he wondered, preferring other thoughts to his own.

Lounel blinked, shook his head slightly, turned and looked at Aragon. What *was* he thinking?

He saw a wolf too young for leadership.

What was he thinking?

He saw a wolf troubled with uncertain love of one too mature and strong for him.

What was he thinking?

He saw a wolf who had too little vision for the task that fate had thrust upon him.

What was he thinking?

He saw a wolf too ordinary yet for an extraordinary time; but one he had journeyed far with, and who somehow he was sure would be there almost to the end.

What was he thinking?

He saw . . . Aragon.

'Well?'

'I am thinking wolf, that when we met and began our journey together from the Auvergne, our purpose was to reach the Heartland. What is our purpose now? What is the Heartland that we sought? This rough stretch of territory that lies between a fell we crossed to satisfy a dream, and a scarp you do not wish to go beyond? Where is our Heartland now? I am thinking, wolf, that I am growing weary with the wait!'

'You're free to travel on alone, Lounel,' said Aragon amiably enough.

'I am thinking, wolf, that I am not. It is with this pack that I belong. My task has not yet begun.'

It was Lounel's turn to be amiable, and he even smiled one of his vague and crooked smiles, and adjusted his awkward limbs.

'I am thinking, Aragon, that in time you will be a greater wolf than you can be now. That is what I am thinking.'

'Lounel . . .' began Aragon warningly.

The scarp loomed nearer the darker it became. A raven

called from out of it. A November night wind gusted and drove in a wet mist that brought the wolves huddling closer together.

'Lounel,' whispered Aragon. 'Do you remember those Mennen we found dead in the Bavarian forest?'

'I do.'

'Huddled together in a mist?'

'I do.'

'Do you ever think of them?'

'Yes, I do. There will be more of those, many more. Dead Mennen breed more dead.'

The wind gusted more, trees bent, and Stry came in. His face was enough to have the whole pack up, alert and more than uneasy.

'What is it?'

'The Magyars are about, Aragon, silent and dark,' he said urgently.

'Numbers?'

'Three at least. More certainly. Below us . . .'

'We all know what to do,' said Aragon, calm. In such a situation he *was* at his best.

'We do,' they muttered.

'Then do it, wolves,' he said, and he led two of them one way, while Morten led the others by a different route.

In a matter of moments, where they had been there was nothing left but the gusting wind, the strain of trees, a raven's call, and a lingering scent of wolves.

A short while later, up from the slopes below, out into the darkening place where the pack had been, Hassler appeared, several male subordinates at his flank.

They examined the ground, scented at rocks and trees, looked at each other and then at Hassler.

'How many?' he asked.

531

'Six.'

'Let us follow them now, my friends.'

He barked sharply to right and left; and then he howled, a cruel, unpleasant howl to which the others joined their own to make it full and ugly.

'Our wolves know what we are doing and have their orders; *their* wolves know that we are coming. Only six! So much for the fabled Wolves of Time!' He laughed deeply. 'When we catch up with them, the leader of these upstarts shall be mine; the rest are yours, my friends.'

'Follow them!' cried one of Hassler's sons.

'Follow?' snarled Hassler, buffeting him to the ground. '*Follow?* The Magyar do not follow. We are *driving* them, as the Mennen drive their sheep and cows. And we shall drive and trouble them here and there this night, and tomorrow and the night after that, until they are dispirited, lost, forlorn and have nowhere else to go but back to the lake, where they escaped from us before and made fools of us. There we shall have our revenge on them, which is most fitting. There you shall take the pack and I shall kill their leader.'

'Yes, yes . . .' they whined and snarled and mocked. 'These things we shall do, Führer.'

'Yes,' purred Hassler. 'These things we shall.' He liked being called by the old term Führer, it held more menace than mere 'leader'. Let the Wolves of Time have a new leader: the Magyars had a Führer.

He looked around at the gusty night, then towards the way the pack's scent trail seemed to lead, and the Magyars too were gone, one by one, to wreak their revenge on wolves who had made fools of them, but would not be allowed to do so for much longer now.

Then the patter of paws in a grim November night; winter coming; the pursued and the pursuers; and waiting for them all a red lake, by whose holy waters the pack of the

Wolves of Time had once been formed, and might now meet its final end.

Yet in the waters of that lake, for wolves who knew how to see, was the reflection, even on a lowering night like this, of a wolfway to the stars that might lead wolves of faith to a territory that had awaited them through so many centuries of time. If only they could reach out and grasp the moment.

The patter of paws; the warning barks of those who chase and those who are chased; tiredness and fatigue, and the options diminishing, one by one, until at last, whichever the pack, whichever the wolf, whatever the purpose, there is but one way to go.

A night or two later, below the moraines, across the Southern Fell, in the northern lee of the cirque in which the lake lay, and towards which the Magyars 'drove' Aragon and his pack, three wolves waited. Jicin in hope, Kobrin for war, Klimt with leadership.

They had crept under cover of rain and driving mist, and they had dug a scrape large enough for each of them to lie almost out of sight in an area of rock whose shards and shadows hid them well. They had eaten of food stored a day before, and now would not eat again until their task was done. They did not talk, for talk was forbidden. They did not move, for moving was forbidden. They did not clean the mud and filth that covered their heads and bodies, for that too was forbidden.

'We shall become the dust we lie in, the rocks that shelter us, the dirt with which we have covered ourselves,' Kobrin had said. 'We shall be the wind when it blows on us, and the rain when it falls on us, the sun when it rises and the night when it overtakes us. Thus we shall wait, as if we are nothing but the elements that surround us. We shall forget all that we are until the right moment comes. When it comes it will surprise us, and in that surprise will be our advantage, and the foundation of our victory.'

So now they lay and awaited the coming of the chased and the coming of the chasers, forbidden to do anything but think, though even that Kobrin would have preferred them not to do . . .

'*I* shall not be thinking,' he said, 'because it saps my energy for an action to come. I have done my thinking. My task now is simply to wait for what we know – what we hope – will happen. But you Klimt . . . and you Jicin . . . you will think. You will try not to because I have told you to try not to. But you will still think . . . which being so, try to think not of what might be, but of fulfilment of the objectives we have set . . . *If* you can!'

Hope, war, leadership . . . three wolves waiting in the dark: Kobrin almost asleep, calm, because he had been through such waits for action so many times before; and the other two, Klimt and Jicin, trying not to think, trying to drift towards a vision of the future, of objectives achieved. Learning the art of waiting, remembering all that Kobrin had taught them, remembering through the night, and the next day and the evening after that . . .

Sleep elusive, hunger gnawing, limbs aching, and as rain and gusting winds, and night and day overtook them, they drifted with the change, became the change, remained utterly immobile and unnoticed – even by the rooks that settled on a rock nearby at dawn, and by rabbits that scuttered but a paw-reach away – through it all the images of the months since they had come together surfaced for a while, drifted before them, before they let them go . . .

The months since the meeting with Kobrin had been exhilarating and dangerous.

Kobrin had persuaded them that their enemy was the Mennen, and Klimt had quickly understood this paradox: that while the Magyar regarded them as aliens, and would probably now kill them if they could, yet Klimt's pack – if it was to be his again – must seek to turn the Magyar enemy into friends. Division meant subordination to the Mennen; unity offered the only possibility of dominating them.

'I say dominating, not defeating. The objective of war is to gain control, not to destroy those in your path. We all see in the Mennen's battle with the earth the pointlessness of destruction, do we not!'

'Do we?' wondered Jicin, who never having travelled beyond the Heartland had seen less than either of them of the Mennen's ruination of the environment.

'Tell her, Klimt,' said Kobrin.

Klimt had already told Jicin of his journey down through Scandinavia, but mainly in terms of his escape from the Mennen; now he talked of some of the things he had seen on the way, and especially once he had crossed the Baltic Sea to the North European Plain – of the deadlands along the Mennen roads, the despoliation where Mennen lived, the dumps of broken, rotten things, the clearings of vegetation, the poisoning of soil, the pollution of the waters.

'So you see, Jicin, the Mennen are at war with the earth, and their purpose is to destroy it. Or, as they hope, to defeat it so that it slowly dies.'

'But we are the earth, or part of it,' said Jicin quietly.

'We are the wolves we always have been. The Mennen are at war with us, with all of us, and with the life that gives us life. Yet, they seem not to understand that they are at war with themselves and in defeating the earth they will destroy themselves. But dominating, well . . . they did that long before they took to destruction. In the Russias, dominance only turned to destruction in recent times, within the living memory of the Pechora pack into which I was born . . .'

So Kobrin had talked of the nature of Mennen and of war, and different kinds of war, and how he had begun to understand that the wolves' true enemy was the Mennen, not other wolves. Which, being so, meant that they must achieve unity within wolfkind before a war on the Mennen could be started with hope of success.

'I do not say we will not need to kill other wolves to gain a territory, because we shall. But if the territory we gain is unoccupied then such fighting and killing as we must do is simply to reach it and retain it. There *is* such a territory . . .'

'The Scarpfeld!' said Jicin.

Kobrin nodded.

'Could it be that Wulf kept it free of wolfkind so that it would be available when we came back?' said Klimt.

Kobrin shrugged and said, 'Could be. You are the leader I believe, the one who will seek reasons why and explain to others why they should be loyal, and into what they should put their faith. All I can say, as one who has seen too much war and fighting for one lifetime, is that if there is such a territory then we should take possession of it. The fewer we hurt, displace or kill in doing so the easier it will be to win such tribes as the Magyars to our side . . . But to do that we must find out what we can about the Magyars. I have discovered a good deal myself, but I would welcome others at my flanks to confirm what I have seen. The winning of a war is no different from the winning of an individual contest: the more you know about the opponent the easier it becomes.

'Now Jicin, soon we shall travel to find out what we can but first you must tell us all you know . . .'

Jicin did so, describing the four main divisions of the Magyar tribe, and how in recent times Dendrine's sons by Hassler had been put in place in many of the packs.

'They said that when he was younger my father, Hassler, travelled regularly between each of the main regions, maintaining his personal control over them and making sure that the leader of each of the local packs remained subservient to him. Naturally he exercised his rights of mating with their respective ledrenes, and made sure he was with them during their breeding periods . . .'

'He must have been a busy wolf during January and February!' remarked Kobrin jovially.

Klimt added, though without a smile, 'And a tired one. It might have been the right time to make a move into the Heartland itself, if he was off in a different part of the Carpathians . . .'

'I'm too young to remember, but in those days he had a Ratgeber . . .'

'Ratgeber?' said Klimt. She had used the word occasionally and usually tearfully, and he had thought it was the name of a wolf.

But Kobrin seemed to recognize the word, for before Jicin could reply he said, 'That must be a counsellor, an adviser . . . we use the same word with the bigger Russian packs, and the Kobrin himself always has a Ratgeber.'

Jicin nodded, continuing, 'It's an old Teutonic word the Magyar used . . . *rat* for advice, *geber* for giver . . . well, anyway, Hassler's Ratgeber was a female wolf called Raute, who was the previous leader's Ratgeber . . .'

'A *female*?' exclaimed Kobrin, astonished. 'There the similarity ends with Russian Ratgebers. Ours were always male.'

'Well, anyway . . .' continued Jicin again, 'Hassler kept Raute on as his Ratgeber and this will probably seem even stranger to a wolf like you, Kobrin, but *she* was the one who kept order when the Führer was away. She seemed to have no difficulty, though that was before she began to age. But then . . .'

'Yes, Jicin?' said Klimt softly, his eyes gentle, for he knew she was talking of things close to her heart. There was something easy and generous about Kobrin that made Klimt unafraid to show his feelings for Jicin.

'Well, I was too young to remember, you see, Klimt,' she said, coming closer to him, glad to be near enough to touch him once more, and also unembarrassed to show her affection. 'All I can say is what I was told, but it came from a good source, my grandfather. He was the one whom Dendrine killed . . . My grandfather said that Raute was liked and respected and never used unnecessary force. She took precedence over the ledrene when the Führer was away . . .'

'A remarkable wolf,' said Kobrin. 'She might have been a good Führer had she been male! Did she never try to oust the ledrene?'

Jicin shook her head. 'For one thing she was not a breeding wolf, and for another my grandfather always said she was too honourable. She served no individual Führer, you see, but the wolf she regarded as guardian of guardians who was, she thought, the Führer of the Magyar . . .'

'You say "she thought" as if you mean she had doubts,' said Klimt. Kobrin nodded his interest in the same question.

'I can only repeat what I was told: I first met Raute when I was very young . . . She came to see me, to look at me. My grandfather was there. It was the last time I saw him. She spoke to me a little, she said strange things, she . . . well, it was a long time ago and I was young, too young to understand I think. It was only much later . . .

'After she was gone, my grandfather confided that Raute was beginning to think that perhaps the Magyars were no longer acting as guardians should, or even knew what it was they were guardians of. By then Dendrine was ledrene and was successfully undermining her authority as Ratgeber. She finally lost power at the same time as Dendrine killed my grandfather . . . The two things were connected in some way.'

Jicin's voice wavered, and a look of pain came across her face.

'So Raute was killed as well,' said Klimt sombrely.

'Oh no, Raute the Ratgeber was never killed. Every Magyar knows that. She's still alive, or she was still alive at the beginning of this summer when I found the courage to leave the Magyar and join you . . .'

'Still alive!' said Kobrin, astonished. 'But why? If Dendrine so hated her . . .'

'Hassler would not allow Raute to be killed: he respected her too much, and he was superstitious, thinking that if she died unnaturally it would bring misfortune to the Magyars. So my father stood up for her. And anyway, she was going blind. What threat could she be? Dendrine took her place as Ratgeber and Hassler ordered Raute to be cared for until she died . . .'

'And you say she was still alive this spring past. You actually saw her?' said Kobrin. He exchanged a glance with Klimt. If what Jicin said was true then this was a wolf to try to reach; this was a wolf who might help them reach into the heart of the Magyar and turn it towards the Wolves of Time, avoiding prolonged war and bloodshed. If only . . .

'Of course I saw her!' said Jicin as if she felt she was doubted. 'You see, when she spoke to me when I was young it was to tell me that if I ever needed her advice, I was to seek it and she would give it. I went to find her and it was not difficult. But she seemed so old, Klimt, and though she had lost all her sight, she was a wise wolf. You could tell! Two young males looked after her, and when I went to her I was allowed to talk to her alone. She told me then that it was already too late for me to go back. Another who had been to her had been killed by Dendrine on her way back to the pack.

'"You have made your choice already, my dear," she told me. "Now, tell me about these wolves you met . . ."

'It was then I told her of that brief meeting with you and the others up above the lake, when you made such fools of Hassler by fleeing from him, and I told her of Klimt's reference to the Wolves of Time. Raute grew excited when I mentioned that and said that I must follow my instincts and seek you out . . . Anyway, she said, there was nothing else I could do. Her aides gave me help to escape, and so I got away without detection by Dendrine or her spies, and so reached your pack. But then . . .'

'There is no need to tell Kobrin of all that,' said Klimt, thinking of the cubs and how they were lost. 'I have told him and he understands. Now you have told us of Raute and it is surely plain that . . .'

He looked again at Kobrin and Kobrin looked at him.

'We must find her, wolf,' said Kobrin. 'None will know better than her what we shall need to know of the Magyar . . . Now, where was it that she lived . . . ?'

'Why, at the head of the Poprad valley, where Hassler's core pack of Magyars lives. Raute herself lives in obscurity some way to the north-east, on high ground where she can influence no wolf. Except that she influenced me! That is where you will find her if she is still alive, but it is well guarded . . .'

So it had been that the three wolves had begun their covert journey into Magyar territory at the end of August, to assess the strength of the 'enemy' Kobrin believed they must find a way of turning into allies before beginning a campaign against the Mennen, and also in the hope of contacting Raute, and gaining her help.

But they went carefully, for they could not doubt that if Jicin was caught she would be killed, perhaps cruelly. Dendrine would not spare her torments from which Hassler would be unable to protect her. This need for caution meant that though they learned much, they prudently turned back from the headland of the River Poprad, the main route being too full of Magyar, and the side routes carefully watched and defended, so that any wolf entering into the territory would have great difficulty doing so without being seen.

It was Kobrin who decided to abort this part of their reconnaissance.

'Mind you,' he said, whispering the words, for they were but a short distance from a patrol when they decided not to go on, all other ways having been equally well-protected, 'whoever has arranged this defence does not perhaps realize that it is harder to get in than out. I do not say, Jicin, that you did not do well to escape from this region without being seen, but the fact is that the way they have positioned their watchers offers opportunities to any already behind their lines . . .

'It is one of the hardest things in war, Klimt, to turn defence into offence, and the Magyars have made it especially hard for themselves. A determined assault by a small group of wolves on one of their positions, and successful infiltration behind their lines, would give their much larger numbers great problems . . .

'But meanwhile, we must retreat and explore elsewhere, and delay any attempt to contact this wolf Raute until we have wolves good at this kind of covert operation, more forces at our command, and a territory of our own to retreat back to.'

After that, such encounters as they had along the way diverted them to other places, other regions, other thoughts. The weeks turned to months as they journeyed into new areas of the Heartland, and then south-eastward into its Carpathian peripheries.

Here, at least, they were able to pass themselves off as vagrants without fear that Jicin would be recognized. Indeed, even had they met wolves who had known her as an abused female to satisfy the whims of Hassler's subordinates and Dendrine's spite, she might easily have not been recognized. She had put on weight, the journeying had made her fitter and much stronger, and most of all, Klimt had given her self-confidence. Sometimes, when tired perhaps, or near other wolves' young, her old doubts and sadnesses returned, but such moments soon passed. She looked the different wolf she was, and travelling with Klimt and Kobrin she successfully made up the third part of a formidable trio.

They were in the Muntii Rodnei to the east when the first snows came in late October, hesitating about whether to journey on for a few more days to seek out Tervicz's kin among the Bukov. But the ground proved too complex and formidable, with gorges to traverse, and great ascents to make, and they decided to retreat. But at Klimt's insistence they decided to howl down Tervicz's name and lineage on the last night before they turned back westward, hoping that their howl might be heard, and answered by Bukov wolves. It was an action that reminded Klimt how much he missed the wolf who had been his friend from the beginning of his adventure with the Wolves of Time and long after the other two had grown tired, and fearful that others heard, he continued to howl out the name of Tervicz.

'He has a sister called Szaba,' explained Klimt to the others, 'and a brother Kubrat who is crippled. And his father is Zcale, a wolf to respect. I would have liked to be able to tell him we had met them, or simply that they had responded to our howl . . .'

'Listen! What was that?' said Jicin, her head cocked as

she strained to look and listen eastward in the night. But the wind was from behind them, and though it might carry their own howl far, it made it less likely they would hear anything in return. A snatch of an answering howl perhaps, a brief moment of reply.

'Nothing,' sighed Klimt, shaking his head as they listened a little more. 'Nothing significant . . .'

Yet, afterwards, on the long journey back, he often remembered that moment, and felt that he had honoured something Tervicz had given him, and that in the attempt to contact others beyond the Heartland was the beginning of something new. They had reached out, and perhaps they had been heard, and one day, if Wulf was with them, reaching out would be the only way to go.

'The more who know of us the better,' he said later. 'We shall be as seeds upon the autumn wind, scattered and sown far and wide, unseen in the long winter yet to come, but then, when spring overtakes us, those seeds will grow and bloom, and wolfkind will find strength and place to grow again. Such may be our role.'

Kobrin nodded and said, 'In such a way will our war with the Mennen be won.'

'War or the discovery of peace?' responded Jicin quietly, looking from one wolf to the other.

'Both,' they all agreed . . .

It was gusty November when they returned to the Southern Fell to find the Magyar massing and heading up towards the moraines. It was not hard to drift in and out of groups of unsuspecting wolves, for many vagrants were on the move as well, and find out what was happening. They were told that alien wolves were up there in the moraines, false wolves who called themselves the Wolves of Time. They were to be driven east, herded like cattle to the shores of the lake, and there killed by Hassler's strongest . . .

'Our best chance is here and now, then,' said Kobrin, taking command of this last part of their long journey. 'I know the ground and it is not easy, but it offers possibilities . . . Come and I shall tell you what I think we must do . . .'

Two days later, under cover of darkness and bad weather, they were in position above the lake. They had not moved, for moving was forbidden. They had not cleaned the mud and filth that covered their heads and bodies, for that was forbidden. They had not talked until this moment . . .

'Ready yourselves for my command,' rasped Kobrin. For out of the morning mist that drove in from the east came four Magyars, scurrying down towards the lake, to hide and wait. 'I may give it in moments from now, or not for hours, but be ready. Eh, Jicin?'

She nodded, face set with determination and purpose, heart abeat with nervousness. There would be one chance, one chance only, and with her the manoeuvre would begin.

'Look!' whispered Kobrin.

The Magyars had gone to ground among the rocks, others scurried down from the other sides of the cirque to add to what was quite evidently an ambush; none approached from the plateau, which began a few paces above where the three wolves lay.

Driving mist. Droplets of water on shivery moss. Wet rock. The surface of the lake below in and out of sight as the mist shifted with the doubting wind. A hush, and all wolves out of sight. Waiting. The slip of paw on rock. A warning bark, tired and desperate. Another bark, further back, this one of command, and confident.

'There!'

Out of the mist they came from the east, too tired to run, to fatigued to look back, too near death to hope for much more life.

Morten led them, a limping Stry followed. Behind him, Elhana, her head low with near-defeat. Tervicz next, bloodied on the shoulders and his back from a fight; then Lounel, awkward as ever, benumbed. And finally Aragon, a leader in defeat, yet still proud, still determined, looking about that dread place for some inspiration, for some way out. None of them knowing that the route they took led them straight to waiting wolves.

While after them, out of the mist, strong and confident, came Hassler and a mass of wolves, taking their time, slowing their pace, that they might watch with pleasure the last moments of a pack that had hoped for too much, and succeeded in too little.

'*Not yet!*' hissed Kobrin, 'not yet . . .'

Below them, from some instinct that all was not well, Morten stopped and the others grouped. Aragon caught up with them. Yet it was Lounel who caught the eye, Lounel upon whom such light as there was that dull day, shone.

He looked around, he looked passingly upslope at where Kobrin and the other two lay, though Wulf knew they were invisible to ordinary eyes, and he seemed to shake his head as if he could not quite believe where he was, or what was happening, or what he saw . . .

Then he laughed, the mad, wild laugh of a wolf at play, delighted with a world all others see as black.

Even as this strange laugh echoed and then began to die and, all about the pack wolves rose up in ambush upon them, Kobrin, still unseen, all unknown, whispered this command to Jicin: 'Now, wolf, do it now! And may Wulf be with us all!

'*Now!*'

VI

BIRTH
INCARNATE

*In which Wulfin stands guardian to a holy birth,
as He who is more than wolf is born again*

CHAPTER THIRTY-FIVE

*The Wolves of Time find
a territory at last*

AT KOBRIN'S COMMAND Jicin slowly rose from where she lay, as strange and terrifying a figure as any who then saw her, friend or foe, afterwards remembered ever having seen; or were ever likely to see again.

Out of driving skeins of mist she rose, fur filthy and matted, eyes pale and intense, from a place no wolf had been, for a purpose none could guess, and her cry, which was a single word, was an accusation, a barb through the heart of all who heard it.

'You!'

It was more than a cry, it was a scream, a scream from hell. It was more than a scream, it was an invitation, and one to which no wolf would ever have wished to respond. An invitation to turn and face an evil past.

'Yes, *you*!'

It was so simply and yet powerfully made that all those who heard it thought it was meant for them; and all who heard it, and were too far off to see clearly the wolf that made it, peered and turned, and scurried forward a shade, the better to see whose voice it was.

'Oh yes, Hassler, Führer, Father, *you.*'

As Jicin said this, she moved downslope a little, to be better seen, and better heard as well, though so focused were the acoustics of the place, so strange the moment, that nothing but her voice could be heard at all. Not the blustering wind, nor the tumble and roar of streamlets down the rocks, nor the slide and crack and shattering of rockfalls far away. Nothing but her voice, and the howl it now sent forth as, around them, that final dreadful accusation echoed, and broke into a thousand profane, suggestive morsels of sinister ends and vile conclusions.

Of that screaming howl, what more need be said of the shock and horror it engendered than that it was born of Dendrine's cruelty, fed on Dendrine's murder of those that Jicin loved, larded with the taint of Hassler's compliance, and ended here and now in the very midst of Hassler's pack, as grim and undeniable as the steepest of the slippery rock-faces that loomed in the country thereabout.

In consequence, the ambush faltered and then stopped. Indeed, like all else, it came to an *absolute* stop as if the wolves who had risen in its service, like its victims, Tervicz, Morten, Aragon and the others, had all been frozen by a blizzard where they stood. But for this: wherever they did stand, or lay, or hunched ready to attack and defend, whether on the slopes around the place, or by the lake that lurked below in shifting mist, their heads turned slowly while their bodies stayed still, turned as one to look towards Hassler and see what his response might be.

Jicin's howl stopped as suddenly as it had begun and she said, with terrible clarity, and before Hassler could think how he should respond, 'By the ancient lore of Magyar, by the rights that any member of an ancient pack possesses, before the judgement of Wulf and Wulfin themselves, I declare that you, Hassler, Führer, *Father* have betrayed your task, which is to protect your pack, and protect the Heartland and protect *me*.'

It must be said at once that these words, concocted by Kobrin and Klimt together, came out a little stilted, for they were not ones that Jicin would normally have spoken.

Before Hassler could open his mouth to reply, Jicin added this most startling challenge: 'Therefore, Hassler, false Führer of our pack, I challenge your right to lead us now or in the future.'

'Challenge?' cried Hassler, recovering himself a little, now that Jicin had said her piece. 'Me?!'

He laughed, a somewhat hollow laugh, for there was something fundamental and unavoidable about the charge she had made; yet, the minions who stood about him echoed his laughter hollowly back.

'Tell me,' he said more firmly, trying to gain a dominance once more. 'Are *you* going to challenge me as leader? A female, fight me? A *daughter* fight me?'

He tried to raise a laugh among his pack once more, but more openly this time, more mockingly, and his pack was getting restive and the initiative swinging his way.

'Oh no!' she cried, and Kobrin, sensitive to every moment of this vital exchange, knowing its effect depended entirely on the element of surprise, now waning, and the awe it generated, considerable, yet waning too, was impressed by the power she still had over them. The laughter died immediately she spoke. 'Not I, father, another wolf. One greater than us both.'

'And where . . . ?'

This was his cue, and Klimt rose to it, massive, slow and sure, hunching forward behind Jicin who, at Kobrin's earlier command, now lowered herself a shade to make Klimt's size seem all the more. The mist could not have moved and heaved more conveniently, nor the wind have whined so well in the rocks about them.

'I challenge you, Hassler,' said Klimt, 'to show that you are able to defeat one stronger than yourself, without recourse to trickery or others to help you win . . .'

It was Lounel, not Tervicz, who was the first to recognize

who this wolf of grime and filth, massive-seeming, wild of eye, actually was, and he laughed as he had laughed before, madly, wildly, strangely. But it was Tervicz who understood the nature of the opportunity and made the rest possible. For as Hassler stood challenged, weighing up what he should do, Tervicz herded first one of the pack and then another upslope towards where Jicin and Klimt stood. It had to be done quickly and smoothly, almost as if it was not happening at all, or as if it was incidental, apologetic, fleeting.

So up they came, and not without difficulty, for they were tired and the slope was steep, nor without two or three of the Magyar wolves starting after them.

'So!' cried Klimt as this began to happen. 'You are ordering your minions up to do your dirty work . . .'

'No!' cried Hassler, meaning no he was not ordering them.

As Kobrin had hoped this 'no' was taken as an order not to follow the wolves. It was enough, for it gave the pack time to reach where Klimt stood, and to hear, to their surprise, the command from nearly-invisible Kobrin: 'Keep on running wolves, keep on! Run for your lives! Falter on the plateau and they'll come up after you. Keep on!'

Klimt wanted to turn round, to see them all once more, to group with them, but Kobrin's warning had been grim: 'If they stop and group around us we shall look like the weak pack we are, compared to the mass of Magyars we can expect to face us. Our wolves must pass on by, onto the plateau and out of sight, almost as if they had never been. Jicin can follow them, for her work will have been done. You must stand alone, Klimt, and never take your eyes off Hassler. Transfix him! Then you will know what you must do.'

The mist shifted, and Lounel, the last of the pack to reach Klimt, passed on by, and Jicin turned to follow him, as she had been told to do. So then Klimt seemed to be the last one there, alone.

'Well, Hassler, here I am. Klimt of Tornesdal. The wolf who made a fool of you before.'

'You challenge me for leadership of the Magyars?'

The moment had come and Klimt must not tell a lie.

'You heard what Jicin your daughter said,' he said. 'Is it true?'

It sounded just weak enough, and impressive though he was Klimt looked just weak enough, for Hassler to start up the slope towards him.

'You cannot expect me to fight you at all, least of all upon a slope and in conditions such as this . . .'

He advanced a little way more, still alone, and still his pack stayed where they were. He looked behind himself and down at them, perhaps feeling suddenly exposed.

'Afraid, Hassler, *Führer*?' said Klimt coldly and with contempt. Neither his voice nor his face betrayed the doubt he felt, or the way his heart beat within his chest. He had saved his pack for the time being; now he must save himself and squash any inclination the Magyars might have to follow. If they followed it would mean his pack were fleeing, if they were fleeing they would be overwhelmed and killed.

Hassler took one more step, then another, and finally one more which though hesitant now, was just enough.

Klimt retreated a single step, and then another sideways – enough to signal weakness, but not so many as to signal flight.

Hassler took his final step, more confident now, a laugh beginning to form on his face as he turned to order his wolves to . . .

To what?

No wolf will ever know. As he turned, the earth seemed to open up before him, massive and cruel and filled with flying retribution. It was Kobrin, and Klimt dived forward even as Kobrin broke cover and savaged hard at Hassler's turned neck. Hard and brutal . . .

'There must be no doubt, no delay, Klimt,' he had said. 'You must do it so absolutely that that wolf is dying or dead before either of us have let go our first bite. It is the only way. Surprise, shock, brutality. To save your pack and frighten the Magyars into passivity it will be the only way . . .'

So Kobrin had spoken, and so the two wolves now did. The shock of Kobrin's appearance and savage attack was so acute that Hassler stood no chance. He saw his own belly opened, he saw the blood begin to gout, and even as his gaze began to wobble, and his legs to go soft and all awry, he saw intestines that were his own, lolloping, rolling, spewing out bloody onto the rough slope.

Then teeth took his throat, teeth not of a wolf but of life itself, a life that had turned and turned and turned into blood-red darkness before all life was gone.

'Not a challenge for leadership!' cried Klimt, as Hassler fell from him.

'The beginning of a war!' roared Kobrin who, bigger still than Klimt, and more bloody too, seemed so terrifying to the Magyar wolves below that they backed away muttering, terrified, appalled.

'For we,' said Klimt almost in a whisper, 'we are the Wolves of Time and we claim now our rightful territory, which is the Scarpfeld, the place of gods. For that we shall make war, for all else we come in peace . . .'

The Führer's blood dripped from his mouth, his fur was wild, but his eyes were the calmest and coldest they had ever seen. And at his flank stood a wolf so terrible to look at, so powerful of effect, that none dared moved at all, except backwards and to flee.

The mist shifted, Hassler's body slipped and rolled upon the slope, his head was half off, his belly all agape, and the two who had done it stood, stared and slowly turned, and were gone.

Hassler slithered down some more. Grey, pink, all intertwined, his intestines slithered further still, like snakes, alive perhaps, certainly not yet quite dead.

But the Führer *was* dead, and pack had lost its head, and the Magyars felt as weak and insubstantial as the mist that enveloped them. None moved. None took the lead. Not one set off in pursuit.

The Wolves of Time had come, they had killed, and now they had gone, gone up to claim their rightful territory and none dared challenge them.

Klimt and Kobrin found the pack huddled and weary in the shelter of a small outcrop of rock, beneath a forlorn mountain ash, its leaves long since gone, and the last of its red berries, brown and puckered now, rattling with the wind.

Thus far Kobrin had advised Klimt what to do, and how to do it, and all had gone well. But from here, and where reclaiming leadership of the pack was concerned, Klimt was on his own, and he knew it.

He had brooded over much during the long covert wait above the lake, including whether or not to take back the leadership. He felt a duty to help save the pack if he could, but leadership . . . he had not felt any pleasure or comfort in it before, and now he had discovered companionship and . . . affection – he did not dare say love – with Jicin, he was loth to jeopardize it by taking on the responsibility of leadership once more.

His mind would have to turn to other things, and if Elhana remained ledrene as seemed most likely, what then of Jicin? What of those times they had had alone, drifting together in thought and emotion, answerable to none but themselves, unobtrusive and content? Klimt knew such things would be diminished, perhaps quite gone. He would drift apart from Jicin, she from him, or worse: they would long for one another across the great void that would be their different positions in the pack, and much that was dark and miserable would follow from that.

So Klimt brooded, and was doubtful. And yet . . . how could he ever forget the promise he had made to Wulf that night in Helsingborg when Wulf had guided him and let him live?

'I shall serve you always . . .' he had vowed, and in his heart Klimt knew that meant as leader of the pack.

'Yet not quite leader,' he had once confided to Jicin in those good days of high summer. 'I see myself as creator of a pack, and as guardian of its sense of purpose, for surely another will take over from me who shall be stronger, greater, and will see the completion of the task that I began. It is not for me to be sole leader of so great a pack, not for an ordinary wolf like me who does not even know how to love . . . who knows the tightness and the coldness of his heart and yet does not know how to release it, or how to dare let love run free . . .'

Such were his doubts and conflicts. And yet, the moment Klimt had seen the pack drift in towards the lake so wearily, so near defeat, he knew he loved them *as a pack*. Individually he felt more for some than others . . . Tervicz, still so proud and strong, certain in his destiny as the Bukov wolf who would one day guide them back to the WulfRock itself; Elhana, ledrene born and bred, hurt by so much, near defeat now, and yet . . . how he admired her, and how he longed to give her what she longed for; Lounel, wise wolf, whose greatness was yet to show itself; Morten, Stry . . . dependable, sent by Wulf and Wulfin, wolves to trust; and Aragon, oh Aragon, did you take over the leadership that I left vacant? Did I give you too much too soon? Yet, did you give Elhana the love she craved and the companionship . . .

To which, he saw in the last moment before Jicin sprang their surprise, that the answer had been this: 'Yes, Aragon had given Elhana more than he, Klimt, had been able.' For as the Magyar rose about them in ambush, the first thing Elhana and Aragon did was to glance at each other, and their eyes spoke not of fear, not even of loss, but of love found, of passion remembered, of gratitude for what had been.

Seeing them again, thinking of them, Klimt knew how much he cared, and knew in that moment of destiny that for better or for worse the leadership was something he must take up again. It was his task and no other wolf's, unless one came who was stronger than him . . . and one *would* come, a wolf as pure in heart as he would be great in love, a leader before whom all other leaders would bow their heads.

As Aragon and Elhana had shared a glance, so then did Klimt and Jicin, and in it was remembrance of love found, of friendship made, of hearts as open to each other's care as the sky is open to the earth, and the sea is open to the wind; and in that final glance, as well, was sadness that all might now be lost, and confusion that the way of duty was not always the way of happiness, and that the play of justice did not always bring the pleasures of content. Then . . .

Then all was lost in that play of feint and battle planned by Kobrin, and the beginning of a war whose purpose was to avoid a bloody battle with the Magyar that their lives might be saved for the coming war against the Mennen. Then . . .

That was then.

Now was *now* . . .

Now Klimt must be as resolute in dealing with Aragon as he had been with Hassler. One would have to suffer in the cause of many, the strike must be where it would have most effect in stopping strife thereafter. Now . . .

They huddled and they turned when Klimt and Kobrin loomed out of the mist, bark having been answered by bark of recognition, rill by answering rill, and no sound of chase.

Jicin stood off to one side, Elhana to another and Tervicz, certain where his loyalties lay, stood off from all of them. While Aragon stood proud, dangerously ready to protect what he had fairly won, and fairly held.

Klimt had no doubt that it was thanks to Aragon that the wolves had reached the lake in one piece. A less clever wolf in fighting and escape would have turned and faced the Magyars, and then all would have been lost. But times change, moments come and go, the leader may be to the hour born, but it is in the day and month and the gathering year that his worthiness must prove itself. The pack had a greater task than merely to survive and breed, and perhaps they had forgotten it. Now they stood divided and uncertain, and the issue of who led them could not be delayed.

Klimt moved ahead of Kobrin and began his charge out of the mist and down into the sheltered spot where they stood, hard and fast at Aragon, as terrifying now as he had been before with Hassler.

Aragon saw and did not flinch. Indeed, he moved a little to one side to give himself greater freedom to move and feint, and too, that none in the sheltering pack be hurt by the coming fray. This done he placed his paws on the ground, coolly watched Klimt's charge, and went to go one way before sliding another, to mislead Klimt and gain the chance of attacking him as he went by.

But he was slow in his movement, and Klimt was fast. Klimt saw the feint, understood it and went the right way, and half-lifted Aragon off his feet, his teeth catching at the fur and skin of his shoulder, his forward movement so powerful that Aragon was pulled down and along and then up and out into the darkness beyond the gully and its leafless mountain ash.

The pack watched, and Kobrin too, as the wolves fought in and out of shifting mist, the colour of their fur the same dark grey, the meeting of their bodies like silhouettes crossing and criss-crossing against a white sky, two bodies become one, limbs confused, none sure which was which. One thing only was certain: Aragon did not give up his rank easily. He might have lost the initiative, but he made up for that, came back, found strength out of his fatigue and tiredness and fought as well as he was able.

But at last he faltered and fell, and one silhouetted wolf stood over another, and demanded obeisance or death.

There was stillness for a time and then the victor rose from off the vanquished and turned towards the pack from out of the murk, and they saw that it was Klimt. Behind him, Aragon struggled and rose, limping and wounded, and came to stand nearby where all could see.

'I have said to him,' growled Klimt, 'that he may stay with the pack for now, provided he admits his lesser rank . . .'

Aragon's head lowered, and his tail curled in. It was enough. Words were not needed to confirm what all could see.

'I have said to him we need him, for his strength and his courage. He did no more than any of us would have done, no more than that . . . But . . .'

Here an awesome coldness and grim purpose came to Klimt's pale eyes, and his face hardened in a way that Aragon's could not and never had. One had the face of a leader, the other of a proud lover. One, they could see, had fought for duty and for pack, and he had won; the other had fought for pride and love, and he had lost.

'. . . but when the spring comes once again, and Aragon has served us and helped us through the winter, I shall exile him from our territory for a time. Let him journey as a vagrant once again. Let him learn as I have done. Let him then decide if he wishes to return to a lesser place not from the need of the moment, but from loyalty to our shared future. This is my decision as your leader.'

He looked boldly at each of them in turn, and each returned his gaze, even Elhana, even Aragon, and they murmured their assent. But more than that, they grouped closer to each other, they grouped as one.

Except for Kobrin, who had stayed just where he was before the fight began.

Then Klimt said, 'This is Kobrin of all the Russias. He is my adviser in war. He is the wolf to whom most of you owe your lives. Therefore honour him.'

They looked around at Kobrin who now squatted down, his forelegs supporting his massive weight, his head seeming to move against the mist, though it was the wind and mist that really moved. His eyes were narrowed, and his gaze though fierce remained benign.

'Honour him!!'

One by one the wolves did so, going to him and touching a paw to his, or sometimes a muzzle, and he accepted their obeisance with good grace, smiling at some, speaking a greeting to others, sharing a chuckle with Stry. But for Jicin he had a smile, and a touch of cheek to cheek, for she had done well, better than any of them perhaps, and shown a coolness and courage that would never be forgotten.

'So . . .' said Klimt, his pack once more his own, the Wolves of Time together again, and more than they were before, 'we shall head on across the plateau, seeking a way to the beginning of the Scarpfeld. There we shall rest, and in the morning, by when the mist may well have cleared, we shall press on into territory which only Lounel has visited before – except for Ambato of blessed memory – and find out what it consists of, and what it means for us. Tervicz, you travel in the front with myself and Lounel.

Kobrin, you take up the rear with Morten. Aragon, you can travel in our midst, with the females . . .'

It was the nearest Klimt came to verbal retribution of his vanquished rival, and none could blame him for it. He was leader, and he could dispose them as he felt fit. Anyway, most were so tired that what he said mattered less than that he had come back, he had taken command, and they felt safer and more assured than they had for months past.

A day of bad weather turned to a worse evening; and that evening to a foul night.

The wolves reached what they hoped were screes at the foot of the first escarpment, and among the fallen boulders there found what shelter they could from the driving rain and mist. Shivering with cold and fatigue, carried forward for the most part only by the fear of what they left behind, and a hope of what might lie ahead, they slept where they staggered down, but for Klimt and Kobrin who kept watch; and Tervicz later, who insisted on taking the watch of the deepest night, that his master might find rest.

Not that there was much to see. No moon, no stars, no shadows in the black, no sky against which to set a dim horizon; no light at all.

Nothing to see, and yet there were things to fear. During Tervicz's watch the night seemed to shift and move, up to the fastness above, across the plateau just below. Odd cries and calls. Movement unseen, eyes opening to snoop and peer.

It was the longest watch Tervicz ever took, and when dawn came, which it did slow and crawlingly, he saw the mist had lifted but a little, so that when he looked up towards the scarp its upper half was lost in swirl.

Lounel awoke, peered about, and said he had no idea

which route he and Ambato had taken before. All looked different, all looked the same.

'So you can see into the future but not the present,' joked Stry.

'Hmmph!' muttered Lounel, his fur shiny with the wet.

'Even so, we shall have to press on,' said Klimt, 'for if I were the Magyars I would be recovering now and be angry, and I would be saying that when the weather eases I would set forth across the plateau at least to the foot of the Scarpfeld, which is here. Therefore we shall move on and lose ourselves above. Fear and superstition, and the need to get back to the heart of their own territory before worse winter weather comes will drive the Magyars away again. So, Lounel, you keep your eyes open for something familiar – a boulder you passed before, perhaps, or a run of grass, or the way the wind sounds up into a gully above. We'll find the way to go. But, wolves . . . stay close, and you, Stry, keep central to us all, barking your whereabouts and howling us back if need be. There's darkness in this place and we should avoid getting separated.'

It never came to that. The rain eased and ceased, the mist lifted a little more, and in mid-morning Lounel found a way on, which took them up a stone chute and thence between great buttresses of black rock which marked a point which seemed to lead on up and through the scarp.

In the shelter there the pack grouped once again, all present and correct, and, looking at the looming gully sides about them and up ahead, Klimt said, 'Good! Forward then! Follow . . . and this time, Kobrin, you keep up the rear. We want no more surprises, and Wulf willing, once this day is done, we shall have found a place that is safe where we can find food and shelter, and plan our strategy for the winter months to come . . . *what was that?*'

What he had heard – what they had all heard – was a

thin and distant cry which in such a wind might be nothing at all, just fancy. Yet, given the gloom of the place where they had paused, and the circumstance of their journey, and their growing confidence that they had left their troubles behind them and needed now only to exert themselves for a day or two more before they gained a new security, and time to rest . . . given all that, it was a shock that the cry came from somewhere above them. Magyar? Dying deer? Mennen?

Klimt shook his head, others muttered to each other and, shouting against the wind, he told them, 'Whatever it was it cannot have been much. We shall press on as fast as we . . . *what!?*'

The cry again, a little louder, most terrible, definitely wolf, and then only wind.

'Come!' commanded Klimt, leading them forward, one after another, with Morten and Stry taking the flanks, and Kobrin and Tervicz the rear. 'Come, wolves, hesitation is the food of fear! It sounds like a solitary wolf but it could be a trap. Well then . . . stay grouped, stay ready and advance with me!'

The sides of the gully narrowed, the wind funnelled and strengthened and drove up behind them. Whatever it was had cried must be near to be heard against such a wind. Grass and scree formed the path they took, and above their heads the gully sides were lost in mist.

Wulf knows what a terrifying sight they would have seemed to any creature coming down that way, a pack of wolves, purposeful and well led, climbing up from the misty depths below. Yet the sight they made was surely nothing compared to the sight they saw, which *was* a wolf. It lay across the slope above them, and was most terrible, most sad . . .

A fallen wolf, limbs trembling in death, its sides raw-red, its fur all gone but around its head, a strange dwarf of a wolf, mouth open with its final breath, and on its face a look of interminable suffering.

So strange and horrible did it seem that their fur ruffed about their necks, their eyes narrowed. Had Mennen done this? Malevolent gods? Was this a warning not to go further?

Klimt went to it and it spoke.

'Do not hurt me,' it said.

'We shall not hurt you, wolf,' whispered Klimt, 'we shall not hurt you . . .'

A look of surprise came to the broken creature's eyes, and then of hope.

'Wulf sent you,' it whispered. 'He sent you to guide me to the stars. That's where I was trying to escape to, there where he will . . .'

'What wolf are you?' asked Klimt.

'Brother, I am brother. Dendrine's son's brother and his food . . .'

'Jicin!' said Klimt urgently, summoning her.

She came, she looked, she stared into the dying wolf's eyes, and she knew what wolf it was. Brother. She went to hold the poor, torn, un-grown thing, and said she was the stars, and that Wulf was waiting there, and at his flank was Wulfin and together they would heal hi . . .

The wolf died as she held him, staring into mist, and seeing more than they of the moment's goodness and kindness they had brought, and knowing at the end of life, of joy an eternity.

Jicin wept and the others stood in silence and respect. Its parts were eaten raw, though when they looked they saw its paws were whole, its pads untouched. But . . . both ears had gone, much of what seemed raw was healed into scar tissue, and yet some was fresh-chewed.

'What has happened to it?'

'What is this place?'

Klimt's expression did not change, nor his purpose falter. Never were eyes so cold.

'Did you think the place we are going would yield up its secrets pleasantly?' he said at last. 'This is the Scarpfeld we are entering. Even the guardians avoided this ancient place. Eh, Lounel?'

Lounel nodded and came forward. He looked curiously at the wolf and touched its head. 'It lived until we came. For it *we* shall live . . .'

'Yes . . .' whispered Klimt. 'Yes, Lounel . . .'

There was pity in Lounel's eyes and no fear at all. 'Let me lead,' he said gently, 'for this way I have come before and whatever waits ahead shall not harm me, nor should we harm it, however evil it may be. Peace shall be our way in this lost place in which we have found peace, only peace . . .'

He repeated the word several times, as if to soothe the place that lay ahead, and make the mist less murky, less troubled in the wind. Each touched the fallen wolf with respect, that they might not forget what they had seen and heard, a life stolen which they must try to live.

Then on went Lounel, quite fast, so they scrambled on after him to keep up, and they left the corpse behind. On and on he climbed, faster and faster . . .

'Lounel!'

He was gone on into mist which swirled him out of sight, too far.

'Lounel!'

Klimt ran the last few paces after him, the others close behind, running towards fear and dread, running to catch him up before . . .

'*Lounel!*'

There he stood, unveiled by mist, solid, certain, stopped quite still. The bluffs of the gully had opened out, the ascent had shallowed and then flattened to lush, sodden grass, the mist ahead was clearing, clearing, and as if coming towards them out of it, though all they were doing was standing still, were two wolves, living, more terrible in life than the victim they had seen in death.

A thin hag of a wolf, fur wisped and torn at by the wind, eyes savage and belligerent, on her face a mother's madness to think her young was threatened. In her eyes cold cruelty, mockery, crudeness, vileness.

Dendrine.

'Get out of here you shits, you turds, you . . .' and then she laughed, and laughed.

Was it their expressions she laughed at, to see the male who stood at her side and who was already a little taller and broader than she was? Was she delighted at their shock? She laughed and cackled and they stared.

'My last-born son,' she hissed by way of introduction. 'My sweetling and my dear. Harm him and you shall be cursed by me. Hurt him and you shall be torn by me. Harass him and . . .'

The son-wolf moved, quite suddenly. His head, huge and monstrous, darkly misshapen, which had been staring closely at the ground, though whether peering at it like a fool, or scenting at it, they could not tell . . . moved up and they saw its eyes, and its eyes stared. And then it charged at them, savage and fast, as if they were a world it raged against, moving with the speed and grace of youth, the head, so terrible, so contorted in its shape and savage in its look, coming nearer and nearer and nearer still, so that all of them got ready to take its assault, for at all of them it seemed to charge.

Then, when it seemed it could not stop, it turned to one side, ran up a slope, towards some scree and was gone, gone into mist, a foul vision turned suddenly to the sound of paws pattering on rock.

The sound of Dendrine's laughter returned to them.

'Now my sweetling will come back,' she whispered hoarsely, and with evident pride and delight. 'Soon.'

They waited in a silence broken only by the wisping wind, and the run of water beyond the mist, up in the crags, unsure from where he would come.

Then her sweetling did come back, though how it came from the *other* side of the gully, how it got there quite so fast, none could tell. But come it did, faster and faster and then slowing, bounding hugely, dog-like, deer-like, rabbit-like, mocking all creatures in its mimicking; and then it spoke.

'My brother is dead,' it said, 'but I live, I live . . .'

Its voice was youthful and deep, and it sounded uncertain, a little lost. Fearful perhaps.

'I live!' and this was a roar, and intimidating.

Dendrine laughed and said, 'Sweetling, brother ran away and died that you might live; telling you it was time to leave; wolves have come that you might go. Don't eat *them!*'

She laughed and came towards them. They drew aside as if she was plague personified and as she passed Jicin, she stared into her eyes and said, 'Why, it is *you*, you my dear, my changeling! One day I'll see that he eats *you* alive. But watch him, he likes teats and is inclined to rip such things off.'

That laugh again as she went on down, utterly indifferent, her foul son now at her foul flank, eyeing her floppy dugs and thinking better of it. He stopped on the slope below, stood staring up at them fearlessly, his paws fretting as if he might charge again.

'Who are they?' he demanded.

'Them?' she said without looking back. 'Wolves my dear, the Wolves of Time. Klimt made a fool of your father and has probably killed the thick bastard by now so that you may take his place. The others, but for your sister Jicin, their names I do not know.'

'What's "sister"?'

'A sister? A fool.'

Dendrine laughed softly, touched him with real love, turned briefly to look back like a mother who is proud to show off her favourite-born and then said, 'Come along, it is time you met your pack. Your time here is done.'

'We should kill them . . .' said Morten and Stry together. 'Such creatures should not live. They will be trouble if we let them live.'

'No,' said Klimt, not knowing why he said it, but that Lounel had warned that they must come in peace. Killing was not the way.

Then more wind and driving mist, and Dendrine and her son were gone, and Klimt and the others were left alone to their new territory.

CHAPTER THIRTY-SIX

*The pack explores its territory, and its
ledrene gets with cub*

FIVE DAYS PASSED before the driving wind and rain eased off into colder, clearer weather, and the wolves were able for the first time to see the extent and nature of their new domain. It did not disappoint them.

Few areas are so noble and so mysterious as the fabled Scarpfeld of the Tatra. Higher than the Southern Fell, lower than the Tatra peaks themselves, the area has all a pack might need, comprising as it does a series of steep, connected scarps, some large, some less impressive, many fissured and strange, some continuing round and out of sight, some being no more than steps to bigger scarps formed by rock that once lay overhead and has been raised, tilted and eroded.

The rocks are variable, of a stratified and sedimentary nature, but with intrusions of volcanic lava that have twisted and turned the steps of rock to form plugs and dykes, which being harder than the surrounding rock, form strange stacks and protrusions, all dark, sometimes fractured.

Broken land then, whose main drift is east to west, but whose fissured nature draws a wolf upward, to see what lives above. But in trying to grasp a pattern where patterns are so complex, heights and lows so unpredictable, dark and light so intermingled, a wolf's head aches, the more so if he seeks to understand. This is the nature of the Scarpfeld.

Added to which are the sheltered corners where a few battered mountain ash survive, though as dwarfs compared to their lowland cousins, and strange rafts of alpine flowers, saxifrage and stonecrop, alpine mantle and dwarf gentians as blue as the deepest, shiniest blue of clear June skies. All of which, literally, is overlain by a micro-climate as varied as the ground it swirls and forms about: pockets of dew, depressions of mist, wild winds around a rocky corner on a day that seemed quite still, and all the variations of sun in summer, and of snow in winter. This is a whole world in miniature; this is indeed a place where gods might have once been born into the mortal world.

Here, too, is what a new pack needs: cover, of rock, of scree, of undulation and of void. Cover of bush and stunted tree, cover of fissured gap and rushing stream. Cover of cloud and mist which, the landscape turning the wind as it does, forms and reforms, drifts and slides, in patterns that frighten a wolf until he understands them.

Here, too, is prey, for ground such as this, its drift and rock dust forming all kinds of soils, some acid and some more mild, makes for many micro-habitats. And rabbits thrive, their white ribs and skulls scattered across the sward, evidence of past lives, and ravens' picking – the ravens: dark emperors of the skies in that strange place. And a natural home for deer. Down from the mountain they come, and up from the fell, down to rut and mate, up to have their young.

To east and west the Scarpfeld stretches, a day or two's journey either way, though its higher, rougher, wilder section, where the gullies are near-gorges, and the cliffs are almost mountains, and on a dark night or a misty day a wolf might turn a corner and fancy he is lost forever, so confusing are the ways, this part is the centre.

It is somewhere in this central part, up there among the cliffs, between one buttress and another, up that scree and round behind that great fallen boulder, *there*. . . a grassy way runs to a place holy and mysterious. A place where wise wolves do not venture. A place of echoing rises, and strange light. A place through which, if a wolf journeys, and if he is pure of heart, he – so wolves say, so many believe – or she, may find the WulfRock.

November moved darkly to December, and it was here, on the flatter slopes beneath the boulder which marked the entrance to a way none but Lounel had ever ventured far along (and even he turned back while Ambato went ahead and was lost in the darkness and light that lay beyond) . . . here the pack made their denning ground. Plenty of places to overwatch the territory and give warning if aliens came. A wide and sheltered area, space enough for wolves to be alone if they needed solitude, and yet still be on call; space enough as well to raise cubs in safety if their ledrene was blessed to bear them.

But which ledrene? Elhana, so far not displaced, so far taking precedence, or Jicin, Klimt's friend? All the males in the pack sensed that just as Klimt had had to affirm his leadership, so with Jicin's coming Elhana must affirm herself as well, or give way. Not that Jicin gave her positive cause to, for the younger, smaller wolf was respectful, and gave way on all things that mattered – food, lying ground, and her position at Klimt's flank when the pack was together. No, her fault was that sometimes she spoke to Klimt alone, quietly confident, companionable, and Elhana did not like it.

When she went to break them up, Jicin retreated, but not subserviently. Rather, she made it seem that Elhana did not understand, could not understand, would *never* understand, and this was what Elhana did not like. Even though these moments of companionship between two friends were rare enough, for Klimt was discreet and understood he gave offence.

To make it worse, Klimt was more forgiving of Aragon's friendship with her than she was able to be of his with Jicin. Aragon did not rankle with him at all and though once in a random while he charged him down and set him running, just to remind the pack who was who, he bore no grudge; he understood. Dominance was leadership; understanding and tolerance was leadership as well. Klimt was now beginning to handle such dilemmas well.

Which, irrationally perhaps, rankled still more with Elhana, who would have wished him to be less reasonable where Aragon was concerned. Tolerance from Klimt was not quite what she wanted if she was to turn finally from her lover and commit herself to her leader. A little jealousy from Klimt would have helped much more.

Through the weeks of December, when the clear days gave way once more to low cloud and rain, these thoughts swirled like mist and low cloud in Elhana's mind and nagged at her, while in Klimt's there were other concerns, and more immediate needs, to take his mind off such thoughts. For one thing he wished, so far as the members of the pack were able, to get to know the Scarpfeld before winter ice and snow came in.

'We need to know its ways, its dangers and its opportunities, well enough that when the winter truly starts we can safely avoid trouble, hide from danger, and make sure we have enough food to see the hard times through,' he told the assembled pack. 'There is the danger of the Magyar, though I believe that for the next few months at least that danger may be past. In the longer term I shall wish to make them into allies . . .'

There was a murmur of astonishment at this, for Kobrin's

notion of a war against the Mennen, and the importance of establishing peace with the Magyars before that began, was not one either wolf had discussed with others, except for Jicin, who had kept their confidence. Their needs now were more immediate and more local, and their priority, as Klimt knew well, was to breed more young. Wulf knew how hard it might yet be for him and Elhana, but lore was lore and so long as she was his ledrene she must be the one to bear the pack's new cubs.

'All I shall say now of the Magyars is that we shall be watchful, and cautious, and see the winter through before we engage with them again, howsoever we do it, and in whatever form,' Klimt declared. 'Meanwhile, we shall take a different area of the Scarpfeld in pairs, and each pair shall explore it, report back about it, show what we know about it to the others, and so as a pack help each other to begin to get to know our territory.

'Of the boulder which lies above our denning ground, which Lounel has told us is on the way Ambato went when he was last seen alive, and which instinct tells us all is the way through to a holy place, the WulfRock itself perhaps, I command that none of you ever go beyond it. Our task is here, to learn and feel our way forward, to discover what it is that Wulf and Wulfin wish us to do, and why it is from the base of this strange territory that we must do it.

'In the weeks ahead, as we get to know the Scarpfeld, I shall be watching you all and doing my best to do what I did but ill before: which is to listen, and to learn, and to be there for those who need me. I am not a leader born: no wolf is. One day another greater than myself will come, and I shall yield up my place to him. Meanwhile, reflect on this: our pack is what we make it, and your leader is what you make him, as is your ledrene. Therefore try to help us as we shall try to help you.

'Meanwhile, as the season darkens into a new year and

we journey through winter towards spring, it is important that we know each other's strengths and weaknesses. Some are best at fighting, some at route-finding, some at taking prey. Some at giving advice . . .'

He smiled and they laughed, for what member of a pack was there who did not prefer sometimes to give advice than take it, or advise rather than act . . . ?

'We can laugh,' said Klimt easily, seeming more assured in his position with each day that passed, 'and we can learn. The Magyar traditionally had an adviser to the leader whom they called the Ratgeber. It is a good idea and one I may adopt. Nor is it any secret that of us all, Kobrin has the greatest experience of war, and indeed, of leadership. Listen to him, as I have in the months just past, and learn from him, for he has much to teach us.'

'Have I?' growled Kobrin.

'You have,' said Klimt. 'Now, about those pairs . . . Morten, I wish you to work with Lounel . . . I know, I know . . . your preference is to be with your brother, Stry.'

The two brothers nodded ruefully.

'Well, Lounel's no fool, though he sometimes chooses to look like one . . . and we must strive to get to know each other better. Habits of companionship form divisions, and divisions weaken a pack. Therefore, Morten and Lounel will be together for a time . . .'

They nodded and moved nearer to each other.

'You, Stry, will be with . . .' he continued to give orders, putting them together in a way that meant wolf mixed with wolf, and the areas adjacent to the denning ground beyond what they had already investigated could be methodically reconnoitred.

Klimt left Kobrin and Tervicz until the last, and called them over to him privily.

'For you I have a special task, and one that will not be easy. But understand this from the first: your lives are more important than the task itself, so take no risks, or not any that do not give you a more than even chance of clear escape. Kobrin, you know of this already but Tervicz, you do not, so listen, and listen well . . .'

What their task was Klimt did not make generally known, and none of the others had a chance to ask the two wolves, even had they been willing to talk. For no sooner were they briefed by Klimt than he instructed them to rest, and sometime before nightfall they had set off back down scarp and slope, to where the gullies led back down towards the Southern Fell.

'How long will they be?' asked Aragon, whose partner in reconnaissance was Klimt himself.

'Days, even weeks,' said Klimt, noncommittally. 'Now . . .' and their time of working to get to know the Scarpfeld before hard winter set in began.

Perhaps there was a part of this wiser and more realistic Klimt that still hoped that Elhana and Jicin could come to an understanding, a way of living together, which would not involve violent confrontation, and inevitable humiliation for one or other of them. Had Jicin not spent time with Klimt after his departure from the pack, and were their relationship not so obviously affectionate and deep – and had not Elhana been the ledrene she was – it might have been possible. But that was not the case.

The days grew colder, shorter and less pleasant as December advanced, and both the female wolves grew restive in the way females do as January approaches and their need to mate begins. It is in the coldest weather that they go on heat and then neither rhyme nor reason is their friend. Increasingly Elhana resented Jicin, and increasingly Jicin saw that if she did not fight for what she wanted, then it might never be hers.

'All I want,' she was inclined to tell herself, for she confided in no other, 'is what I had before with Klimt, which hurt no wolf, which was good and true for each of us, which could surely be again . . .'

But times had changed, and Klimt was a free wolf no more, but emblem, symbol, figurehead of the pack, all in one. It greatly saddened him that he could no longer simply be himself.

So Jicin must fight in the hope that she might win, not wanting what that fight would force on her if she did, which was to be ledrene. Whereas Elhana, her hope of love with Klimt all gone, sought to be what she knew she could be well – ledrene of the pack of packs. So, wanting different things, they had to fight, and one must win and one must lose, and the world and wolfkind be a little worse off than it might have been.

The end of December came with days of wrangling between the two, and the males keeping clear, seeing what was coming though not quite certain when.

'Jicin doesn't stand a chance,' observed Morten, 'but I suppose she's got to go through with it; yet I'm not so sure . . . Jicin's younger and a different wolf than when she first came among us. Who would have thought she would change so much, or grow so strong? A wolf like that goes on growing within herself. She would make a good ledrene if only she began to think that way.'

'Hmmm,' muttered Stry, gnawing ruminatively at a bone whose meat was long gone. 'At least if they have a go at each other it'll clear the air. A pack's no place to be when leadership is in dispute.'

'Ledreneship,' said Morten. 'Isn't that the word? Lounel? You're the intelligent one.'

'Leadership,' said Lounel, 'is neuter and it will do.'

'What do you think about it all?'

'I think that afterwards, when it is decided, Klimt will

have a difficult decision about Jicin to make. I also think that he will make it, and make it well. We have a wise wolf as leader of the pack, and perhaps a great one.'

'He's a strong one, that's for sure,' said Morten with respect. 'He's dependable as well!'

'I wish he laughed a shade more often than he does,' said Stry with a grin, 'but I'll give him this: he's been trying to do more of it of late.'

'That's Jicin's doing,' said Morten.

'And that's the tragedy,' said Lounel. 'But then . . .' He paused and then said no more.

'But then . . . But *then*, Lounel?' said Morten, whose understanding and affection for Lounel had grown in the weeks of working together, just as Klimt had hoped. 'You can't keep muttering out your thoughts and then not share them with us.'

'But then,' said Lounel, acidly, 'a wolf should not think in the short term, especially in *this* pack.'

'A wolf's only got one lifetime, chum,' said Stry.

'That's quite enough,' said Lounel, 'and their love may have need of all of it . . .'

The fight between Elhana and Jicin began quite suddenly one morning, though Wulf knows there was trouble in the air. The air was heavy with it, pulled down by it, so that the assembled pack – and naturally Elhana made sure they were all there to see her exercise in wrath and retribution – were low and huddled, lacking energy, awaiting new orders and impetus from Klimt.

Jicin was eating to one side, Elhana brooding to another, and Klimt watching the lurid sky and wondering if the first heavy snow was due, to mark the start of real winter.

Elhana picked herself up, turned, and charged, as brutally and purposefully as she knew how. She had not survived as ledrene of the Benevento pack so long and so successfully for nothing, nor had she forgotten how her daughter had wrested the right to be ledrene from her. So in she went, and had Jicin by the throat before she had time to let go what she was eating.

But then, nor had Jicin survived her mother Dendrine's attentions, and those of her brothers, for nothing. She knew how to twist and turn, she knew how to run and counter-charge, she knew how to put up a good defence. Defeat might be her lot that day, but she knew how to accept it honourably. Indeed, the longer she fought and the more effective her defence, the less potent Elhana's victory.

The males retreated, some watching with open interest, others affecting no interest at all, their seeming calmness making all the more dramatic and horrible, the bloody, bitter struggle that had broken out.

It was obvious, as Jicin began to weaken, and as Elhana's assault on her grew more brutal, that one was going to win well, and the other lose cruelly.

Unwilling to witness so horrible a spectacle, Klimt walked away. Lounel dropped his gaze. Morten and Stry, who had seen worse, watched and waited: such matters sometimes got out of hand and victorious ledrenes had been known to go too far and kill their rivals. Bloodlust is a terrible thing, and Morten would not allow it to take over. If that began he would invoke lore greater than that which says that females must be left to sort their own kind out, which is the rule that life should be preserved if possible. So he and his brother watched on, prepared to step in.

Aragon, too, was ready to intervene, though his feelings were mixed and troublesome: he liked to see the wolf he loved triumph, it stirred him, he liked it much. He was aroused by what he saw. But he was also uncomfortable. He did not move, nor drop his gaze from the sweating, bleeding, bloodied, struggling and snarling female forms. He wanted Elhana to himself. He watched . . .

While Stry saw only Jicin's tragedy, and felt for her, and for Klimt too. He watched the death of Jicin's hope, he watched her weakening struggling to keep a hold on a love that gave so much and hurt so few; he watched a good wolf drowning in a sea of destiny too rough and wild for her. His eyes filled with tears as he watched.

Then, as suddenly as it began, it was over, and not a word spoken, just a struggle, long and terrible, and Elhana left standing, breathing heavily in and out, her body bloodied as much by Jicin's wounds as her own; and Jicin, crawling away now, hurt too much to go with pride, yet her spirit still unbowed, her courage never questioned. Struggling to her feet, turning to look at where the pack watched, gone off among the rocks to shiver and recover, and to contemplate the final humiliation which was yet to come: returning to the circle of the pack for Elhana to gloat.

No sooner had Jicin retreated than Klimt, who must have been near enough to hear what had finally happened, joined the pack once more.

'Leave us!' he said firmly, commanding all the others to go but Elhana.

She stood there, tired but triumphant, yet not quite exultant. She had fairly done what a ledrene must, and she was sorry for what it must mean to him, but lore is lore, packs are packs, and she had done no more than she should.

'Elhana,' he began, 'you are my ledrene now, indisputably so, and I am your leader. Last time it was thus we did ill by the pack. Now we must do well, and more than well.'

She nodded her agreement sombrely.

'A leader and ledrene do not have to share love for one another,' he continued, his voice quieter now and more resigned, 'but they can strive to like each other, they can show respect, and they can always honour one another . . .'

'Yes,' she said, as quietly as himself, as miserably too, perhaps.

'Well, then, wolf,' he said more affectionately, going near to her yet unable to bring himself to quite touch her. 'We must learn to live together as a leader and ledrene should, and we must ask Wulf and Wulfin's help that we do it well.'

'Jicin . . .' she began.

'You take precedence over Jicin now, now and always, so long as you are ledrene,' he said. She saw that he meant it, and she knew it too: Klimt was Klimt, and she never knew a wolf whose words were as true as his. But it gave her no pleasure.

'But you love her, Klimt, you love her as *I* would have wanted to be loved.'

She sat down now, tired from the fight, her bruises beginning to hurt, and her cuts beginning to smart.

'You are my ledrene,' said Klimt carefully.

'Oh, but my dear, you love her and always will, and to see her will be painful.'

'And Aragon?'

She smiled the weary, affectionate smile more of a mother for an adult son than for a lover. Almost . . .

'I loved him and he me, but . . . things have changed. He is young. You said you were to exile him when spring came, and when you do, and he has travelled far, he will meet another wolf to love. He was not ready to be leader of the pack. Of another perhaps, but not this one. Yet he is a good wolf, Klimt, perhaps a great one . . .'

'I know it,' said Klimt, 'I know it well. He is of the fraternity of the Wolves of Time.'

'Fraternity? Not sisterhood!'

'Sorority,' he said, correctly.

They shared a smile, their first for a very long time.

'With Jicin here it will be hard – hard for all of us,' he conceded. 'But it is not right that she leaves the pack, not now at any rate. Injured as she must be, robbed of the love we share, with Magyars ready to kill her, she would not live long. Therefore Elhana, ledrene, now you have asserted your dominance I ask you to be generous and great-hearted. Let her stay here in peace, let she and I talk as we did before I returned to the pack. Let us be friends without pressure or interference from you until the spring. Then we shall talk again. Much may have changed . . . and all of us may see things a little differently.'

He meant, of course, that Elhana might have cubs, and that if she did, the pack's whole perspective would change and the matter of Jicin be less important.

'And in return?' she said coolly. She, who had been ledrene before, knew that there is a time to make a stand, to gain the most, and this was it. What they agreed now would be honoured, *must* be honoured, for in that honouring was the kernel of the pack's worth.

'In return,' said Klimt, 'I shall not stand in the way of your companionship with Aragon, whatever its nature might be. I ask for discretion but . . . well, I understand the hurts of love, and its demands . . .'

'Let it be so, Klimt,' she said quickly, before he changed his mind. It was more than she or Aragon could have hoped. 'And Klimt . . . ?'

'Wolf?'

'I shall need two or three days to recover my well-being, but then January will be on us and the winter setting in. A time of darkness and of secrets, a time to brood, a time for a leader and his ledrene to . . . to do their duty by the pack, however hard it may sometimes seem. You understand that I desire mating, and cubs? With you if Wulfin wills it.'

'Yes,' said Klimt, reluctantly. 'Let it be so. I shall come to you.'

He left her then, and he left a sad wolf. He had given

her latitude with Aragon, saying that he understood love. Well so he might, and she envied him that he had found love. But love is one thing, lust another, and nothing wrong with either. She might no longer call her feelings for Aragon love but . . . whatever their name she felt them still, and she yearned for him – the more for having talked to Klimt and seen the depth of his feeling for Jicin, and how he had put duty before love.

'Oh . . .' she sighed, and turning, she saw Klimt pace away, while off to one side was Aragon watching her, with a look that told as much of one thing as Klimt's wise words and action told of many.

'Oh,' she sighed again, and settled down to rest as the pack drifted back about her.

Oh . . .

Each was as good as their word in the weeks that followed, which were weeks of harsh weather, when the snowy sky descended, and blizzards came, and the wolves moved their denning ground to a lower site on the south-west lee of the Scarpfeld, which gave them access to a wide-spread of forested land, and the prey that sheltered there.

Klimt met alone with Jicin in those dark weeks, without hindrance from Elhana, though the two said little, for they had memories of a summer of liberty and friendship, and hopes, unspoken, that one distant day, if they were blessed, they might know another summer of liberty, and one in which the friendship might by then openly be called love.

'I'll be old by then,' Jicin whispered, the wind icy beyond the shelter they took and fluting the ice that had formed, 'and so shall you, my dear.'

'Old, my best days done,' he said softly, always so light when he was with her, always so free to be himself.

Stry, who had taken to watching over Klimt's needs in

the absence of Tervicz, was not far off, far enough to be discreet, near enough to be the one to bring him news of danger or opportunity. But that first winter in their territory the dangers were few, the opportunities were many, though the greatest, which was fulfilled love, had been stolen from them.

'Klimt?'

'Mmm?'

'It is nothing.'

'*It has been everything*,' he said with feeling.

'Yes, my dear, it has.'

Meanwhile, with his ledrene, in their interludes, there was a new affection and more enjoyment of the mating that they did. She was, it must be said, beautiful; and he, she felt, was more masterful than before, and yet more caring. So . . . so they made love, by rock and by wind-bent forest tree; by iced-over pool, and underneath the stars.

'It is enough,' she would sigh, and she felt his tenderness sometimes, which she felt to be stolen from another. She felt his sadness.

'I am your ledrene,' she would sometimes cry, for ecstasy was theirs occasionally, brief moments of forgetting . . .

'And I your leader . . . !' he would sigh, wishing for something he could no longer have.

So, slowly, they found an understanding, and respect, and enough of it at least to become the seeds of affection.

He, too, was as good as his word, and let her be with Aragon in those strange, half-sleeping weeks. Where they went, or what they did, he did not care. The times were not often, nor for long, less indeed than his times with Jicin. They were, as all the pack knew, mating times, but the pack understood.

The pack did not suffer by these discretions: the pack

found health in compromise. And if just once, Elhana let Aragon's passion carry her with it too, towards that place where she had once started for with him but had not quite reached . . . if on a night at the beginning of February they dared try that journey once again and found that the gods were with them, guiding them to a time of utter forgetting, guiding them beyond the night and on into a day that was not yet come, the pack could pretend it did not hear her howls of ecstasy. But they knew, and the gods knew, it was just that once the moment of goodbye in which all they had been trying to say with lust was finally said.

'Aragon,' she sighed afterwards.

'Elhana?'

But though she knew what that act that night meant, she did not say; there was no need for him, or Klimt, to know that that day with Klimt or that night with Aragon, the gods were with them all. She felt she knew what was made that night, though who the father was she could not tell.

'I am with cub, Klimt.'

Their eyes met and she saw that in his gaze there was no query nor even interest in whose cubs they might be. It was not that he did not care, but rather that he cared more that she was with cub, than whose they might be. Duty. Love. Leader. Ledrene . . .

He smiled and said, 'It is well, it is well, and this time, Elhana, your leader will protect your cubs as a true leader should.'

'It is well,' she mimicked, and they laughed naturally and with pleasure, for affection was growing between them, and they were surviving their dark winter.

'When, my dear?' he said, and he had come close, and touched her quite naturally for a moment in a way he never had before, and she touched him.

'April, May perhaps. The snows will be melting and I shall prefer to bear them up in the centre of the Scarpfeld, in our home denning ground. They shall be the cubs of the pack, and the pack shall guard them.'

'Let us hope the weather is mild enough for you to have them up in the centre of the Scarpfeld,' he said. 'They shall be the cubs of the Wolves of Time, and as the gods made them, they shall lead us to the gods.'

'Come, my dear,' and they summoned the pack and told them what was to be, and even Aragon, Elhana's lover, even Jicin, love of Klimt's life, were both glad. The gods had given the pack a second chance, and destiny was rolling in the stars, whispering in the wind, and it was theirs now, if they had the courage and the faith to make their sacrifices and the patience to be wise.

CHAPTER THIRTY-SEVEN

*The gods send a wolf to join the pack
and take another on a wolfway to the stars*

YET, THOUGH JICIN WAS truly glad for the pack
that cubs were on the way, she felt a deepening
sadness too. Klimt was hers no more, nor could ever
be, and as time passed by, and the cubs that Elhana carried
began to show, she knew that the pack's interest and loyalty
would centre upon them, and must. Despite herself, she
felt a return of loss and grief for her own lost cubs, and it
seemed that none could allay her suffering, even Klimt
himself. Time, perhaps, was the only healer left to her.

Or was it? For sad though she was there was strange
comfort in Klimt's silent confidence, even his good humour,
as if he knew something she did not, a secret that would
give her pleasure; a coming circumstance that might give
her relief from the old sadness she felt.

'You've got to try to remember that this grim winter will
one day be over,' he would say. 'Then maybe there'll be a
task for you that will give you other things to think
about . . .'

'What task?'

'Some task . . .' he would say evasively, and she could
only smile despite herself, for if ever there was a wolf who
was bad at being evasive it was Klimt of Tornesdal. Evas-
iveness, deceit, lies . . . these were not in his nature, and
barely within his understanding.

586

'You're not telling the truth,' she would say.

'Well . . . I am not exactly telling a lie either . . . I mean
. . . I . . .'

No, Klimt was not much good at evasion, and so she
found comfort in the fact that for her, at least, he was trying.

But as January advanced, other more serious concerns
beset them. Lounel was ill for a time, all aching and shivering, and muttering about the past and present, confusing
the Auvergne with Aragon, warning of a future none could
know . . .

Days later Stry suffered the same illness, though less
severely, and the leg he had injured in August began aching
again, particularly on damp or freezing days. From that
time on it never quite stopped aching; an injury to remind
him if he ever reached old age, of the trials and tribulations
that came with reaching for the stars.

'Age,' he grumbled to Morten. 'I'm growing old. What
have *I* ever done?'

'Old be buggered,' said Morten, irritably.

Then too, prey got more scarce and there were days when
they went hungry. But these never lasted long, for their
territory was well-based, and the more they explored the
lower ground which formed its periphery, the easier it
became to know where and when to hunt. Not that Elhana
was ever allowed to go long without food, even on scarce
days, and though Klimt always took precedence, he made
sure there was food enough for her, and for the ill ones
too, if they had need.

But by the end of January what concerned the pack most
of all was the continuing absence of Kobrin and Tervicz.
All Klimt had ever said about it was that he had thought
they would be gone 'a few more days'. But days had
stretched to weeks, and the weather was steadily worsen-

ing, so that if they had gone far it was growing less and less likely that they would get back safely, or before winter was done. As for what task they had set off to perform, Klimt never said, though when he was asked about it, he was ready to smile a little at his own reluctance to talk.

'Forgive me, but it is a mission that should not be too dangerous unless they are unlucky. But I concede it seems to be taking rather longer than I would have wished.'

It was a few days after this, at the beginning of February, that Lounel grew restive in the way he often did before he gained some insight, or premonition of change, or need.

'Well, wolf, what is it?' demanded Klimt, used to him by now.

'Hmmph!' said Lounel grumpily. 'If I knew I'd say. Since I don't, I wish the pack would give me space to think . . . Klimt?'

'Lounel?'

'When did you last go up to our old denning ground?'

'Me? Some days since, a week or more. But Morten was there the day before yesterday . . .'

'You should go there again.'

Klimt looked at Lounel and knew him to be serious. He knew as well that at moments like this Lounel had no idea what impelled him to say such things. It was just something he knew.

'I shall go with . . .'

'Go alone, I think,' said Lounel. 'You are leader after all.'

'Alone,' said Klimt with resignation. 'Lounel, do you know what a Ratgeber is?'

'I do not.'

'Then ask Jicin to tell you. I think perhaps that that will be your role in this pack.'

'Aah!' said Lounel, dubiously. 'But . . .'

He was frowning again, thinking. His head half-cocked towards the wind whose voice he normally understood so well, though this time its whispers were not quite clear enough, not to him at least.

'But what?' demanded Klimt.

'I . . . I'm not sure . . . I . . .'

'But I am!' said Klimt, suddenly very sure indeed. 'There's worse weather by far on the way now. Just smell the air, Lounel. You don't need second sight for that! It's a day away, two days at most and then . . . then access to the centre of the Scarpfeld will grow more difficult. Therefore, I shall not go alone.'

'Ah!' said Lounel, light dawning, though more slowly than it seemed to have done with Klimt.

'Yes, yes, wolf,' went on Klimt. 'I see what we shall do. The whole pack shall come with me.'

'The whole pack,' repeated Lounel.

'Your idea wolf, you mentioned it.'

'I mentioned the Scarpfeld,' said Lounel stiffly.

'Quite. So . . . let us be assembled, and let's go.'

'What *for?*' asked Lounel, much exasperated. He sometimes thought that few wolves had such capacity to surprise him as Klimt.

'I don't know, but I'm sure we'll find out soon enough.'

They could all sense the worsening of the weather. The wind was fretful and impatient, as if it wanted to get them up to the Scarpfeld and back down again as quickly as it could. The temperature of the air went up sharply for a short time and then dropped back quite suddenly as they neared their destination, and the sky began to turn to that lurid, shiny greyness that presages snow. Like a weight that was upon them all, but one they could not release.

'Not much change up here but for a little more ice and snow!' muttered Stry. 'What's he brought us up for?'

Morten shrugged and looked over towards Elhana.

'Our beloved ledrene is not well-pleased to be dragged up here. She has not felt well these days past.'

Lounel broke a long silence and said, 'It's going to snow,' and did not understand why they all laughed.

The pack grew easier with itself, glad to be back to where they all felt they belonged, grateful to Klimt for thinking what none of them had – that a final time together up here would be a memory to hold on to until they all returned for good in spring.

'With cubs, perhaps,' suggested Jicin quietly.

'Oh before then, wolf,' said Lounel. 'I think you'll find Elhana bears her cubs up there within range of the boulder. But look, here . . .'

The first snowflakes of the new fall came, dancing on the light wind, small at first and then thickening and growing heavier and driving up the gullies from off the plateau.

The pack was skittish and content, safe where they were for now, happy to know they had a safe and sheltered denning ground lower down. Only Klimt was uneasy and restless, pacing about, glancing here and there. Did he sense danger?

'No, no, not danger no . . . something, I am not sure . . . ask Lounel.'

'What, because he foresaw the coming of the snow?' laughed Morten.

'No, because . . . because . . .'

Out of the driving snow they came, just as it began to settle on the ground. Up from the gullies loomed one wolf first, dark and massive. Turning back, calling down behind him, encouraging . . .

'Look!'

'Kobrin . . .' whispered Klimt, relieved at last, his restlessness all gone.

Then another caught him up and two loomed there.

'It's Tervicz with him, Wulf be praised! They are home at last.'

But as the two came nearer they saw there was a third as well, a stranger.

Out of the drifting snow she came now, a lame wolf, very old, and they saw that she was guided at either flank by Kobrin and Tervicz. They led her as if she was the most precious thing that had ever been cared for.

Old and grey, her head bowed down until, sensing perhaps that there were wolves ahead, she turned a little to Tervicz, and spoke to him, as if to ask if they had finally reached their destination . . .

'Yes,' said Tervicz gently, 'we are here and the pack awaits us.'

It was then that she raised her head, and they saw through the driving, drifting, shifting flakes of snow, white snow, that each flake was as white as her blind eyes.

'It is Raute,' whispered Jicin, her voice breaking with emotion, not quite believing what she saw.

Then she understood what it was that Klimt had asked Kobrin and Tervicz to do: to find a wolf she loved, a wolf who needed her, a wolf who might yet have so much to give. Then Klimt nodded to her to go forward and welcome the old wolf, to the Scarpfeld, to the pack, to a final task perhaps, on behalf of them all . . .

As Jicin went forward and embraced Raute, she understood the depth of Klimt's love for her. What he could not himself now so easily give, another might herself bring, which was comfort and companionship, need and care; and more than that, a wolf who having turned from the Magyars after so many years of loyalty to them, had survived long enough to join the Wolves of Time. Klimt was wiser than she knew. With Raute's coming came a seed of peace.

591

The three travellers came forward, weary now that their long trial was complete. Whatever troubles they had faced, whatever depth of courage and tenacity they had shown, would be a story told to the pack before too long, to become part of its own history and lore: how two of its members set off into Magyar territory and bravely brought out from a living death an old, wise wolf who yet had much to give to life. How a pack that had only a present to create, and a future to look forward to, was shown by its leader that it must not forget the past.

'There, Klimt, master, our pack is now complete,' said Tervicz, a smile on his tired face.

'Nearly complete, wolf, nearly so,' said Klimt, welcoming Kobrin too. 'There are some young wolves shall join us in the spring . . .'

He nodded towards Elhana and they understood what had happened in their absence.

'Now,' said Klimt, and he raised his head to begin the pack's first howl into the Scarpfeld, to welcome an old wolf, and to wish a safe journey to the new ones who were already on their way. A howl to tell of journeys completed, and journeys still to come. A howl to welcome winter, and look forward to the spring.

'Welcome, Raute, friend of Jicin, I know much about you . . .' said Klimt later.

She reached out a faltering paw to him, touched his flank and then his face.

'You are the Führer of the Wolves of Time,' she said, her voice gentle.

'Leader, not Führer,' responded Klimt with great respect. 'We say *leader* here. The days of your Führer are over.'

'I had heard,' she replied. 'Hassler is dead but his last

son has come. You know that, don't you, and what it may mean?'

Here shadows seemed to cross her white eyes, night owls across still lakes.

'Yes,' said Klimt. 'I know, I saw him.'

'He is evil,' she whispered.

'A threat to Wulf himself.'

'And Wulfin too. Believe me, wolf, Dendrine's last-born by Hassler is a threat to all of us.'

'It is partly for that I asked that you come here. We shall need your help. Did Tervicz tell you that?'

'Oh yes he did, and yet he had no need. For you, and your pack, I have been waiting all my life. I know that now that I am here.'

'Will you help us?'

'*We* shall help us.'

'Will you join us?'

She laughed a frail cracked laugh and her face wrinkled into merriment. She reached out a paw to him again.

'I am old to be asked to join a pack.'

'But I ask it,' said Klimt, formal, formidable, even to her. 'We have need of a wolf to give advice . . .'

'You want me as Ratgeber?' she whispered, astonished.

He shook his head. 'No, though there is a wolf here you can help towards such a role among us. His name is Lounel. Join us to be the wolf you are . . .'

'Old and in need of care?'

'Old and wise and in need of care,' said Klimt softly.

She reached to him again and touched his face, as if to feel the nature of his heart.

'You are a strange wolf, Klimt, but a leader born. And you are something else as well.'

'What's that?' wondered Klimt.

'Jicin's friend,' said Raute softly, and gentle tears came to her white eyes.

'Yes,' said Klimt, with love.

'Well then, if only for that, I shall join your pack, my dear, and do so gladly. Certainly I am old and in need of care; as for wisdom, well, you shall be the judge of that.'

He turned then to address them all, the snow thickening on the ground about them and settling on their coats. Darkness began to close in.

He looked at each one in turn.

At Tervicz, for loyalty.

At Morten, for strength.

At Stry, for fraternity.

At Jicin, for friendship.

At Kobrin, for war.

At Raute, for care.

At Elhana, for life.

And at Lounel, for an understanding of the stars.

Finally his gaze returned to Tervicz. The first to join him . . . and one distant day, he would be the last to leave, for he was the Bukov wolf and he would live until a wolf came whom he would lead back to the WulfRock, and the wolf-way to the stars.

The pack stood watching and waiting on Klimt's words. They saw a great wolf and on his face, noble and forbidding, and in his bleak eyes especially, they saw a swirling drift of life's challenges accepted, like the myriad flakes of snow that fell among them. They saw in him loyalty and strength; fraternity and friendship; war and care. And sometimes weaknesses.

Klimt was life itself to them.

Finally he spoke: 'Wulf willing, when we return here in spring it shall be to see the birth of the pack's young. Meanwhile, with Raute's coming, our pack is complete and winter setting in. Follow me now, for our task together has begun.'

Then one by one they followed him, as he led them

south-east down to safer ground, and behind them the driving snow filled in their tracks, and the night-time of winter came.

But before the pack could begin to enjoy the hope of spring, and new birth, they had to suffer bitter weather, and the reality of something worse.

It was Klimt's instruction that once every few days two of the wolves should ascend the snow and ice back to the centre of the Scarpfeld to see whether Magyar or even the Mennen had ventured there, and if in any way they posed a threat. At first these ventures had been easy enough, taking no more than a few hours of daylight, which was enough for a pair of wolves to reach the centre and quarter the ground to east and west, and south to the gully that led down towards the plateau and fells, then back to join the pack.

North of the centre rose the steepest and most fractured of the scarps, and many of the wolves always felt that their duty was only complete when they had ascended to just below the boulder which marked the entrance to that divide wherein none of them were allowed to venture. At the boulder they could turn and settle down for a time if the weather was clear, and survey all the central Scarpfeld, and gain a prospect of part of the Southern Fell.

As the first snows came, this view became magnificent, especially towards the end of the day, when the sun set in the west and its glancing rays brought out the lines of snowy scarp after scarp, and gullies, and fallen boulders, and the flat grassland areas, now all pure white, except for where the holes of rabbit warrens showed. A prospect made all the more awesome by the rumbles and trickles of shifting snow and rock in the heights above or, sometimes, in a lesser way, among the small cliffs below.

All of this was set off by mauve shadows which lengthened and darkened even as a wolf watched, to warn him that the time was coming to return to the pack, and lower, safer ground.

But as the winter deepened and February brought blizzards and deep drifts of snow, whose surfaces shone when they froze, and gave no purchase to a wolf's paw, visiting the central Scarpfeld became more onerous. Though any of the wolves would have agreed to go, Klimt now gave the duty only to the stronger members of the pack, which were Morten and Stry, Aragon and himself. These four were therefore the only ones who saw how with the coming of the snows, and the shifting falls of rocks and ice, the highest part of the Scarpfeld changed its character. It was awesome now, all the more so on a dark and swirling day of mist and snow, when rocks loomed out of the freezing murk like cliffs, and the ground could open up beneath a wolf's feet without warning, to bring him teetering over a void he had not realized was there.

So dangerous did the ground become that Klimt forbade any wolf to venture off the main way up into the Scarpfeld, and in some conditions, especially in the dark days at the end of February and the beginning of March, the journey was not made at all.

Yet, by then, there was much else to occupy the wolves. The cubs Elhana was carrying were now beginning to show, and with each day that passed a new ease and comfort settled upon her, and the pack's occasional troubles and strifes eased as well. It was too early yet for her to make preparations for the den, and anyway, she had long since declared that if the conditions permitted it by late April, when the cubs were due, she would return to their original denning ground and make a place there to have them. It would be fitting that their cubs were born as near to the centre of the Scarpfeld as possible.

In mid-March the last of the true blizzards blew, and within days the first hints of the coming of spring began to show. The days now were growing perceptibly brighter, and the skies, when they were clear, were more blue. The snow on the south-facing slopes and in the more sunny and sheltered nooks, grew wet, and soft, and dripped by day and froze by night. While here and there, drawn out by the coming new-found brightness were the first trembling flowers of spring: snowdrops, and in one lone place near the wolves' denning ground, a solitary blue crocus reached up towards the skies.

A few days into April it was the turn of Morten and Stry to make the journey up into the Scarpfeld, a task they accepted with pleasure, for the day was bright and all over the forest and the lower slopes beneath the scree-line which they traversed there was the rilling of running streamlets underfoot. The thaw had not yet fully begun, but it was on the way, and in a few more days at most snow-water would be streaming off the mountain sides, and the snow in the Scarpfeld would begin to disappear.

They climbed higher into cooler temperatures, the snow still hard and firm where there was shade and they dallied on the way, marvelling at the sun and shadows that travelled over the scarps and vales.

'It won't be long now before Elhana will be wanting to come up here. She grows heavier by the day!'

They laughed as brother bounded after brother, up the slopes, over slushy snow, slipping on the hard-frozen drifts, tussling and rolling, just as when they were young.

'Come on, Morten!' called Stry, for Morten was always a little slower than him, and more puffed.

'Dammit, wolf, you go too fast!'

'Dammit, wolf, you go too slow,' mocked Stry and bounded on.

The sudden crack and rumble of falling ice and rock

above them stopped them both, and brought them hurrying together. The sliding, dangerous sound ceased as suddenly as it began.

'We'll stay low and go carefully,' said Morten soberly. 'Spring always brings such falls and landslides in its wake. Stay low and on the flat . . .'

They hurried on to the centre of the Scarpfeld and found it filled with sun, and the tinkling sound of running water. They carefully explored the routes in and out of it and saw no sign of alien life.

'There is nothing untoward at all,' said Stry.

'Nothing,' said Morten, his eyes cautious upon the distant, steeper scarps that hung above them to the north, their cliffs black and shiny with the thaw, the snowdrifts in their fissures speckled black and grey with fallen rock and dust.

'We have seen enough, let's head back,' he said.

Their route took them upslope to the area of their summer denning ground near where, if the thaw continued as it was, Elhana might choose to have her young.

'It's a grand place to raise cubs,' said Stry. 'Better than the place we had.'

'Yes . . .' said Morten, remembering their grim past. Wulf had done well by them, very well.

'Come on!' said Stry, running ahead, and then, as he always did, he turned to run on upslope to sit for a few moments beneath the boulder, and survey their territory.

Morten laughed and watched his brother run rapidly up ahead of him over the slushy snow, between the rocks, and then on to the steep, ice-covered scree and up.

'Stry . . .' he began doubtfully, and then, 'Stry!'

'Come on!' cried Stry. The sounds of his own running and the mountain breeze was too loud for him to hear the warning in Morten's cries.

'All right then . . .' muttered Morten and followed his brother.

The slope was steep, the going slippery, but the boulder loomed above them, summoning them on.

'Come on, old wolf!' called Stry again, turning to stop and stare down at where Morten struggled up after him.

Morten stopped to gain his breath and stared up towards Stry, both laughing, the sun on each of them.

Then a shake and a rumble and whatever Morten saw beyond Stry it took the smile from his eyes. He began running up towards Stry shouting, 'Make for the boulder's lee, Stry! Run, wolf, run for your life!'

Stry turned, saw the smoking landslide beginning up above, and began to run, each upward step seeming to take a lifetime, each upward movement taking him closer to the roar and the rage of ice and rock tumbling, tearing down towards them.

'Run, and may Wulf be with us!' cried Morten behind, his voice faint against the mounting noise.

Stry's heart and lungs were bursting as he threw himself into the shelter of the boulder, and the first great mass of the landslide swept by with gathering speed on either flank. He immediately turned to guide Morten up to him, but overhead, with a roar like a river in spate, the sky was blotted out with the rush of rock and ice that had mounted the boulder and ridden over it.

Darkness was there, confusion, and a last brief glimpse of Morten reaching up to Stry and safety, before he was overwhelmed and pulled down, rolled over and under the landslide that rushed by. The roaring was the roar of death. Then silence, a silence as massive as the slide that had overtaken them, but for the dying echo of the roar, and far above where Stry now lay, the last patter and scatter of rock on rock up on the scarp where the landslide had begun.

'Morten!' he cried, running out among the rocks and ice that now lay jumbled where Morten had been.

Morten . . .

But wherever he was, he was no more, and muttering and moaning his lost brother's name, Stry clambered here and there across the fallen rocks, frantic at first, then aimless, and finally still with shock and grief, disconsolate.

It was his later, single dreadful howl of loss that first alerted the others and some of them came running up from the lower ground, up and up to find him standing there, staring at where he felt Morten to be buried, which was beneath rocks bigger than wolves, immovable, and ice as grey as a dead wolf's eyes.

'Morten . . .' he whispered when they took him away for his own protection, for the rocks still rumbled and shifted and held no life that lived.

But 'Morten' he would whisper in the days of spring that followed, when he came and searched the area of landslip for a brother he would never see alive again.

And 'Morten' when, tiring, hopeless, helpless, he would slump finally into the lee of the boulder, and look down upon the place where he last saw his brother alive.

While of them all, only Jicin could comfort him, though not with words, just with her presence. She too had once lost those she loved, and she had journeyed into a heartland of sorrow where Stry now wept alone. So she stayed near him, settled by him, and if he talked she responded, and if he was silent, she was still.

'Morten . . .' he would whisper, and he did not mind if it was Jicin who saw his tears.

CHAPTER THIRTY-EIGHT

*The pack discovers its great task
and says farewell to those who will be the first
to wander the wolfways in its name*

APRIL ADVANCED, and a few days before its end
Elhana grew restless, and asked that they take her
back to the centre of the Scarpfeld.

They led her there, and watched over her as she turned
one way and another, climbing the moist snow-free slopes,
seeking out a place to bear her young.

By a rock she made a birthing den, where rabbits in time
gone by, and then something larger for a time, many years
before, had taken residence. Empty now, ready to be occupied once more, needing only a small change here and some
burrowing there, and the nesting material she brought in
by herself, and the place was made ready for new life again.

The pack was restless too, watching, checking, protecting, while Klimt travelled more widely, sometimes with
Kobrin, at other times with Tervicz, planning a future for
them all.

Then when he returned, he would ask, 'Has she started?'

A shaking of heads.

'Have they come?'

Not yet, Klimt, not yet . . .

'Not yet?' he would ask again, and again.

Not quite yet.

They came, finally, at the start of May, by dawn and by

morning, all five of them. A male, three females and then a final male. A quintet of cubs to give the pack purpose.

Days of quiet watching would follow, for until they were weaned all would be quiet. And then . . . all would be busy.

The pack hunted and waited. The pack slept and waited. The pack watched and waited, each to nurture, each to protect, all to help raise what Elhana had borne.

'Can we see?'

A shake of heads.

'Can we watch?'

Not yet, wolf, be patient . . .

Finally Klimt was allowed to see them and declared himself pleased.

Raute next, and she was allowed to touch them.

Jicin was kept at a distance.

Tervicz caught a glimpse – just a soft paw, a brief show of a snout, wide blue eyes.

'You're to come back here, my love . . .'

'No, no . . .' and the pack heard Elhana's laughter, and her tired voice, as the cubs grew in the darkness of her den, fed and slept and grew, and she knew motherhood once more.

They heard the cubs' mewings and their first bleats. They heard Elhana's voice more and more as the cubs gained confidence and she sought to control them. Finally they saw her tired and haggard form when she came out from feeding them, leaving them for a time while she breathed the Scarpfeld air, stared at the fresh day, and saw that all was well and safe.

The first time they came out was at midday, peering and shoving one over another, ears pricked and eyes as wide as skies. Then they went back down again.

The second was a morning, and they ventured further from the den, and onto the green and growing grass, and over to a rock. Then they tumbled and played a little before Elhana called them back, allowing them to scrabble and pull at old Raute's flanks before she shooed them down once more.

Two or three days later, after a day of contemplation and private talk with Raute and Lounel, and then a long talk with Aragon, Klimt summoned the pack together.

'Well then, our cubs are growing and there are plenty of us to look after them. Too many perhaps . . . But you know already that Aragon is leaving us. It is better that he does so for a time, better for us all.'

They nodded and Aragon as well. A pack cannot be divided, and their leader and his ledrene needed time now, time without the interference of matters that might not serve the pack's need. Time to bond alone with their cubs.

'I have decided,' continued Klimt, 'that Aragon should not go alone, and also that he should not go without a purpose. For those of us who stay behind there is the task, the great task, of raising these new cubs we have. We shall protect them and nurture them, and we shall teach them.

'But the pack has another need which is to go out into the world and wander the wolfways once again. To see and feel a way forward for wolfkind. I have said that the Mennen are our enemy, not other wolves. Here in the Heartland our pack's task shall be to raise our cubs and seek an alliance with the Magyar.

'But beyond the Heartland it shall now be Aragon's task to lead a smaller group to learn what he can of the Mennen ways and places, to try to understand things which we have only thought of in passing. Wolfkind is in change; so too do the Mennen seem to be. I do not know what he will discover from such change, but I do know it is important, and also that he should not go alone. It would be too unsafe for him to do so, and if he were lost – and he knows how dangerous his mission is – how would we learn again what he has learnt? Therefore two wolves will go with him. Stry, you will be one of them. Jicin, you the other. One for fraternity, one for friendship . . .'

They looked at each other and nodded their agreement. Jicin especially, for now the cubs were born she understood that Klimt could not easily continue their friendship. Raute was settled in and thriving, and could do without her for a time. As Aragon must leave, so must she. While Stry, mourning his brother as he was, might learn new things, and recover his sense of life, if he journeyed with them too.

'So, now . . .' continued Klimt, and they talked on as a pack should, sharing their doubts and fears, saying their farewells, offering their wishes and their prayers.

'But remember, Aragon,' said Klimt finally, 'a year at most will I give you, until another spring. Come back then and bring Stry and Jicin safely home. Or, if the opportunity presents itself, send information back to us . . .'

'I will,' said Aragon, much moved by the trust placed in him, and the wisdom Klimt had shown in choosing such a task in such a way. 'And Stry and Jicin shall be safe with me.'

'And him with us!' said Stry stoutly, a little like his former self.

'You three shall leave tomorrow then,' said Klimt.

In the late afternoon of that same day the cubs came out once more. It was a grey day, a heavier day, when tiny flecks of snow, light and almost floating, came out of the sky, winter's last farewell, and the cubs saw them and tried to catch them but could not. The snow powdered down onto the ground, settling on rocks and soil, grass and scree, a covering as thin as gossamer and all gone the moment a cub pawed at it or chased a brother or sister, or fled before one.

Five cubs in powdery evening snow, three females and two males, each as soft and gentle as the others, except that one of the males was a touch larger now, a touch paler, and one of the females smaller, slighter. Slowly differences were beginning to show.

Tiring at last, the cubs turned back to Elhana by the entrance to her den, and there they nuzzled at her, wanting milk, wanting sleep, wanting to go back down to darkness. And the tiny snowflakes danced down, hovered, shifted, dusted the surface of everything, even the cubs' soft heads.

And then, quite suddenly, the pack all stilled, even the cubs. Still, silent, and filled with awe. Not fear but awe, for here where they were, here and now, they felt their pack was one; and that One was with them.

They turned and saw a wolf standing still, on the slope above them, in the lee of the boulder.

Her eyes shone like stars as she stared down at them, her eyes were whole galaxies of stars. She moved, and her movement was as silent as the drift of clouds across the sky.

The pack grouped about Elhana and the cubs, Klimt solid at their head.

The She-wolf came down the slope towards them and none of them could think, nor move of their own free will.

Her eyes were gentle with love and their hearts beat and they felt great awe.

'Show me,' she said, or seemed to say. 'Show me what you have made.'

The pack parted to let her come by, and come by she did, gentler than a summer wind, bringing with her a world in which all fear is gone and only love remains.

'Show me . . .'

She reached a paw to each cub in turn, and she touched them as a mother would.

'Yes,' she whispered in a voice that held the endless, ageless lilting of a sea, and the cliffs and undulations of the Scarpfeld echoed with that voice, 'oh yes . . .'

'Klimt!'

He came to her.

'Elhana and you others, leave us be for a little while, leave us be . . .' she commanded them.

'My cubs,' whispered Elhana . . .

'They shall be safe with me.'

Elhana let them be.

'Klimt,' she said, 'do you know what wolf is born amongst these five?'

'Yes,' said Klimt, who knew now that he did.

'Do you know which of the two males he is?'

He looked at them and did not know. The larger? The smaller? He knew not.

'That is as it should be, wolf,' she said. 'Raise them equally, or as equally as they allow. Teach them all you know, and let the others teach them all they know as well.'

'I will,' whispered Klimt.

'I know it,' she said to him, and she touched his bowed head and he knew for certain what wolf it was who touched him then.

'Now, listen well,' she said. 'The dark millennium is nearly over and with it his last life will be complete. Through the centuries I have followed him and watched over him, but now I am tired and I must leave. I too shall be reborn, though where I cannot know. So . . . I must entrust him to the Wolves of Time, whose task this has always been. To fulfil this task you have all been summoned.

'Raise him wisely for he will know nothing but what you teach him, and what he can remember of his past lives.

Teach him as I would have tried to do. His last life has begun, and with it his last chance to reach the WulfRock once again, to find the wolfway to the stars, and to restore our world, which is the world of wolfkind and the gods. To you I entrust him, you and the pack you lead. Teach him all you can, and yet Klimt . . . love him too, first and last, as I have done . . .'

'I shall,' said Klimt.

She smiled an ancient smile and said, 'You'll know one day which one he is, you'll know. For you are the leader of the Wolves of Time until one greater than yourself shall find his strength. He who has been born again, here, in the Heartland, where all began and all will end, He will take on the leadership from you. Have faith and courage to lead the others and know that he whom you raise here shall replace you only when the time is right.'

With this she turned from him and went to where Stry stood some way off, watching in awe, just as the others did.

She seemed to speak no word to him, yet all seemed to know that he must go with her.

'Come,' she seemed to say.

Stry followed in her wake towards the slope that led up to the boulder that loomed and shimmered now in the evening air, its top sloping part pale with a dusting of snow. There the She-wolf paused.

'Wait here, wolf, and have faith. Hold vigil to the dawn, and be still, for your brother knows a greater peace, and he will wait for you. The last wolfway you shall take together.'

She went on then, on into the darkening air, and when she came to the boulder she turned and stared down a final time. Her eyes shone with love itself. Then round it she went towards the bluffs of the great gully there, and on and up between them, until they saw her no more.

* * *

Slowly the pack came to life again and Elhana took the cubs back down into the den. The others assembled around Klimt near the den itself and settled down to await the dawn, except for Stry, who stayed where she had shown him. None spoke: a peace was with them, and only Jicin moved. Feeling that she might be needed in the night by Stry, she settled on the slope nearby him, to share his vigil through to dawn.

The pack slept as if they had travelled a thousand miles and needed rest. But it was a thousand years they had travelled, and they had come home. Darkness came, and peace.

Then a cry, and it was dawn. A cry and it was Stry, standing where he had first settled down and pointing at something on the slope.

Jicin ran up to where he stood and she saw as he did the paw-prints of a wolf, large and male: tracks made sometime in the night in the powdered snow which led up towards the boulder and beyond.

'Morten,' whispered Stry in awe.

They followed the tracks upslope, the rest of the pack in their wake and as they climbed the sun rose to the east and glanced across the way they went. Up and up to the boulder which had saved Stry's life, and the tracks went round and beyond into the gully entrance, in between the rises of the rock, into the shadows there and on, on to where the pack had never been. Before that they stopped.

Then Klimt said, 'She told me that she would show us how things would be if our pack's faith is great enough, and she has done so. Ambato was the first to go on to find the WulfRock; now Morten has gone on ahead. Each of us has journeyed here and must one day journey on. May we serve Wulf and Wulfin well . . .'

A great cry then came forth, and it seemed to come from the world itself, the cry of a wolf giving birth as Elhana had done, the cry of life new-born . . .

'Re-born,' whispered Klimt, 'Somewhere she too is reborn. The dark millennium now begins its end and our gods have come back to us that we may nurture them and raise them to be strong. Wulf our god has been born among us; and Wulfin, somewhere she is born again as well. Though he has us, she has none at all. For a thousand years she watched through his lives, but now she has given him up to us to be our task, and our sacred secret.

'May we be with her in spirit, as with him in body . . . for this were we each born, for this were we summoned back to form our pack. For this . . .'

They turned then, back down the slope up which they had trekked, a slope now filled with sun, and as they went, the last dusting of the snow faded before their eyes, and the tracks of a wolf who had gone ahead of them to the WulfRock and beyond, melted away into pack memory.

But waiting for them by the den, watching, their eyes blue and wide, were five cubs, three females and two males, and they ran forward, tumbled, timid and impulsive all at once. Then they scampered back to Elhana's flank.

At the pack's approach the two males separated from their sisters, rolled and fought, bleated and played, and stopped only when they came up against the cliff-like paws and escarpments of the chests and heads of two adult males: Klimt and Aragon. One cub was larger and lighter, one smaller and darker, both had eyes as bright as life itself. They stopped and they stared before turning to run for safety back to Elhana.

'Which one is He?' whispered Klimt. 'Which one?'

He did not know, and nor did Aragon.

Later that morning those of the pack who were staying behind gathered to watch Aragon, Stry and Jicin leave. They did so quietly, their farewells said the day before.

The air was filled with the sounds of spring, of running water, of cubs at play, while high in the scarps the ravens turned and cawed.

'Farewell,' they too seemed to say. 'Farewell.'

As the three wolves set off, one of the male cubs chose to watch the travellers, but one turned away from them all towards the scarps, to watch the way the white clouds drifted across the spring-blue sky. Then He dropped His gaze to where sun lit up the boulder on the slope above, and the gully beyond it and though He stared with the eyes of a cub, it was as if He sought a She-wolf He had lost there. She whom He had sought for a whole millennium, and now had one last chance to find.

THE WOLVES OF TIME
Wanderers of the Wolfways

William Horwood

A NEW AGE IS BEGINNING...

*'I am a Wanderer, and it is to Klimt of Tornesdal that I have jour-
neyed these long years to speak,' the old wolf said, his voice like the
whisper of the wind through the ancient trees of the far distant land
whence he had come. 'Therefore, lead me to him now...'*

Under the austere yet inspiring leadership of Klimt, the
Wolves of Time have taken back the Heartland. They have
defeated the treacherous Magyar wolves, successfully avoided
a confrontation with the Mennen, and their first cubs have
been raised, one of whom is the god Wulf, in mortal form.

But now, in addition to this awesome responsibility, Klimt
faces a new challenge. As the Magyar regain their strength
under Fuhrer, their loathsome leader, and the Mennen enter a
phase of war and anarchy that threatens to engulf Europe, the
Wolves lose their spiritual direction and purpose. Help comes
in the form of a wolf - a Wanderer - from the mysterious lands
of the watersheds, north of the holy Lake Baikal, far to the east
and further than any ordinary wolf has ever travelled.

Can Klimt accept the challenge the Wanderer gives him, and
himself set off on a spiritual quest upon the lost and forgotton
Wolfways?

To do so he must give up control of the pack he leads, aban-
don the Heartland territory he has won at such a cost, and,
worst of all, risk the lives of his two sons, upon one of whom
the fulfilment of Wolfkind's destiny depends...

THE WOLVES OF TIME
Wanderers of the Wolfways
is now available in hardback from
HarperCollins*Publishers*

The Willows in Winter

William Horwood

Illustrated by Patrick Benson

The bestselling sequel to *The Wind in the Willows*

Kenneth Grahame's classic story has been a source of delight for generations of readers. Now, in this bestselling sequel, William Horwood returns to Grahame's idyllic world and brings to life once more his much-loved characters: Mole, Ratty, Badger and, of course, the irresistible Toad.

The result is a magnificent new tale, enlivened by the delightful illustrations of Patrick Benson, in which all the joy, magic and good humour of the original has been recaptured – and Toad is still as exasperatingly lovable as he ever was.

'Horwood has really got into the minds and souls of the characters, and caught the flavour of Grahame's prose. Lovers of *The Wind in the Willows* will feel at home and will laugh a lot with sheer pleasure.'
The Times

Available now in paperback from HarperCollins
ISBN 0 00 647873 5

Also available on tape from
HarperCollinsAudioBooks
Read by Richard Briers

Toad Triumphant

William Horwood

Illustrated by Patrick Benson

In *The Willows in Winter*, his bestselling sequel to Kenneth Grahame's classic *The Wind in the Willows*, William Horwood successfully brought to life once more some of the best-loved characters in British literature.

Now in this new tale, the comfortable bachelor world of the River Bank is thrown into turmoil by the arrival of a formidable female character, who seems to win Toad's heart. Recognising the familiar danger signals, his long-suffering companions Mole, Ratty and Badger must do all they can to save the infatuated Toad from himself.

Enriched once again by the delightful illustrations of Patrick Benson, *Toad Triumphant* is another captivating story, in which Toad's capacity for finding trouble and making miraculous escapes is tested as never before.

'**I found myself becoming exasperated all over again by the conceit, cheek and impossible behaviour of Toad. A thoroughly faithful re-creation, more than a bit inspired by enjoyment of the original.**' *Daily Mail*

Available now in hardback from HarperCollins
ISBN 0 00 225309 7

Also available on tape from
HarperCollinsAudioBooks
Read by Richard Briers

THE BOOK OF SILENCE

Duncton Tales
Duncton Rising
Duncton Stone

William Horwood

A million readers revelled in William Horwood's first classic trilogy about the brave moles of Duncton, *The Duncton Chronicles*, which told how Moledom's Stone followers struggled to find peace and truth for allmole.

In *The Book of Silence*, his hugely popular second Duncton trilogy, their remarkable story continues with Moledom's greatest tale, an unforgettable story of courage, love and faith that has firmly established William Horwood as one of the best-loved storytellers writing today.

If you have never read a Duncton story before, then start here. If you are already a Stone follower, then prepare for the greatest pilgrimage of your life.

'More readable and rewarding than *The Lord of the Rings*.' *The Times*

'A magnificent achievement.' *Independent*

All three volumes are available now
in paperback from HarperCollins

We hope you have enjoyed THE WOLVES OF TIME *Journeys to the Heartland*. The concluding volume entitled THE WOLVES OF TIME *Seekers at the WulfRock* is to be published very shortly and readers who would like full publication details, and information about how to obtain a copy personally signed by the author, are invited to write to

William Horwood at
PO Box 446, Oxford, OX1 5YS